Lipstick's Legacy

BY

Jeffrey Rosin

Tom,
enjoy and
all of my best,
Jeffrey Rosin

PublishAmerica
Baltimore

At the specific preference of the author, PublishAmerica allowed this work to remain exactly as the author intended, verbatim, without editorial input.

First printing

ISBN: 1-4137-8240-X
PUBLISHED BY PUBLISHAMERICA, LLLP
www.publishamerica.com
Baltimore

Printed in the United States of America

To those held captive by the past…

Acknowledgements

I have many people to thank, all those who played a role from Draft Number 1 to Draft Number…well, whatever. I'll try to go from memory, and if I missed someone, I sincerely apologize: to Allison Harris, for getting me started with a used computer; to my parents and sister, for being my first readers and advisors; to Alan Nadel, for being one of the first as well; to Rob Kean, Melissa Jerace and Melinda Jason, for providing a path to encouragement; to Elissa Wald, for inspiring me to reach deeper and for all of her editing help; and while I'm on that topic, I need to thank many others, not just for editing, but for advice and encouragement as well—my parents and sister again, Robert Ostfeld, Adam Goldberg, Kathleen Morgan, Jessica Pollack, Rachel Solar-Tuttle, Garrett Solomon, Alison Frydman, Mike Aronson, Emily Wolk and Alison Wolk, my writing group, Krista Anderson in particular and Toni Amato especially; to Henry Dane, for capturing my image of Lipstick for the cover; and to Publish America, for making this more than a subset of my hard drive.

Although written in first person, *Lipstick's Legacy* is pure fiction. Notwithstanding that, where would I be without Sara, my wife, and a sparkling blend of Lucy, Jayme and Victoria.

PART I

Lucy Polowski

Chapter One

August 2000.

In a small, undecorated office in Quantico, Virginia, Robert O'Donnell re-introduced himself to me as the Assistant Special Agent in Charge of the Organized Crime Unit in Boston. He told me we'd met before. I remembered, of course, and I thanked him again for believing in me. He backhanded the air in a disinterested gesture and congratulated me for making it through. After a few more words, he then told me he wanted to get right to it.

"I'd like to talk with you about Lucy Polowski—or '*Lipstick*' as you sometimes called her," he said, but his words did not immediately conjure her untimely death. Instead, they brought me back to high school and to Tremont Heights Park. For long before I had ever considered a career with the FBI, I was both an admirer and friend of Lucy Polowski's.

* * *

The first time I ever saw her was at the start of my sophomore year in high school, early September of 1993 to be exact. I had just gotten off the bus when Jason Terio's high-pitched *whoop* and outstretched arm directed my gaze to the lower parking lot. Lucy was cutting across the pavement, walking alone and swinging one spiral notebook between her thumb and index finger. From the path she wove through the array of vehicles, she was clearly new and unassuming, but not unsure. Two of her features struck me right away: her hair, a tassel of radiant orange flames, and her not so subtle sway.

Has to be a senior, I thought, *with that body.*

At lunchtime that same day, though, I learned otherwise. Lucy was in my class, which made her even more astounding. She stood in the cafeteria snack line with her back to me, wearing navy jeans and a white top that was riding up on her. The edge of a green design was visible on her lower back where the color of cloth gave way to skin. It was a butterfly tattoo, I later learned, and she said she didn't mind the pain.

Nathan Marks was in line right behind her and, feeling the instant urge for a Drakes cake, I rose from my seat and meandered around the cafeteria tables toward my best friend. I didn't draw much attention as I moved, nor did I expect to. By my sophomore year, it was already clear to me that I was no Nathan Marks, but rather one of those who would go through life as woodwork, blending mostly unnoticed wherever I went.

Nathan, on the other hand, drew more than his fair share of stares. Thick, wavy, brown hair fell in front of his wide dark eyes, and he had the raw-boned face most other guys tried to contrive in the mirror by sneaking in from the side and sucking their cheeks between their molars. A steady regimen of push-ups and chin-ups at the park defined Nathan's broad shoulders and brought his developing pectorals into sharp relief beneath the tight t-shirts he wore. But the blue veins that scored his arms and the knuckled bones that jutted from his long fingers cautioned anyone who might have labeled him a pretty-boy.

I nudged him when I reached the snack line. "Hey buddy. You got me?" I said, thrusting a handful of silver in his direction and looking pointedly at the new girl's butterfly.

Lucy Polowski didn't look like most redheads. She had no freckles. Her skin was pure, seemingly bloodless, the kind that seemed to dare the sun to try. Her rounded lips were painted a dark rouge, the color she would end up branding several willing seniors at the first weekend parties, and the color that would earn her the nickname, '*Lipstick*,' she loved to hate.

Lucy turned when she heard me speak, and she might have caught me in a dead stare had she not looked right at Nathan…and smiled.

Man, did she smile!

I still don't know why Nathan didn't return Lucy's smile that day, but maybe that's why he was Nathan, and I was not. Sometimes, I wondered if he was just slow, unable to react quickly to sudden stimuli. Other times, though, Nathan's expressionless, dark eyes seemed to serve him perfectly. Whatever may or may not have been going through Nathan's head when Lucy eyed him, it became clear she would respond to those who offered her humility. Although her smile faded, and she turned back around, as she did, I caught a tightening in her jaw and a cat-like, half wink of her left eye.

I looked to Nathan to see if he'd noticed, but he only rolled his eyes at me, as if Lucy Polowski was just another girl smiling his way. After fourteen years of friendship, though, I knew better. I knew that underneath Nathan's chiseled features and feigned indifference, he had a thing for Lucy Polowski from the first time he saw her. He confirmed it a few weeks later.

"Don't call her Lipstick," Nathan demanded when I first referred to her that way.

Nathan never liked Lucy's nickname, probably because he didn't like to admit she had kissed other guys. But that did not mean Nathan would make his own move, or invite her into his life in any way. That wasn't his style. Instead, while some would circle and smile, and others would simply pounce, Nathan would take her when he was ready.

Chapter Two

We grew up in an area outside of Boston known as Tremont Heights, more a no man's land than a neighborhood unto itself. We had the prep schools and mansions of Milton on one side, and the auto shops, bus stops, personal injury attorneys and corner stores of Mattapan on the other. To many, Tremont Heights was just the bridge between the two and best known as 'that place' where the big chocolate ice cream cone stood.

Addison Parker's convenience store, The Chocolate Cone, stood about a half mile off the highway into Tremont Heights, but the fifty-foot cone statue in front of the store was visible from at least a mile away. Although very few of the drivers barreling down the expressway knew anything about Tremont Heights, those who did pay attention knew that The Chocolate Cone was our Empire State Building, our Tour D'Eiffel. Seeing it meant we were home, for better or for worse.

Six blocks from The Chocolate Cone was Tremont Heights Park, a well-kept oasis in an otherwise run-down community. The benefit of having Milton on one side of Tremont Heights was its overflow of beautiful parks. Sometimes, I imagined that the Town of Milton funded the clean-up and maintenance of the parks in Tremont Heights, just to keep a buffer zone between itself and Mattapan. Tremont Heights Park was a haven for the neighborhood kids, and we took advantage of it every afternoon the weather allowed.

Yet, traditional playground games did not prevail there. Tremont Heights Park did have two full basketball courts, but they tended to be used by children on tricycles or fathers teaching their sons to shoot. The guys from the Heights just didn't get up for full-court games of five on five. The Park had a decent baseball diamond too, but instead of breeding sluggers and shortstops, it was rutted from puddles and hardened from disuse.

I always knew that our neighborhood was different from those surrounding it, but it wasn't until I went away to college that I realized its differences were manifest in the game we played. We weren't the jawing baseball jocks from Milton, and we weren't the thumping basketball heads from Mattapan. We'd found our own game. We called it 'bruise-ball,' and Tremont Heights Park was where it was lost and won.

I don't really recall which of us made it up, but I distinctly remember how it came about. A couple of guys challenged Nathan and I to a game of handball and the four of us decided to alter one rule of the game and add another. Instead of slapping the ball with our palms, we had to catch it cleanly off the wall after the other team's throw, no matter where it bounced or what it hit. The team who missed a pick-up had to suffer a penalty: face against the wall and hands behind the head while the other team got three free shots. We tallied up points not by whether a team missed the pick-up off the wall, but how often we nailed our opponents.

It wasn't long before the bruise-ball court became the cement center-stage of Tremont Heights Park and an after school haven for our competitive thrills. Nathan and I played so much that there wasn't a team in the Heights, nor Milton or Mattapan, who didn't have to get lucky to take us.

Nathan had an incredible arm. His shoulder strength and precision aim were simply lethal. We figured his height gave him an edge, and he was always the one who would throw if the match were remotely close. I was smaller. At fifteen, my size was a burden in just about every way, but in bruise-ball, coupled with a gift for lateral movement, it enabled me to scoop any grounder within thirty feet.

Nothing could stop Nathan and I on the bruise-ball court, not even the best efforts of Lucy Polowski.

* * *

I remember our game that afternoon so well, and I have played it over and over in my mind: a crisp October day, brown crunching leaves and the skid of rubber soles beneath my feet, a single line of sweat listing down my cheek, sprinting, crouching, darting and stretching, all for a pink rubber ball ricocheting off a cement wall. It was 4:30 p.m., and the sky was already leaning in the direction of darkness. Yet, we had a full hour ahead of us before my dinner call.

Lucy Polowski was watching us play that day. She had been in town for just over two months.

For me, Lucy's presence was inspiring, but if Nathan felt the same way, there was no indication of it. He was used to the attention of every female teen in Tremont Heights, and Lucy would have to do more than watch his after school sport if she wanted to turn his head. It seemed that this was something she was beginning to understand.

Nathan and I were battling a couple of overweight juniors, and punishing red welts marked their bodies. We were well into our game when Nathan went into the third of three wind-ups, and then pink rubber blurred the air. This time, the ball struck between the shoulder blades of the guy who called himself 'BF Goods' before bouncing off toward the bleachers where Lucy Polowski pretended to be sunning her face.

"Good shot!" I heard from her painted mouth.

"I'll get it!" I shouted and started in her direction.

Lucy sat on the bottom bleacher, a lime green t-shirt tight across her chest beneath a mostly unzipped black satin jacket. She slid forward as the ball came her way and stretched to stop it with her right foot. I was grateful for her gesture, as it saved me from having to crawl beneath the ascending metal benches.

Lucy hopped from her spot and bent over to get the ball, and she shot us a cock-eyed smile as she rose. I reached out to take it from her, but she would not let go.

"Give it up," I said, but Lucy looked over my shoulder at Nathan.

"Get the ball, Billy!" Nathan called, as he wiped his forehead with his sleeve.

Now, the other guys were watching. BF Goods was massaging his back. They started to laugh.

"Give it up, Lipstick!" I tried again, but using her nickname was a mistake.

Nathan walked over to attempt to resolve the growing crisis. "Give him the ball, Lucy," he said in that deep smooth voice I was at least a year from even trying to imitate.

When Lucy Polowski heard her real name from Nathan's mouth, she became even more brazen.

"Take it from me," she dared.

By then, BF Goods had come over with his buddy. "I'll take it from you, bitch!" he said.

Nathan put up his left hand to silence the upstart. With a level look at Lucy, Nathan spoke again.

"Come on guys, let's leave," he said, and then he turned and started to walk away.

Nathan had gone about fifteen paces before Lucy's arm stretched back. She fired the ball at his head with a shocking velocity, missing her target by less than an inch. Nathan hesitated and his body stiffened, but he never turned, and he never stopped walking.

That was when Lucy said it: "Has Nathan told you he's afraid of girls?"

Nathan seemed to have heard her because his step suddenly faltered.

"That's right," she went on. "Nathan's afraid of these!!"

When I looked back at Lucy, she was clutching her chest. Her ears grew hot as she waited for Nathan to turn, but he never did.

And then, in apparently the only act of defiance she could summon to match his, and shouting something about Nathan's mother and how he would never dare ignore her again, she actually lifted her shirt right there in front of us.

Right there! Right there in full, broad daylight view!

Exposed and tyrannical, Lucy's eyes darted back and forth between us. She called out something dirty to Nathan's departing form, but I didn't hear a thing. Her breasts were the first I had ever seen on a live girl, and to this day, I have never stopped staring.

Chapter Three

The reckless reputation Lucy had earned on the bruise-ball court that day took a little over a year to subside. Eventually, people found other things to talk about. Nathan's seeming indifference to her, though, had not changed.

But in the middle of our junior year, our class ranks came out. I was ranked 42 out of just under 400. Nathan wouldn't tell me his rank at first, but it wasn't long before I learned that it was 287. It shouldn't have been a surprise to me that Nathan was that low. In all our years together, I never knew his score on any test, or his grade on any paper. He had always refused to share that kind of information with me.

"That stuff's not important," he would say, but his jaw would tighten as he did.

I don't really know why Nathan decided to reveal his class rank to me, but I suppose it was because it represented the end of something to him, some competition I was never aware of.

"All of sudden, it's like everything I'm proud of is nothing at all," he said.

Had Nathan not been a hard worker, he probably wouldn't have taken it so hard. I tried to tell him it didn't matter, just as he had been saying all along.

"What's in a number anyway?" I said.

"Enough to tell me I'm going nowhere fast," he said, walking away as if we hadn't been pals for ten plus years.

Somehow after our class ranks came out, the most charismatic and best looking guy I had ever known had found a streak of jealousy for me. I couldn't believe it. To spend one month in his shoes—hell, to spend a day—I would have traded places with Nathan in an instant.

It wasn't as if my rank was going to raise my high school social status. The way I saw it, there were still forty-one people who had bragging rights over me.

But if the class ranks had altered Nathan's thoughts about me, it was nothing compared to what it did for his feelings about Lucy. When the numbers came out, '*Lipstick*' Polowski was the talk of the school at number 7.

All of sudden, Nathan Marks needed her company like the air he breathed.

* * *

Toward the end of our junior year, I threw a party at my house. Nathan arrived first, and we celebrated the start of the evening together with three shotgun guzzles. For the first time in weeks, Number 42 and 287 bonded as if we were 1.

But Nathan had Lucy on his mind and, looking back at the vigor with which he drained the Budweisers, he'd made his decision well before he hit my front steps that night. He eyed the door with an eager expression every time it opened but dropped his chin and fingered the aluminum tab atop his can each time it wasn't her.

The friends and classmates who arrived early all made a point of coming into the kitchen to say hello. I stood up for most of them, but Nathan just checked a nod and, sometimes, extended a hand their way.

Before long, my living room was full. My radio had decent speakers, but nobody was dancing. There were card games, quarters, conversations, and laughs. When Lucy finally arrived, though, there wasn't much else to do but stare. She was wearing a sky blue dress with patches of white and her body seemed taken from the heavens as well.

Lucy had a wide smile and friendly hello for several others, but it was as if she had seen Nathan through the window from outside, taken note of his vantage point and planned her path into my living room accordingly. Nathan's hand tightened around his beer when he saw her, and the blue veins in his arms stood out, but she never looked his way.

Instead, after a few laughs, she grabbed Henry Wilkins by both of his hands, smiled playfully as he shrugged, and began dancing. Wilkins, newly anointed the fifth smartest person in our class, hardly knew what was going on, but when he was out there, it was clear to everyone else in the room that Lucy Polowski was dancing with herself and her chosen partner was nothing but a prop.

And that was fine. There wasn't a person in the room, male or female, who didn't just want to watch Lucy Polowski move to the music of Crazy Town in that dress.

Come my lady. Come, come my lady.
You're my butterfly, sugar baby....

I stepped toward the living room to watch as well and the words of the song seemed to carry on timelessly. Somewhere in the middle of the third verse, when I looked back at the kitchen table to find Nathan, his head was tipped back as far as it could go as he filled his throat with beer. When he was done, he crushed the tin can, let it drop to the floor, and repeated the process with what remained at the bottom of the bottle of Jack Daniels. And then Nathan Marks was moving across the kitchen, by me, and into the living room.

He grabbed Lucy's arm and turned her toward him. She gasped and feigned surprise, but her eyes were expectant. Nathan's grip was more than welcome, and she did not hesitate as he guided her out my front door.

A week later, after a few beers on his porch, Nathan told me they hadn't even made it through the Park before they were naked on the cool cement of the bruise-ball court.

"Ahh-mazing," was all Nathan said, letting my imagination fill in the rest.

Chapter Four

Nathan and Lucy became an inseparable pair in the months that followed. In the fall of our senior year, October 1995, we had a costume ball for Halloween. Neither Nathan nor Lucy told me what they were going to wear, but they did tell me that they would be sure to turn heads. They wanted their costumes to be a surprise to everybody, even me, so I tagged along with a few others to the party ahead of them. When I got there, I got into some small talk with a guy from my social studies class. He asked what I was supposed to be.

"I'm a crime scene," I said, as if the yellow tape around me and the white tape in the shape of a body on my chest should make it obvious.

"Cool," he said, through his football helmet.

"Are you any player in particular?" I asked.

"No," he said. "Then I'd have had to buy a real jersey. I didn't want to put out the fifty bucks."

We then stood together admiring, or ridiculing, the others in the room. I checked my watch once or twice. It was 10:30 already and the party would be over at midnight. I wondered if I would ever see Nathan or Lucy at all and began to think that they'd ditched the party in favor of a night alone.

But then, there was a tap on my shoulder. I turned to face the two of them in hooded blankets. They were smiling devilishly at me, and both clearly reeling from a few shots of something strong.

"That's it?" I asked. "You're coming as monks?"

They looked at each other and laughed.

"No," said Nathan.

"No," giggled Lucy.

"This was just to get us by the chaperones at the door," Nathan said. "You can bet we wouldn't have gotten inside without the robes." He and Lucy smiled at each other, and she clung to his arm.

"You ready, babe?" she asked Nathan.

"It's got to happen sometime," he answered, before turning and looking her in the eyes as if I wasn't there at all. "On the count of three. One, two, three!"

They pulled at the rope around their waists, removed their hoods and dropped their blankets. I didn't know where to look first.

Nathan was naked, other than two large leaves, one covering his manhood and one attempting to cover his backside. Better yet, only four leaves covered Lucy. They stood there before me for a moment of admiration, and then came forward to hug me together.

"It was her idea, buddy," Nathan yelled over the music.

My arm went around the small of Lucy's back, and I caught my breath as my hand accidentally rested against the upper curve of her buttock. When they released me, they walked straight to the center of the dance floor, hand in hand, Adam and Eve, envoys of creation. They were able to dance for one and a half songs as people circled them, wide-eyed and opened-mouthed, trying to prevent the chaperones from getting a look. In the meantime, I held their blankets and watched, and when the chaperones finally came for them, I was there to help them cover back up. Both of them were suspended. Neither of them cared.

When they returned to school the following Wednesday, they walked arm and arm down the ramp into the cafeteria. As soon as the first few students realized who had entered, the standing ovation began, and it didn't stop until they sat down with me.

Chapter Five

When Nathan and Lucy started dating, my life changed too. I got to know Lucy real well because I was a regular third wheel when she and Nathan were together. But I was also the confidante for each of them when the other was not around.

Lucy was embarrassed to tell me that her mother had left her alone with her father long ago.

"She was a *'night-time dancer,'*" Lucy said, making quotation symbols with her fingers which told me she didn't believe it.

"My mother slept all morning, and she complained all afternoon. She always seemed to reenergize at nightfall, but she barely stayed around long enough to tuck me in."

Those times, Lucy said, her mother would come into her room, and the bedroom air would be awash in cheap perfume.

"They were the most tender moments we had," she said. "I'd give anything for one more."

But then Ginny Polowski would be off, never available when Lucy couldn't sleep or when a nightmare woke her. She went looking for her father sometimes, only to find him snoring in his easy chair surrounded by crushed beer cans. But if Lucy felt any resentment toward him, she never revealed it.

"When I was a little girl, he used to bring me handfuls of dandelions in the spring," she told me, and then she lowered her chin.

"One morning when I was eight," Lucy told me, "my mother didn't come home. Every day, I asked my father where she was, but he could never give me a straight answer. Finally, I got tired of asking, and when my father took a transfer to Boston, I said goodbye to my old life, goodbye to Fort Lauderdale and goodbye to any hope I had of seeing my mother again."

"I cry sometimes thinking about it, but my Pop takes pretty good care of me. He manages to hold a job, bring home food, and throw me a little extra here and there to shop. He complains about the cost of living up here, but for me, a bed, a desk, a radio and some spending money are all that matter right now. I'll make my own way when I'm old enough. Someday, I'll be taking care of him, better than he ever could have imagined taking care of me."

"My dreams were born in Florida, Billy. You ought to see the second homes people have down there. I was 10 years old when I learned to ride a bike, and that was the way I spent my Saturdays; roaming the neighborhoods, looking on, imagining. Someday, that will be me. You mark my words."

It frustrated Lucy that I was not as forthcoming when we talked, but I just didn't feel like I had that much to say. She wanted to know my dreams, and it wasn't that I didn't have any. I just couldn't think of any when she asked. Around Lucy, I wasn't capable. I was just plain dull.

"Who do you like, Billy?" she asked me more than once.

I would look into the distance as if I was picturing the secret object of my desire right then.

"That's for me to know," I would respond, only to be nudged or shoved.

"Who am I going to tell?" she would say, and then pause as if the silence would provoke my confession. "I'll bet it's Krista. I've caught you looking in math class."

The truth was, Krista sat near Lucy, and I would shift my gaze to her whenever Lucy turned.

"You'll know some day," I told her. "Maybe."

Lucy never pushed too hard. In that way, her time alone with her father had turned her into a natural companion to men, and she well understood the value of non-verbal communication. She also understood something I had never seen before.

When I was alone with Nathan, he opened up about it.

"She messes with me, Billy," he told me once, incredulous and frustrated.

"What do you mean?" I asked.

Then, Nathan told me just the kind of story that made me wince and wonder, but definitely shake my head and know it's no good. Lucy was a reader, so she could pull off the use of flowery prose as if she were as sophisticated as one of the characters from her favorite book. Lucy would make some off-hand remark and use a word like 'enigmatic,' then study Nathan's face and delight in watching his forehead furrow.

You know what I mean by that, right Nathan?

Unlike Lucy, the only things Nathan read were street signs. If Nathan wasn't hanging around the Park, he was glued to game shows and sitcoms. He had absolutely no idea what she meant.

When he didn't answer her, Lucy would continue: *You stupid thug! Why do I let you near this body?*

Even as Nathan told me the story, his eyes narrowed and his fists clenched, and I knew he was feeling a slow burn. He told me that he'd raised his hand to her a couple of times, but just couldn't bring himself to slap her.

"It's not in me," he said, and I believed it.

Instead, Nathan told me, he would storm out, her laugh and taunting words echoing in his ears.

Where are you going dumb-ass? To study?

Lucy always knew he would come back. Once she had him, she knew she was the biggest part of his dumb gorgeous pride.

Chapter Six

I left Tremont Heights for college in August 1996, and I was relieved for the chance to move on and find my own identity. Before I left, I sat with Nathan on the bleachers in Tremont Heights Park soaking up the Saturday sun and attempting to reminisce with him about some of the better matches we'd had on the court before us. Nathan seemed not to care at all. All he really wanted to talk about was his fight with Lucy the night before.

"You'll work it out," I told him. "She needs you. She always has."

And then, as if her ears were ringing, Lucy appeared in the distance, and started to skip right for us. She came at me first and offered a long hug.

"I can't believe you're off," she said.

"I can't believe you're not," I responded, noting Nathan's cringe.

"Maybe someday," Lucy added, tossing her eyes at her boyfriend.

* * *

Lucy and I had talked about college a lot. Her class rank and GPA gave her a shot at some great schools, she knew, but her father never pushed her and Lucy didn't know enough to care.

"He needs me around here," Lucy once said, but I didn't know if she was referring to her father or Nathan. I didn't ask. It didn't matter. I was moving on, headed to Drexel University in West Philadelphia.

"Drexel borders the University of Pennsylvania," I once told Lucy. "That's about as close as I'll get to the Ivy League."

Lucy shook her head and nudged.

"You, on the other hand," I added, trying to motivate her.

"Forget it, Billy. There's too many men in college. Too many Billy Tuckers," she teased in that sadistic way of hers. "How could a girl concentrate?"

A part of me wanted to believe there was some truth to Lucy's words. A part of me fantasized that she and I were the ones who were truly made for each other. Someday, I told myself, Lucy would tire of Nathan's chiseled features and find her way to me.

In the meantime, I knew I needed to get away. I would not—and could not as long as Nathan was around—grow or flourish in Tremont Heights. In Tremont Heights, I was at best destined to be Nathan's side-kick.

Lucy's words always reminded me: "You're such a sweet guy," she defaulted, anytime she wanted to throw me a bone.

* * *

"College is a waste of time," Nathan piped in. "Especially for me. My calling is in the cards."

In our last couple years of high school, Nathan and I had been getting together with a few classmates roughly once a week to crush a few beers and play seven card stud, mostly for pocket change, because that's all we had. While the rest of us grew tired around midnight, though, Nathan always tried to prolong the action.

One on one? he would suggest at the end of the night to the guy who had won the most money. *Come on. High card? A buck a flip? Come on. What are you going to do with pocket change?* he would taunt. *Buy gum?*

Nathan wouldn't stop until he was broke, or until he had cleaned out everyone else. If he won, he was on the phone with his bookmaker the next minute trying to parlay his poker winnings on the next NBA game.

This behavior was all too familiar to Lucy. Her father seemed to build his life around the scores on ESPN after her mother left. But it was his whispered calls to distant relatives that bothered her the most.

Lucy's great, her father would say, but then his voice grew hush. *Can you spare a little money?*

* * *

I sat and stared at Robert O'Donnell, my high school days with Nathan and Lucy so vivid despite so much time having passed. He cleared his throat, shook his head and said her nickname again.

"Lipstick." He paused and tried to laugh. "What right-minded girl puts up with a name like that?"

The Assistant Special Agent in Charge then began to fill me in on what he'd learned from his investigation and the bits and pieces he put together about the rest.

He suspected that when Lucy began to see her father's gambling habits developing in Nathan, and when classmates like me were out in the world doing other things, Lucy started to feel an urge to explore.

Chapter Seven

March 1999.

Bordering Fenway Park, just on the other side of the left field menace batters had named '*the Green Monster*,' was Lansdowne Street and a dance club called '*Fire!*' *Fire!* had it all: a wide dance floor, a beat that shook the walls, stiff cocktails handed over by beautiful bartenders, and best of all, wealthy-looking men in silk Armani suits.

Lucy hadn't talked to Nathan all day, and he refused to pick up the phone during the NCAA finals. She pouted on her couch at home as she awaited Heather Connors and watched her father struggle emotionally over Duke's second half performance against UConn.

When Heather finally arrived, Lucy followed her out the door, and the two of them went straight to the bus stop. Their destination: Kenmore Square.

"We're going to rip it up tonight!" Lucy said as the bus hauled up the expressway.

The driver glanced in his rear view mirror, admiring the sparkles on the red head's face.

Heather eyed her friend, whose stare seemed purposeful, but distant. "He doesn't know what he's missing, Lucy."

Heather Connors had been to *Fire!* once before. She couldn't stop telling Lucy about it, and the two of them had decided to keep their eyes out for the next under 21 night. This was it.

"When's the last bus back?" Lucy called up to the driver. She was only a month from her 21st birthday, so she would need to learn how to take the 66 local to Kenmore alone, whenever she needed a break.

The bus jerked and angled its way into the Kenmore station before the driver responded: "One o'clock ladies," he said. "After that, you're walking."

Heather and Lucy stepped off the bus and strode arm and arm, shivering in the nighttime chill. It was Lucy's idea to go without jackets. "We won't have to pay for the coat check, and we'll be a hit from the moment we step in."

Heather was impressed. Lucy had never even been to *Fire!* before, but it was as if she instinctively knew how to be sexy.

They could hear the music from the corner as they turned onto Lansdowne Street, and it took on an insistent pull as they approached the doorman.

"ID's girls," he said, stepping forward.

Lucy smiled, her card ready and in hand. Heather had to fumble for hers in her purse.

* * *

Joey Luca noticed Lucy from the moment she stepped inside, and he watched her make her way to the dance floor.

New chick, he thought, resting one elbow on the bar. "Hey watch it buddy," he snapped, as a sweaty dancer brushed up against him. "You know who I am?"

Later, he would ask around about her, even talk to Frankie at the door. It wasn't often he saw a real redhead, not to mention the way she danced.

For now, though, he was content to enjoy the view. Joey Luca didn't move for chicks. They moved for him. He pulled a roll of bills from his wallet and slapped a twenty on the bar.

"Another round!" he called. "This time with a shot of SoCo!"

Twenty-seven and just out of night school, Joey Luca had a lot on his mind. His father's hauling business was starting to take over his time. He'd had a good thing going at school with the bookmaking, especially with his father's backing, but now his father was insisting that he broaden his endeavors.

It's small time junk, Joey. Leave it to others and take a cut. That's what we do, his father would tell him. It nagged Joey every time he did.

Joey watched as Lucy centered herself on the dance floor, tossing her head from side to side, smiling at her friend. A few amateurs did their best to put the moves on, and Joey watched them with disdain.

You meet a girl, you talk to her, Joey thought. *We're human beings, for Christ's sake, not animals.*

He watched Lucy tease her admirers with her body, and then turn her back. They vied for her attention, tried to work their way in front of her again, but time after time, she kept turning them around. Joey waited for an opportunity to approach her, but Lucy never moved from the middle of the dance floor, not until the moment she was ready to go. Joey swore she looked at him on her way out.

"Don't tell me you don't remember her name," he begged Frankie at the door.

"It was something Polish. That I know," Frankie replied, and it was the best he could do for his older cousin until he saw her again.

Chapter Eight

I got a call at school from Nathan soon after that night. It had been months since I'd heard from him, so I was surprised to hear his voice at all. He needed to talk about Lucy. He'd hit a hot streak and decided to use some of his winnings on a night out with her.

"I took her to Giovanni's in the North End," he told me. "Reserved us a corner table, ordered a $35 bottle of Chianti. We had eclairs and cappuccinos to finish it off."

He told me every detail. I had a research paper due the next day, so I wasn't in much of a mood to talk.

But then it got interesting: "When we got home, Billy, I did everything right. I lit candles, played soft music, kissed her lightly the way she likes, even massaged the back of her head. Nothing worked. Nothing," he repeated. "I couldn't get her going. I couldn't believe it."

"Maybe the wine made her tired," I offered, but Nathan wouldn't hear it.

"I'm losing her, man, I know it. I mean, it's been bad for a while, but I'm usually too wrapped up in my business—my bets I mean—to care. Now I'm winning, but I'm losing her."

"She liked dancing at that club?" I asked.

"She loved it."

"Take her back there," I suggested, hoping to end the conversation and get back to work.

A long pause on the other end of the phone made me wonder whether the connection had been cut.

"You know that's not my scene," he tried, but even as Nathan said it, I could tell he hoped I was right.

* * *

More than two months after her foray into town with Heather, Lucy rode shotgun to Kenmore Square in Nathan's car. "*Fire!* was supposed to be my own escape," she told Heather. "I don't think I want him there."

Lucy couldn't contain her agitation as the rusting Chevy trembled and kicked.

"You don't know where you're going!" she snapped at Nathan.

"I'm following the bus, Lucy. Why don't you get out and squawk at him?"

"You keep talking to me like that, Nathan, and I'm going to leave you."

Since her first trip to *Fire!*, Lucy's passive aggressive ways had given way to flat threats. Her night at *Fire!* had shown her that there was a world out there that did not involve endless hours on the couch or a desperation for ESPN news.

When she arrived at the club with Nathan, Lucy recognized the bouncer, and Frankie Stephano recognized her.

"ID's girls," he said, emasculating Nathan in an instant.

Lucy laughed as she flashed her card and walked in ahead of Nathan.

"Billy's bright idea. What a bright idea, Billy," Nathan mumbled.

* * *

Joey Luca got a call the moment they stepped into the club. He had been seated in front of the television in boxers and his bathrobe. After two straight nights on the town, he had planned to spend the evening in his easy chair sipping a Glen Fidich and sucking on a Cuban, but he was up out of his LA-Z-BOY in an instant when he heard Frankie's words.

"It's the redhead?"

"None other. I'm sure of it," Frankie replied. "Lucy Polowski. That's her name, Joey. Write it down, but don't come tonight. She's with a sailor. He looks cool."

Without even considering Frankie's advice, Joey crushed out his cigar and took the stairs to his bedroom three at a time. He threw on his black jeans, slipped his feet into wing-tipped Ferragamo's and removed his white, flair-collared silk shirt from its hanger. He sprayed on some Stetson, ran a comb through his hair and noticed that he could barely breathe.

What's this? he thought. *She's just a chick!*

Then he remembered how she moved. *What would she be wearing tonight? Who was this guy? He must be the reason she hadn't been back in so long. Thank the Virgin Mother she was from around here and not some out-of-towner enjoying the local scene for one night.*

"Lucy. Lucy. Lucy," he said under his breath. "Po—low—ski."

By 11:00 o'clock sharp, Joey was in his black Corvette, newly painted by Mick at the body shop in lieu of a broken nose. The car actually skidded on the road in front of his house as he wheeled it around into drive.

Joey couldn't get to town fast enough from Revere, but at least he wouldn't have to waste time parking. At *Fire!*, Joey Luca got special treatment, a valet when there was really no such thing on Landsdowne Street. That was the benefit of being a Luca, and the only son to Ronnie himself.

"Good stuff, kid," he told Frankie when he arrived, slipping his cousin twenty bucks. "Have a couple on me later. Who's the sailor?"

"Looks like her local," Frankie answered. "He seemed kind of lost. No trouble in there, though, okay, Joey? I'm kind of tired tonight."

Joey grabbed his cousin's face and squeezed his cheeks. "You ain't got to worry about me."

Fire! was packed as Joey made his way inside. Usually, he refused to fight his way through the club, but tonight was different. He had to find this Lucy and somehow make himself known to her.

She wasn't dancing when Joey saw her. Instead, she was in the lounge above the bar sipping the remains of a cocktail from a straw, studying the ice at the bottom of her glass. There was an empty chair next to her, where her man must have been sitting, but it was turned slightly outward, as if he had just gotten up.

How close is he? Joey wondered, considering his next move.

But then, Lucy looked down and met his eyes. Joey froze, but his expression never changed. Her eyes lingered on his, but still, he did not avert his gaze. He had come armed with the biggest roll of bills he could gather, and he held her stare as he ordered three drinks: a shot for himself, a beer for her sailor, and a sweet vodka tonic laced with Sloe Gin for her.

All the chicks loved 'em.

Joey nodded at her as he instructed the bartender.

"Don't tell nobody who bought these, you hear me?" Joey threatened, and then he downed the shot and made his way out of the club.

"What's this?" Nathan asked Lucy when he returned to his seat. "Did you order?"

"Yeah, it was me," she said.

While Nathan tried not to mind that she had spent another $15, Lucy smiled into her glass and drained her drink.

Chapter Nine

For the next several weeks, Lucy began a streak of Thursday nights at *Fire!* and a life away from Nathan.

"You go alone?" Heather asked her when she found out.

"I have no one else," Lucy responded. "We need to get you a fake ID."

The first time she showed up, Frankie felt there was something different about her. She looked unsettled as she fumbled for ID, and she struggled with her purse searching for money to give the girl behind the counter. Lucy did not have the brassy confidence she'd shown in her other two appearances at the club.

Frankie Stephano placed another call. "She's here again," he told Joey. "This time alone."

Of the many men who approached Lucy, none of them had the finesse of the man who knew Sloe Gin. But she wanted to dance, and she knew better than to let the whole night pass hoping he would come around. Setting her empty glass on the bar, she made her way to the middle of the floor. Out there, she was never alone. There were others doing the same thing, caught up in their own world, a sea of stimulus around them while they expressed in different ways a love for the music. One admirer after another made his way toward her, with a smile, a nod, and an attempt at eye contact. Each of them imagined he had a chance with her. Only one of them actually did.

He was there when she came out of a spin, wearing exactly what he had worn before. Her eyes found his. The corners of her lips curled upward.

Joey Luca had been around enough to know that whatever she was looking for, he had it. *Thank sweet Jesus Christ, I have it!* he thought and almost kissed the cross around his neck then and there.

A few moves, a tug of her hand toward the bar and two drinks later, and they were kissing in the lounge. Within the hour, she left with him.

Lucy Polowski had kissed a lot of guys in Tremont Heights, but she had never done this kind of thing before.

"Do you date a lot?" she asked, nestling comfortably into the leather passenger seat of his Corvette.

"All the time," he answered. "In fact, too much," he added jovially, then noticed the troubled expression on her face.

"You do this all the time, don't you?"

"What?" Joey asked.

"I'm just another one to you, aren't I?"

Joey Luca spent the next twenty minutes confessing that he'd first seen her months before, that his cousin was the bouncer, that he'd watched for her, waited for her, and feared he might never see her again. When he was done, he didn't quite feel like Joey Luca. He had emptied himself on this chick.

Wasn't this the way it was supposed to be, though? he thought. *Now what?*

"What about me?" he asked, unable to believe the note of pleading in his own tone. "Did you feel the same when you saw me that night?"

Joey's question brought Lucy into familiar territory: the insecurity of men.

"You looked cool," Lucy told him. "I was intrigued, but it was the music that was euphonious."

Joey Luca wrinkled his nose. *What did she just say? What was that about the music? It was better than me? What the fuck?* He didn't dare ask. Once he had her in the sack, she would come around. *Nothing phony or phonyous about that, for Christ's sake!*

When they ascended the stairs to the loft above the garage, Joey held her hand, leading her behind him.

"This isn't a good idea. I have a boyfriend," Lucy told him, and Joey felt a pain in his chest as he turned to her. "Please take me home," she said at the top of the stairs.

But even as she spoke, Lucy was peeling off her shirt. As Joey reached for her, Lucy threw her shirt to the ground, grabbed his belt buckle and pushed him onto the couch.

* * *

When Joey dropped Lucy off in Tremont Heights at 6:30 a.m., he had never felt more awake in his life.

It's true, he thought, as he considered the dozens of women he had bedded without a moment of real emotion. *This is what I've been hearing about. This is what it feels like. What they've all been saying is true.*

For the next several Thursdays, Lucy's cover was provided for, as were her drinks, three new cocktail dresses, a bottle of perfume, and late night Champagne at the Top of the Hub. It was endless extravagance, endless magic. Joey Luca was in love.

Chapter Ten

It was a rainy Saturday in mid-October when Lucy decided she had been leading a double life too long. She couldn't keep Joey happy seeing him only once a week, especially when he knew she hadn't fully broken up with her boyfriend back home.

"It's going to take awhile," she had told Joey the night before. "I mean, we practically live together and we've been going out for a long time. I haven't even known you six months. You can't ask me to drop him just like that."

"What's his name?" Joey asked.

But knowing what Joey did to make money, Lucy wondered whether Nathan's name might be familiar. "None of your business."

Joey had never competed for a girl in his life. He tried to tell himself that now was no different, that Lucy's other guy was on his way out with the morning trash. But Joey had also never been in love before.

"You aren't sleeping with him anymore, are you?" he asked, but Lucy shot him a look.

"Take back that question, Joey Luca. You're a thug for thinking it."

Joey wanted to smack her when she got like that, but as long as she had another man in her life, he couldn't risk a wrong move.

Meanwhile, Lucy regularly confessed to Heather that her heart was still frustratingly tied to the boy back home—the same boy she wished had half the will of some others she knew.

"Nathan Marks!" Lucy yelled at him that Saturday afternoon. "Get off that rear end of yours and do something, anything. Anything at all! You have a television tan for Christ's sake. Why can't you be like Billy?"

Nathan was in no mood for her nagging. It was an important night for his business.

"I hate to break it to you, sweetheart," he snapped, "but Billy doesn't give a damn about you or anyone else around here. And Billy only remembers you for your tits on the playground!"

Lucy stormed out, and that night, she decided to go to *Fire!* alone. There was a boxing match on T.V., and Nathan had planned his whole week around it. He had suffered two straight weeks of losses, he was down eighteen grand and feared he might never see his way out. His bookie was coming down on him, demanding payment, so he had a lot riding on the middleweight championship match. Lucy told him she couldn't bear to stay and watch. She didn't even tell Joey that she was going.

"I need a night away from everyone," she told Heather, now of age, and able to go.

"You sure, hon?" Heather said, holding back a cough. "I'll go with you."

"Forget that," said Lucy. "You're still sick and I really want to just lose myself in the music. I just want to dance alone. All alone."

When Lucy got to the club, she nearly turned around when she saw Frankie at the door. It was supposed to be his night off. But then, she thought better of it: "Don't tell Joey I'm here, okay, Frankie? I need a night to myself, you know."

Frankie Stephano was on the phone the minute she passed.

"She's there alone?" Joey asked Frankie in disbelief.

"I think she just wants a girls' night, you know?" Frankie said.

"How could she want a frigging girls' night, Frankie? She ain't there with any girls."

"Maybe they're coming. I don't know."

"You dumb mother, Frankie. I'm coming down there. She told me to meet her," Joey said, attempting to save face. *Who was this girl to insult him like this? After the way he'd treated her!*

Joey threw on his black leather jacket and crushed out his cigarette. He took one last look at the television before turning off the fight in the middle of the seventh round. At least *that* was looking like it would end his way. Tomorrow could be a big day for collections. That moron from Tremont Heights owed him eighteen grand already.

Close your books and put your time into the business, Joey could hear his father carping. *When I was doing what you're doing, nobody got away with owing me that kind of money. You've got to collect what you're owed, Joey. That's a basic rule. I think this little chickie has you distracted, and that ain't a good thing.*

Frankie Stephano knew that his cousin was lying. Lucy hadn't told Joey to meet her. *This is bad,* Frankie thought. The girl was going to be angry with him. Joey was already. He should have just pretended he never saw her.

Lost in his thoughts, Frankie checked the ID's of several newcomers. He was too anxious to pay attention to their faces.

Chapter Eleven

Nathan saw his fighter fall in the eighth round, and it was as if the floor had dropped out from under him. He couldn't move. He couldn't breathe. He couldn't feel his own knees.

What was I thinking? This can't be. Are there any more games tonight? Please, let there be something on the west coast. He searched in vain for the newspaper. *My bookie will take another bet*, Nathan figured. *He has to.*

Then: *Where's Lucy? How could he have exploded at her like that? She was the best thing in his life. She always would be. He had to find her.*

Nathan began heading to the bathroom to shave, but then thought better of wasting any more time.

* * *

When Joey Luca showed up at *Fire!,* he was half relieved to know that Lucy was within reach and half ready to explode.

"Is she still in there, Frankie?"

"I don't know."

Joey clutched his cousin's collar and stared into his eyes. "What do you mean, you don't know?"

"I mean, yeah, yeah, she's in there. Chill out Joey, will you?"

* * *

"Lucy! Lucy!"

She froze as she recognized Nathan's voice, but didn't turn around.

"Lucy!" he said again, reaching her.

She turned. "What are you doing here?"

"I came for you. Lucy, I'm sorry. I'm sorry I yelled at you."

"Shove it, stupid. And get out of here."

Nathan felt dizzy. He was down $25,000. He was sure to get a visit tomorrow morning. He needed Lucy more than ever, and there was no way to hide it.

"You lost tonight, didn't you?" she demanded.

His eyes confirmed it.

"Away! Get out of here Nathan Marks. You're ruining my life. We're through. You can take yourself straight to hell."

Nathan reached for her. She tried to pull back. He kissed her hard, and he swore she gave in for a moment, but then she tore away.

* * *

Years earlier, Joey Luca had seen his neighbor hanging by the neck in a closet, eyes swollen open in shock, and he never once averted his gaze. His father had been proud of him for that. He had also seen his Uncle Vinnie face down on the floor with a bullet through his temple and a pool of blood beneath his head. Again, he hadn't turned.

But when he saw Lucy—his Lucy—in a passionate kiss with another man and when he considered this along with the fact that she hadn't invited him to meet her out, Joey Luca had to turn away.

Who had seen? Who was watching? This couldn't be. It was all around the club that she was his girl. She was humiliating him! She must be drunk, deliriously drunk. That's the only way he could forgive her. She would have to be puking in the middle of the dance floor in an hour for all this to be okay, for him to save face.

He turned back for another look, but she was gone. *Where was she? Had she ducked into the bathroom? Was she headed for the exit?*

Joey pushed his way through the crowd toward where he'd seen her a moment ago. He had not gotten a good look at the guy.

* * *

When Lucy turned from his kiss, Nathan felt empty. He looked at the faces around him. They were smiling, flirting and plotting their next moves. Nathan imagined how out of place he must look: exhausted, unshaven, and smelling like the bed sheets he'd slept in. His only solace lay in his anonymity—that is, until a familiar and unwelcome face loomed before him, lips curled in a sadistic smile.

Nathan had only met Joey Luca twice before, but he recognized him instantly: the soft, fatty skin on his cheeks, the slicked back hair, the angled eye brows, the gold chains on his hairless chest. Nathan had Joey by an inch or two, enough to look down on him, but not quite enough to look by.

Nathan figured his luck couldn't get worse this night.

"Well, if it isn't Mr. Eighteen Grand," Joey Luca snapped, his eyes unfocused as he continued to look for Lucy.

Nathan figured that Joey hadn't seen the end of the boxing match. He stayed silent.

"I'm coming for it tomorrow, Marks. Noon. Your bets with me and any other bookie are done if you don't have it. So's your frigging face," Joey added, his dark brows now accenting his wide and wild eyes.

Nathan watched the veins pulsing in Joey's neck and swallowed hard. There was only one way he could come up with that kind of money and on his honor, he promised himself never to resort to it.

As Joey walked away and turned to a dark-haired girl nearby, the next thing Nathan heard practically broke him in half.

"Have you seen a redhead over here?" Joey asked her. "I can't find my girl."

Nathan stood frozen, wondering what his face looked like bloodless.

Chapter Twelve

Robert O'Donnell stopped talking for a moment and clasped his hands behind his head. My eyes settled uncomfortably on the hairs jutting from his short sleeves. His biceps were has-beens, the sign of a guy who'd decided in the not too distant past he no longer needed the confidence offered by a good workout. But that didn't mean he was above flexing them.

"And there you have it, Billy," he said. "The next thing anybody knows, Lucy turns up dead under the expressway."

"The city cops arrived first. Some patrolman just happened to be driving by. He passes under the expressway and sees a body in a heap off to the side, legs as gray and cold as the damn cement, red hair in disarray. He finds her ID, radios in the information, and minutes later, the ambulance arrives, flashing lights but not bothering with its siren."

O'Donnell paused.

"There was no rush, of course," he shrugged.

"The EMT's show up with nothing more than a burlap blanket and a yellow body bag, coffee cups in hand. Her father then gets the call."

I swallowed hard, shaking my head.

"Can you imagine? Denny Polowski went to sleep thinking his daughter was just out for another late night, but he wakes up to that. He hops into his car, races to the scene, flings open the door, and mouths an internal prayer or two as he rushes over."

"Then, when his prayer isn't answered, he screams. He screams so loud that the cars above him on the highway screech to a halt. He falls to his knees, shaking, and then he begins calling out her name, stroking her dry, lifeless hair and sobbing uncontrollably."

Robert O'Donnell did not hold back as his voice filled the barren room.

"Lucy! My Lucy! My baby girl, Lucy! Not my baby girl!"

My skin prickled as O'Donnell's words echoed off the walls. I thought back to Lucy's funeral, and her father's tilted, somber expression, his large frame a silent mass at the time, unable to vocalize even an appreciation for those who came to pay their respects.

"Poor Denny's yelling her name over and over until the cops pull him away. It took three men to do it."

O'Donnell paused before continuing. "I used to head up the Violent Crimes Unit, Billy." He looked away, lost in a memory, maybe several, he preferred not to share.

"After the local cops realized the dust was settling around young Joey Luca, I ended up getting the call. This one straddles both of my areas."

"The way I see it, Billy, your old friend Lucy was bopping Ronnie Luca's only son, the heir to his influence, and the kid had a motive. It's simple, straightforward and neat. But almost too neat, if you ask me. A guy as savvy as Ronnie—or anyone close to him for that matter—would not leave a body like that."

I cringed hearing his stale reference to Lucy. O'Donnell noticed, but continued unconcerned.

"What's more intriguing to me about the whole thing, Billy, more than the shooting itself, is that Nathan went straight after that night. No more gambling. None at all. Now, I shouldn't need to tell you, kid, that Nathan Marks had a motive of his own to kill Lucy. But it may surprise you to hear that I don't really care. For a reason I can't fully grasp, after that night, Ronnie Luca took Nathan under his wing. Stranger still, Nathan fell right into role. Hell, he's happy to be there."

I nodded. It wasn't the first time I'd heard word about Nathan's new life. But before I even had time to absorb what O'Donnell was telling me, he continued.

"That's what I care about now, Billy. Like you, I care a lot about Nathan…except my angle is different. I've been after Ronnie Luca for years Billy. *Y-e-a-r-s*," he emphasized. "And the way I now see it, Nathan Marks is my ticket in."

An instinctive fear told me where O'Donnell was going with all this, but his next words confirmed it: "That brings me to you."

PART II
Billy Tucker

Chapter Thirteen

August 1996.

Four years before I sat with Robert O'Donnell in Quantico, I never would have imagined myself an FBI agent. In fact, I left Tremont Heights for college that year thinking that I was leaving Nathan and Lucy behind, perhaps forever.

I arrived at Drexel's campus with nothing more than a battered brown suitcase. In it, I'd shoved two pairs of jeans, no-wrinkle khaki pants, one wool sweater, five T-shirts and a bunch of ratty underwear and socks. Most of my classmates arrived with much more. One of them was Roger Norman, my first friend.

I met Roger in passing. It was early in the afternoon of my second day on campus, and I was wandering around trying to figure out how to find my classes. Roger recognized the bewildered look on my face, told me he was a freshman too, and asked me to join him that night.

"We can get a jump on fraternity rush," he said. "I'm a legacy at Sigma Phi Delta. They're having a beer pong tournament tonight."

"Beer pong?" I asked.

"Ping pong. But with beer!" he boasted. "I visited in high school once. Guys play it all night. It's nuts."

"I wasn't really thinking about fraternities."

Roger shrugged, and smiled. "It's free beer," he said, turning away. "That should be good enough for now."

* * *

When Roger and I got to the fraternity house that night, he poured his legacy story on everyone. I had to hand it to Roger, though. He included me in all of his conversations.

"Billy's from Boston," he said, and about every fourth person responded with an annoying request.

"Say, 'Park the car in Harvard Yard.'"

I obliged for the most part, only because I wanted to fit in. Before I knew it, three beer pong games later, I had done just that.

"Serve it up Boston Billy!" someone yelled. "The bean-town kid's a natural."

They were right. Somehow, I had a knack for the lob and *poof!*—something everyone yelled when I sank the ball into the opposing player's cup. It was a shot worth five points and always required the opposing team to chug the beer on the table. I thought of bruise-ball the entire time, and I knew Nathan would have been proud.

At the end of a five-week period and after regular visits to the Sigma house, Roger and I both ended up getting bids. I was given a pledge pin and warned to wear it every day: "On the outermost piece of clothing!" the brothers yelled.

And for four months after that, I was a Sigma pledge, and a proud and diligent one at that. I lined up with my pledge brothers at midnight. I wore my underwear outside my jeans. I learned how to open my throat to chug a sixteen-ounce beer in two monster gulps. I formed pyramid poses with my pledge brothers on historic monuments throughout the city. I ran naked up the Art Museum steps. I ate a live goldfish. All of this in the spirit of my quest for Brotherhood and belonging.

By the time spring rolled around, I had settled into my new life. With the rigors of pledging and my academic schedule, though, I didn't have much time for anything else. Early into my second semester, Nathan and I had talked about a visit. I figured the annual spring beach bash would be the right time to bring him around. By then, pledging would be over and I'd be a Brother, able to come and go as I pleased. I would also have the chance to show off my new life. I told Nathan to bring Lucy, figuring her presence would yield a lot of advantages. She could keep Nathan occupied when I wanted to spend time with my Brothers, and even better, Lucy might be able to help me find a girl of my own.

But as soon as I saw Lucy stepping off the bus that April afternoon, the setting sun glowing behind her, I knew I'd made a mistake. Lucy wore an undersized, sleeveless T-shirt and form-fitting jeans. Her shoulders and stomach were toned, accented boldly by a sparkling, silver ring in her belly. When Lucy hit the pavement, she released her hair from its pony-tail in one defiant gesture, and my legs felt paralyzed. I knew then that I was in trouble, and that no other girl at the party would matter to me. It would be Lucy, just as it always had been, and I would have to hide my emotions the entire time.

"Billy!" she screamed when she saw me.

She jumped into my arms, straddled my hips and planted a kiss on my cheek.

"I am psyched for a frat party!" she called to the sky.

"Billy boy, college boy!" Nathan said, as he lugged two duffel bags with one arm and tried to maintain a straight gait. His forearm bulged and the veins in his wrist pulsed with the weight. I felt the strength in his grip as he tugged me toward him.

"I assume you're buying the beers," he said.

I had borrowed a car to meet them at the bus stop. We loaded in, and Lucy insisted that all three of us ride up front.

"So cool!" she called to no one in particular. "Back between my two guys. You said they're putting sand on the floors?"

"Already have," I answered. "My pledge class carted wheel-barrels of white sand in all day. Dye the bath water turquoise, and it'll feel just like the Caribbean."

"Reggae band?" Nathan asked.

I nodded. "And frozen drinks too."

"Just like the movies," Lucy added.

We didn't say much else in the fifteen minutes it took to get back to campus. Nathan and Lucy were looking around as we rode up the side streets, but both were quiet. I couldn't help but think how they must have felt as outsiders. I'd known that feeling myself only months ago. Students were darting across the street and down the sidewalks, and all of them had a purpose. Their expressions were different than those of the two seated next to me.

Sure, Nathan and Lucy were on the same streets, and that night, they would be sharing the same music, but for them, it all had a different purpose: a weekend taste of entitlement, a frozen drink, some dancing in the sand, and then a tired drive back to nowhere. When I saw that recognition in their eyes, I couldn't wait for the alcohol to hit. I just wanted us all to relax together and share a few laughs again.

Apparently, so did they. When we got to my room, Nathan dropped their bags on the floor, opened the mini-fridge and cracked two cans.

"Let the good times roll," he said, raising his beer and passing one to Lucy. "Buddy," he added turning to me. "I assume you'll join us in a toast."

I did. I pulled out a can for myself, touched it briefly to theirs, and then we each took a long gulp to start the night.

"Hey preppy chicks!" Nathan yelled out my window.

I laughed. When I first started, I'd seen it the same way. I guess my sensitivity to it had dulled over time.

"You want some beers!" he continued when he had their attention.

"Oh, that's good, Nathan," Lucy snapped.

"Hey handsome," came a call from the street.

Nathan brought his head back in and smiled. "I still got it," he said. "Even with these preppy brainiacs."

Lucy's sour look turned cold, and she stood up to cross the room. She stopped in front of my full-length mirror, leaned in and sucked in her cheeks, checking her makeup.

"Let's get going," she said.

Nathan and I only looked at each other, drained our beers and complied.

"It's a good time to head over to the house anyway," I added. "We can pre-party, and you two can meet some of the guys."

Lucy only offered a devilish smile.

* * *

When we arrived at the fraternity house, a sorry excuse for a once beautiful Southern style abode, I walked in first, my strides certain and my purpose determined. I surveyed a quiet living room and pointed to the sand on the floor and the amplifiers at the end of the room.

"It's going to be good," I bragged.

Nathan and Lucy then got my two-cent tour. A couple of the in-house Brothers—sophomores—had just finished showering and were shaving in an open bathroom, clad only in towels. Lucy, who entered the hallway first, smiled and waved, then turned, feigning embarrassment.

"Are you going to live here next year, Billy?" Lucy asked.

"Cheapest rent on campus," I said. "You bet I am."

"I'm losing my buzz," Nathan chimed. "Where is this basement and this continuous run of kegs you were talking about?"

I shook my head. "You can take a man out of the basement, but you can't take the basement out of the man."

Lucy burst out laughing, and Nathan shot her a dirty look. We rounded the hallway and descended the rotten wooden staircase into the cellar where the keg cooler awaited and a putrid odor of stale beer and bleach mixed the air.

I introduced my hometown friends to the Brothers standing around the ping-pong table, and Nathan and I challenged the winners. While we waited, Nathan studied the art of beer pong. Somehow, I knew he would dominate this foolish game just as he had the bruise-ball court. Lucy seemed to know it too. When Nathan and I took on the winning team, Lucy took the opportunity to cheer against her boyfriend.

"Sorry, Billy," she said, recognizing that she was routing against me too. "But this boy can still use a little humility."

Nathan pretended not to hear her, which prompted Lucy to turn-up the music.

As our game wore on, and we emptied one cup after another, the beer became tasteless. At one point, I looked up to see an unusual number of my Brothers gathering around. They threw back their beers with us, but none of them were focusing on the game. Their eyes were riveted on Lucy.

She was perched on the back of the couch with her feet resting on the seat cushions. Whenever there was a point in the game for our opponents, Lucy would jump and wiggle her hips, turning all heads. Then, all glasses were raised in a toast. Guys chugged for Lucy, and not for Brotherhood or ping-pong prowess.

Lucy knew exactly what she was doing. She was an expert at it. After one great shot by our opponents, when Lucy knew she had everyone's attention, she stopped in the middle of her victory dance, turned and reached up to the ledge for the radio. Her shirt rode up her back, revealing the top of her underwear and, of course, her butterfly tattoo. I saw. A bunch of the other guys saw as well. They quickly and quietly elbowed and signaled to those who did not. Lucy acted as if no one was looking and then began to move her rear end slowly, side to side, moving to the music.

I turned to Nathan. He pretended not to see.

"Service!" he called before lobbing the ball into play.

The game started to break up as more and more people arrived at the party. The basement was soon filled with too many distractions to play, but Nathan begged me to finish.

"Come on, Billy," he said. "We're about to whip these guys. We'll go upstairs and listen to Reggae later."

I didn't want to let him down, but I had no choice. People were crowding around the table, and there was barely enough room to move.

"Hey!" Nathan seethed at someone who came too close. "Clear away from the table, will you!"

His anger stunned us all.

Then he glared at our opponents. "Afraid you're going to lose?!"

"Nathan!" I stammered, wide-eyed. "What are you doing?"

"Finishing the God-damned game!" he snapped.

The guys across the table looked at each other and shrugged, then one of them turned to me.

"Billy, we're out. This isn't cool. We'll see you upstairs."

"Chicken-shits," Nathan muttered, jarring me to look their way in fear that they had heard.

In the meantime, Lucy had disappeared. The last I'd seen her, she was holding a conversation with three of the senior guys in the house. My guess was that she was upstairs dancing. It was 10:30 already and I could feel the vibrations from the band above.

"Where's Lip—stick?" Nathan asked, dragging her nickname, and it was the first time I'd ever heard him refer to that way.

I shrugged, as if Lucy's whereabouts should be irrelevant to us.

"Let's go up," he said, starting toward the stairwell.

Nathan and I jostled our way up and into the living room. Bob Marley's voice filled the air, and there was Lucy, crooking her index finger at her dance partners as she sang along and moved her body to the slow beat.

...I wanna love ya.
And treat you right.

I turned away and motioned for Nathan to come with me to the back patio. "Let's grab a frozen drink," I said. "They're loaded with 151-proof rum. That should keep us for a while."

Why I ever thought that 151 was a good idea is something I'll never know. We finished our drinks alone together in the cool evening air, but I was edgy, and it seemed Nathan felt the same way. At the very least, the hard stuff inspired him to finally open up.

"You've got a good thing going here, Billy," he said. "Better than I have back home, that's for sure."

I hoped he couldn't tell how fervently I agreed. "I don't know about that, Nathan. You've got a certain freedom back home. Here, in school, I never feel I can really relax. And let's not forget about Lucy," I added. "You have her."

Nathan shook his head. "Naah," he said. "Lucy's got me. I'm just hanging on for dear life."

Just then, the band announced they were taking a break. The DJ took over and the fast, frenetic beat of Modjo began to blast through the house. It was then that Lucy Polowski took over the party.

Lady, hear me tonight.
'Cause my feeling, is just so right.

Nathan and I heard a joyful scream. He met my look of bewilderment with one of grim recognition. We headed immediately toward the living room, but I wish we never had.

Bobby Reed, who had come to the party late and was delighted to see the new redhead, had won the war for Lucy's attention. That came as no surprise to me. At 6 foot 2 inches, with his California golden-boy glow, his family wealth and wide smile, he had women lining up for his attention wherever he went. But Bobby was a loyal fraternity Brother, and he would throw a girl aside in a second if it meant standing by one of his own. So when Bobby began to dance alone with Lucy, the rest of the guys begrudgingly backed off.

Bobby Reed was no match for Lucy on the dance floor, though. When he recognized the power of her presence, he tried to take control by stepping behind her, wrapping his arms around her mid-section and holding her tight. Lucy let him have his way for a while, but then she turned to him and jumped up onto his hips. Bobby placed his hands under her upper thighs and began to swing her around. As Lucy's legs straddled him, her arms released from his neck, and she leaned back to clear the dance floor. At some point, perhaps about the fifth turn, Bobby Reed's smile turned to wolfish intensity, and Lucy's face relaxed in an orgasmic frame.

That was when Nathan rushed him. I wasn't quick enough to grab him, to prevent the disaster about to befall my future with Sigma Phi Delta or to keep Bobby's head from crashing into the wall.

Seven guys jumped Nathan. I followed in a futile effort to pull them off. Two of the senior Brothers pinned me against a wall.

By the time Nathan sprung free, his shirt was tattered, and his right eye was bleeding. He looked around wildly, but the best way out was directly behind him. Nathan turned and leaped out the French doors to the porch. Before vaulting over the rail, though, he took out three of the guys in his way: one with his right elbow, one with his left leg, and one with his left hook.

I should have known Nathan would deal the last blow, and I should have just let him do it and go. Instead, breaking free from my Brothers, I ran after him. I raced across the living room, out onto the porch and over the rail. I did all of this without thinking, never considering the possibility that this move, a sudden and unforgivable shift in loyalty from the Brotherhood, would mean the end of me in Sigma, the organization I'd just spent the last several months pledging undying support.

Chapter Fourteen

I didn't dare go back to the fraternity house that night, or even the next day. I had violated the fraternity's code—'Our Creed,' as it was called—and sided against my Brothers. I knew that Nathan was wrong, but I also knew that Lucy had provoked the whole thing.

That night, none of us slept. After finding each other outside my dorm room, and after listening to Nathan and Lucy bicker for hours, we decided they should take the next bus back home. It left at 5:30 a.m., and I called a cab to take them to the station.

Nathan refused to stand with Lucy as we waited, so I did the honors.

"Not a good scene," I said, breaking the silence.

"Fuck it all, Billy," she blurted, startling me. "He just makes me so mad. He does whatever the hell he wants, whenever the hell he wants to. It's like I have no control."

I couldn't believe what I was hearing. As I saw it, control is exactly what Lucy always had.

"You?" I questioned.

"Oh, so you're on his side?" she challenged, but I pushed back.

"I'm not taking sides Lucy. I just can't imagine anyone ever having control of you."

"Everyone does," she stammered, her lower lip quivering. "My father does. Nathan does. You're the only one who let's me be me."

I was stunned. "Me? What do I do? I don't do anything."

"Exactly. That's exactly it, Billy. You don't do anything. And I love you for it."

Under any other circumstance, I would have killed to hear those words from her. This, I knew, was casual b.s.

"Nathan would do anything for you," I said, reflecting on what he'd told me. "He's yours. You have control. He's pathetic around you," I said, unable to resist the dig.

"Yeah, well screw him," she finished crossing her arms. "Him and everybody else. He's not going to be controlling me much longer."

A part of me smiled at the thought. The other part pitied Nathan and feared how he'd fare without her. I was used to loneliness when it came to love. I couldn't imagine Nathan in my shoes.

But we ran out of time. Nathan came up behind us as the cab pulled up.

"Sorry again, bud," Nathan said, reaching for my hand, pulling me in for a quick hug, and then trudging to the car with his bag. "Carry your own," he called back to Lucy.

She rolled her eyes at me, mouthed the word, 'see' and then bent down to reach for her belongings. I stepped in her way.

"I got it," I said, lifting her bag.

She offered me a smile. "Some lucky girl, Billy. I'm telling you. She'll be thanking the stars."

Lucy had spoken words like those before. They felt just as empty now.

I dropped her bag in the open trunk and slammed it shut. We embraced, and the touch of her body erased everything else from my mind.

She has to know, I told myself as the cab pulled away. *I'm so damn obvious.*

I went to the campus diner for some coffee and eggs, my head throbbing from the alcohol. I was too worried about what I had done to try to sleep. When the sun came up, I went straight to Roger's dorm room.

During pledging, Roger and I had come to rely on one another to get through Sigma's late-night line-ups and hazing events. His nickname throughout pledging had been Gimlet. The Brothers used to joke that he drank like an old lady, so they named him after a drink old ladies supposedly liked. Since my pledge name was Geyser, and since we constantly had to line up in alphabetical order by pledge name, Roger and I became natural companions.

My knock on his door was met with his typical response. "If you're not a hot chick, go away."

"It's me, Gimlet, open up."

"Geyser?" he asked.

"None other," I said.

I had earned my pledge name one night at a drinking event. My leg of our relay race required that I build a five-story house of cards, downing a beer and a shot of tequila with each level that stood without falling. If any story fell, and I had to re-build, I got no credit for the alcohol I had already consumed. I puked three times during this effort, and each time was *like a Geyser in the air*, I was told.

His voice changed to a whisper. "Are you alone?"

"Yes."

"I'm not supposed to talk to you, Billy," he said. "They told me to have you go straight to the house. Bring all of your trinkets."

By trinkets, I knew that Gimlet meant my pledge pin, Brother's pin, Brother's handbook and Sigma shield.

"What?" I was stunned. "Come on, Roger," I said, now serious. "Open up."

"You can't stay, Billy," he said as he opened the door. "If they even know I'm talking to you, I'm in big trouble."

I didn't care. "I got caught up in the moment, Roger. They can understand that, can't they? I mean, Christ, I've known the guy all my life. I've known you guys less than a year. Hell, if Nathan were here in college with me, he'd be a Sigma too."

"No good, Billy. If Nathan were a Sigma, he wouldn't have rushed Bobby Reed. That was about the worst thing he could have done."

I knew Roger was right. He continued, now angry.

"You think I'm happy about this?" he went on. "I mean, what the heck were you thinking? Couldn't you just have left quietly? Why did you have to bust through the living room and jump the rail. Now look at what you've done to yourself. Not to mention our friendship."

I shrugged his last comment off. I was sure Gimlet and I would stay friends through college, regardless of whether I honored 'the Shield' or lived by 'Our Creed.'

"Now, go," he demanded. "I'm not supposed to talk to you."

When I left Roger's dorm room, I didn't go to the house. I headed home. I badly needed sleep and decided that the fraternity that was about to throw me out could wait.

Hours later, I woke disoriented, and it was a moment before I remembered the events of the night before. I considered whether there was any chance it hadn't happened at all, but my chest actually started to hurt when I recognized the dramatic change my life was about to take.

I considered not going. *Maybe, if I put it off some more, I could avoid it altogether. Maybe I could just walk away.* Without Sigma, I couldn't think of any identity I'd have. To everyone I knew on campus, I was Billy Tucker, Sigma pledge, Sigma Brother. That made me a solid guy, gave me instant credibility. I was fun, but studious; vocal, but unintrusive; and serious, although never too much so.

Without Sigma, I was an outcast, nothing but the same half-wit from Tremont Heights who'd arrived on campus in September. The whole year's effort was about to go up in smoke. The pain in my heart started to spread.

Damn you, Nathan, I thought. *Damn you, Lucy and damn you, Billy, for even thinking of bringing them here*. I should have known better.

But then again, the fraternity to which I had pledged my loyalty should be a little more forgiving. A little more understanding.

"And more supportive!" I actually said out loud, thinking of all of the emphasis on 'mutual moral aid and support' in Sigma's Creed.

The truth, though, was that I could never submit to that code again. In the heat of the moment, I had made my choice, however instinctual or reflexive.

So I knew I had to go over to the house and let this drama run its course. I had to swallow a humiliation pill. That was what we all used to call it during pledging whenever the Brothers yelled at us. I knew that by taking my humiliation pill, I would relieve the organization of any further obligation to me, and myself of any further obligation to it. I walked to the house, wondering which of the Brothers would take the lead in emasculating me. I prayed it would not be Bobby Reed. I prayed that Bobby Reed wouldn't even be there.

And when I arrived at Sigma, it seemed my prayer had been answered. There was no cadre of Brothers waiting for me. In fact, when I opened the door with my key, there wasn't a soul in sight. I called out, but there was no answer. The house had been cleaned of the sand. It was as if the chaos of the night before had never happened at all.

I walked into the living room where the band had been. Maybe Gimlet was wrong. Maybe no one was expecting me, and everyone understood that alcohol-driven passions had gotten the better of a few of us the night before.

But then I saw it. There, on the French doors leading to the porch, the same doors through which I had followed Nathan the night before, was a sign with my name on it. Beneath the sign were five buckets, and each of the buckets had a label.

1. Billy Tucker's key to the house.
2. Billy Tucker's pledge pin.
3. Billy Tucker's Brother's pin.
4. Billy Tucker's Brother's handbook.
5. Billy Tucker's Sigma shield.

I stared at the signs like a traveler lost. It was easy to read the words, and they were easy enough to understand, but still, they made no sense to me at all.

This was it, I knew. This was my humiliation pill. No one wanted to see me or talk to me. There was no need for a formal or ceremonial dismissal. I was done, dead to the Brotherhood. They wanted nothing from me, other than the return of the symbols of my membership. I complied. I placed each symbol in its bucket, all the while wondering what I had truly done wrong.

Would any of them have done differently? I considered.

Maybe my bewilderment was proof that I deserved to be kicked out. If everyone else in Sigma felt I had let them down, maybe I didn't have a true understanding of the organization. Obviously, I had been missing something the entire time.

When I left and walked out into the night, I realized that this method of casting me out had been as effective as any ceremony. I did feel exiled, and I did feel shamed. Most of all, I felt lonely. It was the end of the year, and I was worse off than when I'd started. I would be infamous within Sigma, and maybe even beyond it. They would make me an example in the next year's line-ups.

Don't end up like pledge Geyser, you hear! Live by Our Creed. Obey the Brotherhood!!

* * *

Three years later, despite this record of my past, I was invited to join a new organization—the Federal Bureau of Investigation.

Chapter Fifteen

It was early December 1999 when the FBI introduced itself to me. I was a senior, and the last week of fall classes had passed, but I still had three finals and a paper to complete.

Lucy had been buried nearly two months. I tried getting by with denial, but mostly, my denial gave way to despair. My eyes looked expressionless in the mirror. I found it hard to smile. I tried to write it off to finals season, tried to assure myself that the look on my face was no different than that of my passing classmates: grim, lowered heads, preoccupied expressions, fear and anxiety. All would be better come winter break, I promised myself. But I knew better. A flare in my life had died with Lucy, I was sure.

My grades had been horrible my freshman year, courtesy of the distractions of Sigma. My sophomore year was much better, probably because I had opted for isolation. I found a classmate to have a beer with on occasion, but for my own sanity, I didn't want to be around the social scene. It was infested with students from the Greek system, a wider circle in which I was no longer welcome. So through that year and into the next, I was happy living like a hermit, finding a corner carrel on the top floor of the library and burying myself in class readings. My grade point average flourished, and by the end of my junior year, I had managed to reach a 3.35 GPA. I was hoping to pull it up into the A- range in this last year. That, I felt, would help me land a decent job, although doing what, I had no idea. I hated the thought of sales, consulting, banking or accounting. The thought of graduate school was even more distasteful. Professor Adams, my research director, once tried to talk me into going for a Ph.D in American history. Although I admired the Professor, and the way he took comfort in a torn chair, pipe smoke and tattered books, I just knew that wasn't for me. After the way I had been living the last couple of years, I needed to be in the world, not studying it.

The FBI's December information session was only supposed to be a study break. Their brochure was an intriguing addition to the monthly package of materials we received from the recruitment center, particularly after Lucy's shooting, but I didn't exactly consider myself FBI material.

I read the FBI's Mission Statement inside the front cover of the brochure:

The mission of the FBI is to uphold the law through the investigation of violations of federal criminal law; to protect the United States from foreign intelligence and terrorist activities; to provide leadership and law enforcement assistance to federal, state, local and international agencies; and to perform these responsibilities in a manner that is responsive to the needs of the public and is faithful to the Constitution of the United States.

On the back cover, I read the FBI's core values:

In performing its mission, the FBI must preserve and defend its core values: rigorous obedience to the Constitution; respect for the dignity of all those we protect; compassion; fairness; uncompromising personal and institutional integrity. Observance of these core values is our guarantee of excellence and propriety in performing the FBI's national security and criminal investigative functions.

It all seemed so high and mighty to me at the time. I wasn't sure I had the stomach for it. My disdain for core values and mission statements, anything resembling a 'Creed' for that matter, had long since passed.

Nonetheless, I called the number listed to register my attendance. "William G. Tucker," I said. "I'll be there."

The "G" was for Gerard. I hated it. There was a Gerard in my class in grade school, and he'd been kind of a slob. So to me, Gerard was a sloppy name, and sloppy people bothered me. I'd had very little growing up, and my mother once told me that if I was organized and tidy, I would always have room for more. To me, those who were sloppy weren't ready for more. They couldn't handle what they had.

* * *

Drexel's largest auditorium was a massive cathedral-like hall with plush red chairs and long flowing drapes. It was the oldest building on campus, and always the place for significant events. That night, the auditorium was filled with the buzz of frenzied seniors, echoing laughter and rising voices as people waited for the FBI's recruitment session to begin.

"My mom would kill me if I came out of college a policeman," someone said.

On the auditorium stage was a long table, and on either side of it were two flags, the American flag and that of the Department of Justice. Three people stood behind the table, and the man in the middle asked us politely but firmly to take our seats. I found a chair in the center section, directly in front of them. I wanted to feel that they were talking directly to me.

"Good evening, and thank you for coming," the man in the middle began. "My name is Francis Keiler. I'm the Director of the Recruitment and Public Affairs division of the Federal Bureau of Investigation. On my right is Marianne Delaney and on my left is Bryce Cardin. Both Marianne and Bryce are special agents. They will each have some unique issues about the FBI to present. You'll see that there are some more of us milling around in the back and on the sides. Don't worry. You're free to leave if you want."

This last comment drew a chuckle from the crowd.

"I'm glad you recognize I'm kidding," Francis Keiler continued. "But I want you know I'm also serious. I'm here not only to brag about the Bureau—which is how we within the FBI tend to refer to it—but also to clear up some misconceptions about the world's most powerful law enforcement agency."

Francis Keiler's words commanded instant attention.

"Now it might be of interest to you that I've referred to Marianne and Bryce as special agents instead of just plain old agents, but what is an agent really? Anyone?"

No one responded.

"I figured. Four years of college and you're all math majors right?"

Again, a chuckle from certain members of the crowd, including me.

"Well, an agent is someone who acts on behalf of another with the other's express or implied authority to do so. Think about it. Agents are anybody. Lay persons. Someone you ask to run an errand." There was a pause. "Okay, I'll put it to you in your own terms. Someone you ask to make a beer run!"

This time, the audience roared, and Keiler paused to savor the moment, stroking his goatee.

"If the FBI was made up of plain old agents, you wouldn't know who they were answering to. So in the FBI, we refer to everyone who makes it through Quantico as 'special agents.' They're special because they act on behalf of the FBI, the Department of Justice and the United States of America. They're special because they answer only to the Bureau. It is the Bureau that answers directly to you, the citizens of the United States of America."

"Ladies and gentlemen," Keiler intoned. "I present to you *your Bureau,* the Federal Bureau of Investigation."

The hair on my arms and neck rose to attention. The lights went down and a filmed presentation began. It was the scene of a bank robbery, and it was electrifying.

Down, heads down, nobody move!

Three masked gunmen yelled orders at the people in the bank. The man near the teller called out.

Money in the bag. Put the money in the bag!

The men were carrying automatic machine guns. In the corner was a security guard who appeared to work for the bank. He was bound and gagged against the leg of a desk. Sweat streamed from his forehead.

Who wants to die! one of the gunmen yelled.

He pointed his rifle at the ceiling and fired. The plaster splattered on the floor below.

The scene shifted to just outside the building. In the back of a van, labeled 'FBI, SWAT,' sat ten armed individuals. They exchanged confident looks and nodded as they clutched their firearms and filed out of the van. They took positions at the bank's entrances, exchanging hand signals.

Next, the bank robbers were making their way toward the front door, lugging bags. A car, apparently driven by another member of the robbery team, pulled up to the front of the bank. When he saw the FBI jackets, he hit the gas hard and took off. One of the agents pulled out his radio and dispatched a description of the vehicle. The members of the SWAT team held their ground and their rifles, waiting for the front doors of the bank to open.

Down the street, away from the bank, there was an explosion. The entire SWAT team turned toward it as the bank robbers came through the doors.

The film stopped, and the lights in the auditorium went on. My body pulsed with adrenaline.

"Ladies and gentlemen," Keiler began above the buzz in the crowd. "What you have just witnessed was a crime in progress in a town called Hogan's Alley. The Bank of Hogan is a frequent target for criminals. It is held up at least twice a week."

The audience looked puzzled.

"No joke, my friends. Hogan's Alley is a five-million dollar training ground for prospective FBI agents. It's located at the FBI Academy in Quantico, Virginia. Mock crimes are held there daily, but the scene you just saw was as real to those trainees in the FBI jackets as it felt to you just now. A trainee's failure to treat, react and respond appropriately to every scenario presented at Hogan's Alley results in failure. At the academy, failure is not taken lightly, because on the streets, failure costs lives."

A heavy murmur reverberated in the dome-shaped room.

"I'm going to give the floor to Marianne," Keiler said, and he stepped back, allowing a stiff-lipped woman with a cropped haircut to step forward.

"Good evening, everyone. As Fran told you, my name is Marianne Delaney. I'm here to tell you something I bet ninety-nine percent of you don't know about the FBI. Less than five percent of our work involves a situation where we are required to draw a gun. Contrary to popular belief, the FBI is not about drawing weapons, kicking in doors, hand to hand combat, high-speed car chases and acrobatic arrests. In fact, across the nation, there are less than fifty incidents of gun discharges by the FBI per year."

Disappointment was evident on many faces in the crowd, but I didn't share it. That part of the job did not intrigue me.

"The FBI builds its cases through years of investigation. That requires teamwork and extensive cooperation. As special agents, we are required to listen to telephone conversations on tapped lines, plow through piles of financial reports, execute search warrants and interview witnesses, whether by subpoena or voluntary consent. These duties require a wide variety of skills—skills the FBI looks for when recruiting."

"The FBI needs people with language skills, people skills, book smarts, street smarts, common sense, balanced judgment, mathematical abilities and computer proficiency. We like athletes, artists, musicians, lookers, jerks, bullies and geeks."

"That's right, ladies and gentlemen. The FBI has never once in its history employed an agent who met all of its criteria. Through our recruiting program, however, we seek to develop an FBI family that is educated and trained to meet any situation."

"The FBI is about gathering information and proving cases. In order to do that, we need to gain people's confidence, trust and respect. If a private citizen is more comfortable dealing with an agent of his or her own race or gender, that's what the Bureau is going to provide. If we need information from someone whose first language is Swahili, the FBI will bring an agent who speaks Swahili."

"If you ask FBI agents what they like best about their job, many will say the diversity. Not only do we get to work with all kinds of people and do the things that movies are made about, but we appear in nearly every professional context you can imagine. We dress in everything from jeans and sweats to business suits. We testify in court and work closely with prosecutors and judges. We move from the darkest city streets to the conference tables of corporate boardrooms."

"And we use handcuffs in both situations."

The crowd roared with its approval.

Special Agent Delaney waited for the noise to settle down.

"We have a tremendous amount of authority, ladies and gentlemen, but that authority brings responsibility. Take it away, Bryce."

Special Agent Bryce Cardin, a handsome, caramel-skinned African American, stepped forward.

"If you think this job is about the blunt assertion of force or power, ladies and gentlemen, think again. When you're an FBI agent, you enjoy a tremendous amount of power, but what separates the best from the worst is the way it is wielded. As a special agent, you carry a responsibility twenty-four hours a day. That is not easy, and we know it. In our jobs and in our daily decisions and interactions, the constant exercise of discretion is required. Sure, the FBI has guidelines for how an agent must act, but they are just that: guidelines. We rely on our own judgment nearly every moment of the day."

"For those who don't handle their power responsibly, the FBI has set up an official division, the Office of Professional Responsibility—or OPR—to specifically address breaches by agents both on and off the job. That's right, ladies and gentlemen, whether you're on duty or off, you're always a representative of the Bureau."

"And in the FBI, responsibility comes in many forms, only some of which involve arrests, the protection of witnesses and the cultivation and management of informants. Other forms of responsibility are not as well known. As an FBI agent, you have a responsibility to extend the ideals of the Bureau to the citizens you protect. Our field offices provide programs such as academic tutoring, drug education and safety on the streets. We are committed not only to live by our ideals, but to use them to empower others."

"The initials F-B-I have meaning beyond the one you know so well. The 'F' is for Fidelity. The 'B' is for Bravery. And the 'I' is for Integrity. We look for agents who will be loyal to the cause and courageous and honest in the battle. We seek individuals who will—with Fidelity, Bravery and Integrity—work proudly to seek justice and to protect the American way of life. My question for you is whether you have what it takes."

When Bryce Cardin finished, the room was silent. Francis Keiler stepped forward and shook hands with the other two agents who spoke before addressing us again.

"That's it, folks. That's our speech, and we don't want to take up any more of your time in finals season. But one last thing before you go: we have representatives in the lobby who can address any questions you have. You should also pick up a brochure and application as you leave. Thank you for coming. Thank you all."

I couldn't believe it was over. I wanted more. As the audience rose and murmurs gave way to high-fives, hand grabs and playful jostling, I stayed seated. I had been to fourteen corporate information sessions over the last few months and had never felt so complete.

That night, I filled out the application I had picked up outside the auditorium. I nearly cried when I went to sleep, though, thinking about what I had done at Sigma. I was sure the FBI would never want me.

Chapter Sixteen

The letter that came in the mail telling to me to contact the FBI's local field office for an interview was a shocker. It was also how I came to meet Assistant Special Agent in Charge Robert O'Donnell.

He said he didn't typically conduct interviews for the Bureau, but every now and then, he liked to pitch in for recruitment. He said he was impressed with me. I couldn't think of any time I had heard those words before.

I told him about Sigma. He told me my bravery was admirable. I asked him if I was disloyal. He said just the opposite.

"Your commitment to Nathan should have been admired by the Brotherhood, not scorned."

I felt vindicated.

When we shook hands after our meeting, I had a good feeling, and I received the acceptance letter eleven days later. I jumped up and down pumping my fist. I felt relief, pride and honor, all at once. Robert O'Donnell had given me the break of a lifetime, I was sure, a career overflowing with action, but requiring intellectual acumen. Best of all, Robert O'Donnell had given me power. I had never been a part of something so important before. Three days after graduation, I departed for Quantico.

* * *

The FBI's training academy in Quantico, Virginia was not a place for the faint-hearted, weak-minded or physically unfit. It was a place where determination begat discipline, and where authority mocked its disciples. My goal going in, as eager as I felt, was to simply stay afloat.

As the Greyhound bus made its way down the winding Virginia road, my hands shook. I had heard that the next sixteen weeks of my life would be grueling, and that the physical challenges were tremendous, but that intellectual discipline was critical to succeed. Signs along the road spelled out warnings about live ammunition being fired in the area. I thought about stray bullets and whether, in my new life, I would ever really feel safe again. As we pulled up to the gated entrance, there was a flutter in my chest. I was soon to become an integral part of it all.

"I'm Billy Tucker," I said to the guard with the clipboard at the gate. "One of the new trainees, reporting as scheduled."

I half expected my name to be missing from the list, that I had not really been accepted into the FBI at all. But the man flipped a few pages, smiled, extended his clipboard to me, handed me his pen and asked me to sign. Then, he went back into his booth and placed a call. When he hung up, he told me to wait for my ride.

It wasn't long before a golf cart screeched to a stop before me. Although the guy behind the steering wheel looked serious and stern, as soon as he had secured his vehicle, he extended his hand with a warm, wide smile.

"Billy Tucker?"

"Yes sir."

"Hop in."

I placed my duffel bag into the back of the cart and settled in. When my driver saw me seated, he stepped on the gas and steered toward what looked like the main campus of a university. Then he broke the silence.

"There are going to be a lot of people here welcoming you Billy, but I wanted to be the first. My name is Max Fulton, and I act as a mentor here at Quantico. You should always feel free to come to me with any problems, questions or just to shoot the shit. My job is to look out for you. While you are very much alone when you participate in training segments and examinations, you should take comfort in the fact that you can always talk to me. I've been told I give some pretty darn good advice."

Though Max seemed like a nice guy, the whole instant confidante act seemed forced. "I barely know you, Max," I said casually, expecting him to handle my comment with a shrug or a joke.

Instead, Max Fulton stopped the cart short. I lurched forward and my bag slammed into my back. Startled, I looked at my driver, but even when the cart was completely still, Max Fulton didn't look at me. He looked down. He stared at his feet and nodded slowly as if collecting his thoughts. Then, he turned to me and put his hand on my shoulder.

Looking me in the eye, he said, "you do now."

It was a simple statement, and it said so much. I had never met Max before and he had never met me, but the look in his eye, his grip and the sincerity of his words reminded me that we shared a bond: one forged not by years of friendship and shared adventures, nor from whipping other guys on a bruise-ball court or drinking heavily together into the night. It was bond conferred by the organization whose grounds we were on.

After letting his message sink in and watching me nod in understanding, Max Fulton turned back to the road, stepped on the gas and began his introduction.

"I don't know what you know already, Billy," he began, "but I'll give you a little background. The FBI academy opened here in Quantico, Virginia in 1972, almost twenty-five years after former FBI Director J. Edgar Hoover started the FBI's first formal training course for new agents. Initially, the FBI's program consisted of some classroom work in Washington, D.C. and a three week study in the use of firearms and making arrests on a Marine base in Quantico. Today, all of that has changed. In the next sixteen weeks of your life, you're about to see just how."

"There are more than twenty buildings in the camp here, Billy. All of them are interconnected by glass-walled corridors. Inside, you'll find just about everything you could ever need. The camp here at Quantico operates as a world unto itself."

Max pulled up to one of the buildings.

"I'm going to drop you off here. Inside, they'll have your name on a list. They'll give you a key. A room has already been assigned, and it's yours for the duration. Set your alarm so that you'll make class at eight tomorrow morning. Report to the Classroom Building then, because—surprise, surprise—that's where all your classes will be. There'll be a notebook and pens waiting for you at the seat you've been assigned."

That seat is where I first got to know Victoria Summers.

Chapter Seventeen

From that first day at Quantico, I felt as if I had joined a new fraternity. There were time-honored secrets and traditions I knew I would learn, and the FBI had a set of ideals and standards I knew I would be asked to uphold and live by. If I could not, I knew I would be gone. It was that simple, just as it had been for me in Sigma.

Max Fulton had probably described it best: "In the Bureau there's a hierarchy. In the hierarchy, there's certainty. In certainty, there's comfort—and in comfort, we can grow as individuals within the structure given to us. We have boundaries. We know our limits. We know our role. We play that role until we are asked and are ready to play another role. The system works, Billy. If you don't see that yet, you will."

I understood what he was saying all too well. I had watched guys like Roger Norman, who had managed to live within Sigma's boundaries, assume leadership positions in the years that followed pledging, both among the Brotherhood and in campus and community organizations. They could do that because they had confidence from belonging to something, and a base of support to build upon. Without Sigma, I lost the structure and boundaries it offered, and I never replaced it. I had no boundaries, and found a wholly inadequate substitute in the library carrels. Now that I was being asked to devote my loyalty to another organization—a real and lasting one—I wanted it to work. I swore I would do whatever it took to make sure that it did.

But still, I wondered whether I was up to the task. The reality was, in Sigma, I had failed my duty of loyalty the first moment I'd been confronted with a real choice.

Had I learned my lesson? Would the FBI's sixteen weeks and five million dollar training facility be wasted on me?

All of these thoughts plagued me as I turned the key to my room, not knowing what to expect inside.

As the door opened wide, though, I felt a strange sense of *de ja vu,* flashing back to when I'd first glanced around my freshman dorm room at Drexel. The room made efficient use of its small space. Against the right wall was a thin, low bed. Against the left, next to a closet, stood a wooden dresser with six drawers, and a mirror that did a better job of distorting than reflecting.

At the foot of the bed, I noticed three folded t-shirts. They were navy blue with yellow lettering and the Department of Justice crest across the left portion of the chest. I remembered the many forms I'd filled out once I'd been accepted into the FBI's training program. One indicated that the required uniform during training was khaki pants and a t-shirt, the color of which was subject to vote by the class of trainees. Navy had apparently been the color of choice. It was the one I had voted for, and I smiled.

I unfolded one of the shirts, and I immediately noticed the slogan.

STRENGTH IN SILENCE
WISDOM IN OBSERVATION

I supposed I would learn a higher meaning in those words in the weeks to come. I dropped my duffel bag on the bed and headed back outside. My fellow trainees apparently shared this desire, because the courtyard was filled with fresh, direction-less faces.

I eventually found my way into the Central Building and its decorated rotunda. There, carved into the walls was the FBI's slogan: F-fidelity. B-bravery. I-integrity. Underneath each letter, a colorful and inspiring quotation followed.

Under Fidelity: "Prosperity asks for fidelity; adversity exacts it."

Under Bravery: "Courage is the resistance to fear, mastery of fear—not absence of fear."

Under Integrity: "Integrity without knowledge is weak and useless, and knowledge without integrity is dangerous and dreadful."

Lost in thought about the words I saw and what they would mean to me as the weeks wore on, I was startled to hear a voice behind me.

"Impressive, eh sport."

I turned. There, before me, was an older man with a graying crewcut and icy blue eyes. He was shorter than me, but carried himself as if he were six feet, five inches tall. I responded politely though I wanted to remark that the past hour in Quantico had seemed a study in prose and slogans.

"Inspiring, I'd say. I'm Billy Tucker. I just arrived today for training."

"Welcome. Welcome, young man. You're going to see a lot of me over the next several weeks. I'm your firearms instructor, Gil Pickens."

"Hello Mr. Pickens," I said, extending my hand and maintaining eye contact.

"Gil. Gil is fine."

I nodded.

"Well," Gil continued drawing a deep breath. "You've found my favorite spot. I do admit I come here daily for inspiration. Those letters up there stand for everything that's in those carvings and more. They make me proud to work for the Bureau."

Gil was silent for a moment while he stared up at the words, and I felt a little awkward. I considered excusing myself when he turned to me with a smile.

"But I'm going to tell you another three initials you can count on in the Bureau that are pretty helpful too, Billy." He paused and looked at me with a grin. "You ready?"

"Shoot," I said, then felt a little silly when the firearms instructor smiled at the irony of my response.

"C-D-I."

"C-D-I?" I repeated.

"C-D-I," Gil affirmed, nodding his head. "Do you know what it stands for?"

"I have no idea."

"Take a guess."

I looked away, staring over Gil's shoulder and trying to concentrate.

"Common?"

I looked at Gil for approval, but his expression didn't change.

"Crime? Criminal?"

Gil still didn't move.

"Common Desires..." I continued to look away. "Crime Duties...Criminal Defendants..."

Finally, I gave up. "You got me. What is it?"

Gil's face lit up. "C-D-I, Billy. C-D-I. Chicks Dig It."

He let out a boisterous laugh. "Chicks dig the Bureau. It's romance. It's danger. It's excitement. It's machismo! I'll tell you, Billy, there are a lot of perks that come with being an FBI agent, but none of them please me more than the fact that Chicks Dig It."

I chuckled and smiled so as not to hurt his feelings, but a different three words came to my mind.

God help me, I thought.

Chapter Eighteen

I stepped into the Classroom Building the next morning not knowing which way to turn. The angular and freckle-faced woman behind me shared my confusion.

"Anyone have a map?" she asked, the pleading sparkle of her eyes a welcome distraction from the determination in her jaw. She looked more uptight than I felt.

"My guess is left," I ventured.

"I say right," she snapped, pursing her lips.

I would have insisted on my way, but I wanted to get off to a good start. "I'll go with your instinct then," I added. "Right it is."

And right she was. I turned to her and smiled as we rounded the corner in the corridor and noticed the commotion outside one of the rooms. "Billy Tucker," I said, extending my hand.

"Victoria," she responded, gripping my hand firmly in hers. "Victoria Summers," she added. "I'm from San Diego."

I nodded, though I had never been there. "Long way from home, I guess. I'm from outside of Boston, which isn't so close either."

"It doesn't matter," she said. "We're both here now."

We got to the door of the classroom and I stepped aside to let Victoria pass through first. She turned to me, tilted her head and narrowed her eyes.

"After you, Billy Tucker," she said.

I dared not disobey, and I wondered what Gil Pickens was going to think of her. I passed through the doors ahead of her without a backward glance. I found my seat, which was five rows up and the seventh seat in. We were seated alphabetically, I learned, when Victoria Summers settled into seat six.

"Guess we're neighbors," she said.

"I guess so," I answered. "No cheating off me," I added with a smile.

She smirked, then added: "Don't worry about it."

I looked around the room and watched as many of my classmates introduced themselves to one another. Everyone seemed to have the same respectful, friendly manner. Everyone, including Victoria, looked a lot older than me.

I turned to her. "I think I'm the youngest here," I said.

"I'm twenty-six," she answered. "The average student is supposed to be twenty-nine. So I'm probably one of the youngest too."

"I'm twenty-two," I told her.

"Cut it out," she snapped. "You're right out of college?"

"Fresh."

"I was told they didn't do that," she questioned. "I waited three years to apply. Heck, I nearly bored myself to death in an accounting firm."

"You were an accountant?"

"Don't look so surprised, Billy *boy*."

"No, no," I said, ignoring her slight. "If anything, I'm impressed."

"Well, I'm told that most of the people here have already been professionals in some capacity."

I couldn't help but feel intimidated. The most I could brag about was an 'A' on a final exam. Wondering whether I was ready for what I was about to face, I barely noticed the instructor stride into the room. His first words, though, were enough to bring anyone to attention.

"Please stand," he said firmly, before even introducing himself.

We all shot to our feet. Victoria Summers rose just ahead of me, and I noticed the shapely curvature of her waist.

Athletic, I assumed, and the future would prove me right. Victoria would have the edge on me, and nearly everyone else, for the next sixteen weeks when it came to field work. When we were all standing, the instructor spoke again.

"The weeks to come will challenge you like you've never been challenged before, but we expect each and every one of you to come away from our program prepared to protect the FBI's ideals. Repeat after me," he finished, and we all did so in unison.

I do solemnly swear that I will support and defend the Constitution of the United States against all enemies, foreign and domestic.

As we echoed his words, the room resonated with pride.

"Thank you. Now please sit down," he said.

I would come to see that all our instructors shared one characteristic: they were very direct, so direct that for sixteen straight weeks, none of us dared not follow instructions.

"Now," he said. "My name is Marvin Baxter. I promise you that by the end of this first week, I will know each of yours. For now, let's get right to it."

I turned to Victoria to check her reaction. She did not turn to look at me.

For the next two hours, we received an introductory lecture on the history of the FBI and its various initiatives under directors ranging from J. Edgar Hoover to William Sessions. We learned about Hoover's obsession with crime statistics and his dislike of lengthy investigations because they absorbed resources and produced limited results. We learned about the shift in the FBI's focus under the Kennedy presidency and the pressure to engage in long-term battles against organized crime.

By the time Marvin Baxter was through, I felt as if he had been an FBI agent for sixty years. I took copious notes, trying to get it all down, yet unable to keep up with all the information he provided. I quickly realized that the classroom work in Quantico was going to be harder than anything I had experienced at Drexel. Unlike the material in college, all of it mattered and very little was theoretical. So much information was condensed into such short sessions that I was drained at the end of every day from the classroom work alone.

Victoria Summers seemed to handle it better than me. She focused only on key points. Her handwriting was clear and concise. From our first lecture, I admired the organization on her notepad out of the corner of my eye as I wrung out my cramping hand. By the time we were released for our morning break, I was spent. I closed my eyes and sighed as Victoria got up. She seemed to take a certain pleasure in my fatigue.

"Do that at an all-day client meeting, Billy, and you'll know why I left accounting."

"I can't believe it's only ten in the morning."

"I need the bathroom and a coffee. You need a shot of adrenaline," she said, apparently now comfortable enough to tease.

I took a shot of my own. "You know what they say about bladders," I said, prompting her to eye me suspiciously. "They shrink with age," I finished with a smile. Despite herself, Victoria Summers smiled back.

"You're all right, Billy-boy," she said. "Just don't even think about trying to switch notes."

The instructor then called out to the class. "You have ten minutes," he said checking his watch. "Ten minutes exactly."

Victoria turned, and I followed her to the end of our aisle. As we hustled our way into the hall and got separated in the mass of classmates, I realized that, in the few short hours I knew her, Victoria Summers had earned my respect.

* * *

I was almost the last to come through the door at ten minutes past the hour. The only one behind me was a southern hick who'd introduced himself as Jimmy-Joe in the hall. He'd heard Victoria call me Billy-boy, and he'd figured I was a southerner as well.

Jimmy-Joe had come to the FBI from the Charlottesville Police Force. He told me he was a nine-year veteran and had been trying to get into the FBI since he was eighteen. Jimmy-Joe had never been to college, but he said that he devoured history books like a "hog in the mud."

He also said he had spent his free time on the force studying the country's "Most Wanted" lists. He'd hoped that one day, just by chance and the "hand of God," he would get his break.

"Well, I did, Billy. I did get my break," he said. "Lester Chavez was a Mexican drug lord, wanted in his home country and the United States for multiple violent murders—two of them American tourists. Lester had last been seen in Jasper, Tennessee. He was said to be running around as an insurance salesman, always on the road. I slept with his picture by my bedside, Billy-boy. And you should have seen his face when I spotted him at a strip mall licking the cream out of the belly of a donut. I was in plain clothes, off-duty, but it was like he knew what was coming. Of course, my voice might have tipped him off…"

"Jimmy-Joe," I interrupted. "I want to hear the end of this, but we'd better get back to class. It's ten past now."

When we walked inside—the last two to enter—the instructor had a satisfied smile on his face. He had found his first two victims.

In Quantico, we learned a lot through role playing. Jimmy-Joe Carlisle and Billy Tucker would be the first to give it a try. The scenario: an administrative assistant who won't let an FBI agent through the doors despite the agent's possession of a warrant. We were told that the admin had been warned by his boss, Sonny Hugo, that he was fired if the agent made it through the doors.

Jimmy-Joe played the admin. I played the agent.

"You just wait right here," Jimmy Joe said as he pretended to close a door in my face. The classroom erupted with laughter as Jimmy-Joe walked away, took a seat by the exit door and pretended to file his nails. I looked up to notice the expression of intense amusement on Victoria's face.

I pretended to knock. "FBI sir. You need to open this door right now. I have a warrant."

Jimmy-Joe continued to file his nails. The classroom continued to laugh. I tried to think creatively, but my mind was completely blank.

"You tell Sonny Hugo that this warrant is for his arrest," I called. "You hear me?!"

Jimmy-Joe stomped across the room toward me. He pretended to open the door again.

"Excuse me!" he boomed. "Let me see that warrant," he said, ripping it from my hand. "This warrant is defective. You go back to your damn coffee cake and computers and you stay out of here unless and until you've got a lawful reason to be here. You hear me!"

Jimmy-Joe's voice roared with such authority that I actually took a step backward. After that, I didn't even need to hear the end of the story of Lester Chavez. I was speechless. The class was silent. The instructor asked me to step aside and then, approaching Jimmy-Joe, he leaned in, nose to nose with the eager Charlottesville recruit.

"I'm going to say this once more politely, sir, and then I'm not going to say it again." Marvin Baxter held a piece of paper in front of Jimmy-Joe's face. "This warrant has been signed by a federal judge. That federal judge is named Peter Thomas Meehan. When I was in Judge Meehan's courtroom yesterday, speaking to His Honor, I told him about the evidence the FBI has gathered against Sonny Hugo. I told him about the wiretaps, the statements, the eyewitnesses and the paper trail."

The class was dead silent as the instructor continued to speak.

"And you know what he told me? He said, 'Agent Baxter. It appears you've done some thorough work. In my courtroom, all are presumed innocent, but Sonny Hugo's days of presumptions seem to be numbered.'"

"So you know what pal? Unless you've got a mind to challenge the signature of that federal judge, unless you think your job is worth five years in prison for being an accessory after the fact and impeding a federal investigation, you show some respect and some brains and step aside."

And then, the instructor said a final word. "Now!!" he roared, and this time, Jimmy-Joe Carlisle flinched and did as he was told.

The role play was over. The instructor waited for us to take our seats.

"Jimmy-Joe Carlisle and Billy Tucker: Congratulations!" he emphasized. "You've passed your first test. Now the rest of you, those who watched, but didn't have the opportunity to participate, tell me what you saw."

At least ten hands went up. Jimmy-Joe Carlisle and I found ourselves legends for the night, at least until the next day's role play and the new lessons that came with it.

Through role playing, we learned how to conduct interviews, confront adversity and develop informants. Marvin Baxter told us that, while other instructors in Quantico might disagree with him, he felt that the art of eliciting information from those who didn't want to divulge it was the most essential skill we would learn. And he emphasized the importance of demonstrating integrity.

"When people respect you," Baxter said, "they'll tell you their life story, even if you don't ask."

Marvin Baxter loved the role playing. It was obvious from the energy he put into the scenes he invented. And he provided exactly what a group of naïve students needed in order to feel comfortable play-acting in front of one another. He tolerated no ridicule whatsoever.

"From now on," he said, "save your laughter for comedy clubs. What we're doing here will keep you functional and safe on the streets."

But our training had only begun.

Chapter Nineteen

Over the next sixteen weeks, with four to six hours of classroom sessions per day, we were taught academic subjects such as criminal procedure, forensic science, foreign counterintelligence and computer database analysis. We were also given hard and fast rules about subpoenas, warrants, background investigations and the various methods of polygraph examination. Mixed in with all of it was further historical background about the FBI.

We learned about Congress' weapons to fight organized crime, including the passing of Title III of the Omnibus Crime Control and Safe Streets Act of 1968 which gave the government authority for electronic eavesdropping—wiretapping—in criminal cases, and the Racketeer Influenced and Corrupt Organizations Act, or RICO.

"Three cheers for Title III and RICO," our instructor said. "They are the two most critical tools we have for gathering information and seeing that information through to prosecution and conviction today."

We also had ethics and sensitivity training. We learned about agents who had fallen prey to corruption and abuse of power. Apparently, the danger was greatest among new agents, and we were tested with numerous hypothetical questions and scenarios so that the instructors in Quantico could predict our reactions to ethical pressure and adversity. While answers to some of the questions were obvious, others required tortured analysis and constant second-guessing. The tests were timed, though, so inevitably, we had to go with our gut reactions.

You're invited to a dinner party with your significant other. You are meeting his/her friends for the first time, and you want to make a good impression. You've been told that these are the friends whose opinion matters. You arrive at the party and the two couples present are passing around a joint filled with marijuana. You smell it, and you know it. The introductions and small talk are short. Your significant other takes a smoke. The joint is passed to you. You are witnessing a federal crime. You are now asked to participate in the federal crime.

Do you particpate?

And that was the easy question.

What do you do about the federal crime you are witnessing?

That was the killer. It was questions like these that made me wonder if I was going to make it through, because the 'right' answer seemed too heavy handed. *Arrest five people? Including my significant other?*

The instructions said to answer this second question in two sentences, not to exceed three lines of handwriting. I ended up going with my gut.

I would tell them that I apologized for intruding on their private lives, but they had to immediately stop and dispose of the substance. I would tell them that if they continued, I could not look the other way.

I was sure that when I answered this question, I was doomed. The FBI had a New Agent Review Board specifically set up to eliminate those it deemed weak and susceptible to corruption. For all I knew, as I wrote my answer to this question, I was going to go through sixteen weeks of grueling work only to be told at the end that I didn't have the proper morals to serve the United States with fidelity and integrity. To me, though, the situation called for discretion, even if the 'right' answer meant five arrests.

Other hypotheticals were less emotional, but no less challenging. The instructors made it clear that as part of the FBI, we had an obligation to look out for ourselves, but it was more important to look out for the public we protected. What struck me most was how the instructors emphasized that the public included the accused.

"The accused," the ethics instructor told us, "is entitled to equal justice and due process. I assure you that there will be no sweeter victory as an investigator than when you can prove that someone whom everyone else believes 'did it', clearly and undoubtedly did not."

We were also taught that while it was critical to maintain control in all situations, it was also critical never to overestimate our personal power.

"You are not an army," we were told again and again. "You have power because of the organization and the law behind you. You need that organization and the law behind you more than anything else you have."

Outside the classroom, we participated in a daily, rigorous physical training program. Our fitness instructor taught us that physical control reduced panic and helped maintain composure under stress.

"And physical control means psychological control," he added.

This was another area where Victoria seemed to have the edge. I had always considered myself a decent athlete, but I was nothing next to Victoria—a misplaced accountant to say the least.

It didn't take long for Victoria to distinguish herself. She had a strong upper body, but it was her legs that were especially impressive. She had actually complained to me about them once, but they were truly a sight to behold. In the shorts she wore, her quadriceps and calves were sharply sculpted and defined.

At the end of our second week, we were asked to race through the obstacle course in pairs, and the first one to finish could rest for as long as it took the second to cross the line. At the end, we were told to engage in hand-to-hand combat until one of us was pinned.

I ended up paired with Victoria. The FBI didn't distinguish by gender that way. As the FBI saw it, a man could just as easily end up chasing a fleeing female felon or vice versa. We had to learn how to handle every situation.

We started up the steep incline of the first hill, and it was not more than a few strides before I found myself staring at Victoria's rear—a lovely view, but not the one I needed in front of everyone. I had never seen anyone move up a hill on foot that fast. It had to be her calves propelling her. From the top of the hill, we reached the ropes and climbed twenty feet hand over hand, then crossed a footbridge built between two trees. There, we had a choice: either jump to a thick mat below or slide down a fireman's pole. It was initially faster to jump, but we had already learned that it could be cumbersome and time-consuming to try to get off the mat. Next, it was a half-mile run to the climbing wall, and this is where Victoria truly left me in the dust.

When I reached the end and launched my body over the wall, Victoria was waiting for me. She'd already had a full minute to catch her breath. No sooner did I gain my footing than she came up behind me, swept my legs from beneath me, and had me pinned and breathless in her grasp.

The instructor was shaking his head—whether in disgust toward me or in disbelief at Victoria's prowess, I couldn't tell. Either way, as I looked up into her eyes and as she triumphantly whispered, "Gotcha Billy-boy," I knew that I was falling for her.

Chapter Twenty

Over the next several weeks, my classmates and I also spent one hour a day under the tutelage of Gil Pickens, learning the use of firearms. Training with Gil was particularly intense. He had the air and bearing of a wartime drill sergeant.

"Shoulder steady, Tucker! Keep that left arm straight! Chin down! Head cocked! You're taking aim, for Christ's sake, not bird watching!"

Gil showered everyone with his attitude, even Victoria Summers.

"Center of the mass, Summers!" he yelled, as she sprayed bullets along the edges of her target. "You want to stop an attack, you *must* aim for the center of the mass!"

Then, moments later: "Christ, Summers, don't tell me you're too delicate a flower to put a bullet in some drug dealer's heart!"

Victoria flushed with anger hearing those words. She didn't look at him though.

"I know the type," she told me later over a game of pool in the recreation room. "Hates women. Homophobic. Bad in bed. Probably twice divorced with two kids who despise him."

I didn't dare tell Victoria about my C-D-I conversation with Gil. I was afraid she would escalate it to a full-scale ethics review. Instead, I tried to calm her.

"You don't know that," I said. "He yells at women and men alike. You know it's true."

"Oh, it's true all right," Victoria replied. "Except when he yells at women he does it this way."

And then, Victoria stood, silently mouthing reprimands as she looked me up and down, undressing me with her eyes.

I laughed.

"Don't laugh, Billy-boy. You can't *feel* the way he yells at me when I'm shooting."

And then, she moved close to me. “Come on,” she said. “Hold the pool stick like a rifle. Pretend you’re shooting at the wall.”

I did as she said. Then, she leaned in behind me, talking into my left ear. “Center of the mass,” she said, holding my waist in both of her hands. “That’s it. Center of the mass.”

And as Victoria walked away, she passed her right hand over my rump.

I blushed. I turned to her, but she resumed her usual demeanor.

“See what I mean, Billy-boy,” she said. “I’m just counting the days until the end of this.”

I agreed with her, but I spent the rest of the night thinking about the way her hand felt on me.

To pass the firearms tests, we had to demonstrate proficiency with handguns, shotguns and semiautomatic weapons. We also spent a lot of time in Hogan’s Alley, where we repeatedly fell victim to booby traps, bombs and criminals with hidden guns. Despite the contrived nature of these scenarios, it was never a laughing matter, and Gil Pickens was all we needed to stay serious and focused.

The Firearms Training Simulator—or FATS—machine, was also part of Gil’s course. Armed with a weapon that fired a laser, and yet felt and responded like a true nine-millimeter handgun, we took turns standing in front of a large video screen while a taped scene played itself out. We were asked to react and to protect ourselves and civilians in either a shoot or no-shoot situation.

Firearms testing was as frequent as academic and physical testing. Our days were full, exhausting and stressful. The days wore on, and the classes and drills seemed to blend into one, but I paid close attention to everything. I knew that five percent of those invited to Quantico didn’t survive the cut, and with Victoria motivating me, I wanted to be sure to make this one work.

Chapter Twenty-One

Quantico offered a humid summer, with brutal days but with air conditioning that spared us unbearable nights. The FBI gave us a few weekends off, but the first one felt disorienting. Until then, all our time had been claimed by training, and we didn't have to decide how to spend any of it. So with a weekend off, I wasn't sure what to do with myself. Home was simply too far away for a two day journey.

Victoria Summers seemed to feel the same way about San Diego, and a few weeks in, we made a plan to spend Friday night in the social room. They were showing an old James Bond movie and, naturally, both of us were big fans of 007. We weren't the only ones who'd decided to relax with some alcohol and a flick. But we were the only ones left in the social room at the end of the night.

"Why did you apply?" she asked, as we walked out of the movie hall together.

"Nothing else seemed to fit," I responded.

"Process of elimination?"

"No. Well maybe. I don't view it like that though. Something just clicked. It felt right from the beginning."

Kind of like I felt when I met you, I wanted to say.

"I know exactly what you mean. I was a fish out of water doing the corporate accounting thing. Then I would read a book, see a movie, or something. But it was all glorified, I feared. I worried that I was getting caught up in the romance of it, that I didn't understand the day-to-day. So I started reading non-fiction. I started trying to learn everything I could. I looked for the bad press. I tried to simulate the worst case scenario. But none of it mattered. It was like I was born to be in the FBI. It was almost like the United States had made up the whole organization just for me. I became obsessed. I had to apply. It had to work for me. Thank all of the powers that exist that it did!"

Victoria made my interest in the FBI seem like a passing fad.

"That's great," I added. "It's great it worked out."

"I'd do anything for the FBI, Billy. Wouldn't you?"

I nodded, but felt perplexed. I'd certainly heard plenty of stories of people who got caught up in their careers. Victoria would settle down, I was sure. This was just the beginning of training. From what she said, she had been waiting for it so long. It was no wonder she felt such passion.

Victoria changed the subject. I was pleased.

"So no Mom and Dad for you either?" she asked, not waiting for a response. "Mine are divorced, badly divorced as they say. My father's in Texas. My mother's in San Francisco. I really don't see either of them much," she finished quickly, as if to keep me from asking any questions.

I knew better than to push. Her two-line answer was the same type of response I always offered when I didn't want to open up. This was different, though. I wanted Victoria to know me. Very few people did. I waited silently, until the question finally came.

"Are you close with your parents, Billy?"

I shook my head. "You don't want to know."

"Really?"

"Yes, really. But you know what?"

I didn't wait for an answer. "I want to tell you."

We took a couple of stools at an open table, and I hesitated before opening up to Victoria about the story of my life.

* * *

On my twelfth birthday, February 24, 1990, my mother came home with a bicycle from the local thrift shop; a red one, as luck would have it, with a silver banana seat, high handle bars and chrome spokes. She put a blue ribbon around it in the garage and let Jayme, my seven-year old sister, tie a blindfold around my head to help with the surprise. My father had died when I was five, so my mother often did little things like that to keep the three of us together.

I knew I was in for something special when, in her excitement, she forgot to make me put on a jacket. My heart lifted in my chest when Jayme removed the cloth from my eyes.

"There's still snow on the ground, Billy," my mother said, "so you're going to have to wait until the spring to ride it."

That was okay. I admired it with a pounding heart for two months. Come April, though, I was all over the place with my new toy, pumping up hills, doing wheelies over curbs and mastering the skidding stop. One horsepower. Total control. The sidewalks, the curbs and the road were all mine.

On the second Sunday in May, it was Mother's Day, but that did not matter to me. "I'm going over to Nathan's!" I called.

"Billy? Not today. I wanted to be with you and Jayme today."

"Maaahm!?"

That was the end of our argument. I didn't ask again. I pulled my sweatshirt over my head with my right hand and opened the garage door with my left. I was hovering above the silver seat in no time, and out of the driveway and down the street I pumped.

In order to get to Nathan's, I needed to take Brody Hill, the sharpest incline in our neighborhood. Nathan lived on the other side, around the corner to be exact, and my goal had always been to be able to glide all the way from the top of Brody Hill to Nathan's house. The faster I took the incline of the Hill, I knew, the more likely I'd have top speed on the decline. The last time I'd tried, I had built up so much speed that I was almost able to glide all the way. I was only about a house and a half short. This time, I was convinced I could make it.

"Slow down, Billy!" Mrs. Parker cried out when she saw me approach the intersection for the incline.

"Whatever," I muttered, tilting my head downward.

My eyes narrowed, focusing intently on my churning feet. I tried to count the rotations of my legs. *One and two and three and four and...One and two and three and four and...*

Then, suddenly, I felt an uncontrollable tug. My front wheel hit a pothole, then turned sharply left and dipped forward as the back of my bike hurled me over its handlebars. I didn't even have time to say, "holy shit," before my right shoulder slammed into the pavement, and I slid about ten feet to a burning stop.

I was stunned. My right arm was bleeding. My shoulder felt like it had exploded. I didn't even hear Mrs. Parker scream and go running to phone my mother. I sat there delirious, moving my left arm and my legs to see if they were still attached. They were. I managed to get myself to the corner, dragging my bike with my good arm as I did.

Look at my bike. Look at me! What will I tell my mother? I feared, beginning to cry.

I was tending to my wounds when I heard a high-pitched screech. Mr. Greaney, at the wheel of his family wagon, must have been late for something important. Other neighbors would say that he was barreling down Oak Street much faster than any car should have been driven in our pseudosuburban neighborhood. I looked up to see Mr. Greaney's stricken face through the windshield as his hands gripped his steering wheel in recognition that he was about to hit a blue Datsun—my mother's blue Datsun. She wasn't even looking at the intersection. Her wide and worried eyes were focused the other way on me.

I heard the loud clash of metal and watched my mother's body jolt forward as her car buckled and spun. The reverberating noise brought people to their windows, Mrs. Parker rushing to the scene and, to my wonder, Nathan to me. He had hopped on his bike when he knew I was on my way to try to meet me halfway.

Mr. Greaney jumped out of the driver's seat and ran to my mother's car. I tried to lift my body from the corner, the knifing pain in my shoulder barely noticeable now from what I had just seen.

My mother wasn't moving.

"Call an ambulance," Mr. Greaney cried, reaching her first.

Mrs. Parker's face went pale. I wanted to turn back time.

My mother was still in the flowered bathrobe Jayme and I had given to her that morning for Mother's Day. She had put it on when she took it out of the box.

I knew what was happening before I could comprehend it. Nathan grabbed me, and held onto me as I tried to stand.

"What did you do, man!?" Nathan yelled across the road at Mr. Greaney. "You drive like a mad man." And then, as we walked together to the crushed side of my mother's car: "Mrs. Tucker! Mrs. Tucker!" Nathan called. "Where's the fucking ambulance!"

I remember thinking at that moment that Nathan was a man. He swore with such authority and control.

Mr. Greaney got my mother out of the car, and Nathan let go of me and lunged beside her. He started pounding her chest and blowing air into her mouth. I froze and swallowed hard.

"Mrs. Tucker. Mrs. Tucker!" Nathan called again, and his eyes were wild as he searched around.

"Jesus, Linda!" Mr. Greaney moaned, circling my mother helplessly.

"Mom!" I cried, kneeling down and reaching for her hand.

It was then that Nathan turned and clung to me in a desperate, but belated attempt to stop me from watching my mother die.

It took eight weeks for my cast to come off. My shoulder would be better. My life would not. Jayme was seven, newly orphaned, and old enough to know she'd never forgive her older brother.

* * *

"Whoa," was all Victoria could say when I finished. "I'm so sorry."

"You know when you've got someone in your corner?" I asked.

"I suppose," she said.

"Well, that's how it was with my mother. I miss her so much."

"What about your father?" Victoria asked, perhaps hopefully.

I shrugged. "Another tragedy. Although that time, I wasn't to blame. He was a construction worker. My mother used to say I had his build, but I was too young to remember much about him. I only knew that I felt a void in my life when he was gone. Just five years after he married my mother, he was at a work site, striding across the steel beams that would support the 37th floor, when he lost his balance in a gust of January wind. Supposedly, nobody he worked with could believe it. My mother said he was the best climber they had."

"This is just so awful, Billy."

I agreed. Nearly ten years later I hadn't found a way to reconcile the fate Jayme and I had found.

"So it's just you and your sister now?" Victoria asked gingerly.

"In some ways," I responded vaguely, not needing Victoria to know that much right now.

"Where is she these days?"

I paused. I really didn't want to get into it. Victoria seemed to notice.

"Back home," I said, vaguely again. Then, I stood and walked over to the jukebox.

"I'll pick three and you pick two," I suggested, slipping my money into the slot.

"Why do you get three?" Victoria demanded, seeming to appreciate our return to the superficial.

"Because you've had the edge on me in everything else. You've got to give me something!"

Victoria laughed. "Most people that meet me just think I'm a dumb blond."

"How little they know," I added, admiring her delicate, light hair.

But when Victoria raised her eyebrows to mine, I knew I'd been holding my stare too long.

"Dye it! Dye it purple. I dare you!" I blurted in an effort to lighten the moment.

Victoria then joined me at the jukebox. "Very funny," she said. "Now give me that buck so we can get some music going here."

We spent the next several moments viewing titles and choosing songs, awkwardly close as we jibed each other about our picks. In the end, we settled on a mix of tunes by The Rolling Stones, Madonna, Elvis Presley, Whitesnake and Millie Vanilli. We played pool until our songs had finished.

"I wouldn't be surprised if this place had a camera," Victoria said.

I looked around. "That's a pretty paranoid thought."

"You never know, Billy. They say they judge you on everything here."

"Well, I don't see it if there is one. I think that would be ridiculous, don't you?"

"Shouldn't the FBI make sure its recruits have decent social skills?"

I thought a moment. "Yes. Which means you're out! You blew it when you picked Whitesnake. All of that studying and training and kicking my ass on the obstacle course just went up in smoke. You blew it in the social room *Vicky!*"

"Watch it, Billy-boy," she smiled. "Nobody calls me Vicky. And nobody is going to let you graduate ahead of me."

"We'll see," I continued. "Wait until they hear you picked Whitesnake *and* Millie Vanilli."

Victoria and I walked together to our rooms. It was 2:30 a.m., Friday night, July 28th. We were nine weeks in. It was a cool night, a welcome break from the prior two weeks of humidity.

"How gentlemanly of you," Victoria said at her door as she reached for her keys.

Victoria was twenty-six. She had to recognize the look in my eyes. In the endless seconds that passed, I wavered between instinct and better judgment, the latter being the valuable lesson drilled into all of us on a daily basis.

Victoria waited, making my decision all the harder. Mercifully, she turned to her door and fumbled to put the key in the lock.

"Good night, Victoria," I said, and she stiffened before looking back around.

Turning to face me, she leaned in to press her lips to my cheek. I turned just in time. We hesitated for no more than a second before our lips met, tenderly.

"Leave," Victoria said, as we pulled away. "Go home before it gets worse. And don't mention a word of this to anyone."

I did as I was told.

Chapter Twenty-Two

Victoria's paranoia and my complete lack of experience in romantic endeavors were a tortuous combination for me over the next several days. She ignored me the first day, pretended nothing had happened the next, and by the following Friday, when we had another weekend off, she didn't even seem to care what I might be doing.

I re-lived the night, over and over. *What had I done wrong?* By that Friday, I was sure I had the answer: *everything.*

I shouldn't have kissed her. I shouldn't have beaten her at pool. She likes to win. She's used to winning everything. I must have hurt her pride. She must not have liked the kiss. Maybe I had bad breath. She's angry with me for trying. Maybe she thinks I've been stand-offish all week. Maybe she thinks I'm just trying to sleep with her.

Finally, I arrived at the unavoidable conclusion: *She hates me. She absolutely and positively hates me.*

That Friday, in the hallway outside our 10:30 class, I decided to confront her with my feelings. I did so in the most direct and pointed way I could think of.

"I can ask to switch seats," I told her. "I can say I'm having trouble hearing from our row. Nobody will know it has anything to do with us."

Victoria looked at me. "Keep your voice down," she said. "And watch how you use that word, 'us.'"

I nodded.

"Is that what you want?" she asked.

"That's not what I want, Victoria. I want you. But I don't think you want me, and I just want to make this easier for you."

Victoria smiled, and then she laughed.

"You're pathetic, Billy-boy," she said, and I knew she was right. I had no idea how to handle what I was feeling. Victoria was my captor, and I desperately needed direction from her.

"Join me for a run?" she said.

"Now?"

"Yes, now."

As I left her to retrieve my workout clothes, I fought the urge to skip the entire way home.

* * *

We ran shoulder to shoulder down one of the trails, our feet pounding out a rhythm of anxiety and pent-up emotion. It wasn't a quarter of a mile before the humidity got to me and the beads of sweat on my forehead began to drip. Running with Victoria was a perfect way to have this conversation, I decided. It would raise no suspicions; to onlookers, we just looked like two recruits keeping in shape. She started with small talk.

"Five weeks left," she said.

"I can't believe it."

"Before we know it, we're going to be putting in our preferences for field offices," she added.

And then I realized that Victoria was not making small talk at all. In the second to last week of training, we had to rank our top ten choices out of the FBI's fifty-six field offices and four hundred satellite or resident agencies. It was well-known that agents almost always got one of their first three choices, but we had to specify ten nevertheless. Soon, Victoria and I could very well be going separate ways.

"I take it you're going to want to head back to California."

She didn't respond. Instead, she picked up her pace, which made me angry. We continued in silence for another quarter of a mile before I decided to press the issue. It was simply too important to me to let it lie.

"I've never been to California," I said. "I've always wanted to go there."

Victoria now slowed to a stop.

"I'm four years older than you, Billy," she said, bending over to stretch, not looking at me. "I'm at a different place in my life."

I wavered between shock, lack of comprehension and anger. *She brought me out for a run to tell me that she didn't like me after all.* I considered turning around and never looking back. Instead, I found myself arguing.

"What place is that?" I demanded. "You and I are standing here together in Quantico, Virginia. We're both training to be FBI agents. God willing, in five weeks, we're both going to graduate and be sent to a field office somewhere. Now, it's one thing if you pick the West Coast and I pick the East, but you being four years older than me is not a different place, Victoria.

No way. In fact, if you feel in any way for me the way I feel for you, I would say we're in exactly the same place."

Victoria swallowed hard. She looked around, then turned and ducked onto a path that had been worn into the woods. She motioned for me to follow, and I did. About fifteen paces in, Victoria turned and stepped toward me, the outline of her shoulders reminding me of her strength. We embraced, our body sweat blending at every limb. Then, as she looked up at me, her eyes sparkling and honest, we kissed. We held each other without saying a word until we both caught our breath.

Then, she laughed out loud.

"How about this!"

I shook my head, smiled in both relief and disbelief and took her hand to walk out of the woods. We started back down the road holding hands until better judgment took over. It was then, it seemed, we could let go. A greater connection had been established.

For the next four weeks, without much talking, without intimate chatter, and with barely a moment to ourselves, I knew that Victoria and I were together. Every day, every hour and every moment that I was awake, the world was a perfect place. I felt a sense of peace unlike any I had experienced. My body felt stronger, my heart felt lighter, and nothing bothered me at all.

My only fear was that she and I would be forced to separate at the end of our time at Quantico. The FBI had brought me to Victoria Summers, I knew, but it could just as easily take me away. I had the remaining weeks to hope that this would not be so, and to consider whether there was any way that we could stay together. While it would take the two of us to make it work, there was an uncontrollable and unpredictable wild card. It was the organization to whom we had pledged our loyalty many weeks ago.

So as the days wore on and the time to specify our field office choices drew near, I became more anxious and endured more sleepless hours. And because Victoria insisted we keep our relationship secret, Max Fulton, the self-proclaimed sage of Quantico, was useless.

Chapter Twenty-Three

I rushed to class the day they were handing out our field office assignments and, by the time I arrived, thought my heart was going to burst through my chest. I couldn't focus at all as the FBI's Director of Training called out names from the first half of the alphabet. As he began to near "S" and "T," though, my eyes deadlocked on the contours of his mouth.

"Paulson!" he called. Then, in sequence: "Robbins! Santiago! Stern!"

Then, it came.

"Summers!"

Victoria rose and rolled her eyes at me as she stood and turned. My name followed nearly without hesitation.

"Tucker!"

The moment of truth had arrived. I slid from my seat and, following Victoria, rushed down the aisle to the front of the room.

"Warstein!" he continued.

My classmates with names higher in the alphabet were already tearing open envelopes anxious to see where they'd ended up. I was just anxious to find out whether I'd be near Victoria.

"Tucker, sir," was all I said, and I was handed an envelope.

I walked toward the wall at the front of the class, braced my back against the chalkboard and closed my eyes for a few seconds, holding the envelope to my chest. Then, I said a silent prayer, drew a deep breath and inserted my finger into the envelope's ridge, tearing along its end and withdrawing the paper inside. I was confused to see the cryptic message.

> SPECIAL ASSIGNMENT: UC TRAINING...FOLLOW THESE INSTRUCTIONS VERBATIM...LEAVE THE ROOM QUIETLY WITHOUT SAYING A WORD TO ANYONE...DIAL EXTENSION 7290 AND ASK FOR ASAC ROBERT O'DONNELL.

My mind raced, and my face warmed. I searched for Victoria. *Where had she gone? She wasn't even in the room anymore? Special assignment? What did UC training mean?*

I knew what 'ASAC' stood for, but *Robert O'Donnell, Robert O'Donnell,* I repeated. *I know that name. Where do I know that name?*

Then, it came to me. My interview on campus. *The same guy? What was going on? Did I fail?*

All I could do at the moment, though, was follow the directions. I glanced at the rest of my class and watched as they exchanged high five's, shook hands, patted each other's back, or nodded and smiled. I looked around again for Victoria, but the room went blurry. I needed to get out. I needed to re-read what the paper said, somewhere far away from the commotion in front of me.

I tugged the handle of the door to exit and slipped out into the corridor, striding quickly to exit the building. The fresh air enlivened me, and I searched the grounds for any sign of Victoria. More than her, though, I needed a telephone.

My walk quickly turned into a light jog, which then became a full-fledged sprint to my room. For the first one-hundred yards or so, I was sure that I didn't breathe at all. By the time I got to the front door of my dorm, I was gasping for air, doubled over and about to collapse. It took several minutes for me to catch my breath, but when I did, I bolted up the stairs and unlocked the door to my room. Panting, I picked up the telephone and dialed.

"Damn it!" I repeated, pressing the wrong numbers for the second time.

Then, connecting at last, I spoke when I heard a "hello."

"Robert O'Donnell, please," I sputtered.

"O'Donnell here," I heard, and his tone was practically musical.

"Mr. O'Donnell, sir. This is Billy Tucker," I said. "I'm a graduating Special Agent in Quantico. I've been instructed to call you about my assignment."

"I know that, Billy. Slow down a little. I'm the one who gave you the instruction. It's been a long time, son. Since your interview at Drexel, if you remember."

"I do," I said anxiously, relieved that the connection had been made.

"Well, first things first, son. I want to wish you a hearty congratulations. I understand you finished among the top few in your class. I sure know how to pick 'em, don't I?" he laughed.

"Yes sir," I responded, appreciating the flattery, but knowing that it wasn't what I needed.

Robert O'Donnell then began to speak about his days in Quantico, but I interrupted him before he even completed his first sentence.

"My assignment, Mr. O'Donnell," I repeated cautiously. "I'm a bit anxious, and I hope you understand."

"Yes, yes. I know. Well, I want to tell you about your project personally. Luckily, I'm right here in the main office at Quantico today. Why don't you meet me over in the Administrative Building in ten minutes."

"Ten minutes?" I repeated, which seemed eternal.

"Yes Billy. And catch your breath. I think you'll be very pleased with what I have to tell you."

"Really?" I tested.

"Absolutely. Have you ever heard of a rookie getting assigned a high-profile undercover job?"

I thought a moment before responding, now realizing what UC must stand for.

"No sir. In fact, I heard that's impossible. I heard that all new agents have to do the rotations, the wiretaps, the..."

"It just became possible, Billy. I'll see you in nine minutes. Don't you dare be late," he finished before hanging up the phone.

Chapter Twenty-Four

The lobby and hallways of the Administrative Building were stale and dark, and its odor was a mixture of bleach and citrus. I looked at my watch, and it had only taken me four minutes to arrive. Thankfully, I did not have to wait the remainder. Before I could even figure out which office to enter, out of a door to my right strode a smiling Robert O'Donnell, wearing a light gray suit covering a pale blue button down. I recognized him instantly, and my face flushed with gratitude. Not only had O'Donnell given me the chance of a lifetime by inviting me to join the FBI, but his invitation had brought me Victoria. I owed him my life, as I saw it. The Assistant Special Agent in Charge extended his right hand warmly.

"Billy Tucker. Look at you. Those FBI letters become you. Let me see the back."

Robert O'Donnell stepped around me and read aloud. "Strength in silence. Wisdom in observation."

"Yes sir," I said.

"I like that. I really do. It says a lot, don't you think?"

"Yes sir," was all I could say.

"Welcome, son. Come on in. Let's talk. What did you think of training?" he asked, not seeming to care about my response.

It was good to see O'Donnell. It reminded me of how little I'd known about the Bureau when we first met. He still had such a casual, yet sophisticated confidence about him; the kind that probably allowed him to pursue art thieves and gunmen alike. I followed him into an austere office with one window, and he took the chair behind the desk.

"Sit down, Billy. Sit down right there," he said, pointing to the only empty chair in the room.

I did as instructed.

"So where did your classmates end up?" he asked, eyeing me suspiciously.

I recognized the trap.

"I don't really know. I stepped out of the room when I read the instructions you gave me. A couple of people were high-fiving and saying 'New York,' but that's all I heard."

"Good," O'Donnell responded.

With the silence that followed, and the way he stared at me, I grew uncomfortable. He seemed lost in thought, so I broke the ice.

"Mr. O'Donnell," I said.

"Robert. Call me Robert."

"Robert. Okay. I'm extremely anxious about my future right now. I know I'm supposed to be calm under pressure, but I have to admit I'm a little freaked out about what might be in store for me."

"Well, Billy," O'Donnell interrupted. "What do you think of undercover work?"

"What do I think?" I asked, sitting forward.

"Yeah, how would you like to do some?"

"But what about the rotations—the background checks, the wiretaps and all that?"

"Bullshit, Billy. It's all bullshit," O'Donnell said, leaning forward. "Do you want to do that bullshit? It can be arranged."

O'Donnell's tone was firm, almost threatening, and I felt that I'd crossed a line. I sat back, hoping that my new posture told him I was all ears.

"No sir. I'm ready to follow orders."

The veteran agent assumed a relaxed pose. "Do you know how old I am, Billy?"

I shook my head indicating "no."

"Thirty-four next month. Thirty-four. I'm an Assistant Special Agent in Charge."

I nodded.

"I didn't get that way by toiling in background checks and wiretaps, you know. I busted my ass, and I was lucky to get a couple of breaks."

Robert O'Donnell turned toward the window and grew silent.

"Tremont Heights," he said, continuing to look outside. "Have you been back lately?" he questioned, again seeming not to care about the answer.

"Not at all," I said.

"Well then," he continued. "Let's get right to it. I'd like to talk with you about Lucy Polowski—or *Lipstick,* as you sometimes called her."

And just his mention of her name brought me back to high school, to the butterfly tattoo above her jeans, the bruise-ball court and the beautiful, pale, flesh beneath her jersey. Hearing the word '*Lipstick*' from O'Donnell's mouth reminded me of her sky blue dress, the fig leaves barely covering her at the Halloween dance and, of course, Sigma. Lipstick's legs enveloped Bobby Reed on the dance floor in Sigma that night like a tarantula preparing its prey. Like every good predator, it didn't even matter that Nathan got in the way. Lipstick still managed a kill. It just so happened to be me.

All of these memories rushed into my head when O'Donnell mentioned Lucy. Far from my mind, oddly, was the tragedy of her untimely death. I sooner remembered Lucy's class rank and our time together talking than the way I'd heard they found her. But O'Donnell caught me up on all of it, everything that happened in the year before her death: Nathan's gambling, Lucy's journeys into Kenmore square, Joey Luca, and last, Lucy's grief-stricken father having to identify her body.

I shuddered when O'Donnell finished. I had completely forgotten about Victoria, until he brought me back to where I was.

"You're a part of us now, Billy. You're a part of our organization. After tomorrow, after you go through our little ceremony here in Quantico, it will be your organization too. You might not realize it yet, but that's pretty powerful. So I'm going to tell you something that most new agents don't know. Typically, they'll hear rumors some months into the job before they learn what I'm about to tell you. But it's no secret, really. You shouldn't feel that you're privy to something covert. At least within the Bureau."

As O'Donnell's last words lingered, I thought about the oath of confidentiality that I took at the end of every day in training. It was then that O'Donnell started to tell me about the FBI's high-level informant program, which I quickly learned had borders, but when it came to organized crime, very few boundaries.

"As I know you've learned in your weeks here, Billy, the Hoover era is long gone. Today, long term solutions matter, and they require long term planning. Organized crime—the 'mob' for lack of a better word—is a cohesive and sophisticated organization that built force over the years J. Edgar looked the other way. By the time law enforcement woke up, the influence of organized crime was pervasive. So Congress passed Title III and RICO, and gave us the weapons to go to court. Under Title III, we can put listening devices anywhere. Under RICO, two criminal acts constitute a 'pattern' of activity, and we can put criminals away for five times the amount of years than we could under simple extortion and loan sharking laws. We do what it takes to find that pattern, even if it means making some pretty serious criminals, convicts or not, into high-level informants."

"And I have to tell you, Billy..." O'Donnell paused as he built to his climax, "your old friend Nathan Marks is our ticket in Boston."

I felt delirious hearing Nathan's name in this context. Nathan Marks was the friend who held me tight on a street corner. He was my bruise-ball partner, my drinking buddy. Nathan wasn't the FBI's "ticket" in Boston.

This is absurd, I thought, but O'Donnell read my expression.

"Just listen, Billy," he said. "I've been living and breathing the life of Nathan since the Polowski murder. He's a marked man as far as I'm concerned. Now tied to Ronnie Luca, he's the first domino that needs to fall for me to get to the whole Luca crime ring. Who knows? Maybe we can even flip Ronnie Luca as well. He's big, but there may be someone bigger behind him. In my world, there will be a lot of rats, but for me, with this Polowski cover-up, it all starts with Nathan."

My mouth suddenly felt extremely dry. I could barely swallow.

"A marked man?" I repeated.

"Listen, Billy," O'Donnell continued, "when Ronnie Luca met Nathan Marks, he happened to need him. It isn't often that's the case. But in this case, after Lucy Polowski was killed, Ronnie needed Nathan badly. His son, Joey, was in a big mess. Witnesses were telling cops that he left *Fire!* with Lucy. Someone even came forward and claimed that he saw Joey slap her across the face on the sidewalk outside the club before taking her to his car."

"Down at the precinct the next day, after the local cops brought Joey in, Ronnie was able to get a few minutes alone with his son. Their lawyer was present. We have no idea what they said, but we do know this: Nathan's bank account—which had a whopping $812.47 before the night began—never emptied. We also got no robbery reports in the Tremont Heights area. Instead, Nathan traded in his rusting Chevy for a shiny new black T-Bird."

"On the surface, it seems that Nathan's debt to Joey was forgiven for a favor. A big one. Because in one night, Billy—the same night your hot little red head was shot—your old buddy somehow got himself out of a $25,000 debt to Joey Luca and found himself taking his first steps toward becoming a trusted confidante of Ronnie's. And nobody's talking. Even if Nathan had something on them, like he witnessed the crime or something, in all of my time—and I've talked to other agents across the country—if Nathan saw something, he would have been whacked by now. Ronnie Luca would have found a deep hole to bury him in. No doubt."

I continued to listen as my temples throbbed.

"So one of my theories," O'Donnell continued, "but one that might just be too simple to be true, is that Ronnie bought a big lie. An alibi. Joey's claiming that he wasn't with Lucy after the club because he supposedly took Nathan for a ride. Joey's claiming that he took Nathan to Revere Beach and kicked the crap out of him for the gambling debt."

"Meanwhile, Nathan's not talking. The cops didn't get to him for four days anyway. Can you believe it? Local pricks. They wait four days before even interviewing the dead girl's steady boyfriend."

I felt an internal pain as he referenced Lucy Polowski as the '*dead girl.*'

"Anyway, one of the locals—thinks he's a hotshot—said he remembers Nathan having a cut across the bridge of his nose, but he remembers nothing else. That's not exactly a sign of an ass-whipping, so I think the guy was hallucinating. I don't think Nathan had a scratch on him, not even an internal bruise. Nothing."

"So day seven I get the call. Double pricks for waiting that long to contact the FBI. We send our guy in. Day eight before we even find Nathan to talk to him. By this point, even if he had a cut or a bruise, he's got the same pretty-boy look he had in your high school yearbook. We flat out asked him if he is covering for Joey. But Nathan just looks at our guy blankly and says: *You think I would stand up for Joey Luca? I'd bury that bastard if I had the chance.*

"Where did you get the money for the car?" we ask.

I got lucky, was all Nathan said.

O'Donnell laughed. He looked at me eagerly. It was as if he thought I knew something he didn't. Then, his expression changed.

"And that's it, Billy. That's the party line. That's where we are today."

"So what do you want from me? Do you want me in on the investigation?" I asked, praying beyond rationalization that the answer was 'no.'

"Not exactly, Billy," O'Donnell continued, and I sighed with relief before the weight of his next words hit me.

"I want you to *be* the investigation."

At that moment, I wondered what my eyes looked like. I wondered how far they actually extended from their sockets. I parted my lips to speak, paused, and then muttered what seemed like an incredible question.

"You want me to get you to Nathan Marks?" I asked, as if the mere sound of the words would cause Robert O'Donnell to shake his head and laugh with the absurdity of the whole thing.

"You're my man," O'Donnell confirmed. "When we examined the sign up sheet from the FBI's information session on your campus, Billy, the idea struck me like lightning, and I haven't been able to let it alone since."

The sign up sheet at Drexel? I thought confused.

"But I might not have even applied?" I protested.

O'Donnell shrugged. "That was a possibility, I agree," he started. "But we have recruiters. And after I talked to the recruitment center at your school,

I knew we had a good shot. It wasn't as if you had a lot of options."

Drexel's recruitment center? O'Donnell talked to them? They were useless for me!

"And I want you to remember something, Billy," he continued. "You came to us. You felt the same emotion that night at the information session all of us feel here in the Bureau when we sit back and consider our responsibilities. You wanted to be one of us. That just gives me so much confidence that we can help you succeed."

O'Donnell's last words puzzled me. *The FBI helping me?* It was all too overwhelming to grasp.

"New agents might never get assigned undercover work, Billy, but where the situation demands it, any rule can be broken—especially when you have the backing of Director Roth."

"What?" I asked, this meeting more puzzling by the moment. "Director Roth knows me?"

"He knows *of* you," O'Donnell said.

Suddenly, 'overwhelmed' could not sufficiently describe the way I felt.

It was then that O'Donnell began telling me about his proposal to Director Roth, how with his assistance, the project had sailed through the FBI's Undercover Review Board Committee. In Quantico, I had learned that the URBC rejected hundreds of cases each year for all kinds of reasons, but most notably, ethical concerns and conflicts of interest. I was proud of the Bureau when I learned that. Now, I didn't know what to think.

"So I'd ask you what you think, but you haven't even heard the hard part," he continued, shaking his head.

"That was the easy part?" I scoffed.

"Unfortunately," O'Donnell responded, before staring down at the desk in silence for several seconds. "Billy," he then began. "In our lives, I don't care who you are, you look back on your past at some defining moments. These are moments you never forget, because in choosing to go one way at that time, you set in motion a chain of events that bring you inevitably to the place you currently are. In ten, twenty, even fifty years, you'll always remember getting your first assignment with the FBI. No doubt, Billy, if you accept it, you'll look back on this moment as the one which began your incredible success in the Bureau. The assignment I'm about to give you is unprecedented. I've looked into it. If it goes as I know it will, you'll be golden in the Bureau. Trust me."

While those were words I knew any person starting a career would've loved to hear, all I wanted was to escape.

"But consider this," O'Donnell then paused, adjusting his hands like a quarterback standing shotgun in the pocket. "Consider a theory that very few of my colleagues want to credit at all."

I waited for him to continue.

"Consider that it was Nathan who popped her; Nathan who pulled the trigger."

I swallowed hard.

"Just listen," O'Donnell warned. "Why does Nathan want to give Joey an alibi? Sure, $25,000 says a lot, but if Joey's going to be arrested and end up in jail for killing Lucy, the $25,000 debt is probably going to be wiped out anyway. Joey's going to have bigger worries."

"To Nathan, the way I see it, the bigger motivation is Ronnie Luca's sudden interest in him. Ronnie's interest means a job, an important one. It means opportunity and a way to rise up out of the Tremont Heights life. For a guy who looks at the world and sees no good options, a role in Ronnie Luca's organization is a sudden and dramatic step forward."

"But the bigger question is why Ronnie is suddenly so interested. And my theory is one that goes much deeper than Nathan representing just an alibi for Joey. I think there's a collateral motivation happening here."

"So consider this: Ronnie Luca sees something he needs in Nathan. Ronnie needs to spread his influence, outside the North Shore. He needs guys in other places: guys with guts, charisma and most importantly, guys he knows will be loyal. You know Nathan. You've seen his loyalty first hand. I have to tell you that I really don't think a guy like Nathan is going to give that loyalty to Ronnie Luca if Joey Luca shot his girl. I think Nathan *knows* Joey didn't shoot Lucy. And how would he know that?"

I stared at O'Donnell, searching for what I hoped would be a different answer.

"There's only one way, Billy. Nathan's protecting something else. And my theory, Billy, is that Nathan's protecting himself."

I opened my mouth to protest, but O'Donnell wanted to finish. "And I think Ronnie believes that too."

"You see, Ronnie would know if Joey did it. But if he *knows* Joey didn't do it, he also knows that someone else did. The only other person he sees that might have, is the same one I see: Nathan Marks."

"Bottom line: there's something in it for all of them: protection and opportunity for Nathan, an alibi for Joey and a new influence for Ronnie south of Boston in Mattapan."

"So the story behind Polowski's murder, Billy, is our ticket into Ronnie Luca's crime ring. The way I see it, in order for us to bring down Ronnie Luca, we need Nathan Marks. We've been unable to locate a murder weapon, and no witnesses have come forward. We need a confession from Nathan, son, and then we need to flip him into an informant, a high-level informant, as we call it here these days. It's the only way. As the FBI sees it, you're the only man who can get it done."

My body shivered. My stomach rolled.

"What if I say no?" I asked, not caring about the consequences.

Robert O'Donnell shrugged.

"I'm serious. What if I say no?" I repeated, my heart pounding as I challenged the very man I had thanked a thousand nights for giving me this life. "I mean I don't need this assignment in order to prove to the FBI..."

O'Donnell slammed his fist on the table, startling a bird off the windowsill behind him. He shook his head sideways and ground his teeth.

"And bail on us the way you bailed from your fraternity!"

My ears grew hot. Swallowing hard, I could only stare at him in wide-eyed fear. O'Donnell continued.

"I took a gamble on you, Billy Tucker! I took a gamble that you learned your lesson the hard way in Sigma and that you never want to go back. But if a lifetime of loneliness and empty devotions is your calling, then say it now."

He paused. I stayed silent.

"Say it!!" O'Donnell screamed, standing and leaning in at me. "The only reason you're a part of this organization now is Nathan Marks. Make no mistake about that! In case it hasn't been made clear to you now, that *is* the reason I recruited you!"

My eyes bulged as I looked at him. My thoughts wandered back to Nathan, to Mother's Day when I was twelve, and then my thoughts wandered back to Victoria. *Would losing the FBI mean losing her*? *And then what would I have?* I thought back to the emptiness I felt walking out Sigma's door that evening after the beach party.

In an instant, I regained my bearings, and then, looking back at O'Donnell, I nodded rapidly.

"I'm with you sir," I said, my voice seeming to come from outside my body. "I'm with you. And I'm with the Bureau."

O'Donnell nodded, once for emphasis.

"I wouldn't have taken 'no' for an answer anyway," he warned.

Then, his eyes flared: "Make no mistake about it, Billy Tucker. The FBI intends to ride your wings to Ronnie Luca. And that makes you *MY* man!" he emphasized. "I've been waiting a long time for you, Billy Tucker. Welcome aboard. Welcome the *Fuck!* aboard."

Chapter Twenty-Five

O'Donnell got up to excuse me from his office. I couldn't speak. A cool sensation on my back signaled that I had sweated through my T-shirt. I needed fresh air again, and I needed to be alone.

"Some say it's the intensity that's made me successful," O'Donnell said as I turned, a half-witted attempt at reconciliation. "I don't know, though."

I remained speechless as O'Donnell showed me the door, and as he offered one additional light-minded warning: "This undercover assignment is not for sharing, Billy. Neither is the content *or tone* of this meeting."

He waited for my response, but I had none.

"Do you understand me?"

My head moved up and down, but my face felt catatonic. Finally, O'Donnell let me go, and I left the Administrative Building feeling like one-half the man who had entered.

When I got back to my room, I slumped into the corner of my bed, holding my knees tight against my chest and rocking back and forth. Cupping my face in my hands, I began to sob. It started slowly at first, but before long, I was overcome by heaves and sickening noises. I thought about my situation just one year ago—the start of my senior year—so naïve to the circumstances that would befall me. For the first time since I had flipped through the pages of the FBI's brochure I received at school, I noticed a distaste in my mouth. I was in way over my head, I was sure, and there was nothing to do but drown.

* * *

Hours later, Victoria knocked on my door. She told me she'd been looking all over for me and had come by my room twice already.

"New York," she said expectantly, plopping down on my bed and waiting for my response.

But when I shook my head and told her I was being sent to undercover school for a special assignment, she had the nerve to tell me she was jealous. She accused the FBI of sexism. When I offered to tell her what I would be doing—just to make her realize how bad of an assignment I'd actually received—Victoria clamped her hand across my mouth.

"Don't you dare break your oath, Billy Tucker. Don't make me a party to that. You get through that assignment, whatever it is. This is probably the break of your career."

Then, as Victoria removed her hand, we embraced. The strength of my hold must have signaled her.

"Jesus," she snickered. "You'd think you were just handed a death sentence."

If she only knew, I thought, staring over her shoulder at the whitewashed wall in front of me. *If she only knew.* There was so much I wanted to tell her, so much she didn't understand.

"Can't I at least tell you where I'm going to be?"

"Don't you dare," she said again, but this time, I didn't understand. It was only my location.

We had one big secret already. What was one more?

"You're going undercover, Billy. That's serious stuff. We expect you…" she looked at me oddly before shaking her head to correct herself. "Geez, all of this training has me brainwashed. What I mean to say is, *the FBI expects you* to take it seriously."

I knew that Victoria's advice was probably right, *but was that what devotion to an organization really meant? Did I feel that way now? Would I ever be capable of that? Was I overanalyzing?*

Victoria then told me she had to pack. "They're putting all of us going to New York on the same bus tomorrow," she said. "Can you believe it? They're ramping up the staffing on a 10-day wire approval. They say they need a lot of new ears. Isn't it exciting, Billy? It's really happening. It's happening now."

"What about the goodbye gathering tomorrow night?"

"Tough luck," they told us. "Can you believe that? Sixteen weeks and me and the rest of the soon-to-be New Yorkers around here can't even toast our finish."

Victoria seemed giddy. I couldn't believe it. I felt abandoned.

"What are you doing tonight, then?" I asked, trying to stop her growing momentum.

She came forward and took my hands. My head was spinning, but her touch was calming. "Spending it with you and not sleeping a wink," she offered.

The words from her mouth were perfect, but the curl of her lip as she spoke them made me fear that I'd already lost part of her heart.

"That is, if you'll have me," she finished.

I wanted to hold her and never let go. I had been traumatized by my meeting with O'Donnell. I was confused about what the FBI had in store for me. I needed this time with Victoria to be stable. I needed to tell her everything.

"Victoria," I said slowly, shaking my head. "Are we going to make it?"

She then paused and smiled. "You're pathetic, Billy-boy," she said. "Now get your shoes back on and come help me pack."

And in the hours that passed, well into the early hours of our final morning together, I barely thought about my assignment at all. I only considered how lucky I was to be alone with Victoria, her every movement warming my senses, and the soft glare of the moonlight against her freckled skin reminding me of the lightness of being.

"One of these days, I'm going to have tell you all about this girl I grew up with," I said.

At the time, so content in Victoria's arms, I shouldn't have been thinking about Lucy Polowski at all. Robert O'Donnell had ruined it for me, I was sure.

"Why?" Victoria asked.

I paused. "Why? Well, I guess she's the only other girl that's ever struck me like you."

I hoped Victoria would reciprocate, but she didn't say anything for a while.

"Are you still in touch?" she finally asked, and I sensed a certain jealousy.

"Not at all. Impossible, in fact. She was killed."

My meeting with O'Donnell ran wild in my mind. I longed to tell Victoria. I longed for her to probe.

Victoria didn't, though. "How horrible," was all she said. By then, it was 5:45 a.m. I wrote it off to fatigue.

We fell asleep in each others' arms in the minutes that passed. We awoke at noon to a hot sun and breathless, humid air. At 2:30 in the afternoon, I walked Victoria to the front gate of Quantico.

Our hug in the parking lot, surrounded by the others, could only be described as 'official.'

Chapter Twenty-Six

The night Victoria left the training grounds in Quantico, I was miserable and tired. I didn't go to the party, but I knew I couldn't face the celebration of my classmates even if I was rested. As I saw it, the end of Victoria's time with me in Quantico meant an end to everything. I had nothing to celebrate.

I also had little time to reflect. O'Donnell had left me a message about where to report Monday morning. The FBI's undercover training program was a two-week, intensive course, extending from 7:00 a.m. to midnight each day. The first two days would be classroom work, but the rest would be simulation.

I took a look at the manual I had been given at the start of my sixteen weeks and thumbed through to the section at the back I had never had the need—or time—to read. There were some opening paragraphs describing the benefits and dangers of undercover work. The true danger in it, I learned, was not the agent getting caught. That, the Bureau could deal with. In the flash of a signal or a call over a radio, the FBI could be anywhere, anytime, on a mere moment of notice. The true danger in undercover work, the manual said, was losing the agent to the world he was infiltrating.

It was clear from what I read that the FBI's course would teach me how to absorb myself in my project, believe in it, and walk, talk and react as if I was just another citizen on the street. It was also clear, though, that I would be expected to remember that it was only a project, something that served the greater purpose I had trained so hard to represent.

"Danger might dictate pulling out," our instructor told us on the first day of class. "As much as you want to be successful out there, this is perhaps the most difficult decision you will have to make," he challenged.

But O'Donnell was observing class that day, and likely observing my reaction to this possible outcome.

"Oh don't worry, Billy," he said, taking me aside at the break. "*Pulling out* will not be an option for you."

To the extent O'Donnell had not already earned my loathing, this comment sealed it. I thought about the words of Bryce Cardin the night of the FBI's information session at Drexel: *When you think about power, my friends, you must think about responsibility. In the FBI, one cannot exist without the other.*

I spent the next several nights staring at the ceiling and wondering what these words truly meant in the mind of Robert O'Donnell.

PART III

Nathan Marks

Chapter Twenty-Seven

Nathan Marks was an only child, or at least that's what he first told me before we became close. He and his parents moved to Tremont Heights when he was eight years old. They wanted to be closer to the city, he told me, where there were better opportunities to find work.

It wasn't long before each of them found two jobs. With all of the bills they had, though, they decided to cut costs by forgoing a sitter. So even at an early age, Nathan spent a lot of time in his house alone. His parents warned him not to go out while they were gone, and he obeyed. He also obeyed the detailed instructions they gave him about housework that needed to be done and how to make himself meals.

You have to be self sufficient, they told Nathan.

Nathan would come by my house when he got really lonely, but for the most part, he occupied himself with the television. I once asked Nathan how he felt about his parents not being around, but he simply shrugged and told me that he learned a lot of family lessons from daytime television. The way he carried himself, I believed him.

Nathan was honest, as if he knew that at the end of any lie, he would get caught. He was supportive, as if he decided he wanted to emulate one of the stronger characters from one of his shows. And he was obedient and loyal, knowing better than to ever cross authority. Nathan always picked up after himself when he visited my house. My mother used to be so impressed that she sometimes cited him as an example to me.

But I never envied Nathan for that. I too was taken by how polite and mature he seemed next to me. He deserved all of the compliments he got.

One Saturday, I was spending the afternoon at Nathan's. We were seated in front of the television when his mother came home. She was between shifts. She was crying. But when she saw me with her son, she sniffed and stopped.

I asked Nathan what he thought she was crying about. It was then that he opened up to me that it happened all the time. Nathan told me that he'd had an older brother. His parents used to live in a home out in the suburbs. They ran a pizza shop in a strip mall, and spent all of their time there, even with their two boys.

Nathan was a newborn when his brother was four, so he had no memory of his brother at all.

There was a marshy pond behind the strip mall. It was an unusually busy day. Nathan's brother disappeared, and his parents both took off out of the shop to look for him. The ovens caught fire, and someone had to pull Nathan out of the smoke filled parlor. The restaurant was ruined. They called in a search team for Nathan's brother, but it didn't take them long to find him. He'd drowned in the pond, feet stuck in the mud in an apparent pursuit of his favorite orange ball.

For eight years, Nathan's parents tried to resurrect their life, but there were too many reminders of the painful sadness that had befallen them, and they could barely afford the house they lived in. Finally, they gave up and moved closer to the city. Each of them got two jobs not only to pay the bills, but also to distract themselves from the horrors of the past for as many hours a day as possible. They hoped that exhaustion and sleep would get them through the rest.

I don't remember the year Nathan's parents divorced, but I do know that it was soon after my mother died.

It's just two of us, was all Nathan's mother told him when he asked her why his father never even tried to visit. *That's all it's ever going to be now. You're going to be the man around the house.*

Nathan quickly learned otherwise. His mother was a looker and, after his father left, she not only took up heavy drinking, but she also took up with several men. Nathan regularly watched man after man stumble out his front door.

But Nathan stayed obedient. He lived for whatever attention his mother would give him. Every now and then, though, Nathan's emptiness turned to anger. He took to the Park and began working on his throwing arm.

One hundred shots against the wall, he told me. *I only wish it was his face*, he once confessed, referring to his father. *And she doesn't care about me,* he once added. *She's got another son right in front of her, but I might as well be dead too.*

It wasn't as if Nathan didn't hope for a better home life. He used to tell me that, sometimes in the morning, with the sound of his mother shaking the aspirin bottle in the bathroom, he actually felt a moment of peace. *Maybe that feeling she has in the morning will convince her to change the way she spends her nights*, he told me.

Nathan was wrong. The pattern continued, endlessly it seemed.

Her skin looks yellow, he once told me in the days when he actually still cared.

There came a time, though, when it seemed that Nathan stopped caring. It probably occured a couple of years after I'd lost my mother, when Nathan realized that he didn't need that kind of attention to survive. And when Nathan started earning his own paycheck, he became truly self-sufficient.

For the first couple of years, we were about 13 or 14, Nathan did everything he could to make a buck. He was a golf caddy in Milton, a busboy at a pub off the expressway, a bagger at a Mattapan supermarket and, in the summers, part of a clean-up crew for the Parks and Recreation department. Nathan started to know people everywhere he went, it seemed.

With the money he earned and the responsibility he shouldered, Nathan also began to develop into the kind of guy who liked to take care of others. I don't know whether he did it out of a need for control, or whether it was just simple generosity, but I was sure that, at the least, it was an effort to give to others what he never got at home.

But then, somewhere in the middle of our sophomore year, Nathan got tired of the schedule he kept; in school all day, working nearly every afternoon when school was out and waking up early on Saturdays and Sundays to get to work as well. He bailed on the caddy job first.

Too early. Too much time. Not enough money, he said to me.

Next, went the restaurant job.

I'm not getting the shifts I want, and I'm getting home too late so I'm too tired to pay attention in school.

But I knew that Nathan's mind was elsewhere. By then, Lucy Polowski had come around. She had come after Nathan with such an initial surge that he couldn't help but enjoy the attention. Nathan wouldn't talk about it, but I was sure he knew he was the envy of all the guys in school. The seniors even respected him for catching Lucy's eye. Lucy's attention fed Nathan's ego where his mother had turned her head.

Nathan ditched his supermarket job last, probably because I worked there too. As long as we were together, we were able to survive the boredom. We would make up races when we started to bag an order at the same time. We timed our dinner breaks together. We would have push cart competitions in the parking lot if we were ever heading back toward the building at the same time. We did whatever we could to make the time pass. When I was offered a promotion to be a shelf Stocking Clerk before Nathan, though, things changed.

Nathan didn't waste much more time trying to please the Front-End Manager. He started showing up late, taking longer breaks and worse, not showing up at all. It didn't matter to him that I didn't take the position. Nathan felt slighted, and I couldn't blame him for feeling that way. There was no reason for me to get the job offer over him at all.

By then, Nathan had Lucy anyway, and she consumed all of his time, even if the bulk of it was in front of the television. And in front of the television is where Nathan's gambling habit thrived.

By the time Ronnie Luca came around, Nathan was more than ready to channel his energy elsewhere. At the end of my undercover training program, Robert O'Donnell was more than eager to bring me up to speed.

Chapter Twenty-Eight

September 2000.

The day my undercover training program ended, Robert O'Donnell told me to meet him at the FBI's office at One Federal Plaza in lower Manhattan. He said he had to be in New York City for meetings and wanted to brief me there. I tried to reach Victoria to tell her I was coming, but each time I called, I got only her voicemail.

My first trip to The Big Apple was hardly a smooth one. I spent six and one-half hours cramped into a packed Greyhound bus. It was not as if I'd never ridden a crowded bus before, but, on my way to New York City, every person seemed to carry more baggage, gadgets and claim more space than on any other ride I'd ever taken. And the odor of my seat companion was putrid.

I couldn't decide if the fact that I was on an express bus was good or bad. On one hand, I would be there sooner. On the other hand, there was no time to catch a breather or stretch my legs. Worse, the bathroom in the back—which was directly to my right because I'd been the last one to board—stunk more than the guy next to me. I tried to read, and I tried to focus my mind elsewhere, but every thought brought me back to the recognition that I was filler in the middle of a stink sandwich.

I think I was close to passing out when I saw the Manhattan skyline, a massive, competing collection of windows and an impressive organization of steel and concrete. We circled into the City from New Jersey, the bus jerking and shifting through traffic the entire time. As we descended a sharp, rounding decline into the Lincoln Tunnel, I observed the houses on the cliff above, pristine and perfectly perched for a view of the skyline, yet safe observers of the chaos beneath.

From the tunnel, we emerged into life itself, it seemed. People were everywhere. Yellow cabs flew by us on the right, darted around us in the back to the left and crossed uninterrupted across our bow. All of the cars, yellow and otherwise, dropped and lifted with the imperfections in the street, crossed lanes without signals, and raced through green lights, yellow lights and sometimes red, knowing the rules of some hurried game I'd seen nowhere before. Our driver, whose posture livened when he turned onto Ninth Avenue, instantly adapted. Despite the largest collection of people and cars I'd ever seen in a four-block radius, we turned into the Port Authority Bus Terminal in no time. We took the turn into the garage so sharply that I had to press my leg against the bathroom door to prevent myself from ending up in the aisle. I could only imagine what would have happened to me if there had been no door holding me back.

While I waited for my bag to be unloaded from the undercarriage of the bus, I struggled for air in the terminal garage, only to be greeted by the scent of acrid urine inside the terminal. I walked as quickly as I could to the escalator and ascended behind a family who's father carried some of the largest suitcases I'd ever seen. The look on all of their faces spelled misery, especially that of the apparent mother who carried a bottle of water and stroked the hair of a sweating and unhappy blond toddler beside her. Looking at them, and looking around at others in the terminal, I was grateful to only have to think of myself.

As for the rest of the people around, I couldn't find one who was smiling. Everyone was moving, though. Everyone had a place to go.

When I got off the escalator, I searched the ceiling for signs to a subway.

Take the N/R train downtown to City Hall, Robert O'Donnell had told me.

Before I exited the bus, I'd reviewed the crinkled piece of paper in my pocket one more time. Thankfully, the signage was clear, and as I meandered through the direction-less crowd, I found my way to the subway gate in no time. There, despite hearing the rumble of trains below and feeling the anxiety of knowing that I had missed them, I stood in a long line to buy a token. My pride and my position caused me to turn down two offers I received from a couple of child entrepreneurs who sought to charge me $2.00 for the $1.50 token each held in his hand. It was tempting, but the words at our graduation ceremony in Quantico held me back.

Everything you do as an FBI agent, whether on-duty or off, reflects upon this organization. Think about that with every daily decision you make, however small.

By the time I made it to the stairs to the subway platform, the crowd was too thick to move. Worse still, the arrivals and departures of the metal tubes that screeched into the station did nothing to stem the tide. After letting two trains go by, I left my perch on the stairs and joined the masses on the platform. Only small baby steps and a literal jamming of my body against the person in front of me allowed me to fit in. Anywhere else, I was sure, I would be accused of assault.

The crush of bodies on the train was worse. My legs were as one with those around me and my arms were locked at my side. I tried to concentrate on the feeling of my wallet against my rear to avoid being pick-pocketed. Somebody coughed, but he couldn't get his hands to his face in time. I breathed in whatever virus he might have been carrying.

Pleasant, Victoria, I thought sarcastically. *You've gone from sunny San Diego to this. How will you ever be able to last and be there for me when my horrific assignment is through?*

When I got off the train at City Hall, I was ready to strike someone, just for the sake of it. I'd had more offensive body contact on that ride than in my entire time in hand-to-hand combat training in Quantico. As I ascended the stairs into the open air, I was thrilled to see the small park in front of me and the government building overlooking it.

Must be City Hall, I thought, and I was further relieved as a waft of salty air made its way into my nostrils. *The seaport.* O'Donnell had told me that if I rode the train too far, I would be at the seaport.

I removed the mangled piece of paper from my pocket again. *Walk North two blocks*, it said, so I asked a street vendor which way to go.

The two-block walk in the fresher air and the ease with which my credentials got me past the security desk in the lobby of One Federal Plaza relaxed some of the tension in my shoulders. I had expected to see an impressive structure housing the FBI's largest field office, but I was not surprised to find it as basic as an old office building. *The nicer it is,* we were taught in Quantico, *the more likely it could be a target for terrorism.* With these thoughts in mind, I rode the elevator to the reception floor, and found a woman sitting behind a glass walled desk.

"I'm Special Agent Billy Tucker," I said. "I'm here to see a visiting ASAC named Robert O'Donnell. Would you ring Agent Victoria Summers first, though?" I asked. "I'd like to say a quick hello."

The thought of seeing Victoria was the only thing that had kept me sane on the way there. It had been two weeks since I had seen her, and we'd only talked once. It wasn't a particularly satisfying conversation either. We mostly traded stories about what we had been doing in our time apart. The one thing she said which kept me strong was that I'd better not forget about her or run off with some other FBI trainee.

"Never, Victoria," I responded. "I would never even think of doing anything to hurt you."

The receptionist pressed a few buttons on the telephone pad and offered me a pleasant smile as she waited for Victoria to pick up. "Not there," she said. "Do you want me to leave a message?"

"No," I responded, knowing that I already had. "I'll try her again later."

I walked away from the receptionist to wait for Robert O'Donnell, my stomach now fluttering in full fear of the man I never really wanted to see again. I tried to distract myself by looking around the lobby, admiring the pictures on the far wall of the FBI's current top brass, and the pictures on the opposite wall of the FBI's ten most wanted.

It was no good. My mind wandered right back to Quantico, as if I were standing and talking to Special Agent Ed Kelly right there.

Chapter Twenty-Nine

After my third day of undercover training, a few of the guys from our training group went for drinks. I spent most of the night talking to a five-year veteran of the FBI's Boston office. His name was Ed Kelly. Other than knowing his name and where he was from, I never tried to learn much about him. Instead, at my first opportunity, the end of an arrest simulation, I asked him what he knew about ASAC Robert O'Donnell.

"No one really *knows* O'Donnell," he started. But Ed Kelly was generous with what he did know, and what he'd heard from others.

"Supposedly," Ed began, "O'Donnell came to the FBI when he was twenty-three years old, a young guy like yourself, but no one got close to him. For one thing, O'Donnell never talked about his family and, for a while, all the guys assumed he had none. Holidays and weekends would pass, and O'Donnell wouldn't talk about where he was going or what he was doing. For another thing, he was in the office all the time anyway, always intensely focused on whatever investigation was happening at the time. O'Donnell was there even when everyone knew he didn't have to be. He would just sort of *be there,* as sure as the sun will rise. I think in my five years there, the guy took a total of three weeks vacation."

"O'Donnell spent his first two years as an agent in the FBI's New York office. But when things started to heat up in an organized crime investigation in Boston, O'Donnell and a few others were asked to re-locate. There were four of them. They all tossed around the idea of living together, but O'Donnell threw the whole equilibrium off when he leased a studio by himself. He didn't even tell the other guys he did it. No one figured he'd make a fun roommate anyway."

Ed Kelly tipped his head back and drained his beer. He motioned for the bartender to come our way.

"So they got to Boston," he continued. "And I met them all then. Good guys for the most part. The organized crime investigation continued full speed, but the problem was, that was all that it did: *continued.* Months passed. Years passed. There were no arrests. None. After four years, the guys on the team had nothing to show for their work, just boxes of paperwork and boxes of tapes. Morale in the unit was at an all time low. Guys would come to the office, sip some coffee, listen to tapes, plow through bank records, and go home. They started to become the butt of office jokes. Word actually got back to New York. Some nicknames grew out of the experience."

"Most of the guys took it alright, but not O'Donnell. He was bullshit. If there was ever any ribbing in his presence, you could see his shoulders lock and his face go red. Generally, people knew O'Donnell was too sensitive to take it, but one time, a real wise-ass named Mickey Roos decided not to let up."

The bartender placed another bottle in front of Ed, and he took his first sip. I followed suit, and then listened to Ed remember the scene: "*Hey Bobby,*" Ed Kelly said, mimicking Mickey Roos. "And right away, Billy, that was already an offensive start to any conversation with O'Donnell. When O'Donnell didn't look up, Mickey went right over to him. *I'm talking to you Bobby. I heard the mob is having a bar-b-que in Medford this weekend. They're grilling burgers and sausages and for a side dish, they're steaming a pot of FBI wires. They're going to put some red sauce all over the Bureau's wires, sprinkle some mooo-zarella cheese, and have a hell-uv-a meal.*"

"O'Donnell continued to stare at his computer screen and Mickey, who was getting some tentative chuckles from some on-lookers, decided to turn it up a notch."

Ed Kelly stepped back and continued.

"And for salad, Bobby. You know what they're having for salad, don't you? Mixed greens, some FBI tomato heads named Jasper and Fisher—and agents Sam Jasper and Mark Fisher who had come from New York with O'Donnell shook their heads with a smile—*and a thick, watery cucumber grown from the insides of the Boston office itself. The thing has been sitting still quietly and growing large and fat and watery for so long that it took four Luca's to chop it down. It took Ronnie Luca, boy Joey, and Uncles Arnie and Vinny, all standing there with ropes and axes and shit."*

Ed could tell I was soaking up his story, and a smile came across his face.

"Mickey Roos' onlookers laughed aloud with the absurdity of his tale. That egged him on, and he continued."

"They pulled and they chopped, pulled and chopped some more, and did it with all of their strength and all of their might. When that cucumber finally came off the vine, it fell to the ground with such a thud that it shook the

Green Line all the way from Government Center to North Station. But then Ronnie and Joey and Arnie and Vinny all had a lot of explaining to do when they brought it home. Because inside.... You know what was inside Bobby? Do you know?"

"Inside was you!!!"

"Now," Ed Kelly told me, "with the office erupting in laughter, O'Donnell finally turned his head, and Mickey kept going."

"Inside was you, Bobby. Typing away at that frigging computer. You didn't even look up then either. You just kept typing, but your fingers were all wet and slick from cucumber slime that...."

And then Ed Kelly paused in his story. He made a point of looking me right in the eye.

"Whack," he said. "That's all I can say to describe it. We could hear the *whack!* all the way across the room. O'Donnell hit Mickey Roos so hard that he broke his jaw in three places: two at the point of contact and one on the other side, where the vibrations from the blow must have just shattered the bone. Mickey Roos' jaw was wired shut for eleven weeks, and he wasn't able to talk at all. He lost forty pounds in the process sipping apple juice through a straw. When he returned, O'Donnell never even acknowledged him. He also never said he was sorry, and a lot of guys felt that O'Donnell never needed to."

"One thing was sure, though, no one ever teased O'Donnell, or anyone else on the organized crime team, again."

Ed Kelly now rested his elbow against the bar. His story was winding down.

"When a position opened up, O'Donnell was promoted to Assistant Special Agent in Charge of the Violent Crimes Unit. The guy was only twenty-nine years old at the time. It was unheard of. Mickey Roos immediately put in for a transfer. Once O'Donnell got promoted, Mickey knew he had to go. O'Donnell helped make sure that his wish was granted quickly."

"The guys loved Mickey, and everyone hated to see him go, but one thing O'Donnell could do that Mickey Roos never would was lead by example. Sure, O'Donnell would end up leading by fear as well, and that wasn't so healthy sometimes. More importantly, though, with O'Donnell's example to follow, everyone in the office stepped up a notch on their cases. O'Donnell helped successfully lead the Violent Crimes Unit for three years of record prosecutions and convictions. People started claiming he was going to be the next SAC in Boston."

"Then, in an effort to kick-start the laboring investigation into organized crime, ASAC Dan Miller was sent on his way. O'Donnell was made ASAC of the Organized Crime Unit and put back in the saddle chasing Ronnie Luca. This time, though, O'Donnell was calling the shots. The investigation was going to happen *his* way."

I swallowed hard as I began to see where I fit into the picture. Ed Kelly continued.

"I'm still in the Violent Crimes Unit, Billy," he said. "And I'll tell you, O'Donnell knows his stuff, but I also have to tell you that I'm happy he's no longer my boss, no longer in charge of my every day. For three years, I was on pins and needles in that office, in a constant state of inadequacy. How can you measure up to a guy who has no measurements? How can you satisfy the perennially unsatisfied? That was me. That was all of us under O'Donnell."

"You want to know the truth, Billy?"

I nodded, short of breath as Ed Kelly continued to speak.

"The truth is, Billy, Robert O'Donnell is a prick beyond the worst of them. The guy is unrelenting, uncompromising and *unraveling*. Sure, he'll charm you, woo you and cajole you with the best of them, but get this straight, Billy, he won't like you. The guy will take you apart before you even have a chance to get it together. The worst part of it is that he knows what he's doing. When you're working for him, as hard as that is, you do feel a sense of control. O'Donnell is in the office so much, and paying such close attention to every detail that it seems like it can't get out of control. That's a good feeling, sure, but it's also the kind of thing that makes you feel like he's the only one who really knows what's happening, what's supposed to happen and what will happen."

"Maybe that's the secret of his success. Maybe he makes others around him rely on him so much that he has to be the leader, the one calling the shots. In my mind, that's a dangerous way to operate. Some day, O'Donnell could go *ultra vires*, as they say in Latin, *outside his authority*, and there wouldn't be anyone there to stop him, at least until it was too late. That's the only thing I worry about with a guy like Robert O'Donnell."

Ed Kelly shrugged, apparently finished with his diatribe, which was alright with me. I didn't want to know more. I just wanted to be alone. I just wanted to be back in the pool-room picking songs from the jukebox with Victoria. Something told me that the boy within me was slowly dying, and that I would never feel light-hearted and excited about life again.

Chapter Thirty

Lost in thought about Ed Kelly's story, I was startled when Robert O'Donnell peeked his head through a windowless door and called to me from where I stood. My heart sank when I saw him, but I did my best to shake his hand firmly. I then followed him through the door, down a long corridor and into a small room.

O'Donnell must have decided that there was no time for any niceties.

"As I hoped you've now learned, Billy, undercover work is dangerous, and in a lot of ways."

I tried to focus as he spoke, but the pounding in my chest was a distraction. Since I learned of my assignment, my emotions had overwhelmed me several times. Each time, thankfully, I was alone. I struggled to maintain control as I stared at him. I knew that what I was up against would require me to play a role that only Robert O'Donnell truly understood. In the cloud of haze that circled my head, I tried to absorb all that I could.

"We've begun to establish some essentials for your return, but I'm going to wait until you get settled to follow up with the extensions on the Title III approvals. Remember, in this project, you're supposed to be in a self-evaluative, down mood, generally, since you couldn't find a job out of college."

I considered the irony of his words. Compared to what I was going to be sent home to do, I would have felt lucky to have had no career at all when I graduated from Drexel. Hell, I would have felt lucky to have not gone to Drexel, and to have simply stayed in Tremont Heights with Nathan and Lucy. *Maybe I would have been with her that night? Maybe I could have been her ear, her support that fateful night she wanted to be alone?*

O'Donnell paced as he spoke, the intensity of his thoughts now evident on his forehead.

"You've got to have a firm sense of your goal and you've got to always keep it in mind. I don't need to tell you that this assignment will spark some old ghosts for you, but you've got to stay focused on your role, believe in it and keep reminding yourself of it. Most importantly Billy, you've got to remember that it's only a role."

"Role playing myself, you mean," I added, but O'Donnell didn't seem to appreciate my interruption.

"The only way to do this right, Billy, is to believe it. You're going back to Tremont Heights because although you've been given every opportunity in college to succeed, you couldn't buy a job. You're down on your luck, and you have nowhere else to go."

Would anyone believe me? I wondered. *And how would I handle myself around Jayme?*

O'Donnell continued. "You don't know what you want to do, or even what you are capable of doing. You just know that your life has taken a turn for the worse. You're sorry you haven't been through town in a while. You would like nothing better than to get back in touch with your sister. You would like nothing better than just to sit back and have a few beers with your old friend, Nathan. The only thing that can keep you going is to reach back to your roots. You know you'll never be able to get on track until you can get back to the basics of your life again."

"It's going to take some time for people to accept that story—maybe a lot of time. You must be sure not to rush it. You've got to concentrate on being patient or you'll never get this right. Do you understand?"

My nod of approval hid my horror. I felt weak. O'Donnell seemed to notice.

"You've got to believe in your mission, Billy, but you've also got to periodically remind yourself of it. Over time, you might find yourself so comfortable in your role that you forget your mission completely. You've got to be aware that this will happen, and you've got to be able to recognize when it does. It's good to set a point in the day—a specific time—to remind yourself of your role."

"So every time it's 10:00 p.m., I want you to pause for a moment and remember your goals. 10:00 p.m. According to Gary McCormack, it's the time Lucy Polowski hopped off the number 66 bus to get to *Fire!*, and the last time before anyone but Nathan or Joey Luca remember talking to Lucy alive."

I felt as if my body were turning inside out.

"And remember this," O'Donnell continued. "As much as we've lectured to you over the past couple of weeks, a successful undercover performance is something that cannot truly be taught. The training course gave you some great tips and countless drills to go on, but in the end, you need nerves of steel and a near complete divorce from reality. That is something that no book, lecture or role play can accomplish."

My nerves were already on edge, and I had no idea whether the emotions I would encounter when I saw Jayme or Nathan again would allow me to separate my role from reality. Sure, I was devastated when Lucy died, but now that I'd met Victoria, and now that I knew I was going to have to insert myself into Nathan's life, Jayme's life and Lucy's final days and weeks, I really didn't care about my role or reality in Tremont Heights. I just wanted to be as far away as possible. A shoreline in San Diego with Victoria would do just fine.

Robert O'Donnell snapped up from his chair. I was dizzy and nauseous.

"Let me take you down to the audio room," he said, waiving a tape dated January 2000. "I need to let you in on what's been going on with your old pal, Nathan."

Chapter Thirty-One

"Guess who's back?" Nathan said as he slammed through the screen door of 141 Forsyth Street in Mattapan. "We want greenbacks, Roy! We want them now. You've been skimming. We know it. And you're hiding them here."

"No, no, no, you goons," came a cry. "You've got it wrong. I'm all paid. I swear I'm all paid," Roy Hanson pleaded.

"Give it up Roy!" came a call from Nathan's partner, Morty. "Ronnie's got no time for you or your frigging games."

A loud *crack!* and *pop!* filled the tape, and I heard an anguished moan.

"That could be your skull," Nathan called.

"Now, this *is* your skull," Morty called.

Immediately after he finished his words, I heard a shuffling of feet and then a loud thud. Then a wail.

"You want another!" Morty screamed. "I'm going to give you one every ten seconds until you tell us where you're keeping Ronnie Luca's money. That's four, three, two, one!" And then another thud. And another wail.

"Take a shot, Nate," Morty called. Come on, Nate. Let me see that pitcher's arm swing. Get a good one. This low life wants to go lower! Seven, six, five, four, three…"

I heard another shuffling of feet. It was the sound of my childhood buddy moving across a linoleum floor.

"Okay! Wait. Wait. Okay!" came a call from Roy Hanson, and then I heard a skidding stop and five heavy breaths. "Under the sink. In the dishwasher detergent. It's my kid's God-damn graduation money you goons. You God-damn goons."

And then, I heard some sobbing before Roy Hanson continued in a lowered tone.

"I don't need this. I'm earning an honest living. Ronnie doesn't do a damn thing for me. One thing, he did, years ago. Now, he thinks I still owe him. One thing. He got me a permit. It expired, God-damn it. I had to go before the

Board myself to get it renewed. Where was Ronnie then? I lost the permit. I had to pay Hank Billings off myself. Where was Ronnie then, huh? You tell him that. I don't owe him anything more. This is it. This is the last of it, you goons. Next time he sends you two out here, I'm going to shoot you myself!"

And then, another loud *pop!* and a call from Roy Hanson.

"That's my ceiling, you goons! You're going to fix that. I'm taking it out of Ronnie's money! I swear!"

Robert O'Donnell stopped the tape. "We talked to Roy Hanson," he said. "We're still working on him, but we have no leverage. The guy is earning an honest living, and he has two kids to worry about, both of whom he knows Ronnie Luca can find. It's a piece in the puzzle, but one that's not going to fit anywhere yet, unless Roy Hanson can be sure that Ronnie Luca, and many others, are going away for a long time."

Robert O'Donnell then hit the eject button and replaced the tape inside. "This one's arguably even better," he said, waiving a new cassette in his hand. With the press of an excited index finger, the next tape began to roll.

"Morty," I heard as the voice of Nathan Marks began a soft confession. "That felt great. It was easy. It was the way I imagined it."

"Yeah," came the voice of Morton Jamison, a two-time felon who'd been released one year earlier after serving five-to-seven for armed assault. "You ain't seen nothin' yet, Nate. Wait 'til they're really in arrears. Then you'll see 'em beggin', offering their T.V.'s, VCR's, whatever. Whatever it takes. Reduced to nothing. Reduced to beggin' vulnerable rats, that's all. That's my favorite part of the job. That's power. When you see a grown man crawlin' at your words, you'll be thankin' Ronnie Luca for this experience. It'll teach you. It'll teach you good."

"I was never one for academics," Nathan responded to the offer.

"Who needs them," Morty added. "This ain't no brain surgery. You've just got to be sharp. That's it. Sharp as a knife."

"I'm sharp," Nathan added. "I know what's going on."

"I know you do," Morty responded. "Ronnie Luca doesn't take no morons. It's bad for business."

Then, there was a silent pause. I knew Nathan. I knew he felt proud.

"You ever killed a guy over this stuff, Morty?" Nathan asked, and my ears perked high.

"Come on," was Morty's quick response. "Did you kill Lucy Polowski?"

I froze, the gravity of my assignment hitting hard. There was a long pause on the tape. I felt Robert O'Donnell studying me.

"I hear you," was all Nathan said.

I turned to look at the Assistant Special Agent in Charge, but by then, he was studying the floor.

"You see what I'm talking about, Billy," O'Donnell said as he looked up at me and pushed rewind on the machine. "Those are two of many. Now let's take a quick break before we try to piece together how your old pal ended up where he is."

With that, O'Donnell took me into a large room lined with rows of desks in the middle and cubicles around the outside. My fellow agents worked away at their stations, placing calls, gathering information and recording it on their computers. I longed for my assignment to be as simple as theirs appeared. I searched in vain for Victoria. I couldn't believe I was here in New York and I hadn't seen her yet.

We crossed the room to the other side and hugged the far wall all the way to the corner coffee station. Robert O'Donnell poured himself a cup of black.

"You want one," he said.

I took one look at the powdered cream on the counter and wrinkled my nose to say no. O'Donnell followed my eyes.

"You'll learn to drink it without cream and sugar," he told me, as if he was giving me his most important advice of the day. "It's quicker this way. You get your fix easy and then you get back to work."

I then followed the ASAC back across the room and into our private listening chamber. I didn't emerge for over two hours.

Chapter Thirty-Two

"People take a liking to Nathan when they meet him," O'Donnell began. "And I know I don't have to tell you that."

I nodded. Even in grade school, teachers had a soft spot for Nathan. He got help when he never asked for it, and he was allowed to walk in several minutes late while others got chewed out for tardiness. I noticed it, and I was sure others did too. For the most part, I marveled at the difference in treatment, and considered it interesting at best. Other times, though, I felt down right jealous. But Nathan was always good to me. I had no reason to challenge the favoritism he got. I would tease him sometimes, but Nathan was good about shrugging it off.

O'Donnell continued. "There's something about the way the kid looks, walks or smiles that's unassuming, disarming and acceptable, regardless of what he's doing. People just want to help him. And he's got so much talent. It's raw, undeveloped talent, though, and it may always be. Nathan may not be smart enough to channel it in the right direction. But Ronnie Luca has his ideas."

O'Donnell paused as he shook his head. "Ronnie Luca sees what Nathan has loud and clear, particularly since he's got a kid about the same age, and someone to compare against Nathan. And to be honest with you, I think Ronnie's always been a bit disappointed in his only son."

O'Donnell lips flared as he flapped a cassette tape in the air above his head. "Here's the one that gives me that insight. The one getting yelled at is Joey."

The squeaking reel of tape turned to words. "Pah, when do I have time for that!"

"When do you have time? When? How about the weekdays? How about the weeknights? How about the weekends? Do you know how I got to where I was?"

Silence.

"Huh? Take a guess, numb nuts. It wasn't from staying up all hours at night clubs four nights a week. While you're chasing skirts and arriving home at 6:00 a.m. with blood shot eyes, you could be keeping the books, getting organized. Christ, you could just be getting some sleep! Look at you. You either smell like perfume or JD, depending on the kind of night you had. And who do you run with? Who do you call your pals? Huh? When I was your age, I had a pack of boys. We were tight. We were unbreakable. We were loyal to each other. We looked out for each other, supported each other, and they helped me build the business we have today."

"Pah, they work *for* you, not with you."

"Don't you say that Joey. My business partners are just that, partners. I run the show, of course. I wouldn't have it any other way, but these guys are my lifeblood. Trusted. They're my advisors in times of need. You've got no one! Only your own thick head. No one from the neighborhood and no one from that night school you insisted on going to. What did you come out of there with, huh? No loyalties at all."

"I've got me, Pah. And I've got you and yours."

"Freeloader."

"Oh come on," Joey pleaded. "I've been paying my own way for four years now. I can do…"

"I'm not talking about paying," Joey's father interrupted. "I'm talking about building your own base, your own support. You've got to give loyalty to get it, son. And all I see you doing is stepping on toes. Threatening. Intimidating. You do it alone and you do it for pennies too. I've told you once and I'm going to tell you again. Drop the small stuff and get others to do your dirty work. Earn their loyalty. Earn their respect. You'll see what I mean."

"Pah, that's not my way. That's not for me."

"Ahh!"

Then, I heard a sound like that of a chair sliding away from a table.

Silence. Then Ronnie Luca started again. "I'm going to have a cigar. Get out of my sight."

For a moment, when O'Donnell stopped the tape, I wondered what it might have been like to have that kind of dominating influence in my life. I listened for further sounds. There were none, no further clues into the apparently tortured relationship of a father and his son, but O'Donnell waited a few seconds before stopping the tape anyway. He looked at me as he hit the eject button and signaled that he wanted to talk again.

"So when Ronnie Luca met Nathan Marks," O'Donnell started, "he needed him. Or, I guess, he needed a guy like him. From their first meeting,

Nathan struck a chord."

O'Donnell then began to tell me about the strangest of coincidences: Ronnie Luca and Nathan Marks sipping coffee together at a diner in July 1999 and a restaurant server hearing the whole thing. O'Donnell laughed when he told me the catch.

"The server wasn't really a server," he said. "She was undercover and assigned to Ronnie Luca. Apparently, every Saturday morning, Ronnie liked to get the eggs benedict, sip coffee and read the Herald at the counter of Barb's Diner in Southie. Nathan just happened to be there one day when Ronnie was in a talkative mood, and Special Agent Alexandra Tyler took copious notes after they left."

"We all thought it was a waste of paper," O'Donnell laughed again. "Tyler was the butt of a bunch of jokes—outside of my presence, of course," he added, and I thought back to the tale I'd heard from Ed Kelly. "But then, everything changed when Lucy Polowski was killed."

* * *

"Nothing but bad news," Ronnie Luca began to no one in particular as he flipped the pages of the Herald, but Nathan Marks was the only one within ear shot. "And I didn't win Mass Millions again."

Nathan didn't respond.

"Why can't you open the paper and see something good for a change? More coffee, Alex," Ronnie called to Agent Tyler, who played with the pin in her hair before picking up the pot and dragging it over.

"How about you, kid? More coffee?" Ronnie asked. "This one's on me." He laughed when he finished. The bottomless cup of coffee was the rule in Barb's Diner, as in any.

"You that cheap?" Nathan responded with a smile, and as Alexandra Tyler described it, somehow, the way Nathan said it, Ronnie Luca didn't mind the slight. Nevertheless, he paused and studied Nathan Marks.

"You know who I am?" Ronnie responded lightheartedly to the kid beside him, and Agent Tyler said her adrenaline poured into her veins with the question.

"Somebody's mailman?" Nathan added, his sarcasm something even I had rarely seen. I figured he must have gotten it from Lucy, all of those tortured sessions they'd had together.

"Jesus H. Christ," Ronnie added. "Smart-ass kid. Okay kid. You're so smart, tell me what the 'H' is for."

"Tell me why I should," Nathan responded.

Ronnie Luca was having fun. He looked at Nathan's plate of steak and eggs. "I'll buy your breakfast."

"I'm not done ordering," Nathan challenged him. "I was thinking about another round."

"Done," Ronnie responded. "Tell me what the 'H' is for and I'll get you whatever you want to eat."

"Are you serious?" Nathan asked.

"Do I look like I'm kidding? Hey Alex! Am I a man of my word?"

Agent Tyler looked at Nathan Marks. "He never skips out on a check, kid. That's about the best I can vouch for."

"You're going to buy my breakfast if I can tell you what the 'H' is for?" Nathan confirmed.

"That's what I said."

"What if I'm wrong?" Nathan asked. "Then what?"

"It's not an 'either or,' kid. It's trivia. You get it, you win. You don't get it, you don't win." Ronnie Luca paused. "Get it?" He was proud of his little play on words.

"I just got hammered last night at the track in Wonderland," Nathan responded. "I could use a benefactor like yourself...Mr. Mailman," Nathan added warmly as he laughed.

I shook my head when I heard O'Donnell recount that word from Nathan's mouth. I knew where Nathan had learned it. It was from Lucy, of course. Nathan called me that night and told me Lucy had started a shower.

Billy, he said, when I answered the telephone. *Benefactor? What is it? Tell me quick.*

I paused. *What?*

Dude, he repeated. *I don't have time. She's in the bathroom. What does benefactor mean?*

I explained, and as soon as Nathan understood, I heard a click and then a dial tone. I hadn't thought about it since.

O'Donnell continued the story.

"Don't push your luck, kid," Ronnie Luca warned, but only Alexandra Tyler recognized the devil in his eyes.

"Holy," Nathan blurted. "The 'H' stands for Holy. And it's not a middle initial."

Ronnie Luca stared at Nathan, his eyes a cross between astonishment and vengeance. "You think you got it? You think you're right?"

Agent Tyler noted that Ronnie seemed to playing with him.

"How old are you?" Ronnie asked, delaying the ultimate.

"Twenty-one," Nathan Marks responded.

"A little younger than my son."

"Come on," Alexandra piped in. "Did he get it? Is the kid right?"

Ronnie Luca looked at her, curious about the interruption. "I've got to hit the head," he responded. "I'll let you both know when I get back."

Agent Tyler turned her back on Nathan Marks. She did not want to speak with him at all. Her time for listening and engaging was limited to Ronnie Luca when he was around. She thought about using Nathan. She thought about asking him to ask Ronnie some questions. She thought better of it though.

When she heard the bathroom door open, Agent Tyler, coffee shop waitress, turned back around. Like Ronnie Luca, she too was surprised to see that the kid with the steak and eggs had disappeared. There was no money in front of him either. Not a dime.

"Where's the kid?" Ronnie asked.

Alexandra Tyler shook her head, puzzled. "Where's my money?"

"He skipped out?" Ronnie asked, but Tyler only shrugged.

"You going to pay for him or not?"

Ronnie Luca looked around. He walked back to the bathroom door and peaked inside. He went over to the front door and held it with his hand while he looked left across the parking lot. Finally, satisfied that he truly had been abandoned, he went back to the counter. He rolled out a $50 bill for Alexandra Tyler and told her to keep the change.

"This more than covers me and the kid," he said. And then he smiled, nodding his head as he did. "Quite a kid," he added, smiling again. "Lucky for him, he guessed right."

* * *

"No one knows for sure the next time Ronnie and Nathan saw each other," O'Donnell said. "We got lucky that Saturday and, believe me, after Lucy Polowski went down, we had Agent Tyler there every day that followed. We never got that lucky again, though. As far as we can assume, Nathan Marks didn't see Ronnie Luca again until after she died."

It was then that O'Donnell began to tell me about some additional FBI intelligence. Apparently, the day after Lucy Polowski was killed, the G-men who did their best to trail Ronnie Luca followed him out of the police precinct right after he went in to visit his son. Ronnie headed South on Route 93 with two of his muscle men and pulled off at Exit 11, right into Tremont Heights.

"The Bureau's trailers got lost on a side street, but they say Ronnie was in Nathan's general neighborhood. We talked to a couple of neighborhood kids to see if they remembered a car that fit the description," O'Donnell said. "Overall, we've got enough to assume that Ronnie and Nathan met."

"Based on that?" I responded.

"What more do you need Agent Tucker?" O'Donnell snapped.

My head jerked backward hearing the way he addressed me. That was who I was now. I had been taught to think, act and respond like an FBI agent was supposed to. O'Donnell was giving me—no demanding of me—the warning to do so.

"How old were the kids?" I asked, having learned that the memories of youths were often guided by what they thought their listener wanted to hear.

"Irrelevant," O'Donnell responded.

"It's not irrelevant," I tried. "If they flashed their badges…"

"Move on Agent Tucker," O'Donnell interrupted. "What else do you need?"

"Did they shadow the on-ramp back up to 93 North?"

"No."

"Did they interview Nathan?"

"I told you that already. Are you listening? The answer is 'no'."

"Why not?"

"Come on, Tucker. I told you that it took the local cops days to interview Nathan. The locals didn't even tell us he was her boyfriend until several days in. It wasn't until then that we started to understand a reason for Ronnie Luca's drive to Tremont Heights."

"So you've got him driving to Tremont Heights, and you talked to a couple of neighborhood kids. From that, you think Ronnie Luca met with Nathan?"

"Something wrong with that?"

"Well what did the kids say?"

O'Donnell held his arms to the ceiling in what I thought was a gesture of relief. "What did the kids say?" he repeated, but I wasn't sure if he was mocking me. "Right. I never told you, did I? I skipped that. I said that we talked to a couple of neighborhood kids and overall we had enough to go on. I didn't link it up."

I nodded.

"Well the kids didn't say a damn thing!" he belted with evil eyes, and then I knew that he was mocking me. "What's the matter with you, Tucker? I would say that we had enough just from the fact that Ronnie drove from the police precinct to Tremont Heights right after visiting his son, when Nathan Marks was not only indebted to his son but also Lucy's boyfriend! Wouldn't you say that's enough?"

I shrugged, feeling belittled and thinking again of Ed Kelly's description of the man in front of me. O'Donnell shook his head telling me I was supposed to agree.

"We're the FBI, Tucker. We're not the judge and jury. We give the prosecutor enough to make the case. When we can, we give him the script. When we can't give him a slam-dunk, we tell them to do what they were taught to do in law school: *argue*. As long as we give them the ability to do that, we've done our job. In my book, coupled with Nathan being taken under Ronnie's wing after the shooting, I would stake my career on the fact that, from what we have, Ronnie drove out to Tremont Heights to pay a visit to Nathan Marks and that they did talk. Tell me that you disagree and I'll send you right back to Quantico for another round."

My blood now began to boil in a mixture of anger and shame. *I was new. What did he want from me? This was why rookie agents weren't given this kind of responsibility. I hadn't had a chance to make my rookie mistakes yet. I needed a chance to learn how to apply what I was taught in training. O'Donnell wasn't giving me that chance.*

"I'm not ready for this," I blurted, but then it was O'Donnell's turn to boil.

I watched his entire body tighten as he turned back toward the window. Then, in a repressed voice, he spoke.

"You're the *only* one who's ready, Tucker. That, I can assure you. And what I'm telling you is this: don't be the judge and jury when you're back in Tremont Heights. Do your job. Make assumptions where you can. Like I just did. Trust them. Trust yourself."

His words seemed more than just an effort to repair my shattered confidence. They came from a burning need inside of him for me to succeed, I was sure. I looked at the Assistant Special Agent in Charge as he paused. *How many lessons would I have to learn before this assignment was over?* I wished I had something close to a clue about what I was doing. I would have given anything to have a few hours alone with Victoria. She was strong. Her convictions about the Bureau would be able to guide me through this, I knew.

Robert O'Donnell was then called out of the room for a phone call.

"Excuse me, kid," he said rising to depart. "This isn't my only case."

My shoulders felt lighter as the senior agent exited, and I savored the next several minutes alone. From where I sat, the project seemed surreal. I knew that soon, I would be heading back to Tremont Heights. My assignment would officially begin. But I also knew that now, as long as I was not there yet, I could take comfort in the distance, and pretend that this nightmare was not really about to happen.

Chapter Thirty-Three

When Robert O'Donnell returned, he was eager to play a few other tapes that he felt would give me good insight into the psychology of my assignment. I considered it ironic that he even mentioned that topic, because he certainly didn't seem to have given much thought to mine.

He flipped through the pile of tapes before him, but there was a knock on the door. O'Donnell paused and leaned forward, crossing his hands on the table between us.

"Come in," he shouted.

"Sir. Call for you sir."

"Who is it?"

"It's Reggie Williams sir. He's calling from the field."

"Tell him to use his best judgment, whatever it is, and tell him to call me in two hours."

The door shut, and O'Donnell shook his head. "Dumb shit," he muttered, but then looked at me as if he wished I hadn't heard his words.

"Now where was I?" he asked as he began thumbing through the tapes again. Ah! Here it is," he said before filling the recorder once more, this time with one dated December 1999, a month after Lucy's funeral and, ironically, the month of the FBI's information session on Drexel's campus.

* * *

All I heard for the first several seconds was a shuffling of feet and furniture in the room.

"We all here?" came the voice of Ronnie Luca, to which there were a few grunts of acknowledgement in response. "For those of you that don't know him, I want to introduce Nathan Marks."

A few more grunts but no discernible words. Ronnie Luca continued.

"Nathan comes to us from Tremont Heights. You all know where that is.

You all know the latest news from there as well. The girl that fell was Nathan's high school girlfriend."

Ronnie Luca paused for effect, and I heard a shifting of bodies and the sliding of a few chairs.

"We're sorry about Lucy, Nathan. Really, we are. Such a tragedy. Such a young girl. Seven 'Our Father's' for you Nathan. Isn't that right, gang? We're each going to say seven 'Our Father's' before we go to bed tonight. For the girl and for Nathan."

"Yes Ronnie. Uh huh. Seven 'Our Father's'. Bless us Father. Bless Nathan and the girl," came the varied responses from the crowd.

"That's for you, Nathan. We're all doing that for you. We do that for each other. Does everybody have their knife?" Ronnie asked.

"Uh huh. Yes Ronnie. Uh huh," came the varied responses again.

"Okay then. A moment of silence for Nathan and then a drop of blood for his girl. Everybody now. Everybody together."

There was a long pause of silence and some minor shuffling.

"Joey, you too. This has got to include everyone," Ronnie said. "Joey's suffered a loss too, but this is for Nathan right now."

Another long silence.

"Good. Is that everyone? I saw everyone," Ronnie said answering his own question. "Now you, Nathan. Now you. I brought you a knife. Prick the tip of your ring finger. Go ahead. Go ahead and do it."

I looked at Robert O'Donnell in the silence that followed. "How did you ever get this on tape?"

He only put his index finger to his lips and raised his eyebrows in response.

"That's it, Nathan. That's it. Now let a drop fall in the dish there in the middle."

Another pause. Ronnie Luca continued.

"We don't speak about this again my friends. We don't speak about Lucy Polowski. We don't speak about *Fire!*, and we don't go to *Fire!* You got that Joey? The life of this girl sits right here in this dish before us, and if we do talk...CLANG! RIP!," the tape got so loud I had to block my ears. Ronnie Luca raised his voice. "We end up like this!"

I heard a baritone yelp from what must have been one of the men in the room.

"Jesus, Ronnie," someone said.

"Don't Jesus me, Sal! That was some strangely slow driving you did that day! I have a mind to cut your finger right off for that crap. If I didn't know you better, I would have thought you were in cahoots!"

Then, there was a moment of calm and Ronnie Luca lowered his voice. "Nathan?" he asked. "Any questions?"

Silence.

"Anyone else? Do we know who shot Lucy Polowski?"

"No Ronnie. Uh uh Ronnie. No idea Ronnie," came the varied responses.

"Nathan?"

"No Mr. Luca," came the voice of my old friend.

"Were any of us in Tremont Heights the night she was killed?"

"Uh uh. No Ronnie. Where's Tremont Heights?" someone asked, provoking laughter.

"Nathan?"

"I was with Joey, Ronnie. You know that," came the voice of my old friend again.

"That's right Nathan. You and Joey. Joey and you. Together that night. That's my boys. That's my two beautiful boys."

* * *

"This is what you're dealing with, Billy. It doesn't take a brain surgeon to know to keep his mouth shut after something like this."

I nodded, lost in thought. It was inconceivable to me that Nathan could even pretend to forget about Lucy, or not mention her again. As I knew them together, they were one, symbiotic, even if they were dysfunctional. *How could Ronnie Luca squelch that?*

O'Donnell seemed to read my thoughts. "Put yourself in one of those meetings, Billy. Try to imagine yourself there. What would you do?"

But all I could imagine was Lucy. Little did she know she would cause such a mess.

Could she see this? I considered. *And what if she could?* I couldn't decide if she would feel flattered or lonely. *Would she be cheering for Nathan? Would she be cheering for me? Or would it be like that night in Sigma, where Lucy didn't think about anyone but herself.*

Chapter Thirty-Four

When Robert O'Donnell rose from his seat to stretch, I thought he was going to give me a break, let me wander. I figured I would have a full fifteen or twenty minutes to find Victoria. She couldn't be far, I assumed.

But O'Donnell's words interrupted my fantasy. There would be no break at all, only more overload about the elements of Nathan's new life.

"Now Ronnie Luca wasn't handed the influence he has," O'Donnell started again. "As a result of that, he expected Joey to be able to make his own way too. But let me tell you something about genetics, Billy. It doesn't always work that way. They say that socialization has a lot to do with it. Joey Luca never had to fend for himself. He had his father to fall back on. Ronnie, on the other hand, learned how to make it the hard way, and he saw something in Nathan that reminded him of himself, I'm sure."

I could understand what O'Donnell was saying. He was smart for seeing it. To most outsiders, Nathan looked lazy, unmotivated. Those that truly knew him, though, understood that he was an incredibly intense and hard worker. Gambling was a distraction for him, sure, but really, Nathan attacked gambling with the same intensity he attacked everything else. He just needed someone like Ronnie to set him straight, or sort of straight, I guess.

"So what Ronnie said about Nathan at that meeting was true, Billy. He saw Nathan as one of his 'beautiful' boys right from the start; so much so that even Joey began to see it. And to hate what he was seeing."

"How did Ronnie Luca make his name?" I asked, not ready for O'Donnell to turn to Joey.

O'Donnell leered at me. "Loyalty," he said, as if he didn't need to say anything else. "Ronnie Luca was loyal to everybody. It didn't matter who. A stranger's car stalled, Ronnie was there pushing. Someone in the cashier's line came up short, Ronnie offered the money. Somebody's kid needed a ride to work, Ronnie had plenty of room in his car. July 4th barbeque, Ronnie had an extra burger and dog for anyone who wanted one."

"But he was smart, Billy. Ronnie's acts of kindness weren't so random in his mind. He took down everyone's name that he helped, *everyone's*. And when Ronnie's instinct told him the cup was overflowing, he went the other way."

"Hey Jimmy, Ronnie would call across the street to a hulking guy. *Remember when I pushed that car of yours? Well, now I need a favor. I need you to take a walk with me and just look tough when I talk. Don't say anything. Just look the part."*

"Slowly, but surely," O'Donnell continued, "Ronnie Luca found his gang. The guys he felt most comfortable with and who seemed most natural in the role became his henchmen. They couldn't resist. He paid them more than he took himself."

I raised my eyebrows in surprise.

"All for goodwill, Billy," O'Donnell said, shaking his finger. "Ronnie was smart. After one or two years of doing that, he knew he could start tipping the see-saw in the other direction and building his own wealth. Ronnie looked at it like the start of any business. In the first few years, most entrepreneurs just hope to break even. After that, if the right infrastructure is in place, it's all profit."

"And that's all it is now for Ronnie. It's been that way for a long time."

I was impressed. I nearly forgot that Ronnie's business meant loan sharking, black mail and violence.

"But then there's pride," O'Donnell continued. "Pride is what keeps him pushing Joey. Nothing would make Ronnie prouder, I'm convinced, than for Joey to build his own little empire."

"But in Ronnie's mind, and based on his own path, the right to an empire is a meritocracy. He wants Joey to earn it, and he's showing him how to do it, but it's not quite clear if Joey's up to the task. And like I said, Billy, people like Nathan, wherever he goes."

O'Donnell then described how Ronnie's gang, even Ronnie himself, began to choose Nathan over Joey for certain odd jobs, the kind that required a long drive, prolonged surveillance, overnights, and visits to guys like Roy Hanson. It was always under the guise of "teaching the kid" or "showing the kid."

"Can I bring the kid? Ronnie was often asked, and Nathan felt flattered by the attention."

"*Tutelage*, Ronnie would tell Nathan. *It's all in the name of your tutelage, kid.*"

"But the gang was careful not to disrespect Joey in the process. *Let me bring the kid*, they would say, *Joey's got more important fish to fry*."

"And that had a dual effect," O'Donnell explained. "On one hand, Joey was isolated to spend more time close to his father and be on top of the operations he ran. On the other hand, it was Nathan who began to earn the gang's loyalty. One of Ronnie's guys would return from the field with Nathan and have an exciting tale to tell the others. Nathan's role would be trumpeted to justify the request for his presence, to claim some part in Ronnie's idea of 'tutelage.' It got to the point where each guy in the gang began trying to one up the other."

Robert O'Donnell paused and shook his head.

"Over the last couple of months," he continued, "it's been like a bunch of kindergartners fighting over a favorite toy."

O'Donnell paused. "I think Ronnie can sense it," he continued. "My guess: Ronnie's loving every minute of it. He's looking sideways at his son and thinking, '*is he getting this? Does he see what's happening?*' My other guess: Joey gets it and gets it but good. Joey's boiling beneath the surface, but he's not going to give his father the satisfaction."

O'Donnell continued.

"So Joey's all over the map. Sometimes, he actually wants to pal around with Nathan and see what Nathan has to offer. When he does so, though, he realizes that he can't stand his presence, or the jealousy he hasn't quite come to understand. Sometimes, he tries to insist on going out in the field in place of Nathan. '*Let Nathan stay here with Pop,*' we've heard Joey say, '*I need some exercise.*'"

"And sometimes, Joey just falls right into role. *When you and Sal are done, Nathan, come right back. Me and Pop want a full report. You hear?!*"

"Now the times Nathan and Joey are alone, Billy, are probably the most interesting of all. You can imagine why. At least as far as we know, neither of them has ever approached the subject of Lucy Polowski. The times we've been able to catch pieces of their conversation, with trailers and such, it's been tense and forced. A bad date is the only thing I can liken it to. Strained conversations. Strained interest in one another. Strained smiles. They never look each other in the eye. Even their strides are tense. Those two need some serious therapy," O'Donnell finished. "You know what I mean?"

I could imagine the scenario: side by side, co-conspirators in a plot to silence a murder investigation of a girl they both loved, two murder suspects themselves; and perhaps worst of all, bookie and gambling addict walking together as if the power dynamic that defined how they first came to know each other no longer had any meaning at all. I could imagine Joey's resentment. I could imagine Nathan's discomfort. I certainly knew Nathan well enough. We had spent enough time together growing up to have an occasional tense moment ourselves. I was always able to break the tension, though, because I could draw Nathan out and get him to talk about it. I suspected that alone with Joey, there was no outlet. Neither one of them was permitted to talk about Lucy. Nathan probably could sense that Joey would tell his father if he ever raised the subject, and Joey simply was unlikely to ever trust Nathan.

The tension the two of them must have felt walking next to each other far outdid what Nathan and I felt after some bad play on the bruise-ball court, I was sure. That was a game, and there would be a next time. For Nathan and Joey, this was life. This was their future. A misstep could change everything for them. I tried to imagine the way I felt in some of my interviews on campus when I felt that my future was on the line, and then I multiplied it by 50.

"And this new life for Nathan has been good to him," O'Donnell continued.

I learned a lot more about my old friend's life in the conversation that followed. It wasn't long before Nathan decided to slick back his hair and buy a couple of silk shirts for the evenings. It wasn't long before he started rolling out a wad of bills from his pocket to pay for small things, telling people to keep the change. Not so gradually, Nathan Marks grew far apart from the guy who used to pull crinkled singles from various side and back pockets, gather and count the change in his hand and ask the server or clerk, a winning smile plastered across his face, if he or she minded that he was a few cents short.

With the way Nathan grew up, it came as no surprise to me that Nathan had found something that worked under the wing of Ronnie Luca. It was no wonder that he fell right into whatever code of silence Ronnie demanded. He needed the structure and guidance, if not the opportunity. With Ronnie Luca, Nathan no doubt saw a new beginning.

But I still hovered somewhere between disbelief and denial of what I had to do. Under Robert O'Donnell's disguise, I was being asked to intrude into Nathan's new life; not just into his life at present, but into the past that brought him to where he was. I suspected that when my project came to a conclusion, if ever, both Nathan and I would be worse for wear.

And for what? Just when both of us had found our way, me in the FBI and Nathan under the wing of Ronnie Luca, I was sure to tear us both back down. Neither one of us deserved that, and it didn't even matter to me that Nathan had turned to a crime. To me, Nathan Marks was not now, nor would he ever be, a criminal. Destiny had new meaning in my project, and to two kids with tragic pasts, I was sure that all it meant was greater despair.

But deep down, subconsciously perhaps, I think that I always had a different hope: finding a way out for both of us. This, of course, I never told to Robert O'Donnell.

Chapter Thirty-Five

Before I left One Federal Plaza in lower Manhattan, I asked Nancy, the receptionist, to ring Victoria Summers one more time. There was no other noise in the front area as I waited, so I could hear the muffled rings as Nancy held the telephone away from her ear.

One ring. *Please,* I thought, my heart racing with the excitement of being able to see her again.

Two rings. *Just let her be tied up for a second*, I prayed.

Three rings. *Not looking good*, I knew.

Four rings. *Definitely not there*, I was sure.

Five rings. *Just me and my misery*, I concluded. *There would be no bright eyes or smiling face or even a, 'Hey there, Billy-boy' to comfort me*. I was alone.

Sixth ring. "Hello," came a voice I instantly recognized, even if muffled and hurried.

My chest lifted to my chin.

"Ms. Summers?" the receptionist asked.

"Yes Nancy, it's me."

"What's your name again, sir, I'm sorry," Nancy said to me.

"Billy Tucker," I stammered. "Tell her it's Billy Tucker."

"Billy Tucker is here to see you Ms. Summers. Do you want me to send him to you or do you want to come out."

There was a long, silent pause. I strained to listen. The pause was a little too long, I felt, but I didn't view it as anything other than Victoria's speechless surprise.

"I'll come out," she said. "No. No, send him in. No wait. I'll come out."

I smiled. *She was surprised. I had caught her off-guard. She was nervous. She must not have picked up my voicemails.*

It felt like an eternity as I stood in the lobby and waited for Victoria. *She must be freshening up*, I thought.

When the door finally opened, I thought my heart was going to leap from my chest. I nearly dropped when I saw the rugged face that appeared.

"Tucker?" Robert O'Donnell said. "What are you still doing here? You should be on the bus."

Now, I was speechless. "I ah…I was just checking to see if one of my classmates from Quantico was around, and it turns out…"

Just then, Victoria came through the door. She looked brilliant. She was dressed in a pressed navy pants suit, her shoes sparkled and her face lit up the waiting room. She smiled at me. It was a smile that offered such warmth, such comfort.

"Hel—lo there," she said musically, but her hello was accompanied by a strained glance at Robert O'Donnell. "Fancy seeing you here, Billy Tucker. I just picked up my voicemails on the way out. I've been tied up in a wiretap for the last 36 hours. I'm going on four hours of sleep."

She looked fantastic.

"Look at you," I said, conscious of O'Donnell standing by and curiously absorbing the whole exchange. "You look great."

I held back my words, held back my burning desire to reach out to her, and I held back my overwhelming urge to tell O'Donnell to *Bug Off!!*

Victoria came to me and offered me a hug. She squeezed my shoulders extra tight. It was a signal I recognized from our days together in Quantico. It was the *play it cool, nobody knows* warning.

"How was the undercover course?" she asked.

"I learned a few things. Thirty-six hours?" I questioned, directing the attention back to her.

O'Donnell interrupted. "Don't worry, Tucker. Where you're going, that's highly unlikely to be a part of the game."

"Did you find an apartment?"

She started to nod and say "Brooklyn."

The Assistant Special Agent in Charge then looked at his watch. "Tucker," he said, and his words were like hot lava on my skin. "I let you out of here at 2:30 so you could catch that 3:30 express bus. It's now almost a quarter of. I'm serious about you making that bus. Now get moving. You will have time to catch up with all of your old Quantico pals another day."

Victoria and I looked at him. My eyes drooped. She held her pinky and index finger to her ear, as if she was holding a phone.

"We can catch up another time, Billy," she said angling her eyes at O'Donnell. "But best of luck, wherever you're going. Keep in touch and let's grab a coffee when whatever it is you're doing is through."

And then she winked at me with her right eye, the one that O'Donnell couldn't see.

"I can call you to catch up," I blurted, picking up on her cue, but not caring what the Assistant Special Agent in Charge would think or say. I took pleasure in the moment, regardless of the consequence.

Victoria turned to go. So did I. Opposite ways we went this time, but one day I knew, there would be no Robert O'Donnell to interfere.

I walked out of the building aggravated but uplifted. I had seen her. Our bodies had made contact. Most of all, I had engaged in a subtle act of defiance to Robert O'Donnell. I realized in the process that I may have been his pawn, but he needed his pawn. He needed me badly. It felt incredible, and I rode that feeling on a non-stop Peter Pan bus all the way from New York to Boston. I sat in my worn navy blue suit, a white shirt wrinkled from a full day's wear and traveling and a cheap red tie.

O'Donnell had asked me not to change, figuring that a rag tag, pseudo preppy business-man look would work well when I arrived in Tremont Heights.

I followed his instructions, but not for the reasons he hoped. I followed his instructions because the clothes I wore had touched Victoria, and I could smell her beauty on me the whole way home.

PART IV

Coming Home

Chapter Thirty-Six

It was September 2000, and I was ashamed to admit that it had been over nine months since I talked to Jayme, since Lucy's funeral, really. We hadn't been good about keeping in touch while I was at college. Jayme didn't have e-mail and our phone calls were infrequent anyway. My sister was growing up in my absence, I knew, but I tried not to think about it. It was too painful.

We'd had it out at Lucy's funeral. I don't know if it was because of the stress of the day or the tension that had grown with my distance and our lack of contact. Whatever it was, I didn't enjoy it, and I didn't appreciate her attitude. I also felt guilty about it.

It was a sunny, but cold day in Boston. *Fitting for the occasion,* I supposed. *Like Lucy herself.* As Jayme and I walked from Lucy's gravesite together, my body feeling limp and shaking, and my eyes swollen from holding back the tears, Jayme seemed inappropriately upbeat.

"I might have a thing for Nathan," she told me, looking back for him.

And what a time to tell me. Just when my opinion of Nathan was at its worst, Jayme decided to act her age and be the girly teenager she'd suddenly become.

I held my tongue, but she continued: "I can take better care of him than that bitch," Jayme said.

I clenched my jaw, gripped her hand tightly and guided her beyond the fence. "First of all, Jayme. You show some respect. You don't talk like that here, not now. Not ever."

"Oh get over yourself," she muttered with fiery eyes and locked teeth. "You've always been jealous of Nathan. You've always loved *Lipstick*," she added, emphasizing her nickname. "Don't think everyone couldn't tell."

I didn't know what to say first. No one had ever confronted me with these feelings. I really had never done so myself. I took the high road.

"I'll tell you what Jayme. Get over *that thing* you think you have for Nathan. He's going nowhere fast, and he'll only take you down with him. I forbid you to see him."

I don't know why I ever thought I had that kind of authority over Jayme, but it sounded parental at the time to say it. It was also my way out of the conversation.

Jayme saw what I was doing, and she didn't take it too well: "Don't pretend you're my parent, Billy. You took the only one I ever had away from me. You don't know me, so don't pretend to!"

At the time, I knew I had to catch a bus back to Philadelphia. I was also a month from winter finals. I didn't need this as an additional distraction. It was hard enough for me to remember how I'd left her in Tremont Heights in the first place.

* * *

Ruth had been our mother's best friend. In the years before my bike accident and the tragedy that followed on that street corner that morning, Ruth came over nearly every night to chat. Ruth was a chain smoker, and she had a cackle that made me cringe. I hated the sound of her throaty voice drowning out the soft whisper of my mother, and I hated inhaling her secondary poison.

Ruth was always about to lose her home. She didn't have a job, didn't care about finding one and constantly bemoaned her trouble at the unemployment office. She had a 24-year old son named Rick who lived with her, but he had never been able to hold a steady job either. She came knocking the evening after our mother died. Our house was paid for, courtesy of the life insurance policy my father's construction company had provided for its workers.

Ruth said she wanted to move in.

I panicked when she asked. We had no relatives around, and none that we had any relationship with at all, but I was hoping we would end up moving in with Addison Parker.

Addison, proud owner of The Chocolate Cone, was born and raised in Tremont Heights. At 41 years old, he had purchased and remodeled his store almost twenty years earlier and named it after the purest pleasure of his childhood. Everyday, he checked the stock of soda, straightened the candy, filled the shelves to capacity and stood comfortably behind the counter. Although his height was nothing to behold, his upright stature gave him a tall appearance. Coupled with his sturdy jaw and the inquisitive gleam in his eyes beneath his receding hairline, Addison's presence was imposing. Even a stranger could sense a quiet, inner confidence from his exterior glow.

After his youth and years of toiling around Tremont Heights at odd jobs,

Addison was happy to have become an independent businessman. The Chocolate Cone kept him close to his roots, but it also allowed him to keep any external pressures at a comfortable distance.

I don't bother nobody. And nobody bothers me, he would repeat to anyone who would listen. *Cold out there?* he would say when, as kids, we came into his store in the winter. *How's the humidity?* he would say six months later.

Addison was married but had no children, so I thought he'd be a natural fit for us. Addison typically worked fifteen hours a day, yet, he always had a smile for me—and everyone else for that matter—the moment the silver bells signaled a step through his door.

Billy Tucker! he always belted, even if he had just seen me hours before. *You coming for a slush, a snack, or some stimulating conversation from the eyes and ears of this beautiful neighborhood.*

To Addison, Tremont Heights was the most special place in the world, and he was also its self-acclaimed watchman.

Did you hear about that brush fire over behind the Gallagher's last night?

I never needed to answer when Addison raised a supposed topic for discussion. A nod was enough for Addison to finish what he wanted to say.

Damn good thing he kept his hose going through November.

And then, the punch-line.

You know I sold Eddie Gallagher that hose?

Addison was proud of what he had, and what he had accomplished, and he regularly shared that with me as well.

I built this business from nothing, Billy, he would say, extending his arms and eyeing the far walls of his store. *In here, I don't answer to nobody but me. You'll see some day—some day when you find yourself working for the man. But you just say the word. Say the word, Billy, and I've got work for you here. Safe work. Steady work.*

Addison was good like that. He always needed help stocking the shelves or taking inventory. I often took him up on his offer, especially in the winter when the evenings came early. He never pushed too hard. The work he gave to me he could have easily done himself.

After my mother died, I considered asking Addison and his wife to take care of us, but Ruth preempted my plan.

"Billy," she rattled, when I opened the front door. "Don't give me that little look of yours. Your mother and I talked about this once. She would have wanted it."

My arm jerked because I wanted to close the door on her, particularly after she mentioned Rick.

"Ricky won't get in your way," she stammered. "He's always out, and we can give him the basement. We'll tell the DSS I'm a distant relative."

I didn't know what to say. I knew we needed someone to look out for us, and maybe Addison didn't want the responsibility. I didn't want to have to make him turn us down. And there was Ruth, on our front steps, offering. I felt trapped, so I yielded our home and our custody to Ruth.

I also issued a warning, my first step as a twelve-year old man of the house: "You're going to stop smoking if you're going to live under this roof," I said.

Ruth never managed to quit altogether, but she did cut back, and after a few months, when the DSS came knocking, we all were able to grin and bear it and let them know we were getting by just fine.

But as I grew older and began to fill-in my teenage body, Rick's presence in the house—at any time—became increasingly loathsome. Rick was a scrawny guy, and no doubt, viewed my increasing strength as a threat. Anything and everything we did turned into a competition. If we were taking out the trash, it turned into a race. Trimming the hedges immediately became a contest of who could trim the fastest. If I were ever about to win, Rick would either start to poke and punch me, or change the rules altogether. The only way I could gain control of these situations was ignore him. Then, according to Rick, I was too *chicken shit* to take him on.

If I ever ignored Rick's taunting, he upped the ante. Once, he went way too far.

"What's the matter?" he dared when I refused to partake in his trash bag throwing contest, the one where I always ended picking up the inevitable mess. "You miss your mommy!"

I tried to take Rick out at the knees just as he'd finished his words, but he came down on me hard, backhanding my face.

"Don't mess with me, you little bastard!" he yelled, straddling my body.

My tears were instant. I was sure that I could kill him if I had the strength, but at fifteen, I knew I still did not.

Jayme had more success avoiding Rick, probably because Ruth knew her son, and she tried to spread a protective wing. Thanks to Ruth's constant efforts, Jayme barely even had to make eye contact with him, but I knew what she was thinking. Sometimes, it was evident in the simple way she looked at me while he tormented.

"Put some weight on, shit for brains," Rick yelled down to me once from the top of the ladder.

And as she watched from the window, it was as if Jayme could read my thoughts, as if she too envisioned him slipping from the top rung and landing smack on the ground next to me.

While moments like those brought Jayme and me closer, I was constantly racked by guilt. I felt responsible for bringing us Ruth and Rick, but there was nothing I could do to redeem myself, short of getting Rick out of her life for good. There were moments when her eyes seemed to beg me to do it, and I would have considered it, if only to regain favor with my little sister. In the end, I let fate continue its course—one I knew would at least take me away to college.

"Some day it will be your turn," I tried to tell Jayme, but at 11 years old, she could easily do the math and recognize that *some day* might as well have meant *never*.

Chapter Thirty-Seven

In a little over three and one-half hours, the bus pulled off the Massachusetts Turnpike and into South Station, just outside of Boston's financial district. Compared to the Port Authority, South Station allowed for a serene and orderly arrival. I could actually hear the echo of our footsteps as we made our way down the corridor to the escalator. Everyone headed in the same direction this time, probably because that was the only way to get out, and the crowd was less than one-tenth of that in New York City.

My next move involved a transfer to a local MBTA bus to Tremont Heights. That was easier than I expected and, after the day I had, I was nothing short of pleased. During the fifteen minute ride down the expressway, it occurred to me how close I was to my assignment becoming a reality, how close I was to stepping back into Nathan's shadow.

It also occurred to me how close I was to feeling the presence of Lucy Polowski, and all of the passion she inspired. I tried to compare my awe for her to my feelings for Victoria, but the two could not be compared. Lucy Polowski would always be the sexy and potent standard of temptation. But for me, love's pull was more powerful. I knew that for every fantasy I had over the years with Lucy on my mind, it was nothing compared to the uplifting feeling I got when I thought about Victoria.

Before I knew it, the driver turned off onto Exit 11 and, a little over a mile down the road, brought us to a jolting stop. As I stood and reached above my head to pull my duffel bag from the luggage compartment, the driver yelled, "Milton/Mattapan!"

To me, that meant, 'Tremont Heights,' and it meant that I was home.

I strode down the aisle and took two steps to the pavement. *Home it was*, I thought, and as the bus pulled away behind me, I took a moment to absorb my surroundings.

A part of me felt as though I had never been away, but the rest knew better. Much had happened in the life of Billy Tucker in the meantime.

'Home' meant something different to me now. The color of the houses, the height of the fences and the faces in the neighborhood might have been the same, but I looked at them differently. I was back under contrived circumstances.

Good old Addison Parker, I thought as I looked at The Chocolate Cone and the man inside who had given it its name.

As proud as Addison was about his business, he was more proud of the relationship he had built with the kids in Tremont Heights. Growing up, he did everything he could to make us feel comfortable at his store. He wanted us all to have an adult to turn to for advice if there was ever a need. Addison understood that youngsters would only come to him for advice if we could trust him, and we would only trust him if he did not hold himself out as the conscience of the community. As far as Addison was concerned, absent an urgent circumstance, it was better to simply listen and nod and let the Tremont Heights kids grow and learn their lessons on their own.

Nathan and I had spent so many hours together hanging around The Chocolate Cone and passing the time with old Addison. Every now and then, we used to do odd jobs for him to make some money or earn a Coke and a bag of chips. Back then, we were probably closer to Addison than any adult.

I drew a deep breath as I reached for the door handle and pulled, knowing that my assignment had just begun.

* * *

"Billy Tucker!" Addison said with wide-eyed shock, his mouth extending into a welcoming smile.

"You'd better call the cops," I said smiling back. "There's a stranger loitering in your store."

Addison hadn't aged much physically. The lines around his eyes were a little more pronounced. His cheeks drooped a little further around his jaw. Perhaps he had lost a little more hair on top. But his weight looked about the same, and the gleam in his eye hadn't changed at all. He still stood upright and tall. He beamed with pride.

"Billy Tucker. My boy! My man!"

"In the flesh, Addison. You're looking younger than ever."

Addison rounded the counter to me, extended his arms and offered me a lengthy embrace.

"Shame on you for staying away so long," he said, pulling away but gripping my shoulders.

"Shame on me is right, Addison. I should have listened to you when I was fourteen," remembering the advice Addison had given me about learning a trade and having a skill so I would never need to rely on anyone else for work.

"Uh, uh," Addison said shaking his head to disagree. "Look at you. A college graduate. You look like a hard hitting, Wall Street business man."

I looked down at my tattered suit, considered his perspective, and bit my lower lip. "I'm nothing of the sort."

"Come on, Billy. Where did you end up? Who's the lucky company that got Billy Tucker to work for them?"

I shook my head sadly and offered only a surrendering smile.

"It's called unemployment, Addison. The state's paying my rent. I have yet to find work, and I'm home to regroup."

Addison threw his hand up at the ceiling. "Can't find work. You? I thought you did well there."

"It didn't matter."

I walked to the back entrance of the store and looked out at the familiar gravel parking lot. I thought of Lucy Polowski, how after only her fifth day of school in Tremont Heights, I had seen her clashing tongues back there with Kyle Taylor, a senior linebacker for the football team and one of the reasons she had earned her nickname. I continued staring out the door until I spoke again, breaking our short silence.

"It figures, Addison. After all of that studying, test-taking, paper writing and even a little grade grubbing, nobody would hire me. Maybe I'm just not the type to work for someone else."

I wondered whether the wire I wore was picking up the conversation. O'Donnell had wanted me to test it in a neutral situation.

"Addison. I'm in the mood for one of your specialties. Are you still serving up that water-lemon ice?" I asked, remembering how much I liked the cool mix of watermelon and lemon.

"You bet."

"I'll take a large."

"You'll take that large on the house."

Addison took a large paper cup from the pile next to the ice machine, pushed the lever down that sat above the label "Water-Lemon" and released the flavored ice until the cup was full. When I took it in my hand and sipped from the straw, my mouth filled with the flavor of my youth and an unforgettable feeling after a long afternoon in Tremont Heights Park. Although so much had changed in my life, such a simple pleasure of my childhood remained exactly the same.

"So good," I said. "I never understood it before, but it's all clear now."

Addison let out a guttural laugh. "A chocolate ice cream cone, my friend. I've been telling you that for years. That's what does it for me."

I nodded in understanding, but as I closed my eyes and sipped the memories, Addison's question jolted me back into role.

"So what now, son?" he asked.

Addison was the type that needed definition, needed a plan. I shrugged.

"You heading home?"

"I've got to see Jayme. It's been way too long. I haven't been much of a big brother over the last few years, but there's no way around it, other than to face it head on. She might not have me, but I've got to try."

"Do you need to make some money?" he added, indicating with his arm gestures that I could help him around the store.

I pressed my teeth together and shrugged. Thinking about the money I had in my pocket from the FBI, I deferred.

"I've got a little to last me a while. Let me get settled first. I appreciate your offer, and may need to revisit it, depending on how things go."

"Take your time, Billy. I'm not going anywhere."

As I slurped the last bit of liquid from my drink, I knew that the noise offered a good exit strategy.

"Thanks, Addison. Thanks for the drink and being here."

"Always have been."

"I know," I said walking out the door. "I'll catch up with you tomorrow."

I wasn't sure how the encounter had gone, and I wondered whether I looked uncomfortable. Everything that came out of my mouth had felt awkward. There was something different behind my every word—behind the delivery of my message. I wondered whether Addison bought the story. It was an insecurity like no other I had ever experienced before.

* * *

I walked down a car-lined street toward Tremont Heights Park and, for several moments, emptied my mind to enjoy the peaceful evening air. It was a beautiful September evening and the trees swayed gently with the light, end of the summer breeze. I still had a few hours before nightfall, and before Jayme might head out for the night, I figured. I wanted to see her, but as long as it was still daylight, I was in no rush.

When I came upon the entrance to Tremont Heights Park, I noticed that a new playground structure had been added for climbing, but otherwise, things looked about the same. A few young children chased each other around one of the old swing sets in the distance, and I sat down on a nearby bench to watch them. I couldn't help but notice the copper plate on the back of the bench.

It read: "In loving memory of Lucy Polowski, Tremont Heights High School, Class of 1996."

I remembered receiving the mass mailing from Stu Wilegard, our class president, and writing a check donating $25.00 for my part in the purchase of the bench and the plaque.

After a stressful four and one-half months in Quantico and a long day of traveling, I needed a break. I lay back on the bench, Lucy's bench, allowing the setting sun to heat my face and allowing my body to fill with the sensations of my childhood. The sights, sounds and smells in the air reminded me that I was home and made me wonder why I ever went away.

What would my life have been like if I had not? I soaked in a collection of disconnected images of possibilities for the next several minutes, and in so doing, realized that for the first time in as long as I could remember, I felt completely and totally at ease. I even found a bright side in my assignment: I was getting paid to pretend to do what I had needed to do for such a long time anyway. Part of my journey home and back into Nathan's life would include my reconciliation with Jayme, something that was long overdue. It would be good for both of us.

As I stared up at the sky, watching the time tick toward darkness in a bold mixture of orange and pink, my entire body fell limp, and I faded off to sleep.

Chapter Thirty-Eight

It wasn't until the temperature had dropped sufficiently to inspire a shiver that I awoke from the park bench, recognized impending nightfall and headed back to the old house. An unlocked screen door and the music up the stairs led me to Jayme's bedroom.

I stood at the door and, although in another moment, I might have felt regret, shame, or even anger, at that particular moment, I was just simply excited by the sight of a beautiful girl. Jayme Tucker was fully dressed in a tight army green tank top and form fitting khaki pants, a radio blaring rap music next to her as she admired herself in the mirror. It looked like tonight was a dancing night for Jayme, a night for shoulders, hips and for the silver twinkle of a pendant around her neck. With a brush of make-up and a burst of a smile, she stepped back from the dresser and, with her elbows close to her side, propelled herself into a 360-degree spin. She stopped midway though, when she saw who had come through her bedroom door.

I was a bit embarrassed by my intrusion, but managed a faint wave as I nodded hello. I spread my arms in an incredulous gesture, my eyes proudly examining how my little sister had transitioned over the year in my absence.

Jayme said nothing as I stared. She offered no response to my outstretched arms. Her eyes looked at me and while, at first, they radiated joy, they quickly took on a vacancy seeming to remember where we had last left off.

Guilt rushed through every vessel in my body. Jayme turned to shut off her radio and kept her back to me for several tortuous moments. Finally, I broke the ice.

"I was yelling, 'Hello', downstairs but nobody answered," I said, trying to justify my intrusion.

"Must have been the music," Jayme answered without looking at me. "What are you doing here?"

"You look beautiful. I can't believe how long it's been. I should have come home a long time ago."

"You did come home a long time ago."

I felt the bite of Jayme's comment and launched into an apology.

"I've been caught up, Jayme. It's been a tough year. I guess I wanted to just forget…and you…"

"Save it, Billy. Don't be laying any of that heavy stuff on me now. I've got plans tonight, and I'm going out. I'm on my way out now."

Lifting her jean jacket off the bed next to her, Jayme strode toward the door. She stopped in front of me.

"I assume you're going to step aside," she said.

I turned my body, stunned by the sharpness in her words, and allowed her to pass. "You're leaving? We haven't even had a chance to…"

"It's Friday night, Billy," she interrupted, as if it was the only explanation she needed.

Outside, a car engine roared. A horn beeped twice, and the driver revved the engine. A distant, hollow echo of a heavy bass beat broke the evening calm.

I followed Jayme down the stairs toward the front door. There were two boys in the car. I didn't recognize them, and neither one of them smiled. Neither one of them even looked at her as she bounded down the steps and the walkway toward them.

I barely recognize her, I thought.

When she reached the car, she turned back toward the front door. She seemed to know that I had been watching her the entire time.

"Oh, by the way," she started to yell back to me. "Your room is the way you left it. Sleep there if you want…or disappear. It's your choice. Just don't wait up for me. If you do, you'll be saying hello to the sun."

Jayme turned, slung her jacket over her shoulder and stepped into the car, her way of telling me that my visit would not ruin her night. I wondered where she was going and who she was going with. It occurred to me that I didn't even know who Jayme Tucker was anymore.

The boys in the car got a big, sexy smile and a kiss on the cheek before I saw her rear back in the back seat and scream, "Let's have some fun!"

What I didn't know is that silently, my sister wondered how she would ever be able to make it through the night.

Chapter Thirty-Nine

In the second semester of my junior year at Drexel, when Jayme was fifteen, Ruth was hospitalized with emphysema. Jayme called to let me know. She also called to tell me that she was alone in the house with Rick. She was scared, and she figured that I would come home to her rescue.

"I have mid-terms this month, Jayme. I can't come home."

"Can't you study here?" she asked, but she didn't understand what finals meant in a college setting.

"No, Jayme. I have a study group. We share notes and divide up the work. People are counting on me here. I need them too. If I fail, I'm going to have to repeat the classes. I'm already in debt up to my hair line and I need to make each of my classes count."

A still silence on the other end of the telephone line beckoned me to say more.

"Rick's just a creep, you know that. He's harmless. There's no reason to be scared."

But I knew better than to believe my own words. I didn't find out how badly I was mistaken until after Lucy's funeral. Jayme had written me a letter the prior summer, when again, I opted to stay on campus instead of going home. I just didn't want to be around Lucy and Nathan together again. I didn't know at the time it was really my last chance.

Jayme started the letter by telling me that it took her a while to decide whether to mail it or call me. *But, of course,* she wrote. *I tried to call you before. I told you how scared I was. And after our argument at Lucy's funeral, I made my decision.*

Jayme's letter then explained to me why she had to tell me the story she did. She realized that I would feel guilty, and the truth was, she hoped that I would. She was tired of feeling alone and feeling abandoned. She was tired of biting her upper lip the occasional times I called to check on her from school. She was tired of looking out for my feelings. *This time, and from now on,* she said, *I'll be thinking about my own needs only.*

Jayme told me that, in my absence from Tremont Heights, Rick had gone from bad to worse. He tried starting a landscaping business, but he was too cheap and lacking in foresight to invest in the right equipment to do the job professionally. His clients were sparse, particularly in Tremont Heights. Hardly anyone had a yard that was worth landscaping there anyway. Rick always thought that he would be able to tap the business in neighboring Milton, but his losing attitude and poor marketing skills got the better of him. The work he did have was rare and far between, and if ever the weather didn't cooperate with his need to make money, Rick tore into rages. Jayme once told me that his thundering voice could be heard blocks away.

In the meantime, Rick filled his time and assuaged his boredom at the tattoo shop on Route 28 in Mattapan. Jayme wrote that nearly all of his skin had gone green with violent artistry. *A snake, a skull, a red-eyed hawk and tangling vines were some of the highlights,* she said. Jayme described for me how he had become even more unpleasant to look at, his scraggly black hair and his hollow, perpetually unshaven face no longer his dirty trademarks.

Rick's appearance, though, was second only to his evolving violent attitude. During the winter months, when the grass didn't grow and there was no snow to plow, the energy in his rages often turned physical. *Those moments were horrifying,* Jayme wrote. He punched sofa cushions and threw pillows to start, but soon began to find greater release with hard, movable objects.

Rick generally took his frustrations out on his mother, and he actually flung a mustard bottle at her once in the kitchen, but devoted as any mother could be, Ruth put up with it all. He was her one and only, and she let him rule the house. As a result, in my absence, he ruled Jayme too.

Rick took it upon himself to try to mentor Jayme, to try to teach her all the hard lessons he had learned in life, he said. More likely, he was trying to garner her sympathy. But Jayme had no respect and thus, no sympathy, for Rick at all. He would demand her attention, demand her obedience and demand her loyalty, but Jayme would have none of it. She would stare at him blankly, turn away as he spoke and sometimes, if he had her cornered, just close her eyes and block her ears.

Once Ruth went into the hospital for good, Rick had no outlet and Jayme had no buffer. Rick began to channel his hostility directly toward her. Late one afternoon, Rick was yelling at Jayme about the way she folded his t-shirts when they came out of the dryer. She had her eyes tightly closed and her index fingers in her ears as he screamed. She tried to hum a tune in her head to block him out.

Within seconds, his hands were wrapped around her waist, and she opened her eyes to find him two inches from her face. *His breath smelled like human waste,* she wrote. He pulled her hands away from her ears and slapped her cheek hard. Her face stung and her head spun from the blow. She quivered with tears and reached out to stop him, but she was unable to prevent the consecutive blows to her body and head. Worse, she was unable to prevent him from reaching his tattoo stained, bony right hand over her pants in a half-witted effort to stroke her crotch.

Jayme wrote to me that she heaved and choked on her screams for help. She said that she tried to scream my name, forgetting that I was not there.

"Billy's not coming for you, you little bitch!!" Rick screamed between blows as he place his other calloused, dry hand over her mouth. "I own you now. I say what goes. You'll listen to me!!"

Over and over she called my name, she said, and with each cry, her calls became a whimper. She thought that it would never end. At some point, Jayme's thoughts removed her from the scene. She retreated into her own mind. She retreated from the life she had been given—that she had been left to lead by her brother. She wrote to me that she turned to the only person she thought might care. She went to Nathan Marks, the friend I had asked to look out for her in my absence.

Jayme said that she hadn't seen Nathan much since I left for college, but that he occasionally stopped by to say hello. When she first reached out to him for help, she wrote, he was shocked that she and I had lost touch. He said that, after what happened my freshman year when he and Lucy came to visit him, he could understand why he and I had talked less frequently. He could not understand, though, why I would ever let my relationship with my sister fade away.

When Nathan listened to Jayme recounting her situation with Rick, he slowly boiled, and he knew immediately what had to be done. In many ways, Nathan felt that Tremont Heights was his town, particularly when others, like me, left for college. Nathan couldn't stand for this behavior; he wanted to protect Jayme, he said, and he owed it to me.

"Billy asked me to look out for you," Nathan told her, and as I read these words in Jayme's letter, my eyes filled with tears. "If Billy can't be here for you," he said, "I will."

Jayme was alone in the house with Rick late one afternoon when she placed the telephone call. Nathan gave his beeper number—a product of his gambling habit—to very few people, but he made it available to her, and gave her a code to dial when she was ready. With Ruth still in the hospital, but due back any day, that is exactly what Jayme did. She dialed Nathan's pager and punched in the numbers that spelled her code: 'No more tears.'

Rick was watching a re-run on the television and throwing back Budweisers on the living room couch. Jayme stayed upstairs. She listened to the front door open. She listened to the bodies file in. She listened to the words from the living room, and recognized the voice of Nathan Marks say "hello."

"What the Christ?" she then heard from Rick's mouth.

And then she listened to the dull thuds and the cracking of bones. She smiled as she cringed. She even cried, she said, slow silent tears. She came downstairs when she heard the door close, when all she could hear were the quiet groans from the scrawny, bloody and broken runt of a man in the living room.

"You'll never touch me, you'll never speak to me, and you'll never look at me again. Got it?" she whispered into his ear before she dialed the ambulance.

When the police officers arrived to question Jayme about Rick's beating, she lied. She told them that she was with Nathan, and that she hadn't seen anything at all.

"Why wasn't she upset?" they asked.

"I hated him," she replied. "Have you ever hated anyone?"

Nathan was interrogated. They spent hours with him, but he sat in the chair in the interrogation room like a rock, he told her. "I sat there for you. I sat there for Billy. And I sat there for Tremont Heights," he told her with pride.

"Jayme was with me," was the only thing he said in the eight hours they questioned him.

My eyes welled up with tears immediately when I finished. Her letter concluded with a "Love, Jayme," but I didn't understand how she could feel that way for me at all. A 'p.s.' beneath her signature told me that she wrote to me instead of called because she knew I would need time to absorb everything she had to say.

It might seem dry and it might seem cold in the way I wrote this, she concluded, *but I thought you would want to know that Rick is gone and the house is now mine. Ruth passed away in her hospital bed. When I went to pay my last respects, I couldn't bring myself to tell her what had become of her son.*

I'm delaying getting rid of the house as long as I can, Billy. The DSS checks in on me every week and is trying to take control. I've asked for a little space, and since I'm almost seventeen, they're being a little more lenient than they would have been years ago. I don't know how long I'll hold out, but Nathan's 21 and claiming he's a half-brother. It's taking them a while to do the research.

* * *

I tried to call Jayme three times after reading the letter. I even tried to call Nathan. None of my calls were returned.

When Robert O'Donnell sat down with me in Quantico and told me my assignment, none of these memories, this further psychological wrinkle in my assignment, had escaped me. Left alone in my old house, though, all of the emotions I felt when I read Jayme's letter rushed back.

At least there would be no interference by the social services department now, I knew. Jayme's real brother was home. On top of that, Robert O'Donnell had told me he had something important to say to the Massachusetts DSS.

Chapter Forty

Left alone in my old home, I took some time to look around and reacquaint myself. Jayme kept the place well for a teenager. It wasn't particularly clean, but it was neat. The old furniture in the living room was still in its place and a stack of magazines were neatly piled on top of the oak coffee table. I noticed the old chip in the corner of the table Nathan and I had managed to make one day when we were moving the furniture around for a wrestling match. We tried to hide it with brown paint, but two nine year olds without an ounce of artistic talent between them had only made the situation worse.

And then there was my mother's wedding picture, a black and white of her standing alone, a glowing smile and a graceful veil thrown back over her head. That was the only picture my mother would keep up after my father died. She couldn't bare to keep up a picture of both of them and have to look at him next to her in a frame every day. *It was hard enough*, she had told me, *to picture him in my mind.*

I paused on the picture of my mother for some time. I hadn't seen that smile in so long, and water rushed to my eyes when I began thinking, again, about my last memory of her alive. I thought about letting my emotions go, but I knew at the moment that I couldn't. It was all too much at once.

As I walked up the steps and down the hall to my bedroom, I had a flash back to my early morning departure to college, and my goodbye to Jayme. That morning, I remembered trying to hold back the tears as I ascended the stairs and approached Jayme's door. Through the cracked opening, I could hear her quiet breathing as she slept deeply and peacefully. Easing the door open, I stepped into the warmth of her room and knelt beside her bed. At that point, my efforts were useless, and I was instantly overwhelmed by emotion.

Jayme awoke frightened at the sight of me and what this day meant for her. When my tears registered, Jayme also began to cry. We embraced. She cried a soft, sweet melody on my shoulders, and in each other's arms, we held tight our special love. It was one of those rare moments where we both understood that, for better or for worse, we had each other. No words had to be spoken.

I was horrified at how badly I had let that go. I wandered further down the hall into my old room. Very little had changed at all. My navy blue bedspread still covered the most comfortable place I had ever slept, the brass antique car lamp was in its usual place and my corkboard remained filled with favorite baseball cards and cutouts from the Sports page. There was Larry Bird raising his arms over his head as he tossed a towel in the air, a champion again and, at the time, the ultimate symbol in my mind of victory and hope.

Making my way over to my desk, I recognized my favorite snapshot. Nathan and I must have been about fourteen when it was taken because Jayme was between us wearing a paper birthday crown and proudly exhibiting nine fingers as she looked up at me for approval. With his right arm extending above Jayme and touching my far shoulder, Nathan wore a slight, devilish smile. His deep brown eyes and dark hair contrasted with my lighter features and wide smile, one of genuine pleasure in the moment.

I couldn't believe what I was doing home now. The FBI had sent me home to live a lie, giving me an assignment that tore at the essence of my past. I wondered again what the end of this assignment would bring, other than my emotional devastation. I worried about my future with the FBI, and with everybody who had passed through my life. Despite a total of eighteen weeks of training, I feared that I was ill-prepared for the task. Again, I feared that some small detail would blow my cover completely, and I would be exposed to those I cared for the most, well before I was ever ready, as the ultimate emblem of betrayal.

But I tried to re-focus. Even though I had a lot to catch up on with Jayme, what I really needed to think about was how to get close to Nathan again. The last time we talked was about two months after Lucy was killed. When all other conversation had failed, I asked him how he was doing without Lucy.

Billy, he interrupted. *I can't...I don't want to talk about Lucy anymore.*

I got defensive. *Oh I don't mean to bring up...I just thought that you might want to talk about her and...*

Billy, I'm a fucking suspect! he interrupted before slamming down the telephone.

When Nathan hung up, I sat in stunned silence in the several moments that passed. I stared at the receiver. At the time, I figured that it was unlikely I would be talking to Nathan Marks again anytime soon.

So now, I wondered what I would say to Nathan when we met again. I wondered how Nathan would receive me, and whether, with his new status with Ronnie Luca, Nathan would even meet me or talk to me at all. With all of the pressure from the police and the FBI, O'Donnell had told me that Nathan was very cautious about where and with whom he spent his time.

The more time that's gone by, the harder it has been for us to get close to him, O'Donnell said. *If and when you talk to him, you have to draw him out.*

For me, the question could not be an 'if.' It had to be a 'when.' O'Donnell reminded me that I needed to have the right kind of exposure, plant the right seeds with the right people and above all, heed his warning and be patient.

You'll lose every edge by rushing, Billy. You have to be indifferent. You have to occupy yourself in other ways.

One of these ways, I learned in undercover school, was to become an expert in the details of the crime. Inside a zippered pouch in the inner part of my duffel bag, I kept a file filled with copies of all of the police reports, notes of witness interviews, notes of interrogations of Nathan and Joey Luca and several of the more detailed and fully briefed press clippings.

The last two items were of particular importance to me. The notes from interrogations were important because I wanted to be sure that when I did eventually talk to Nathan, I did not approach the subject of Lucy's murder in ways that had been done before. I was sure that if I made that mistake, Nathan would be reminded of the sessions he had with law enforcement and instantly become suspicious. The press clippings were important because I knew that they had likely been Nathan's main source of information. If Nathan knew the details of these stories well, I wanted to make sure that I did too.

So alone in my old house, having made my emotional rounds, I decided that my first Friday night in Tremont Heights would not be spent on the town. Instead, I would use the opportunity to give my copy of the FBI's file one more intense review before securing it someplace safe. Former FBI Director Hoover might have had a couple of bad legacies, but he had a multitude of good ones. One of his best, I had learned, was recognizing that the FBI was about information. Knowledge was power. The more the FBI knew, the better it could function. With better information, the FBI could outsmart its opponent, more effectively prepare itself for battle and react more intelligently to adverse situations. Every trainee in Quantico learned that this was so.

Finding a can of Pepsi in the refrigerator, I sat down on the living room couch with my folder and began to re-read.

Chapter Forty-One

When I awoke the next morning, the house was completely silent. I had slept well and remembered reading the file until one o'clock in the morning before turning in for the night. I also remembered taking time before I went to sleep to hide certain critical belongings.

The file from the case needed to be put in a place where Jayme wouldn't find it, as did my credentials. The loose carpeting in my bedroom closet offered the perfect cover. My weapon was another story. O'Donnell had warned me against keeping it on or around me at all.

The security you get from carrying that weapon, Billy, is exactly the kind of thing that anyone who's street smart will sense in you. I'll be watching out for you, that's for sure, but you won't know I'm there. You just have to trust me. That gun, that sense of security, hinders the role you're playing. We need you to come across without the confidence and security that gun will give you. Otherwise, it'll be over for you, Billy. And if we don't get to your sister first, who knows? It could be over for her too.

I remembered my reaction to O'Donnell's words—the heavy sense that if I failed in my mission, I would also be putting Jayme in danger. Thinking about the facts of a crime story I learned about in Quantico, I hid my handgun inside the back panel of the living room television set.

I did not remember hearing Jayme come home before I went to bed, but I remembered her words.

You'll be saying hello to the sun, I mimicked.

I passed the stairs and looked down the hallway toward Jayme's door, which was closed, a sign to me that she did come home at some point. There were no noises coming from behind the door, though, so I went down to the kitchen and searched the refrigerator. I figured that greeting her with French toast was the best way to start repairing our relationship. Once the smell of egg-soaked bread cooking in the kitchen filled the air, I hoped that I might have a chance at forgiveness and, at the least, a reason to head back upstairs and awake her from her slumber.

Twenty minutes later, I did just that, carefully turning the knob of her door so as not to startle her. The stillness of the air inside her room and her quiet breathing were disarming, and I considered letting her awake naturally, but then I figured it could help to catch her in a relaxed and vulnerable state. It felt strange to whisper her name in the intimacy of the morning moment, but I also felt an excitement inside for the new beginning. Quietly, I actually thanked the FBI for forcing this chance.

"I'm making French toast," I said as Jayme's door hinges creaked and I got the rest of my body inside. "It's almost ready."

"French toast?" Jayme confirmed with a raspy drawl.

"Do you still like it?"

Jayme rolled over in bed and faced me, with a half-opened eye.

"Silly question," she said.

"Well get washed and come down then. It's no good when it's cold."

* * *

Few words were shared during the first several minutes of our breakfast together, but Jayme broke the ice with something neutral.

"Tastes good," she said.

"Not bad," I replied. "I figured the least I could do was to make you a meal."

I looked up from my plate and Jayme was looking right at me. When my eyes met hers, she looked down again and began eating. An awkward silence followed.

"Why are you home now?" she asked. "I assumed you graduated months ago, and I didn't see or hear from you then."

It pained me to think that in my first real conversation with my sister, I already had to lie.

"I'm sorry Jayme," I said, delaying a response to her question. "I'm just so sorry."

I watched Jayme's face flush red and tears come to her eyes. She tried to turn away and tilt her head up to prevent any teardrops, but as she blinked, she lost her battle. She dropped her fork and then quickly wiped her eyes.

"Sorry for what? I'm doing fine," Jayme managed to say as she sniffed and looked back at me.

I looked around the neatly kept kitchen and motioned with my arm.

"I can tell. You're doing real well, Jayme. I'm proud of you. What are you doing for money?"

"This and that," she said. "I work at the grocery store to pay the bills mostly. I used to hate it, but now, I get the hours I want; a lot of Sunday time. It's time and a half then. One twelve-hour Sunday shift will pay for the phone and the heat. The rest is food and drink, and that's just a matter of discipline."

I felt proud of my sister as she spoke. She was talking like our mother.

"So what about you?" she asked.

"What about me?"

"Come on," she said. "What are you doing home now?"

I shrugged.

Jayme rolled her eyes. "How long are you here for?"

"I don't know."

"Don't you have a job?"

It was inevitable and unavoidable. Jayme's entirely innocent question had forced my hand. Special Agent Billy Tucker took over the conversation.

"No. I don't have a job. Nobody would hire me, Jayme."

I stared into her eyes for emphasis and understanding, and she stared back. If I were paranoid, I would have guessed that she already knew I was lying.

"You? I thought you did all right with grades. What happened to my brother the banker?"

I remembered what I had told her early on about the allure of Wall Street. "All rejections," I said. "Rejections across the board. I blew some interviews. A couple went really well, but overall, I didn't even get my foot in the door at enough places to put the odds in my favor. All rejections, Jayme."

She seemed to sense the pain I portrayed, and I was gaining confidence.

"Nothing doing. Nobody wanted me."

"I'm sorry, Billy," she said, but her regret was not yet fully formed. "Why?" she continued.

"I don't know," I answered in feigned, suppressed anger. "I'm sorry too. You know, Mom always used to say that you can't forget where you come from because if you do, everybody else out there will remind you of it."

Jayme looked puzzled. I don't know why I mentioned our mother, but I guess part of it was to remind her of our blood bond, and that we were the only two people in the world who shared it.

"You think not getting a job had to do with Tremont Heights?" Jayme said incredulously. "What's wrong with Tremont Heights?"

I looked down at my plate. It was clean except for the lines of drying syrup across the bottom.

"Nothing Jayme. That's why I'm back. I've got to figure some things out for myself first. You know, kind of regroup."

Jayme smiled reassuringly, and I returned the expression. I was beginning to feel connected again.

"What about you?" I asked, seeking to change the subject.

"What?"

"Are you happy with your life here?"

"Since Rick left?" she asked, reminding me how unhappy she was only a year ago.

"Of course," I jumped in. "Of course. That bastard. That fucking bastard."

I reached across the table to stroke her arm, half expecting her to pull away. Instead, Jayme nodded.

"I'm happy now," she said. "I'm doing pretty well in school, and I was thinking about applying to college too."

I nodded excitedly. "You should. You absolutely should, Jayme. College is great. It would be great for you. I'll help you fill out the applications and…"

"I don't really want to leave Tremont Heights anymore, though, Billy."

Her words reminded me of those of Lucy when I left for college. *What a mistake*, I thought. *If Lucy had only removed herself from the confines of Tremont Heights*, I considered. But then I considered why Lucy had wanted to stay.

"Any guy in your life?" I asked, afraid of the answer.

"I've got a boyfriend," she responded proudly, as if saying the words quickly would make whatever she wanted to say easier.

"Is that right?" I said sitting back in my chair and letting out a short, pleased laugh.

"That's right," Jayme repeated.

"Is he from Tremont Heights?"

"Yep," Jayme said, apparently now enjoying dancing around the final answer.

"Do I know him?"

"I think so."

"Who?" I asked, my heart now fluttering with horror.

Jayme paused and shook her head sideways, so I asked again.

"Who, Jayme?"

"You're not going to believe this one."

"Who?" I asked, suddenly knowing what the answer would be.

"Nathan. I've been dating Nathan," she said.

When I heard her words, I wondered if I would ever be able to swallow again. The knot in my throat was sudden and paralyzing. My mouth actually stuttered as I tried to stay with the conversation. Jayme looked at me with the old 'you're weird' expression.

"Nathan Marks? My Nathan Marks?" I repeated, searching my mind in vain for a way this might not be happening to me, to all of us.

"None other," Jayme said smiling, nodding and offering some light laughter. "*My* Nathan Marks."

She stared at me, seemingly trying to figure out the expression on my face.

"Don't look so freaked, Billy. He's terrific. You know it. And you know what else?" she asked, her eyes turning slightly sadistic.

I shook my head to say 'no' but she continued anyway. "I'm in love," she added defiantly.

Sitting there before my little sister, the lump in my throat became the least of my worries. Her words reminded me of the emotions I held for Victoria, how they knew no boundaries, no restraints. My entire body advanced to the point of numbness, and my head began to spin. I couldn't hear a thing, other than a quiet ringing in my ears. Although I was staring back at Jayme, I felt as if I were floating outside of my body and looking down from a pinned position on the ceiling at both of us. The whole scene became quietly surreal, and I wanted to disappear. I hoped that the sensation I was feeling was death. I hoped for a stroke, or a quick heart attack, anything to pull me out of this nightmare.

Confused, foremost now by how in the world this new revelation affected my assignment, I wondered whether O'Donnell knew what Jayme just told me. As she stared at me, expecting some response, I violently scanned my memory for any hint of this in O'Donnell's undercover instructions. I wondered whether my assignment had just become harder or easier. At the least, I knew one thing for sure. If O'Donnell knew this about Jayme and Nathan and had hidden it from me, I was going to demand to be taken off the case.

Getting somewhat of a grip on myself, I responded weakly, but tried to hang on to my undercover role as best I could until I could sort everything out.

"That's unbelievable, Jayme. That's just unbelievable. I can't wait to see him and talk to him again. You ought to invite him over."

Jayme looked at me dubiously.

"Listen," I continued, knowing that I needed to escape. "I'm going to head outside to take a little walk. The French toast is sitting right here," I said, pointing to the top of my stomach area, and wondering how many minutes would have to pass before I was standing eye-to-eye with Robert O'Donnell.

Chapter Forty-Two

It was 11:00 a.m. when I left the breakfast table with Jayme and began a jog to the bus stop. I figured that O'Donnell had already landed in Boston, and the second I knew I was out of Jayme's view, I paged him.

Emrgcy. Meet at f.o. ASAP, I typed.

Then, looking up from my pager, I opened up into a full-out sprint down the street when I saw the bus pulling up. My legs couldn't move fast enough, neither could the bus on its way to Center Plaza, nor could any of the people that boarded and departed at each stop.

When I reached Government Center and saw the building that housed the FBI's local field office, I wondered whether any rookie agents had ever punched out a manager. I wondered if anyone had ever punched out Robert O'Donnell and what would happen to me if I did. *Maybe the disciplinary committee would bring me up on charges,* I thought. *But my defense would be temporary insanity. They would have to understand. They would have to side with me. Maybe O'Donnell would just take it like a man.*

But then, I paused. I knew that nothing I could complain about on any personal level overrode my duty of loyalty to the Bureau. To the FBI, I was merely on the job—the best man for the job on the job. It occurred to me that nobody would side with me. Sure, some would pity me for being in such a situation and others would talk about me for years, but nobody would side with me.

But maybe, just maybe, I hoped, *there was a small possibility that the man who had been spying on Tremont Heights and Nathan Marks for the last year might not have any idea who Nathan was dating.*

It was a remote hope, but one that flickered nonetheless. This was my way out of the assignment. This was just one conflict too many, I knew, particularly with the FBI's emphasis on ethics I learned in Quantico.

I drew a deep breath when the elevator doors opened, and I tried to remind myself to remain calm, but it was no use. The sight of O'Donnell sent my blood pressure and adrenaline skyrocketing.

"We've hit a glitch, sir. It's a big one—a big psychological glitch," I blurted, exasperated. "A big motherfu.... " I started to say clenching my fists at my side.

"Step inside, Billy. And watch your mouth!"

I followed the Assistant Special Agent in Charge inside and attempted to speak again, but O'Donnell interrupted.

"Jayme, right?" he said calmly, squinting slightly as if to acknowledge the sensitivity of the situation.

"You know?" I asked incredulously.

"I know," he confirmed, and then I lost it.

"This was underhanded, sir. Totally underhanded! It's not fair and I won't be a part of it. I'm out! Project over. Done. Find yourself a different man."

O'Donnell squinted again, gingerly this time, as if I had tread into an area he did not want me to be. He removed a mini cassette tape from his jacket and motioned with his head for me to follow him. My blood boiled in a mixture of anger and anxiety. It was as if he was ready for this encounter when he had left New York. In fact, O'Donnell had been prepared ever since Special Agent Reginald Williams captured Jayme Tucker on tape talking to Nathan and telling him exactly how she lied to the Boston police about her whereabouts when Lucy was killed.

Reggie Williams was a couple of years my senior and had given it a go for the FBI as an undercover agent in Tremont Heights in the months after Lucy was shot. Accordingly to O'Donnell, even though Reggie didn't know about me, he had begun to take a back seat while I was in training—when O'Donnell planned on getting me involved.

We went into the audio-visual room and O'Donnell slapped in the cassette, and I recognized my sister's voice immediately.

"So?" I asked. "So she said she wasn't there and didn't learn about the shooting until the rest of the town knew too. What's the deal?"

"We know she was there, Billy."

"Jayme?"

"Jayme," O'Donnell confirmed.

"She was at the scene of the crime?"

He nodded.

"How do you know that?" I stammered, suddenly finding it worthwhile to challenge everything this man claimed he knew.

O'Donnell picked a piece of lint off of his blue button-down and offered a smug expression. "I've been doing this job nine years, Billy. I know things."

"I've been doing this job two weeks, sir, and I won't accept anything I can't prove. How do you know?"

O'Donnell sat forward and glared. "There's a hierarchy on this case, kid. I know it. I'm telling you I know it. You just accept it and get back to work."

My hands dug into my chair with frustration.

He continued. "Your little sister lied to police investigators, Billy. I'll get her on aiding and abetting if I have to. Hell, maybe she'll lie again to a grand jury. I'll get her on perjury too."

The thought of operating in a state of trust with Robert O'Donnell was loathsome to me at this point. The thought of Jayme going to jail was worse.

"That would be a big case for you," I said sarcastically, but instantly knew that I had crossed a line.

O'Donnell jerked up out of his chair and pointed his finger at me. "Now you're questioning my judgment!" he said.

In the split second before he spoke again, I tried to recover, disarm him with my fear. "I want out. I can't do this, sir. I want out."

O'Donnell lowered his hand and turned toward the window. He was silent for a while. I felt like a child. When he finally spoke, he looked me directly in the eye.

"Can't do it, Billy. You're our man. We're going to get to Ronnie Luca. You're going to get Nathan to roll. And if you bail?" he continued rhetorically. "Well, I would hate to see Jayme caught up in the take down."

I considered the irony of Nathan walking away from murder but Jayme going to jail for obstructing justice. "That's fair," I added sarcastically.

O'Donnell glared. I returned the gesture. We each held firm for several seconds. Then, O'Donnell's face softened, and he spoke again.

"You mean to tell me you want your little sister dating Nathan Marks?" he asked, and when he saw my eyes train downward, he knew he had hit me where it counted.

I opened my mouth to respond, but found nothing to say. O'Donnell, sensing his successful effort at damage control, escorted me to the elevator. We both stayed silent as he pushed the call button, and we awaited my escape.

"You do your job, Billy," were his parting words as the metal doors opened before us. "And you'll see, everything will work out fair for everyone."

Everyone but Nathan and Jayme, I thought, as the doors closed between us. On the ride down, I remembered Victoria, my rock, and my only hope for sanity.

* * *

I rode back to Tremont Heights confused. *My sister at the crime scene? I couldn't believe that neither Nathan nor Jayme had mentioned it. What had gone on? What had I not been privy to? And why couldn't I know?*

O'Donnell felt that I was not supposed to know. He warned me that I was supposed to discover that information myself.

"You act surprised, Billy," he warned. "You did not hear it here first. That's going to be your challenge now. You have to be able to play this one off but good."

Remembering O'Donnell's words as I rode back to Tremont Heights, but not understanding why this had been kept from me, I began to feel a desperate, survival-like need deep in my gut to get off the bus immediately.

"Driver!" I called.

Startled, the bus driver looked up into his rear view mirror. All the passengers in front of me looked back my way. I was already standing up out of my seat.

"Stop the bus. I'm going to be sick!"

All heads turned away. The people closest to me propelled their bodies as far away from mine as possible, some of them letting out long low groans. The bus driver examined the traffic to his right. Seeing that it was clear, he began to pull over into the right lane when the sound of the horn caused him to jerk back. I lurched sideways into the seat on my left and almost lost it right there. The driver of the car in the right lane flipped his middle finger at the bus as he flew past.

When the bus finally stopped, I barely had enough time to get off. Right there, over the guardrail, all in the form of partially digested French toast, I wretched up four years of college, weeks of grueling training in Quantico, the fading hope of repairing my relationship with my only blood relative, and the knowledge that I needed to betray the most loyal friend I had ever encountered in my life, all over the side of the road.

"I'm staying here. Don't wait for me," I managed to say to the driver between heaves.

The bus driver merely nodded, shut the doors and pulled away. As I stepped over the guardrail, I wondered whether I should bother clearing myself out of the way of the speeding, gawking traffic at all. If I stayed on the wrong side of the rail, I figured that I might get lucky; one of the speeding cars before me might veer out of control and save me from the prospect of having to face the rest of my life.

Chapter Forty-Three

The walk home would be a long one, I knew, as I shivered in the raw atmosphere of a sunless autumn day. An early chill had descended upon greater Boston, always the sign of impending winter, shorter days and lower moods.

I estimated that, based on where I had exited the bus, I had about another six or seven miles to go to get back home. I hadn't run in a few days, but after a few minutes of a light warm-up, I hit my stride. The exercise actually felt good and helped calm my troubled mind and soothe the anger that lingered within me. I thought about my conversation with O'Donnell, how he wanted so badly for Nathan to be an informant. I thought about the ideals of the FBI that I had learned and come to admire in Quantico. I wondered if O'Donnell had gone astray.

What if Nathan had committed murder? Could the FBI look the other way? I knew that some things did outweigh others, and only O'Donnell knew just how deeply Ronnie Luca's organization penetrated the Boston underworld. Only O'Donnell knew how many people he had threatened and intimidated. Only O'Donnell knew just how many men like Roy Hanson were living scared under the Luca influence.

But I also knew that only petty crimes were the kind of 'authorized' crimes informants were supposed to be allowed to commit. *But who drew the line?* Agents were trained to use discretion. *Who was to say where the line blurrred? Where would justice lie for Lucy Polowski or her father if the truth behind her shooting was buried somewhere deep in a confidential FBI file?*

Despite all of the training I had in Quantico, I saw no easy answers to these questions. I needed a quiet night with Victoria, I decided. I needed to be lying in her arms in the dark, music playing in the background and soft, calm conversation about responsibility and the ideals of the Bureau guiding us. As I approached Tremont Heights through Mattapan, I searched for a pay phone and dialed. There was no answer, though, only her voicemail.

I hung up the telephone and dropped my hands to my toes to stretch my hamstrings. All I could think about was having the opportunity to get myself out of this. If Victoria Summers saw it the same way I did, her approval would be all I needed. If she would stick by me, I was sure I would drop the FBI in a heartbeat.

I began to run again and didn't stop until I recognized the sign for The Chocolate Cone. I had made it home. *A little over an eight-minute mile*, I figured, looking at my watch and considering the stop I made.

I made my way down the road to Addison's store and reluctantly stepped into role again.

"Billy Tucker," Addison said as he eyed me up and down. "You've been working out?" he questioned.

"Just a light run. I've been keeping in shape for a while now."

"Good for you. I'm in shape too. Feel that," Addison said pointing at his stomach.

I reached over the counter toward Addison's abdomen.

"What are you packing in there?" I said with a tired smile.

"Six cold ones, young man. Two hundred sit-ups a day. I'm as solid as a rock. How far did you run?"

"I don't know. About seven. Do you have any water?"

Addison reached for one of the soda cups on the counter, released some ice from the machine and stuck the cup under the cold tap water from the faucet. "Enjoy."

I gulped eagerly.

"Thanks Addison," I said, finishing and taking in a mouthful of ice. "How's Betsy?" I asked.

"Betsy's doing well; a lot better now, I guess. She was really upset about the whole Polowski thing. She felt terrible that our store was a part of it."

I knew that Addison was referring to the break-in of The Chocolate Cone the night Lucy was shot.

"Married life has always been good to me, Billy. I already told Betsy you were back. She'd love to see you."

"Likewise," I added.

"So how did it go with your sister?"

"Jayme?" I said delaying, afraid of what might come out of my mouth, but Addison only nodded waiting for me to speak.

"We talked this morning. We have a lot of catching up to do. You know what, though? She's doing great. She may have had to fend for herself, but she's doing great."

I paused, not knowing if I should raise the issue, but I tried to picture what I would say if I weren't undercover.

"Do you know what she told me this morning?" I asked, shaking my head back and forth as I looked down at the counter feigning laughter. "She told me that she and Nathan are an item, a serious one too."

"I knew that," he said.

"No kidding," I responded, seeking to control the tide within me. "I guess I'm the last then."

Addison shrugged. "She always held a candle for him, Billy. I used to watch her look at him when you two ran around together in high school."

Addison must have noticed the expression on my face change.

"Nathan's a good boy, Billy. He's always been a good boy."

"Always *was*," I challenged. "What's this I hear about his new wiseguy status?"

Addison looked away. No response.

"What's Denny Polowski doing these days?" I challenged again, trying to bring Addison back to reality.

He responded to that. "Denny's been moping. The poor guy's a wreck. He can barely lift his head when he walks."

"Have he and Nathan ever talked?"

"Denny won't talk to anybody, Billy, especially Nathan."

"I have to tell you, Addison. It worries me if Jayme is running around with a murderer."

Addison shrugged. "Was Nathan ever arrested?" he asked, the tone of his voice now challenging me.

"Not that I know of."

"Well I can tell you that he wasn't." Addison paused, then continued softly. "And maybe there was a reason."

"Sure there was a reason," I piped in. "It was all over the papers. No one to place him at the scene." I let what was unsaid linger because I wanted the opportunity to read Addison's eyes. If the FBI knew Jayme was there, I wondered if Addison did too.

"Yeah, and what else?" Addison asked.

"No murder weapon," I answered staring straight into Addison's eyes.

"That's right son," and as we finished, a couple came strolling through the door laughing. They didn't look like they were from Tremont Heights.

I knew that our conversation was over.

"I think I need a tall one, Addison," considering that after the morning I had, a beer would be soothing—a large one. "What are you getting for the forty ouncers?"

Addison motioned for me to take it and leave and, because the unemployed college graduate would have done so, I did so too.

Chapter Forty-Four

My clothes hung on me a bit, sweat stretched from the run, as I wandered off toward Tremont Heights Park. I took a long gulp from the bottle, eager for the light headed, easy feeling that the alcohol would bring. My stomach was empty from my earlier gymnastics by the guardrail. The buzz hit me quickly, and I decided to give Victoria another try. At the gate to Tremont Heights Park, I went straight for the pay phone. This time, she answered on the first ring.

"Victoria Summers," I heard, and I was instantly relieved.

"Victoria," I said. "It's Billy. I'm calling you from a pay phone."

"Hey there!" she answered enthusiastically. "Where are you? No wait, don't tell me. How are you doing?"

"Been better," I answered. "I've definitely been a lot better. What about you?"

"Oh, you know, still the boring stuff. Nothing exciting and *undercover* like you."

"Trade you," I offered.

"Come on," she said. "It can't be that bad."

"Oh it's bad," I jumped in. "It's bad and getting worse. I really need to talk, *privately*," I emphasized.

"Billy?" she pleaded, even though I knew she could sense something more desperate in my voice.

"I need you to make an exception," I said.

"No exceptions, Billy. It's against the code and you know..."

"Victoria. Drop it, will you? As far as I can tell, I'm way beyond the code as it is."

"What the hell have they got you doing?"

"I..." but I couldn't respond before she interrupted me.

"Stop! Don't tell me. I'm not ready yet. I need to think about this. You have to let me think about this. I'm going to have to call you back."

I was silent. I waited for her to guide me.

"I'm getting another call, Billy. I'm going to have to call you back."

She hung up the telephone quickly as she finished her words. I don't know how she possibly expected to be able to call me back. I did carry an FBI paging device in my pocket, even though O'Donnell had encouraged me not to, but I hadn't given anyone the number, anyone but O'Donnell that is.

* * *

Like me, Special Agent Reginald Williams reported directly to Robert O'Donnell. Periodically, he made reports about his progress, what little there was, but by now, he was just eager to get out of Tremont Heights. After so many months, his investigation had hit a wall, and he hadn't been home to Northern New Jersey more than a handful of times to see his wife and kids. O'Donnell had promised him that he would get the recall any day now, when the transition was smooth. O'Donnell never shared with him what that transition was, though, or who it was. He felt that sharing that kind of information could be dangerous for both of us.

Reggie Williams was a thorough agent, though, one who did not contemplate leaving much to chance, especially when it concerned whether he would be able to see his kids again. After several months on the job, Reggie felt he knew most everything about the streets and people in Tremont Heights, knew their habits and their vices, and he liked it that way. With control like that, Reggie would never have to deal with surprises.

At about 1:30 in the afternoon, Special Agent Williams received a dispatch from Saul Spaco of the Boston Police Department, responsible for patrolling Mattapan and Tremont Heights. Spaco's report detailed a description of an unknown male, early to mid-twenties, heading to the park. The male was reported to be disheveled in appearance and drinking from a brown paper bag. From the swagger in his walk, Spaco thought that the bag covered alcohol.

"Unknown?" Williams said, seeking confirmation.

Unlike me, the police department had been informed about Williams' presence in Tremont Heights. O'Donnell had thought this may give Williams certain advantages. The months that had passed had proven him wrong.

"Confirmed," Spaco said.

"Pick him up."

* * *

The liquid courage I consumed was soothing.

To hell with everyone, I thought. *I'm a federal agent. The United States of America needed me, wanted me, recruited me. I excelled in training camp and was given the toughest assignment out of any of my classmates. I'll get to Nathan. I'll flip him. I'll rescue Jayme, and I'll bury Joey and Ronnie Luca forever. I'll be golden in the Bureau.*

My thoughts were interrupted by the sound of the bullhorn behind me.

"Stop on the sidewalk," the voice said.

I hadn't noticed the police car creeping up behind me. Once the officers had my attention, the driver turned on the red and blue flashing lights and let out a chirp from the siren.

I felt instantly sobered and couldn't believe that I wasn't carrying my credentials. But then I remembered that I couldn't even show them to these guys. I remembered O'Donnell's words.

No leaks. Not to anybody. Nobody. You never know who's on the take in these places.

"Bend down and slowly place the bag on the ground next to you," the voice bellowed.

I knew better than to not obey.

"Now raise your arms over your head and, with your leg, kick the bag away from your body."

I did exactly as I was told, allowing the officers to take control.

"Now turn around with your hands still over your head with your back facing us."

I recognized the maneuver. They didn't know if I was carrying a weapon. They turned me around like this to give themselves that extra split second they might need if I tried to pull a weapon. I heard the car doors open and shut and heard a more human sounding voice as one of the officers spoke without the bullhorn.

"What's your destination?"

"Just out for a walk."

"Looking for some dope?"

I wanted to keep quiet, but the stupidity of the question and the abusive tone in the officer's voice infuriated me.

"Man, what kind of a question is that?"

I felt the hands of one of the two police officers on me. I started to ask what was happening, but when my hands were pulled down from above my head and placed behind my back and locked together in handcuffs, I knew that I was better off not saying a word.

"Look at what we have here," one of the officers said with a sneer.

In the officer's hand, I saw a clear glassine bag containing a couple of vials of something that looked like it was supposed to be illegal.

What I wanted to say was: "That's a plant and you're going to jail," but I knew this was not possible.

In any case, my bladder was starting to throb from the water and beer I had consumed. *Great*, I thought. *These thugs better give me a chance to take a leak.*

I knew that at the station house, assuming the locals played by usual rules, I would have one telephone call. It would be to Robert O'Donnell to get me out of whatever stupid mess was happening. *That son of a bitch*, I thought and realized that it had been about the fourth time in one day I had thought those words.

"I have nothing to say until I have a lawyer present," I said from the back seat, now not sure what these locals were capable of.

The two cops in front looked at one another.

"Did you hear something, Danny?"

"I don't think so, Vin."

I knew that I was in for a hard time, but I also knew that I had to relieve my bladder. Arriving at the station house, I decided that a better tactic might be to ensure satisfaction of my biological needs while my legal needs waited.

"You know, I've got to use the bathroom real bad," I said.

After parking the squad car in an empty area in front of the station, the two cops in the front seat each exited their doors. The one named Vin opened my door and guided me out. He looked me squarely in the eye.

"Hold it."

"That's the problem," I said shaking my head and looking at the pock-marked face of Officer Vincent Solaro. "I really can't. That was beer in that bag I was carrying. But I guess that's fine if you want your interrogation room to smell like urine for two hours when I'm giving you all of the information I have. You could get some awards for the stuff I know."

Officer Solaro squinted at me. He held his stare for a few seconds before abruptly turning me toward the front door of the building and pushing me to walk.

"You'll get your bathroom break. But I'll be right behind you ready to put a fist in your skull if you pull any funny stuff."

Wonderful, I thought. *This guy's supposed to be on my team.*

Nevertheless, I was pleased that I had won the necessary concession, and I was brought immediately to the men's room where I was allowed to relieve the cause of most of my immediate anxiety. I knew that I would feel even better once I was able to call O'Donnell.

After the bathroom, I was brought to a small room with a table and a few chairs. I was placed on one side of the table with the solo chair, and the handcuffs were removed from my wrists. I smiled at the police officer who did so.

"Thanks," I said and he nodded, and oddly, for a brief moment, I considered him my friend.

My interrogation lasted nearly two hours. It was filled with questions about my background, where I had been and what I was doing. Every time they brought up the drugs, I offered a disgusted laugh and shook my head. When they got tired of asking me about me, they turned to what I could offer them.

"What about all of that stuff you promised us, Tucker."

"I lied. I had to take a leak. So if you're not going to arrest me, I'm leaving.

"Don't forget the vial, wise ass."

"Then don't forget my phone call," I retorted.

Without even agreeing to offer me even that small courtesy, they left me alone in the room, surrounded only by the sound of the buzzing lamp overhead, and my own disjointed and anxious thoughts. I was exhausted but startled to hear the abrupt opening of the door. Robert O'Donnell strode into the room.

"Special Agent Tucker," O'Donnell said with a coy smile taking one of the chairs across from me. "Twice in one day for us. Isn't this a treat?"

"O'Donnell," I said, recognizing the dueling tensions within me by the mere mention of his name. "How did you know I was…"

"Got yourself into a little jam, I see," he interrupted, ignoring the question.

I shrugged and exhaled in disgust. "Jayme and Nathan. I can't believe you knew," I said shaking my head. "I can't believe you're pulling this on me."

"I thought we were through this."

"I just can't believe it, that all. That's the heart of the matter. It's not some peripheral issue. I should have been informed."

"Oh yeah?" O'Donnell responded. "And how would you have hidden that natural surprise that suited you so well this morning? How would you have maintained the innocence of your breakfast with your sister with this information in your back pocket, Billy? Would you have awakened her in the morning with French toast simmering in a pan downstairs? What would you have done? Would you have been Jayme's big brother or an FBI agent? It's a pretty tough variable, Billy. I made an educated guess. And you know what, the way this whole day has gone, I'd have to say I was right—even if I have to say so myself."

"Fully informed, sir, I'm fully armed. What else haven't you told me? What other surprises are in store? How much more are you going to tear me apart? How many other times am I going to end up being pushed around by some local morons with badges?"

"Let me tell you something, Tucker," O'Donnell responded. "I'm running this project. As much as you think you might like to be in control, you're not. Part of the reason you were chosen for this assignment is that the local morons with badges would treat you the way they just did. You might not realize it, Tucker, but your project just hit the fast track. That was the best thing that could have happened to you. Guess who we just trailed and who observed you being placed under arrest?"

I stayed silent.

"Nathan."

I felt a chill rise up the back of my neck, considering that Nathan had been watching me.

* * *

Nathan Marks called Jayme in the late morning hours that day. He was upset that she had decided not to spend the night with him. Lucy Polowski's double life had left its mark on his confidence. He was happy to hear from Jayme that everything was all right, but there was something different in her voice. He didn't know what to say when he heard that I was back in town, so he said very little.

"He wants to see you," Jayme told him. "He knows we've been dating."

"Is he there now?" Nathan asked.

"No. I think he went out for a run or a walk or something. He wanted to see the neighborhood again. He's been gone a while."

"And he got there last night?"

"Yes, but…"

"I can't believe you didn't tell me."

"I didn't want to ruin…"

"It's okay," Nathan assured her, "I understand, but listen, baby. Don't tell him you talked to me yet. Can you do that?"

"Why?"

"Can you just do that?"

Jayme paused, and Nathan drew a sigh of relief when she said "yes."

Since his last night with Lucy, Nathan came to believe that suspicion and doubt were the key ingredients to survival. He reminded Jayme that he felt this way, even if he was dealing with me. Hearing that I was out and about Tremont Heights again though, Nathan couldn't resist. He found a secluded spot in Tremont Heights Park and waited, knowing that there were few other places to go in our neighborhood, and that I would eventually return to the scene of our early days. There, Nathan watched me wander into the hands of the police, a situation that, over the last year, he knew all too well.

* * *

"That's right, Tucker," the ASAC said. "Your home phone is tapped, and we put a trailer on Nathan after that call. So trust me, will you? This day may have been hell for you so far, but I couldn't have scripted it better. You're doing an even better job on this than I could have imagined. The FBI's proud of you, son. Stay strong."

"Get me out of here," I said.

Robert O'Donnell paused and looked down, and I knew instantly what that meant.

"No!"

"It's a necessity, Billy."

"Sir! What am I…"

Robert O'Donnell held his finger to his mouth and looked desperately toward the door.

"Shut your mouth, Tucker. Shut it now. You're going to make it worse for yourself. Do you have any priors in this town?"

"Priors?"

"Prior crimes."

"You know damn well I…"

"Relax then," he interrupted calmly. "Get a good night sleep. They've got twenty-four hours to arraign you. When they do, just make sure you plead guilty."

"Guilty! Are you crazy? I'm not going to go to jail for…"

The Assistant Special Agent in Charge shot me a hideous look.

"You do as I say, Tucker. Plead guilty. That's an order. The only other order that I have for you is to call your sister. She should know you're in jail. Both of those orders are called doing your job. Got it!"

I was fuming, although I half understood.

Robert O'Donnell whipped open the door to leave, but just as it was about to close behind him, he peaked his head back into the room and, to my surprise, smiled.

"Tucker," he said. "It gets better, and it's only beginning to get fun."

With that, the door closed, and I was alone. In twenty-four hours, my life had turned completely upside down. As I looked around the walls of the interrogation room thinking forward to my night in a holding cell, I wondered if 'better' would ever really be an option.

Just then, my pager, which had been sitting on the table during O'Donnell's visit, began to buzz. It was a 212 number.

Victoria! I knew. *It had to be her. I had to get to a phone.*

Chapter Forty-Five

By the time I left the interrogation room, I actually looked forward to the solitude and limitations of a night in a prison cell. At the very least, it would be an interesting professional experience. On my way down, I again requested my telephone call.

"Can I let my sister know I won't be home?" thinking of O'Donnell's orders but secretly wanting to reach out to Victoria.

"You already got your call," my escort said.

"Not yet, actually. If I did, you would have already met my lawyer. Ask around, I've had no lawyer in to see me."

The officer turned his head in an aloof manner, letting me know he did not need to talk to me at all. I needed to amplify my case.

"But I don't need a lawyer," I added. "I'm pleading guilty tomorrow anyway. I'm not going to pay some lawyer to help me do that."

I knew the officer would like this. I had learned in Quantico that it was inevitable for law enforcement officers to have a natural distaste for defense attorneys. After all, a defense attorney was actually a police officer's conscience. He brought me over to the telephone.

I had memorized the number that came through on the pager before it was taken from me. I repeated it over and over in my mind. The problem was, the officer was right at my back, right on my side when I wanted to dial.

"Can I have a little privacy?" I asked.

"No," he responded sharply. "You can't. I can also forget about your call."

My faced flushed with frustration, and in a difficult moment of choice, I followed orders and dialed my home number. I prayed that Jayme would not be home, though, and that I could place a second call to Victoria. The last thing I wanted was to have to explain anything about my morning to Jayme. No such luck for me on this day, though.

"Billy?" she said when she heard my hello.

"Yes, it's me."

"Where are you?"

"Don't worry. I'm over at the police station. They're taking me down to a courthouse holding cell for a night. Don't worry though Jayme. It's nothing."

"You got arrested?"

"Yes."

"For what?"

I wanted to tell Jayme I was in for public drinking. I hated to tell her it was for drugs, particularly knowing the charge had no substance. But I stuck with O'Donnell's advice.

"Well," I paused. "Possession of narcotics."

"Billy!"

"It's bullshit Jayme!"

"Billy!"

"Listen. I just wanted to tell you where I am. I'll take care of this myself and try to check in on you tomorrow night."

"Billy, you do drugs?"

The officer looked at me impatiently. "I've got to go," I told Jayme. "I'll have to talk to you later."

"I'll come visit…"

"No Jayme! Don't do that. Do you hear me? I've got to go. Bye," I finished before quickly hanging up the receiver.

"This way champ," the officer said guiding me away.

With my hands again cuffed behind my back, I was led down the hall to a stairwell. I hoped that the mattress on the bed in my cell would be thick enough to sleep comfortably on my side. I hoped I would have a sink with some hot water, particularly since I still hadn't washed since my run. I even wondered what they would serve for dinner.

"Is Jayme your girlfriend?" the officer asked in an apparent effort to make conversation.

"Sister," I responded. "I told you I was calling my *sister*," I hesitated and stopped myself before calling him a "jackass," as if he couldn't already sense it by the tone of my voice.

Reaching the bottom of the stairwell, the officer used his body to shield my view as he pushed a combination on the door. I heard a clicking sound as the door released and the officer pushed it open. The noise from inside was deafening, and I looked around in horror. There were two large cells, each filled with about eight to ten screaming hoodlums. The officer did a quick count and, without hesitation, put me in the one with the fewer number of men. I could barely hear my thoughts amidst the echo of the arguments inside. I looked desperately at my guide, but he could only offer a helpless shrug as he locked the door behind his newest inmate.

I turned and spotted a toilet in one corner of the cell. There was no running water.

"What a wonderful day it's been," I muttered sarcastically. *Corporate boardrooms, my ass*, I thought. I wondered what Marianne Delaney would say at her next campus information session if she ever had a chance to talk to me.

* * *

After I was safely placed in the holding pen, FBI Special Agent Reginald Williams received the telephone call from Saul Spaco.

"Did you get him?" Reggie asked.

"We got him."

"What's his story."

"He's not talking."

"Has he got any links?"

"You're not going to believe this one, Reggie."

"What?"

"He's Jayme Tucker's brother. He's back in town for a visit."

"*Nathan's* Jayme Tucker?"

"You got it."

Reggie Williams was intrigued on the other end of the telephone.

"We can use this," he said. "We can use this. I'll get back to you."

Reggie Williams thought for minute. He figured he would need a little guidance on this one. It was one of those times he should dial Robert O'Donnell.

"O'Donnell," the Assistant Special Agent in Charge said answering his phone.

"Williams here, sir."

"Go ahead."

"Interesting development. It seems that Jayme Tucker's brother is back in town. I just had the locals pick him up on a drug possession charge."

"Yeah, so. What's his profile?"

"College grad, believe it or not. He's one of the few from Tremont Heights," Reggie Williams said laughing.

O'Donnell played dumb. "What's he got?"

"Nothing yet. It could prove fruitless. I thought I'd inform you though.

We're going to keep on the angle."

"Don't waste your time, Williams," O'Donnell responded. "Just keep an eye on him. If he's a college grad, he's not going to be in town for long."

Chapter Forty-Six

When she hung up with me, Jayme telephoned Nathan crying.

"They arrested Billy," she managed between sobs. "He's spending the night in jail."

"I know. I know."

"How do *you* know?" Jayme wondered, not for the first time surprised by how her boyfriend had become the eyes and ears of Tremont Heights.

"It's not important, baby."

Jayme lost it.

"It is important, Nathan. It's my brother!"

"It's a fact of life in Tremont Heights, Jayme. I've been in. Dozens of times. You know that. I could name about ten other guys who have too. Billy will be all right. He's probably got no priors, right?"

"How do I know?" Jayme continued as her sobs softened.

"He'll be all right," Nathan said. "We've got to talk tonight. I need you to come over."

* * *

O'Donnell was ecstatic when he returned to the field office and was handed the tape of Jayme's telephone call.

"I'll take over from here," he told the young agent in the room.

"But sir…"

"Carter!" O'Donnell interrupted, shocking his eager disciple before he repeated his words, slowly and deliberately. "I said, *I'll take it from here!*"

* * *

It wasn't long before Jayme arrived at Nathan's, only to see him pacing in his kitchen. After a long embrace, he led her downstairs into the back room of the basement, a dim lit, leather couch dominated 'chill room,' as they liked to call it. Nathan closed the door behind her and ran his hands through her hair. He held her head to his chest.

Robert O'Donnell watched as Nathan's lips moved. He said a silent thank you to Special Agent Reggie Williams and his skill in installing the FBI's latest technology.

"It must have freaked you out seeing him again," Nathan began. "And now this."

Jayme tilted her head back away from her boyfriend so that she could see his eyes.

"He appeared right there in my bedroom, just as I was getting ready to go out and see you last night."

"I wish you had told me," Nathan remarked.

"I didn't want to ruin the night," she offered. "I didn't know how you would react, and I didn't want to spend the whole night talking about him," she finished defensively.

"Listen. It's okay," Nathan responded in an effort to calm her. "I just wish it, that's all. You know we're in this together."

Not for the first time since Reggie Williams had succeeded in his audio/visual installation, Robert O'Donnell swallowed hard, eagerly focusing on the bigger picture.

"Maybe Billy can help," Jayme offered.

"There is no one that can help, Jayme. You have to understand that. What we're doing is all we can do. We have each other, and we trust each other, so we don't have to trust anyone else."

Nathan waited. Jayme did not speak. "Even *Billy*," he emphasized. "Hell, especially Billy. I'm getting real paranoid, Jayme. I'm starting to feel like Ronnie might even know it's you."

Jayme's eyes bulged and she placed her hand over her gaping mouth.

"How? How Nathan?" she demanded.

Nathan eyed her, shaking his head. "I don't know, babe. Process of elimination? I mean, he knows that it has to be someone who cares about me a lot, someone I trust. It's so obvious when you think about it. Damn it!" Nathan finished.

Jayme changed the subject. "I told Billy about us."

Nathan shook his head back and forth. "That must have made his day."

Jayme opened her mouth as if to protest, but Nathan continued.

"How long is he in town for?"

"I don't know," Jayme answered. "I don't think he's on vacation. He says he couldn't get a job."

"Billy?" Nathan asked incredulously.

"He seems down."

"Billy?" Nathan repeated, stepping away. "What did he say?"

"He said he's going to stick around for a while until he can regroup. He wants to spend some time with me. He wants to hang around for a while. And I told you. He wants to see you too."

Nathan laughed. "How did he react when you told him we were dating?"

"He didn't say much of anything, Nathan. Something like 'amazing' or 'unbelievable' or something. I don't know exactly."

"He didn't say, 'that's terrific,' I bet."

"Have I told you that I love you?" Jayme added.

"Not today."

"Well let me remind you then," she said, stepping forward to kiss him. "Will you come over to see him?" she asked.

"Not yet. Tell him that I'm busy and tough to see. I'm not ready to see Billy again, Jayme. At least not yet," Nathan added.

Jayme walked across the room and ran her index finger along the table. "I have to go to work," she said, looking back at him.

Robert O'Donnell then watched them hold each other tightly in a parting embrace.

Chapter Forty-Seven

That night, huddled against the cold metal bars and an unforgiving cement floor, surrounded by dirt-bags and derelicts, I barely slept. My thoughts turned in sickening circles, from the present to the past, and then back again. Victoria, Lucy, Jayme. In that order. My mother. I couldn't believe how many years had gone by. The FBI had brought all the women in my life together for me, all five of us on one hand. Like a thumb, I could touch them all with the assignment I was given.

I faded off to sleep in the early morning hours. I was actually one of the fortunate ones. Suspecting that sleeping space would be the main issue for the night, I had found a spot early in the evening and didn't move. That way, everyone else in the cell would understand that I had staked my ground. I was right. It was actually a luxury to be able to rest my back against the area in the bars where there were horizontal crosses. There, my head could nestle between the two cold vertical metal poles while my neck rested against the horizontal one. Also, by staking my spot early, I was assured that I would not have to sit in one of the spit-laden areas of the cement floor.

Someone poked me in the shoulder. I awoke startled.

"You an 8:30?" one of my cellmates asked of me, his putrid breath perhaps the most offensive part of this initial encounter.

A guard had started calling out names. Twenty-four hours to be arraigned meant just that. The guys who were called at 8:30 a.m. were those who had been brought in the morning before. Because I hadn't been brought in until the early afternoon, I would have to wait until the afternoon court call, until after the criminal court judge had some lunch and took care of some administrative or personal matters.

I really hadn't talked to anyone at all since I arrived in the cell. I knew better. At Quantico, I learned that inmates who talked to each other inevitably ended up talking about other crimes they had committed. Occasionally, they bragged about the ones they had gotten away with. I had no desire to become a witness against one of my current roommates. I just wanted out of the cell and out of this situation for good, and I figured that the quickest way to do that was to keep my mouth completely shut.

"S'up man? You an 8:30?" the scraggly one in front of me asked again.

I had made up nicknames for a few of the guys during the night for my own entertainment. This guy didn't earn a nickname initially because like me, he basically kept to himself. He came in only a few hours after me anyway. Because he was tall, skinny and awkward looking, I considered 'toothpick,' 'beanpole' and even 'javelin,' but none of those really stuck. But now, with his large teeth and exposed gums in front of my face, and with his breath polluting my nostrils, I had a whole host of new ideas.

I turned my face from his which, for some reason, prompted an introduction.

"Lyle. I'm Lyle," he said.

I offered a head bob, and a bare raise of a finger, but then looked down at my knees.

"You look familiar to me. How do I know you?" Lyle asked.

"You don't," I said sharply, trying to end the conversation.

But Lyle took my response as a challenge. "Uh huh. I know you. I know I know you. Let me see that face."

Lyle tried to tilt his head and peer directly into my eyes. I turned away in a gesture of annoyance.

"Damn, man. Testy this morning, aren't you?"

Lyle stepped over my knees and now reached for my face. I was instantly wide awake and thought about raising my knees into his crotch.

"Hands off, dirt bag," I said instead, pushing Lyle's hands away. "And get out of my personal space."

Lyle stepped back. "Come on. What's your name?"

"What's my name?" I delayed, giving myself a moment to decide whether I should make something up. I quickly dismissed the idea as foolish.

"Billy Tucker."

"Billy Tucker?" he repeated.

"Which word didn't you understand?"

"You're Jayme's brother," Lyle confirmed. "I knew I saw something familiar in your face."

Lyle's demeanor seemed to change. He seemed less edgy.

"You haven't been around this way in a while, have you?" he asked, sitting down next to me.

I had no memory of a guy named Lyle at all. *Had I really been this out of touch?*

"Well if you're Jayme's brother, you must be cool," he said trying to get back his edge.

I had no idea what to say. Lyle seemed to want to control the conversation anyway, and that was just as well.

"Jayme's a fox," he continued.

I smiled.

"Nathan's a lucky man," he said.

I nodded. There was a pause.

"What did you do?" he asked.

"Nothing," I said.

"Me neither, man. It's bullshit that I'm in here. Bullshit!" Lyle finished, turning back toward the cell officer with a yell.

The officer behind the door peaked his head in and shot a dirty look in our direction.

"How come you're in town? The word around the Heights is that you're off making your cake on Wall Street. I thought you finished college?"

"I did finish college."

"Why are you back?"

"Because I'm finished," I said, hoping to end the conversation.

"Smart-ass," Lyle said with a laugh. "So what are you going to do now?"

Thankfully, my need to answer was interrupted.

"Tucker! Billy Tucker!"

I jumped up and figured O'Donnell must have at least pulled a small string to get me called in the morning. I smiled at Lyle and nodded good-bye.

"Plead guilty!" Lyle yelled after me, and I couldn't believe that this was the universal motto.

So much for the presumption of innocence in this town, I thought.

From the holding cell, I was brought through one of the side doors of the courtroom and told to sit down on a beat-up wooden bench inside the door. Some wild-haired, tattered man sitting next to me on the bench and wearing a wrinkled light beige summer suit asked me what I was charged with. Then, he asked whether I had any prior offenses. When he heard that I did not, he asked whether I wanted representation, and I politely declined.

"Are you sure?" the man asked, wearing a cheesy smile. "I've represented hundreds of people like you. You only need to pay me if I get you off with no jail time."

I politely declined again, and the man looked disappointed.

Handcuffed, I remained seated on the bench until the courtroom deputy called my name. I stood abruptly. All of the faces on the benches outside the bar looked my way. I was embarrassed to be wearing the handcuffs. *What if*

I knew someone? I looked quickly at the audience, relieved that Jayme was not there, but wondering why O'Donnell was not.

I felt nauseated and light-headed from my lack of rest and nourishment and was pleased when the court officer guided me to the table in front of the judge and poured me a cup of water.

"Does the Commonwealth have anything to say?" the judge began.

A young woman next to me came out of her hunched position where she was frantically looking through papers.

"Nothing, Your Honor," she responded standing upright and proud.

"Mister Tucker, do you have an attorney?"

"No, Your Honor," I said, imitating the woman next to me, but finding it strange that, having been trained in Quantico how to testify in court, the first time I was addressing the black robe, I was a defendant.

"Do you know that you have the right to an attorney?" the judge asked me.

"Yes, Your Honor."

"Have you chosen to waive that right?"

"Yes, Your Honor."

"Mister Tucker, you are being charged with one count of possession of a class C controlled substance. How do you plead?"

My moment of consideration might have caused the masses to rise-up in protest, but then I thought better of it. "Guilty, Your Honor."

"You plead guilty?" he asked, seeking confirmation.

"Yes, Your Honor."

"Okay then. Before accepting that plea, I have to ask you a series of questions."

I nodded, and he began. "How old are you?"

"Twenty-two."

"What is your level of education?"

"I graduated college."

The people in the courtroom began to murmur. "Frat boy!" I heard from behind me. The judge looked up. "Order. Order!" he called.

He didn't address me again until the courtroom noise settled.

"What is your occupation?"

I hesitated. "Unemployed."

Nobody in the audience reacted to this answer. This one, they must have been used to.

"Have you been under the care of a physician or psychiatrist?"

"No."

"Do you understand what is happening now?"

"Yes."

"Do you understand what you have been charged with?"

"Yes."

"Do you understand that by pleading guilty to the crime with which you've been charged, possession of a class C controlled substance, you face a possible term of imprisonment of up to one year and a fine of up to one thousand dollars?"

O'Donnell better know what he's doing, I thought as I said "yes."

"Do you understand that you have the right to contest the charges against you at a speedy and public trial and that you have the right to an attorney to assist you in this regard?"

"Yes, Your Honor."

"Do you understand that at a trial, you are entitled to a presumption of innocence? That at a trial, you are entitled to present witnesses on your behalf, testify on your behalf, or even do nothing at all and that the Commonwealth must still prove your guilt beyond a reasonable doubt to the satisfaction of unbiased citizens of the county?"

"Yes," I responded.

"Do you understand that by pleading guilty, you waive these rights and that this plea of guilty can later be used against you in a subsequent prosecution?"

"Yes," I said, O'Donnell's advice sounding worse by the minute.

"Okay, Mr. Tucker. On or about September 27th, did you violate section 120.01 of the penal code by possessing two grams of a Class C controlled substance?"

As much as I hated to do it, I nodded.

"I need you to speak for the record, son."

"Yes, Your Honor."

"Your answer to my questions is 'yes'?" the judge asked.

"It is, Your Honor."

"Any priors counselor?" the judge said to the woman standing next to me.

"No, Your Honor."

"Any recommendations?"

"Your Honor, the Commonwealth recommends that in light of the small amount of substance seized and the lack of any prior offenses, Mr. Tucker be sentenced to a continuation without a finding."

"Any rebuttal, Mr. Tucker? That's a pretty good deal."

I paused for a second. Everything was happening so fast.

"What's a continuation without a finding?"

The courtroom roared with laughter. I had no idea why until the judge spoke.

"It means that the handcuffs are removed from you now, you walk out of here a free man, and if you can stay clean for six months, this will all get washed from your record. How does that sound?"

The stupidity of this whole ordeal struck me.

"It's sounds like I shouldn't have had to spend the night in the holding cell in the first place."

A lonely silence invaded the courtroom. The female prosecutor next to me shot me a look of surprise, and the judge pointed his finger at me. My body tensed up, and I figured I had blown it.

"Mister Tucker. I'm going to let you take this deal, but I'll tell you what. If I see you in my courtroom again, I can assure you that you'll have the opportunity to feel a lot more comfortable in that jail the next time we're through."

I appreciated his point and silently feared another transgression by the local police. *Then, I will really need O'Donnell*, I thought.

"Madame Clerk!" the judge bellowed. "Call the next case!"

When the court officer came over and began removing my handcuffs, I sighed with relief. Walking by the benches where I last sat, I caught the eye of the attorney who offered to represent me. I couldn't resist.

"Who do I have to pay now?"

The man just shrugged and turned away to offer his services to the next victim beside him. I couldn't help but think at that moment that criminal justice was no more than a human factory.

Chapter Forty-Eight

When I left the courthouse, I figured that my opportunity to reach Victoria had long since passed. I made my way to a pay phone and tried the number she had paged me from. There was no answer, of course, and I racked my mind for how I could reach her. But then, I remembered our brief conversation in New York, and how she had started to mention Brooklyn. I dialed information, although I didn't expect her to be listed. I was right. The telephone representative told me there were two Summers' listed, one of them a V. Summers, but she could not give out the number.

I nearly walked away from the phone until the thought hit me, and I couldn't believe it hadn't occurred to me before. I was an FBI agent, and I could get any telephone number I wanted. I dialed the main line of the FBI's New York office, gave the person on the other end my code, and had Victoria's home number in an instant. She picked up after only two rings, her voice cracking from a restful night of sleep.

"It's even worse since we talked last," I opened. "I'm two days in, and I'm thinking rock bottom isn't far away."

"Okay," she responded. "I paged you yesterday because I thought about it. I nearly changed my mind last night when you didn't call," she warned, "but tell me all of it; go ahead and lay it on me," she said, and my heart leaped with joy. "But you can't tell a soul you told me."

I then did tell her all of it. I couldn't get the story out fast enough. It was disjointed as I told it. In order for her to understand just how difficult this project was for me, I had to throw in anecdotes about Nathan, our friendship, his loyalty to me, Ruth and Rick, Jayme's distance from me, my distance from her in school, the guilt of a twelve-year old on a street corner, the freshman fraternity party, my teenage lust for Lucy, and everything else I could think of from my entire life. And then, ending with what Jayme had told me about her feelings for Nathan, I said it. I said what I had been thinking for weeks.

"And I love you, Victoria. Your love guided me through training, leads me through this awful assignment, shelters me from my fears, and I can't imagine doing anything that would jeopardize what I feel for you."

The other end of the phone was silent for several seconds. I felt good, but my heart raced with anxiety.

"Wow," she responded heavily. "Holy…wow," she repeated.

Of course, despite my needs, in Victoria's rational and methodical way of handling all information, she responded to the first part first.

"I can't believe that you've gotten that as an assignment."

"Me neither," I jumped in. "I'm devastated, and I'm not sure I'll come out of this sane."

"Just calm down, Billy, okay. Let me think."

I did. The line was silent for a good two minutes. I didn't interrupt. I prayed for the words that would set me free, and finally, she spoke.

"You never shared all of that with me before."

"I should have," I said. "Long ago."

"Wow," she said again, and then, after a deep breath, she continued. "Okay, here's my take: You have got to get this done right," she started. "O'Donnell is right. It may be hard to face, but looking at this objectively, he is right. Jayme is only seventeen. Nathan's become a bad apple. There's bad stuff happening in Boston that we have been unable to break into."

My heart sank when Victoria used the word 'we' to refer to the FBI instead of her and me.

"You are the key, Billy. You are the FBI's ticket. Do you see what kind of an opportunity this is?"

But then I grew angry: "Victoria!" I charged. "He's threatening me, and he's threatening Jayme. You think he's right??!!"

"I don't in that regard, Billy, but remember what we learned in Quantico, about there always being a means to an end, and where there's an end…"

"Fuck Quantico!" I interrupted, and I nearly told her the same.

"Billy!" she stammered. "Stop talking like an infidel. This is an important project for the Bureau and for *you*."

"For me? Just me? I hate to say it, Victoria, but it doesn't sound like you care much about *me* right now."

Still recognizing that she had yet to respond to my expression of my feelings for her, I nearly hung up on her. Just then, she let out an uncharacteristic giggle.

"What," I snapped. "What's that for?"

"In all of the excitement, I almost forgot," she started. "Billy," she said. "I'm in love with you too."

The heat of her words filled my face. My shoulders curled with a light, awakening chill. I drew short, quick breaths, struggling for words. Everything in my past that had led me to my present suddenly had meaning. The alienation I felt in school after my fraternity de-activated me; the warm welcoming arms of the FBI; the sheer luck that Victoria was my seat companion for sixteen weeks in Quantico; and the circumstances of my home life that kept us together on the weekends while others headed for home. It all made sense to me now. It all seemed like a perfectly designed plan. A fate I had been destined for years before.

"You do?"

"I do," she confirmed.

"That is simply the best news I've had in weeks, in years; hell, in my life," I finished, now laughing.

Victoria laughed too. "It's good to say it," she said.

"Say it and feel it," I added.

"Yeah," she said, but her voice suddenly grew distant.

"What is it?" I asked.

"I'm late," she said to my surprise. "I'm supposed to be in at 9:30 this morning for an arrest meeting. Shit!" she added. "I've got to go, Billy. I really have to go."

"Can I call…"

"Yes, yes," she jumped in. "Whenever it's safe. But promise me you'll stick with this. Promise me you'll do your job. It doesn't matter whether O'Donnell is right or wrong at this point. What matters is that you follow orders. They may seem tough for you, but to me, an outsider of sorts, I'm not totally convinced that the higher purpose isn't the better purpose here. I'm sorry you have to go through this, Billy, but it's a long life. It's a long life for you, for your sister and, you know what?" she added. "It's a long life for us. And the life I see for us is a life in the Bureau."

There was so much more I wanted to say to her, to share with her, and to hear from her. As tough as her advice was, our conversation was uplifting. I had called Victoria looking for freedom from the project, but mostly, I had called her looking for guidance. In her words, more sweet than bitter, I had found it.

When I hung up the phone, I smiled at the sky. In the end, when my project was through, I would not have 'nothing,' I realized. I would have love.

Chapter Forty-Nine

In the days that passed, with the strength of my emotions for Victoria behind me, I adjusted to the new wrinkle in my assignment. *My sister would be okay in the end,* I kept telling myself. *But what had Nathan dragged her into?*

With my last thought, one that had started to occur to me more regularly, I had found a way to reconcile what I had to do. Sure, Nathan might have rescued Jayme from Rick and taken care of her in my absence, but look at the situation he was putting her into. It suddenly occurred to me that O'Donnell may have been right. As much as I cared for Nathan and always would, I didn't really want the Nathan I now knew dating my sister.

Yet, despite this subtle shift in my feelings, I was still torn by the notion of having to interfere with love. Now that I had found love, I understood first hand the strength of its pull, the blind faith of its hand and the loyalty it inspired. It was impossible, I thought, for anyone or anything to be able to interfere with it. Worse, would be the wrath upon any person or object who succeeded. Not for the first time, I feared what could happen to Nathan and Jayme if I was successful in my assignment. For the first time, thinking about my own love for Victoria and her last words to me on the telephone, I feared the consequences of my failure.

* * *

Robert O'Donnell wanted a progress report every forty-eight hours, but for the most part, I simply had nothing to give him. He made it very clear to me from the beginning that he was not my therapist and that he had no interest in serving as one.

Your emotional roller coaster is going to be something you deal with alone, he had said, and that was just fine with me. I had no interest in sharing my deepest thoughts with such a loathsome, heartless man, and O'Donnell couldn't know about Victoria yet anyway.

So after that day in the Boston field office and at the police station, I kept all of my emotions to myself. My conversations with O'Donnell were limited to facts, whenever there were any, which was seldom to not at all. Our conversations tended to be short and uneventful, and sometimes I delighted in my lack of progress. The less I learned and the slower my progress in reconnecting with Nathan, the more I could agitate O'Donnell.

Other times, with no progress from my end, I began to feel like I was not doing a good job. At times, I asked O'Donnell for his advice, but he had little to offer.

Stick with the program, kid, he would always say. *Without patience, you're lost undercover.*

In the meantime, I could not tell if Jayme was getting used to having me around or if she was instead, starting to feel annoyed with my presence. She seemed to try to spend less and less time in the house, although I was not sure if this was actually the case, or if I had become so bored that I started to keep track of such mundane details. I pushed to see Nathan, but Jayme was evasive. She reminded me that Nathan was busy and that very few people got to spend any time with him at all. Her time alone with him was special, and he was reluctant to share that with anyone, even me.

When I was alone in the house, I often spent hours rehearsing the conversation I planned to have with Nathan. I pictured Nathan confessing to the crime, my revelation that I was in the FBI, and his begging me to cut him a deal.

Sitting on the living room couch one afternoon, weeks into my assignment, and in the midst of these thoughts, I was startled by the sudden opening of the front door. In walked Jayme, done with her shift at the grocery store.

"Oh, you're still here," she said with her usual flare.

My constant presence had become a running joke between us.

"Any clarity yet?" Jayme asked sarcastically.

Jayme asked me the same question nearly every day, sometimes twice in one day.

"Clarity in boredom," I said, changing my usual response. "I'm growing old lying around like this. I don't think I'm going to be around much longer."

Although I knew that I was lying, after the passage of what was now a few weeks of us living together again, I wanted to test her response. I half expected an uncontrollable smile, even a jumping for joy. Instead, Jayme stopped in her tracks and instantly shed the edge she'd carried into the house. She stared at me for a brief moment before looking away. Her eyes seemed to well up with tears and her lips to quiver, and then she turned and walked away.

I was completely touched by what I saw. Jayme did not want me to go. The way things had gone, she probably figured that I would never come back.

"Where will you go?" she said, as she hung up her coat in the closet.

"I have to get a job, Jayme."

"Get a job here," she said, and her words were, at once, painful but moving.

"I would really like to see Nathan," I said, now thinking that I had lied my way into some leverage. "And I'm tired of sitting around the house like a slug. If he doesn't want to call me or see me, fine, but I'm heading out to the Park. You give him a call for me and tell him I have a pink rubber ball with his name on it. Tell him I challenge him to a game of one-on-one. No sweatshirts. No jeans. Just t-shirts and shorts. Loser wears the welts."

With that, I pushed open the screen door and exited, tossing the rubber ball in the air and bouncing it along the pavement as I went. It was a brisk day, probably a bit cool for a t-shirt and shorts, but it was more the spirit of the attire than the appropriateness of it that made it proper.

The walk to Tremont Height Park from my house was always a pleasant one. The trees that lined the front yards of the houses murmured a comforting whisper in the late, autumn wind. An occasional car passed, the buzz of its engine a reminder of human influence on nature, but for the most part, I took comfort in being able to walk down the middle of the street unimpeded by threatening traffic. I tried not to catch the eyes of any of my old neighbors who might have been on my way. In my time back home, I liked to avoid small talk as much as possible. That was O'Donnell's advice as well.

To loosen up, I began a light jog, but since my house wasn't far, I reached the entrance to the Park in no time. There was no one around, no one using the basketball courts, but more importantly, no one using the backstop we needed for our game. I wondered whether there were any teenagers left in the area, or whether Tremont Heights had become a town of twenty-somethings and has-beens. I wondered whether Jayme had even bothered to call Nathan and hassle him with my challenge. It would simply be offensive, I decided, if he chose not to show. It would also be a sign that he didn't really care for me much at all anymore. That would make my work a lot easier to stomach. Silently, a part of me hoped he wouldn't show.

I began to throw the ball against the wall, lobbing it at first, but gradually throwing harder. As the echoes of my childhood against the wooden backboard grew, I threw it more at an angle than straight, forcing myself to move laterally to get to it. Soon, sliding across the pavement and whipping the pink rubber through the air, I was fourteen again. I was a teenager, a Tremont Heights high school-er, a growing boy scared about the future, focused but confused about his place in the world, no mother to turn to for support, rooted but root-less, eager for something beyond but completely unaware of what it was or how to grasp it, but most of all, comfortably hidden in the certainty of the shadow of Nathan Marks, all that he stood for, and all that I was not.

And then, there was my memory of Lucy Polowski, as if she were right there watching again: the new girl in town with a heart full of sass, a Hollywood body, and a mind that was unattainable and sophisticated beyond our neighborhood. Academia was hers for the taking when she wanted it, but Lucy needed far more than the teachings of any scholar. She needed the attention of the masses; her life blood. Like a young politician headed for the American Presidency, in the time I knew her, Lucy was on a path to something larger than life. Her aura was unmistakable and guiding for those, like me, who watched her with awe. But for a select few, like Nathan Marks and apparently Joey Luca, her hold was gripping. So gripping that she fell to tragedy in their hands before her true potential would be realized.

And now, I was home, to discover and champion her legacy. Would it be as simple as the last laugh on Nathan? Or would it be much more? What would Lucy Polowski have to say to those whose lives she touched before she fell? Each of us, in our own separate ways, were all waiting, and we were all listening.

Nathan never did show up that day to play me. Jayme wouldn't even answer me when I asked her if she called him.

"Times have changed, Billy," she said, "and so have we."

That night, when darkness fell, I decided that I would take a new approach.

Chapter Fifty

I was mentally preparing to implement my new strategy when, late in the next afternoon, I received a page from O'Donnell.

"Tucker. Where are you?" he said when I answered the page.

"Relaxing," I said to confront him.

"No time to relax," he responded sharply.

After my last visit to The Chocolate Cone, I had told O'Donnell about the way Addison defended Nathan when we talked about the crime. O'Donnell now told me that, based on what I'd said, he was able to convince one of the pro-government judges to approve a listening device in Addison's store.

"The judge gave us ten days," O'Donnell said. "He warned me that it would not be renewed."

O'Donnell then told me that he heard Nathan talking to Jayme that afternoon at The Chocolate Cone, and that there might be some trouble for them with the police in Tremont Heights Park.

"You've got to get to the Park."

"What kind of trouble?" I asked him, but he said he didn't have time to explain.

"What the hell sir?"

"Get there Billy. I'll explain later," he finished as he hung up the telephone.

* * *

Just before O'Donnell paged me, he paged Reggie Williams.

"Are you clear?" O'Donnell asked Reggie.

"I'm alone."

"Nathan and Jayme are proceeding out of The Chocolate Cone. They're going to head by Tremont Heights Park. Arrange for your guys to give Nathan a hassle when he gets there. Make it last and make it real, but don't make any arrests. Got it?"

"Sure, but what's going on?"

O'Donnell continued, non-responsive: "Nothing physical, but a little tough talk and even some minor body contact is okay."

"I've got it, Robert, but why?"

"Don't ask Williams. I'll explain later," O'Donnell said, just like he had said to me. "Just stay clear of the whole thing. I don't want you anywhere near Tremont Heights Park. Just arrange to have it done. Pronto!"

* * *

I hung up the telephone and sprinted out the door. I would be damned before my sister would have to spend a night in a holding cell like I just had. Every time my body wanted to let up, I thought of how I did not want to let her down again. In two and one-half minutes flat, I was at the entrance to Tremont Heights Park. I could see Jayme. She was with Nathan and two uniformed officers. Both of the officers had their hands gripped around their batons. Nathan was raising his arms and pointing his fingers, and Jayme was trying to calm him down. I could not hear the conversation between them, but my heart dropped into my stomach when I saw one of the uniformed officers step back, draw his baton and raise it over his head.

Jayme shrieked. Nathan took off and one of the officers started to take off after him. Then, I called out, "Jayme!" but no one responded. "Jayme!!!" I screamed at the top of my lungs.

When I reached my little sister, tears were pouring down her face.

"What's going on," I tried to say calmly, my eyes darting back and forth on full alert, but Jayme couldn't talk.

"Not your business, son. Who are you?" the officer asked.

"I'm her brother," I responded between panting breaths. "Is she being taken into custody? Are you arresting her?"

The officer did not respond. "Are you arresting her?" I demanded again.

Jayme's sobs let up a little as she listened to me speak.

"No," the officer said reluctantly.

"Then I'm taking her home. I'm taking her home right now," I said.

"I may need to speak to her later," the officer said, trying to reclaim some authority.

"About what?" I asked, remembering the scene of my own arrest.

The officer was dumbfounded, and he simply responded, "We'll see."

I was completely rattled as I walked away with Jayme. I was supposed to be composed in arrest situations. I had just trained for moments like these for weeks. What I realized I had never been trained for, though, was an arrest situation involving someone I cared so deeply for. *But how could that skill be taught? How could I ever be objective?*

We walked for several paces before Jayme broke the silence: "That thing you said about 'custody' was good, Billy. How did you know that?" she asked, sniffing and wiping the tears from her eyes.

I thought quickly. "I took a legal studies class in college," I said, and then I embellished. "I always thought it was a waste of time," I lied. "Until now, I guess."

As if to apologize for him, Jayme then told me her deal with Nathan. The events of the last year had made it dangerous for him to be seen in public. The police were looking to bring him in on anything, so he had told her that if she insisted on spending time outside with him during the day, these situations might happen. In these situations, he was better off running for it than risking making matters worse for himself by letting the police add another bogus, petty crime to his record.

I told Jayme my arrest was bogus too, and she understood.

"This whole thing today is going to be tough on Nathan," she added.

"Why?" I asked.

"He's going to be jealous. Don't think Nathan enjoys leaving me standing there. Nathan has been playing the role of my protector for a while now, and he likes it. But when I was talking to him the other day, he was asking me about you. I think he's worried I will need him less now that you're here. I love him, though, Billy. I need him."

My stomach churned with her words. The thought of Nathan being jealous of me was twisted, but the thought of what I was going to have to do to Jayme in my assignment was worse.

* * *

Reggie Williams may have been a loyal special agent, but he was no fool. He knew O'Donnell had been running a back-up plan, but he was told that it was too dangerous for him to know what it was. He also knew he was told to stay clear of the Park, but O'Donnell hadn't pulled something like this in all of Reggie's time in Tremont Heights.

He looked on at the scene in the Park with curiosity, but also with fear.

Something's going on, he thought helplessly wondering just what danger lay in store for him outside O'Donnell's ever-shrinking circle of knowledge.

Chapter Fifty-One

Robert O'Donnell had spent the entire morning prior to his Tremont Heights Park set up in the listening room. The first call was short, but he paid close attention. Lyle Jasper had finally gotten a chance to meet with Ronnie Luca.

You got nothing? Ronnie Luca asked.

Uh uh, came a groan.

I shouldn't even be paying you.

Ronnie, I got in there too late. By the time we started talking, he was called up to court. Who's fault is that?

When did I call you? Ronnie snapped.

Ronnie, I had to drive all the way down from Maine. I couldn't...

Enough Lyle. Enough. I'll talk to Spaco. We've got to set something else up. I don't like the way this smells.

The next call, moments later, was frightening, but it was still Ronnie Luca's voice.

Saul?

This is him.

Saul, it's me.

Hey.

Silence.

What's up? Saul asked.

Our guy came up empty. What's going on? Is it the fibbi?

Robert O'Donnell re-wound the tape. 'Fibbi' meant only one thing.

It is.

His doing?

His doing, Spaco confirmed.

Something's up, Ronnie said.

I don't know, Ronnie. He seemed clueless when he called. Said it was an unknown who was wandering around. Asked me to pick him up. We did.

Something's up, Ronnie said again.

Not in my instinct. Just the fibbi checking everything out.

And?

And he wants to know what our guy, Lyle, got out of him too.

My guy! Ronnie Luca burst. *I sent Lyle in there. Not him.*

Indeed, after I was called up out of the holding cell that night in the jail, the man that introduced himself to me as Lyle followed shortly thereafter. Unlike me, though, Lyle never went up to the courtroom. He just went straight to the street. That was the benefit in being Saul Spaco's 'special collar,' and being ordered in by Ronnie Luca himself.

As far as he knows, Ronnie, Lyle's my guy, and he thinks that the information is coming to me and then going to him. No one else.

When is this stuffed G-man going to realize that we're watching him more than he's watching us?

I don't know, Saul Spaco responded.

Well keep a closer eye on Jayme's brother, Ronnie finished, but then he called out an order as he hung up the phone: *Bring me Nathan*, he demanded to someone who must have been nearby. *Me and the kid need to talk. And where the HELL is my good for nothing son.*

* * *

Robert O'Donnell ran his hands through his hair with the second call. He started to dial my pager, then he stopped. *Think. Think,* he repeated to himself.

Reggie Williams' cover was blown. Ronnie Luca was going to be watching Billy Tucker. Was that a good thing? Or bad? Could he use it to his advantage?

"Think, think," he said again, this time aloud.

But an hour of face-scratching, nail biting and finger twisting did no good. He was actually happy to be interrupted by the opening door.

"Sorry to interrupt sir," the junior special agent said, "but we've finished enhancing this last one."

O'Donnell grabbed the tape and inserted it into the machine. He motioned for the junior man to leave, but not before asking for another cup of coffee.

* * *

Joey, hand me the ashtray, Ronnie said, squinting his eyes through a haze of smoke. *Are we all here? We all settled?*

Yeah, pah. We're all here.

Good. Nathan. How's collections?

Right on, Mr. Luca. We're at eighty percent and by the end of today, I think we'll exceed it.

Eighty percent?

Yeah.

Joey, did you hear that? Eighty fucking percent. I don't remember the last time you were that high. Hell, have you ever been that high, Joey?

There was some laughter in the room. No response came from Ronnie Luca's only son.

We just got there the other day and only because Gunther came up big. I wasn't even there, Nathan added, as if to apologize to Joey.

Yeah, well. Gunther's the man, Joey added, picking up on the clue. *Ain't no Gunther when I was collecting, pah.*

Shush! Ronnie snapped. *I don't want to hear it. You and Gunther run together, right Nathan?*

Yeah.

Well don't be so fucking humble then. You're a big piece of that eighty percent. And Joey, my Joey. I pulled you off of collections to use your talents elsewhere. What are you doing these days, anyway?

More laughter. *Shush!* Ronnie snapped again. *Let me tell you all something. Joey's my heir. There ain't no mistaking that. You show him respect or I'll show you six feet under.*

Total silence. Ronnie continued. *Now, me and Joey are going to talk a bit alone in the next room. Nathan, you come too. The rest of you have some scotch, but not too much. I don't want anyone leaving before I have a chance to talk to them. Got it?*

There were several grunts and acknowledgments and then some shuffling of feet.

* * *

After closing the door behind his son and his disciple and stepping into a private room, Ronnie Luca asked Nathan about me. *Did he know I was in town? What was I doing there? How come he hadn't talked to me yet? Was he happy I was back? Did he think I knew what he was up to? Would I ask a lot of questions?*

You know those college kids can be pretty smart, Ronnie added, testing Nathan's resolve.

Mr. Luca, Nathan responded. *You don't have to worry about me. I'm with you.*

Nobody forgets that first love, Ronnie Luca added. *You loved her, didn't you?*

Nathan offered up his standard answer. *Mr. Luca,* he said. *I hated her. I hated her for the way she made me feel. I've got a better thing now. No question.*

With a level look, Ronnie responded: *You're better thing is your pal's sister.*

Nathan feared that Ronnie would challenge him now, tell him he knew that Jayme was at the scene, that he'd figured it all out. If Ronnie knew that, Nathan well understood that they were both at his mercy.

Where do you think that gets us when Billy starts asking questions? Ronnie asked instead, and Nathan sighed.

Right back where we started, Joey piped in.

Shush Joey, Ronnie snapped. *I'm not talking to you yet.*

Listen, Nathan interrupted. *Billy Tucker and I have long since parted ways. It's over. I'm not like him, and he's not like me. I wouldn't trust him for a bag of beans.*

You better not, Joey added, ignoring his father's advice, but this time Ronnie Luca didn't *shush!* his son.

Joey talks sense, Nathan. You listening?

Nathan was frustrated. He felt that all he ever did was listen. *I'm listening Ronnie,* he said, and then he threw in a kicker. *I'm closer to Joey now than Billy anyway.*

Good, Ronnie jumped in, looking back from Joey to Nathan, both of whom still, even in this crucial moment together, couldn't bare to look each other in the eye. *Good*, Ronnie repeated wrapping his arms around both of their necks, apparently missing the subtlety of the moment. *That's my beautiful boys.*

Now this party, Ronnie continued, addressing Nathan. *This party you're having. I'm going to send my guy in. His name's Lyle. Stay the hell away from him. And Joey. Stay the hell out of there completely. I don't want you within ten miles of Tremont Heights. That's an order. Nathan, I'm only sending my guy to look out for you. I don't want you to end up in some soup with your old friend around.*

On the surface, Nathan knew what Ronnie Luca was doing. He was simply sending a man to watch him. Beneath the surface though, Nathan knew that if Ronnie trusted him completely, he wouldn't need anyone to look out for him. This was a step in the wrong direction as far as Nathan was concerned. It was hard enough to have come as far as he did.

After Lucy was killed, Ronnie needed to keep Nathan close, particularly when Nathan slipped into their first conversation they had that he thought there was a witness at the crime scene.

If I had to bet my life on it, Mr. Luca, Nathan had said, *someone saw, and it was a girl, a teenager, definitely.*

From the little Nathan knew about Ronnie Luca in that first conversation, he was sure that he was gambling with his life—and maybe Jayme's—when he offered that up. But it was the only way, as he saw it, not to get whacked. Addison Parker had once said that every smart man keeps his friends close and his enemies closer. Nathan was betting on that.

But in the months that had passed, after Ronnie Luca took Nathan under his wing, Nathan felt that their relationship had moved beyond that. He was happy about it too. He hoped that Ronnie now wanted him around and trusted him to be around, that whoever 'did it' or 'saw it' that night no longer mattered.

But this was definitely a step backward. Nathan worried whether things would ever be the same. And to Nathan, it was all my fault.

Come on, Nathan challenged. *You don't have to do that with me.* He hoped that he would be able to gauge Ronnie's response, determine from his eyes just how much potential damage their relationship was facing. As usual, though, the eyes of the gangster were cold when cornered. They remained that way until he spoke.

I'm looking out for you, Ronnie finally said, but Nathan wasn't sure who he was addressing. With each word he spoke—and Nathan wasn't sure if it was the angle of his view—Ronnie's eyes seemed to be looking off toward Joey.

And by the way, Ronnie added, purposefully. *We've got an undercover fibbi in Tremont Heights. For all we know, Nathan, he's going to be at your party too. Our guy knows who he is. You don't need to.*

Nathan felt a strange mixture of anxiety and relief at this revelation: anxiety, in that it was now likely that someone unknown to him had been watching him; relief, in that there really was a good reason for Ronnie to be sending in Lyle, or that is, watching the guy who was watching him. Both emotions poured out in Nathan's next question.

What do you mean I don't need to?

Listen Nathan, Ronnie said. *You stick with the program for now. You need to know, that's true, but I've got to figure out what I'm going to do first. And I need more information to do that. Once I get all of that figured out, we'll get you straight.*

Nathan shrugged, helpless and now, suddenly, feeling completely out of control in Ronnie's world. He immediately felt his jealousy for Joey rise.

Nathan had learned long ago that no matter which way it leaked, blood was thicker than water. And Nathan knew he was water, in every aspect of his life, even with Jayme. So knowing Ronnie Luca as he did, Nathan silently feared that the day would never come that Ronnie was comfortable with him again, at least as long as I was in town. And for that matter, as long as I was in town, Nathan feared that he would lose all comfort with Jayme too.

Chapter Fifty-Two

About the same time Nathan was meeting privately with Ronnie and Joey, I decided that the incident in the Park gave me an opportunity and a reason to implement a new strategy. I left our house and headed straight up and over the hill and around the corner to Nathan's.

It was early in the morning, but even with the sun shining and the sky clear, 33 Foster Street looked like an abandoned road shack. That was the thing about Tremont Heights. About every fifth house had a beautifully tailored yard, the sign of a proud homeowner and happy family, but the houses in between generally went from unappealing to worse. The home of Nathan Marks was one of those at the far end of the scale. Strands of dry, tall grass wavered in the wind, and dusty ridges reminded of where there was once dying brush. Blue paint chipped visibly from the woodwork that surrounded drawn and lopsided shades. A dog barked in the distance, a jolting reminder that I really was not supposed to be where I was right then.

I stepped up onto the brick landing and pushed the buzzer. *He's an old friend*, I kept reminding myself, and with the churning in my stomach and pounding of my heart, I wondered why O'Donnell had played any tapes for me at all. *If he was truly looking to engross me in my role*, I considered, *he would have been better off not letting me know a thing.* The way O'Donnell had gone about educating me about Nathan's new life had actually made me nervous to see him.

There was no answer for some time, so I buzzed again. Instead of waiting by the door, I walked over to the garage and stood on my toes to look in through the window. Nathan's car was in there, but again, there was no answer at the door. In a final effort, I pressed the buzzer three quick times in a row, holding down the last for emphasis.

Let me in, damn it, the doorbell's noise rang, *we have something very serious we need to talk about.*

I decided to walk around back to see if there were any shades open on that side. No such luck. My walk around the back was lonelier than the echoes of the doorbell in my ear.

When I came back around front, I fully expected to head straight home. Instead, I found myself ducking behind a bush at the side. At the front of the house, Nathan was exiting a limousine, a black blazer hung over his shoulder. He leaned in to speak with someone inside. He was shaking someone's hand and smiling, although it wasn't the relaxed smile I once knew. As he closed the door behind him and turned, he blew out a full cheek-load of air.

Just then, the window of the limo came down.

"Hey Nathan," the voice of Ronnie Luca called. "You just take your time with that thing we talked about, okay. Patience is the key. Let him come to you."

"Got it Ronnie," Nathan said back.

"That's my man." The window started to rise and the limousine pulled away.

Nathan looked tired, like he had been out all night. It was not the right opportunity to confront him. I suspected that whatever Ronnie Luca had just told Nathan, it had something to do with me.

* * *

When I got back to my house, Jayme told me that Nathan had called her. He was having a party Saturday night.

"He said you should come by," she finished, and I swallowed hard as I searched for the right words.

"Great," was all I could muster at first, but then I grew braver. "Maybe I'll go early so we can catch up?"

"Maybe, maybe not," Jayme responded. "He just said you should come by. You can get there with me."

"Great," I repeated. "Saturday night. It's about time," I added, trying to remind Jayme how ridiculous I had found the delay.

When Jayme stepped out, I contacted Robert O'Donnell right away.

"Billy," he started. "Remember how I told you about how we had a man in Tremont Heights while you were finishing college and getting through Quantico?"

I nodded.

"Well, he's still there," O'Donnell added, and I felt the tiny hairs crawling on the back of my neck. "But I don't want you to know who he is," he continued. "And I don't want him to know who you are."

"But that's kind of an awkward situation…"

"Billy," he interrupted. "I don't think it could possibly help either one of you. His cover's been blown."

"How?" I asked, my eyes now wide as I considered my own situation.

"I don't know. It's a small town. A guy like Ronnie is going to be suspicious anyway. Our guy was an unknown in town before the funeral. Suddenly, he appears. It was the best we could do for a while, at least until we thought about you."

The inevitability of my role seemed so logical, yet so unbelievable.

"Is he in danger?" I asked, an instinctive response to what I learned in Quantico.

"I don't think so. And I think if we pull him, you might be."

To the extent the hairs on my neck were only at half-mast before, now, I felt them at full attention.

"Why are you sharing all of this with me now?"

O'Donnell paused. The silence seemed eternal. "You might be able to use it," he said, but he seemed unsure of his words. "Even if you can't, though, it's going to set off somebody's alarm if we pull our guy out only a few weeks after you've been in town."

"Come on," I jibed, but that only made O'Donnell firmer.

"Are you thinking like a criminal, Tucker? Have you considered what you might be thinking if you knew that the smallest slip-up could mean your loss of freedom? You *come on*," he mimicked.

I waited. "So what should I do?"

"This party at Nathan's," he said. "I'm going to make sure our guy is there. Don't play detective, though. Don't try to figure out who he is. Stick to your game plan, which is getting together with Nathan. Two old friends. That's all. I told you this because I don't want you to be side-swiped if Nathan mentions an undercover FBI agent being in town. I don't want you to panic and think he means you. I'm going to transition our guy out of there when the time is right. I just need the opportunity."

I immediately felt uncomfortable. "Sir, we were taught in Quantico that something like this needs immediate attention. We can't just…"

"Tucker," O'Donnell interrupted. "Spare me the theoretical bullshit. These are the real streets and we've got a real problem."

I, of course, agreed. I had been to numerous parties in my life, but I felt ill-prepared for this scenario. *Perhaps Nathan felt the same,* I considered. Either way, we were both in way over our heads.

Chapter Fifty-Three

Two nights before Nathan's party, I felt a surging desire to see him immediately, to talk to him right away. I couldn't wait for Saturday night. The party was not going to be a good scene for either of us, I was sure. We needed some private time, the kind like we had in the old days. Just one-on-one conversation.

I asked Jayme for his pager number. I figured that if I dialed in our home digits, he would respond, thinking it was Jayme. Instead, he would get me.

"No Billy," she said. "He doesn't give it out."

"Let me explain something to you, Jayme. Nathan may think he's a big shot, but in my mind, he's still the same guy I shared beers with in high school, the same guy I teamed up with in bruise-ball, and the same guy who I suffered with through the aftermath of the '86 World Series. I have the right to call him, and you don't have the right to stand in my way."

"He told me no, Billy. He told me not to give you his number under any circumstances."

"Well how about the circumstance that I'm pissed off? How about the circumstance that I need him? How about that I need to talk to him and he's treating me like a junk yard dog?"

"I'll be right back," she said, and she stomped her way up the stairs.

I waited for her. Five minutes passed, then ten. I figured Jayme was paging him herself, but our telephone never rang.

"Not around," she said as she came back downstairs. "He's not even answering me," she continued. "It happens sometimes."

"Great," I added sarcastically. "The guy that used to never leave the confines of our fifteen block neighborhood is nowhere to be found."

Jayme shrugged. Then, she told me she was off to work. Grabbing her green Supermarket apron from the counter, she headed out the door.

I immediately picked up the telephone and hit re-dial, an old but simple trick we had been taught in Quantico. Nathan would know that this was the second page he was getting from Jayme's number in ten minutes. He might worry that something urgent needed to be addressed.

* * *

"What is it babe?" Nathan asked when he called.

"It's not Jayme, old buddy, it's me."

"Whoa," he responded. "What happened to Jayme? Is she alright?"

I was touched by his concern, but more focused on my own situation.

"Jayme's fine. That's all you have for me after all this time?"

"How did you get this number, Billy?" Nathan asked. "It's supposed to be private."

"Ever hear of re-dial?"

A pause. Silence. Nathan must have been aggravated that he was outsmarted, even in this little way.

"I can't talk," Nathan responded. "I only called because I thought something was wrong. I'm in the middle of a meeting. I really can't talk."

"You haven't been able to talk to me in six weeks now. It's getting old. I'm happy you've found a way to spend your time otherwise, but really, we go back a ways. I didn't expect this kind of welcome."

"Spare me, Billy. When you were in college, you didn't have much time for anyone here either. Now that you were forced to come back home, that doesn't mean your schedule is mine as well."

I choked on the word 'forced' as it came from his mouth.

"You can't just expect us all to drop everything to see you."

"That's ridiculous, Nathan. I'm not talking about 'you all.' I'm just talking about you."

"Yeah, well. I've got to be ready for it too, you know? A lot's happened in the last year. A lot of changes."

"I know. I've heard word. I'm not so sure this is the best thing you can be doing with your time."

"Cut the shit, Billy. I'm hanging up okay."

Nathan's words told me I had gone too far.

"I don't need any lecturing, alright?" he continued. "I'm doing what I've got to do. Just like you did. Just like you did when you went off to college."

"Nathan, I didn't mean to say that finding your way wasn't right; what I meant was…"

"I have to go," he repeated, stopping me mid-sentence.

"Yeah well, when are we going to talk?"

"I don't know. Maybe Saturday."

"Fine," I said. "Saturday. Let the record reflect, though, that you chickened out of my bruise-ball challenge," I added, trying to lighten the moment and cure my apparent mis-step.

"I'm done with that bullshit, Billy. Don't give me that teenage bullshit. You left that life long ago when you went to college, and it isn't going to do either of us any good to re-live it now. Move on, will you? Go live that better life you left us for long ago."

Nathan hung up the telephone, but his last words knifed through my gut. I sat on the couch staring directly in front of me into our kitchen, but seeing only the two of us together, slapping a pink rubber ball against the wall in perfect harmony. Somehow, Nathan had moved beyond the memories that were so precious to me.

How had he done it? I questioned, but then the answer seemed so obvious.

To me, our years together in Tremont Heights Park were frozen in time because I had left them behind. I had moved far away from the Park. While I was darting across Drexel's campus, distracted by whether I would be late to class, Nathan was passing by Tremont Heights Park, no doubt looking on in loneliness, replacing his memories of us together there, and figuring out a way to move on.

In time, I would be able to do the same, but for now, I couldn't. In my role for the FBI, I knew I needed things to be the way they were. My challenge now would be getting there again.

Chapter Fifty-Four

December 2000.

I stood alone in a corner of the basement sipping draft keg beer from a yellow plastic cup. The last time I had done so was senior week at college, a week filled with hugs, smiles and high-fives as we shared a collective hope for the future, as people wished me well in Quantico, and as I wished them well in their endeavors. Roger Norman told me he was headed to Wall Street. I told him he was a shoe-in for success.

Back then, I felt that life was moving on for all of us. I was oblivious to the path Robert O'Donnell had carved out for me. Now, standing in a basement in my own neighborhood in the disguise of my own skin, I considered the irony of where my life had moved: *nowhere.*

As the heavy base beat of the music filled the room, I watched Jayme socialize, observed her laughing and smiling, and I thought about how comfortable and graceful she looked. But I also thought about how she deserved so much more; events like the semi-formal and formal parties I had gone to at school. I thought about how stunning she would look in a form-fitting black dress with spaghetti shoulder straps and spiked-heels, and what a great date she would make for some lucky guy.

Then, I thought about Nathan and how he must feel differently about my sister, the softer, gentler counterpart to the sassy red-head we all used to worship so. Addison was right. Nathan was a lucky man. *And Jayme?* Well, one thing was sure, regardless of how I felt, Jayme felt that she was lucky too.

Everyone at the party left me alone. I wasn't sure if it was because I looked out of place or because Nathan had ordered it. Either way, I felt uncomfortable and struggled to find a way to blend in like I had been taught in undercover school. When I dressed for the evening, I had been sure to keep the door to my room locked. Robert O'Donnell had instructed me to use my judgment about whether to wear the FBI's wire. I decided that I should definitely do so, even in the odd chance that Nathan confessed his role in the crime tonight.

Once again, I could hear O'Donnell's words of advice.

Patience, Billy. You've got to be patient. I know you want this thing done as fast as possible, but if you push it, you'll blow everything you've been working for. You don't want to put your life—or Jayme's—in jeopardy.

I had a hard enough time believing that O'Donnell had any concern for my life, let alone Jayme's, but I quickly put such thoughts out of my head and reminded myself to be patient. It was just time to catch up with Nathan. It wasn't time for anything else. It was time to revisit with an old friend.

As the party began to fill with people, I was able to find shelter in the mass of bodies. I sipped my beer and assumed a relaxed pose against the wall. *Just kick back and enjoy the music*, I told myself. *Just a loner, aiming for a buzz and some good tunes. No need to talk to anyone.* But as the party filled in, the idea of standing alone became worse. I decided that I needed to socialize, shake some hands, pat some backs and become a Tremont Heights local once again.

Across the room, I finally saw a familiar face. Lyle had just come through the basement door and was clashing crossed wrists and exchanging smiles with a lot of the guys on the dance floor. I intended to ask him if he pleaded guilty too. Then I wondered: *could Lyle be the other FBI undercover O'Donnell mentioned?* I shrugged off the notion, figuring that it would be far too coincidental for us both to have been arrested in the same night. There was no reason O'Donnell would have plotted something as odd as that.

Unless he didn't know, it occurred to me. *Unless O'Donnell's other undercover agent didn't know about me.*

I began to study Lyle's movements. I looked for even a hint of the FBI strut we had all assumed in some fashion in Quantico, but there wasn't anything distinct about his neighborhood swagger. The only thing I noticed was that, like me, Lyle seemed to know very few people. Unlike me, though, Lyle never stopped moving. He had fleeting conversations with random party-goers as he passed.

It wasn't long before someone cranked up the radio and the whole room started to shake with the beat of the music. Although no one really seemed to be dancing with each other, there was a tremendous sense of togetherness and community in the movement of the group. There were smiles all around, and I actually felt as if I had been missing out all these years with the good folks from my hometown.

I was lost in thought, contemplating the differences between my last four years and Nathan's, when I realized that I hadn't seen Jayme for a little while. I began to make my way around the room, excusing myself as I softly bumped a few bodies on my way to the keg of beer at the other side.

When I was halfway there, the song that was on the radio began to come to a close, and the alcohol that had settled into my blood was beginning to help me feel more comfortable. I figured I would say hello to Lyle to make myself seem more a part of the party. That way, I might be able to meet some of the others too.

"Lyle," I called out to him when he had his back to me.

Other than Lyle's neck tensing up, I got no response. I tried again, this time reaching to tap him on the back.

"Lyle!" I repeated.

The faces around him turned toward me and then back to him with confused expressions. Lyle stepped forward and away, as if to ignore what had just transpired. He looked back.

"Ain't no Lyle here," he said, but I was sure I recognized him, particularly his remarkably large gums and teeth.

I knew something was awry, but I let it go and turned away, until I heard someone else echo his name.

"Lyle?" this stranger said. "Are you Lyle Jasper?"

"What are you talking about man?" he responded.

"Lyle Jasper," the stranger repeated.

Lyle pulled the stranger aside. I wasn't the only one who was paying attention. I was probably the only one who was actually interested, though. "Well who the *fuck* are you?" Lyle snapped.

"I'm Reggie," the man said.

What Reggie Williams didn't know at the time was that Lyle Jasper knew he was an undercover FBI agent. Reggie figured he could walk the fine line, maybe take their relationship to another level. Reggie sensed that he might not be long for Tremont Heights anyway.

Lyle's eyes narrowed. "I don't know any Reggie," he tried to say, but it was clear to me he did. "But I'll take a beer."

Lyle and Reggie then walked off to the corner of the room and began what seemed to be a strained discussion. They both looked in my direction. I trained my eyes up to the small, hatched window by the ceiling. It was an easy adjustment, and I held my stare long enough, I hoped, to convince them that I wasn't watching them.

Reggie took Lyle a few steps away from another guest that had been encroaching on their conversation. Lyle did not look happy the way Reggie grabbed his elbow, and Lyle shook him off with a violent arm spasm and a hard-set stare. They both looked my way again. *Was that an FBI swagger?*

I thought, but the doorway opening on my left distracted me.

The back room was in full view. The smoke from within brought forth Nathan, guiding Jayme by the hand. Head lowered, he looked strong and imposing as he emerged. His angled face and wide eyes set handsomely beneath his crop of dark hair. A black collared-shirt, the first three buttons undone, exposed a thin but muscular chest. *There he was, once again,* I thought. *The room always moved with him.*

As a slow beat and groove of U2 came over the radio, Nathan turned to Jayme and began to dance, exchanging only unspoken communication as they pressed against one another.

In a little while
Surely you'll be mine.

My body shivered as I watched them together, moving as one, my blood and my childhood now blending together before me.

The song continued, slowly, purposefully, but Nathan never looked in my direction. Instead, he seemed focused on one thing: dancing with my little sister. He held his right hand spread wide and firm on the small of her back. He closed his eyes and rocked and swayed with her to the beat.

Once more, I thought of Lucy and how she was the last person I had seen in the grip of my old friend. I thought about the way she used to cast her arms around Nathan's shoulders, standing upright though, as if she wanted it to seem to the world like he was holding her up. And now, there was Jayme in her place. My initial reaction was that Jayme did not belong, but then, as Lucy's face melted into that of my sister, I watched in envy. The two looked so taken by the music and the comfort they felt in each other's arms. The way Nathan held her and the way Jayme responded said it all: her folded arms around his shoulders and her head guided by his, the way her hair fell across her face, her closed eyes and soft unspeaking lips. I knew exactly what I was looking at. It was love, a love that enabled two human beings to completely co-exist in the unity of a moment.

I thought of Victoria, and an intense sadness overwhelmed me. I did not know whether to feel worse for myself or for Nathan. For Nathan, moments like these, surrounded by his neighborhood friends, were probably some of the most peaceful and protected that he knew. And Nathan's status had become Jayme's, willingly. Jayme was with him in her heart and her mind. She had told me so, and that night, I witnessed it myself. My legs felt heavy.

I looked down at my watch. It was well past 10:00 p.m., and on this night, I didn't need the clock to remind me of my mission. It was all around me, and all it brought was pain. As Nathan and Jayme turned to the music, Nathan opened his eyes and looked right at me. It was as if he knew exactly where I had been the entire time. His facial expression didn't change. His stare never moved. I felt like Nathan was sensing the danger my visit back to Tremont Heights had brought him.

My mouth started to open. My hand started to rise as I intended to wave, but I quickly realized that none of this was necessary. He wore the same frozen expression he offered Lucy Polowski in line at the snack bar on the first day of school that day. I finally understood it. He was saying hello, acknowledging my presence and acknowledging his respect. In so doing, though, Nathan was drawing a line—a line that meant that when we did actually sit down to talk, it would be on his terms. That day in the cafeteria, Lucy must have understood it too, and she never let it go until she had him.

Now, Nathan was showing me that instead of holding Lucy, he was holding Jayme. He was holding her tight, holding her for dear life. I knew at that moment that I wouldn't be talking to Nathan this night. I was invited to the party so that I could see and be seen. My presence was no longer necessary, needed or even wanted. Nathan wanted to look into my eyes and make a judgment. I wondered how Nathan would interpret my stare, or the sadness I was feeling.

I left the party before the last beat of the song. It occurred to me in my walk home that in my path across the floor, I had not seen Lyle or this guy Reggie who had approached him. I dismissed it. I didn't care. I had bigger concerns. When I arrived home, I shed my clothing and the wire, grabbed two beers from the refrigerator, downed them in no time, and lay back on the living room couch. Emotionally spent, I fell soundly asleep.

Chapter Fifty-Five

I awoke to an uncomfortable pressure in my bladder and the vibration of my pager against my leg. I debated this one for very little time. I really needed to get to the bathroom. The pager could wait. Maybe it was the wrong number. It would not have been the first time.

Gathering up the motor skills I needed to move, I sat upright, keeping my eyes closed. I felt that if I were able to make this little journey without adjusting my eyes to any light, I would be able to fall back asleep faster. The urge was too great not to take a peak at the clock, though, even if it meant a florescent digital glare from the VCR across the room. 4:37 a.m.

I'll hit the toilet and then head up to the bedroom, I figured.

When I looked toward my destination, though, I was so startled that I almost emptied my water right there. To my left, in the lazy chair, sat my old friend Nathan, wide awake, in a relaxed pose, and looking directly at me.

"Nathan?" I said, as if I needed to confirm, the adrenaline already coursing through my body.

"Hello Billy," he answered calmly.

"How long have you been there?" I said, feeling a bit violated that he had been watching me sleep.

"A while. Seems like forever."

"Let me hit the bathroom," I said, and Nathan nodded and looked away.

My thoughts raced as I stood over the toilet. *Be calm. Be patient*, I told myself, but then I remembered that I had left the wire in my heap of clothing at the foot of the couch.

With the sound of the flushing toilet at my back, I returned to the living room, thankfully, to find Nathan in the same place I had left him.

"Sort of a weird time to show up, buddy. You could freak a guy out who didn't know you."

"You could freak a guy out dropping into his life unannounced," Nathan returned.

I shook my head slowly back and forth, my effort to say I wanted to start over. "Well it was college that took me away, and now college is over," I said smoothly, having practiced and rehearsed the line with myself so many times before. But then I moved on.

"You and Jayme looked good together tonight. Who would have thought?"

"Not you," Nathan added, but then he paused, as if he were attempting to reconcile a desire to lash out at me with an internal guilt about his own troubled past. "But, I guess not me either originally," he conceded. "At least not with Lucy around."

Nathan then fell silent, so I continued. "A lot of time has passed, Nathan. A lot has changed. I'm happy to hear that you've been finding your way, I guess."

"There wasn't much choice," Nathan said, but I didn't pick up on his cue.

"Yeah, well. You're looking at a guy who was handed a platter of assorted gems and picked the one made of plastic."

Nathan managed a slight smile. "You talk as if you've lost."

"Feels like it right now."

"Not you," Nathan said shaking his head in denial, almost disgust.

Neither of us spoke for a few moments.

"Hey, I'm not here to cry on your shoulder, Nathan. Why did you surprise me like this tonight? What are you doing here?"

"You told me you wanted to talk."

"It's nearly 5:00 a.m."

"Very few people other than the cops have wanted to sit down and talk to me over the last year, Billy. I'm here to find out what you want."

"Just to say hello. That's all. We were best friends, remember?" I added sarcastically, challenging him.

"Do I remember? Me?" he snapped back. "I remember everyday. I remember us doing everything together. Drinking, laughing, kicking some butt in bruise-ball. I remember it all. When you left, my best buddies became the guys from ESPN, but only when they were telling me good news, which wasn't too often. Easy money. That's all I wanted. I didn't want to work for it. I knew I couldn't study for it. I thought hell, if I can do what I do best, sitting back in a recliner and watching games, and earn my keep plus a little, I'll have one up on everybody. Including you."

"Come on, Nathan." I said. "You've always had one up on me. Old woodwork Tucker? You had it all. The looks, the build. The girls. Jesus, Nathan. You might not think so now, but you got Lucy. Everybody wanted Lucy. I wanted Lucy."

Nathan focused on me with my last comment. He shook his head and threw up his hand. I couldn't believe he never knew. "Yeah well," he said. "Nobody's going to 'have' Lucy now."

"How's her dad?" I asked, breaking an uncomfortable pause.

"You're asking the wrong guy," he responded sharply. "I'm surprised the guy hasn't just whacked me yet." Nathan shook his head as he continued. "You know I never wanted any of the attention, Billy. Any of it. I didn't like it in high school. And I certainly don't like it now."

I knew where he was going.

"I can't even go out in public anymore," Nathan continued. "You saw that scene in the Park with Jayme. You were there. That stuff is ridiculous. Hell, it happened to you. And it happens to me all the time. I can't function."

I nodded. Nathan continued again.

"So you're back in town and want to say hello to me. For what? Are you feeling empty? Like you wish you never left? Like you wish you never lost touch with me? Bullshit. That just plain old stinking bullshit, and if that's your line, then you had better come up with something better."

Silently, I agreed, and I realized that I now did need to come up with something better. I decided to play hardball.

"Well, the fact is, Nathan, I'm home now. And while I'm home, I wanted to catch up. But what do I learn? I learn that you've got my sister's heart. So if I'm to come up with the real reason I'm hanging around, I'll tell you that it has nothing to do with you. But it has everything to do with Jayme."

"That has to do with me, then," he tried to interrupt, but I didn't let him.

"Do you think I'm happy that the best thing in her life is you, Nathan? You and I definitely had some great times growing up. I love all of my memories about us. You were a great friend. We were real close, and no one can ever take that away. But I've been thinking about it, and it's like you said on the phone. Life changes, and you have to change with it. Sure, maybe it's my fault for leaving Jayme here under your wing, but where are you taking her? Your problems were your problems alone, but now they're Jayme's too."

I paused. "And when the problems are Jayme's, they're also mine."

Now that I had gone this far, I kept pushing.

"And what's going to happen to Jayme, Nathan? What if she gets tired of the basement life like Lucy did? What if she wants to spread her wings? What if you get angry? What if history repeats itself? You're damn right I'm back. And I'm back to save my sister's life."

Nathan flinched in his chair. His nostrils flared as he eyed my rising temper.

"What are you suggesting, Billy? What are you getting at, college boy? You think you got it all figured out? You think it's that simple? Jealous rage? You think I haven't heard that crap before? Hah," he said as he shook his head.

Nathan's eyes lowered as he examined me. He resumed a relaxed pose.

"You ever heard of a Reggie Williams?" he asked.

I had not, thanks to the work of Robert O'Donnell. "Doesn't ring a bell," I said. "Should it?"

Nathan let out an evil laugh, something I had never heard from him before. I realized just how little I knew my friend anymore. I knew I needed to ask more questions.

"Who is he?"

"Just someone I know. He's been around town. Around for about a year, coincidentally. You might know his latest buddy Lyle."

My jaw clenched with the knowledge that something was going on, but I didn't know what.

"I met Lyle in a holding cell several weeks back," I said, trying to keep what I did know on the table. "And he was at the party tonight."

Nathan nodded.

"Who's Reggie Williams?" I asked, fearing what the answer would be, and remembering what O'Donnell told me about there being another undercover FBI agent in town.

Nathan stood from his position. He looked sideways and took a long drag from his cigarette.

"He's an undercover cop, maybe FBI. I don't know. I just know he's been snooping around here for a long time. Who knows? Maybe like you."

I desperately searched my mind for how Nathan might have a clue about my identity. *Had my cover somehow been blown too?* I heard the words of my instructor from Quantico echoing in my ears.

You've got to know when it's time to pull out. That's crucial in undercover work.

I thought about the handgun I had hidden in the back panel of the television set. *Could I get there fast enough? Could I ever use it on Nathan? Would he ever force me to?* I wondered what this Reggie Williams had given up. I wondered if he had somehow given me up. *O'Donnell had left too much in the dark on this one. This time he had screwed up.*

* * *

Back at the field office, Robert O'Donnell had his hand on the panic button. He had been trying to page me earlier and, with no response, he was a flick of a finger away from arranging for his arrest team to rush in. He notified them the minute one of my contemporaries who, unlike me, was doing the usual rookie rotations, picked up the transmission from my living room. O'Donnell had received his own page the second Reggie Williams hadn't checked in after the party and, for the first time in nine months, was nowhere to be found.

* * *

Nathan continued. "I may not be the sharpest tool in the shed, Billy, but the lessons I've learned have taught me not to be stupid. With Jayme in my life, it all finally has meaning."

Nathan paused, long enough for me to again consider Victoria. Finding his next words, Nathan's face tightened in anger.

"Do you think I'm ever going to let anyone take that away?"

Now, for the first time, I thought O'Donnell had it right. "You did it, didn't you Nathan?"

"You have no idea what you're talking about," he said. And then, Nathan's voice boomed. "No idea!!"

I pointed my finger at him and matched his tone.

"What happened that night, Nathan. Lucy was my friend too!"

* * *

Robert O'Donnell's eyes bulged as he listened. The device in my clothing in a heap on the floor was transmitting loud and clear.

* * *

"It's bigger than anything you can do, Billy. It's bigger than whatever boredom you feel the need to fill while you're passing through town. And you didn't earn the right to know just by dropping in for a few weeks. Don't think I haven't heard your questions before. The cops have been so far up my ass for the last year that even my breath is blue."

He continued. "Don't think I can't read the eyes of every person I know who is too afraid to ask the question either. I know what each one of them is thinking. *Am I looking at a killer?* I haven't told them. I don't need to. And I certainly don't need to tell you."

Nathan was forcing me to step it up even further. I walked toward him.

"When I leave Tremont Heights, Nathan, I'm taking Jayme with me. If you can't give me a reason not to, then that's your problem. You'll rot here alone with your little secret."

In Quantico, I had spent two hours every other day training in defensive tactics and the various ways to react to an aggressive assault. There was the side step, lean and kick; the wrist grab and roll; the open-faced palm punch to the Adam's apple and at least five other methods depending on the angle from which the attack came. I had done well with all of these tactics. My instructor had specifically said so.

The problem was, in the near 100 hours of training I had in these tactics, I had no training at all in the way to react when my whole childhood was coming at me. And that is what happened when Nathan rose. Within a split second, Nathan lowered his shoulder into my gut and flattened me on the carpet.

I would have responded. I would have kicked and clawed, wrestled and twisted my way to the top to gain control, but for one thing, Nathan had knocked the wind out of me. More importantly, the last time he held me that tight, I was twelve years old, and I was sitting on a curbside watching my mother die.

* * *

Robert O'Donnell braced himself on the desk as he fought to listen. He heard a muffled *thud*, and a rapid clicking noise. Then, there was nothing. When he realized he had lost contact, he threw the yellow stress ball at the chalkboard across the room.

* * *

When Nathan realized I wasn't going to react, when he thought he had hurt me, he unlocked his grip. He rolled back onto his knees and grabbed my arm to pull me up.

It was then that Jayme walked in, awakened by the commotion and the rise in our conversation downstairs. She wore blue sweatpants and a Tremont Heights High School athletic department T-shirt. When she saw what had been going on, she cupped her hands over her face and began to cry.

Nathan shook his head at me and went to console her. I stood and watched, long since removed as a supporter in Jayme's life. My head felt cloudy. I took quick breaths to recover the air in my lungs. Then, when I started to feel normal again, I took a step toward both of them. Nathan eyed me at first, but then dropped his chin to tell me it was okay. I felt relieved, forgiven almost.

I put my arms around both of them, ducking my head into the back of Jayme's shoulders. Forgetting all about my assignment in the moments that passed, my chest began to heave as I tried to hold back the sobs.

That night—that morning—Nathan, Jayme and I ended up having the conversation of our lifetimes. I found out more than I ever wanted to know about Lucy's last night. We didn't finish talking until 7:30 a.m.

PART V

Lipstick's Legacy

Chapter Fifty-Six

My body dragged like a deflated raft when I left Jayme and Nathan behind at the house. The potent mixture of emotional trauma, realization and minimal sleep made me dysfunctional. I couldn't answer O'Donnell's page until I had composed myself. This was too much.

Fidelity, Bravery and Integrity? I questioned. *What were those? What did they mean when I'd have nothing else? Victoria,* I reminded myself. *Keep thinking about Victoria.*

Finally, when I came to grips with denial, I answered O'Donnell's page.

"Tucker! Where in the hell have you been? Who's with you? Where are you?" O'Donnell fired off in rapid succession. "I'm coming in to pull you out. Give me your whereabouts and I'll send a car. I'll send two cars."

Not that I had known him that long, but I had never before heard panic in O'Donnell's voice.

"I'm safe. I don't need a car."

"You're not safe!" O'Donnell snapped. "We've got a man down. It's our other uncover agent. He took a beating last night. He's at the Boston City Hospital. It doesn't look like he's going to make it."

"A beating? Who?"

"We don't know. We've been picking up some strange conversations on the wire. The bottom line is that you're not safe anymore. I'm sending in help."

O'Donnell's words would have been music to my ears 24 hours ago. Now, knowing what I knew, they didn't make sense. "What's his name?" I asked. "What the other guy's name? I think I…"

"Never mind," he interrupted. "Ah hell. Reggie. His name is Reggie."

"Okay," I responded. "That makes sense."

"What?" O'Donnell's voice pulled away from the receiver. "What?!" he then called to someone apparently far across the room from him. "What are you jabbering?" he snarled.

We've got a body! I heard in the background. *We've got a body,* the voice repeated.

"Whose?" O'Donnell asked, before putting the receiver back against his mouth to address me. "Hang on Tucker. Don't move an inch. And don't hang up."

It's coming in now, the voice in the background continued. *Hang on. It's coming. Positive ID. Lyle Jasper.*

"Who?" O'Donnell called.

The victim's name is Lyle Jasper. Bullet to the back of the head. Looks like a mob hit, sir.

I hung up the telephone immediately and shut off my pager. As far as I was concerned, I now knew everything I needed to know to figure out what I was going to do with my life, with Nathan's and with Jayme. I thought about what I did know. That guy named Reggie at the party was an undercover FBI agent, and he ended up beaten. As for this Lyle who took the bullet, somehow Reggie knew him, but O'Donnell did not.

An informant? I asked myself. *Quite likely,* I decided. *But for Reggie? For the FBI? How could that be if O'Donnell didn't know him?* More likely, Lyle Jasper was tied to Ronnie Luca. The proof was in his shooting.

I headed straight to the City Hospital in the hopes of learning something more from Special Agent Reginald Williams. I did learn something more, but it was something that dashed every bit of hope I had left inside me.

* * *

Jayme's bicycle was old, but usable, and it was the closest and most certain means of transportation I had at the hour. Before I left the house, I retrieved my credentials from the closet, strapped on my gun belt and went to the television to remove my .38 revolver from the back panel. I was going to Boston City Hospital as a special agent for the Federal Bureau of Investigation, I decided, not as some desperate civilian with no authority, power or control.

I could barely concentrate on the ride to the hospital. *Who really was this Lyle? What did Reggie Williams know about him? What did Reggie know about the crime?* Panting, but within a half hour, I pulled up to the emergency entrance. Two paramedics were leaning against the back of an ambulance smoking a cigarette. They looked exhausted. It was exactly how I felt, but my adrenaline kept me functioning. I hopped off the bike and let it crash onto the concrete sidewalk. It took only two steps for the automatic emergency doors to slide open, creating a wide entrance, and I made my way to a window about twenty feet away. I approached the receptionist's glass, knocked hard and gathered my emotions.

"Can I help you?" the woman behind the counter asked, raising her eyebrows and flashing her painted fingernails toward the glass.

I thought for a minute. I had never pulled out my credentials for anyone before. This would be the first time, and I felt strange as I reached into the inner pocket of my jacket and removed the leather casing.

"Good morning," I started. "My name is William Tucker, and I'm a Special Agent for the Federal Bureau of Investigation. It's my understanding that a man has come in recently, wounded from a brutal beating last night, perhaps within the last couple of hours."

The woman motioned with her head and pointed toward my right. I followed her finger down the hall and, about one hundred feet away, noticed three plain clothed men. The two on the right were sitting and the one on the left was standing against the wall opposite them, his head tilted back. I placed my credentials back inside my jacket and approached them. The one standing up came to attention as I neared.

"Guys," he said. "Guys!" he repeated when the two others didn't immediately respond.

The two men jumped up.

"Can we help you?" the one on my left asked.

I looked back from one man to the other, not knowing what to say, but focusing on the badges hanging around their necks. They were Boston Police Officers, that was clear.

"I'm with the City Police," the same one said. Can we help you?"

In order to get in to see Reggie Williams, I was going to have to reveal that I was law enforcement as well. I reached for my pocket. All three of the men reached for their weapons and pointed them at my head.

"Hold up, hold up," I said removing my hand. "I'm with the FBI." I removed my badge and showed it to them. "Special Agent Billy Tucker. FBI."

The man on my left reached forward and snatched my credentials. The other two looked in his direction for confirmation.

"Who sent you here Tucker?"

"Identify yourselves, please," I said, looking first at the two men to my right.

"I'm Bill Woolsey and this is Evan Murphy. We're with the City Police."

"Anthony Thomas, FBI," the one who held my credentials said. "What are you doing here?"

"I wanted to have a word with Reggie. I came to see him." When they failed to immediately respond, I turned it up a notch. "I've got to get in to see him."

"Tucker, the man's not up to it. Whatever you're here for can wait."

"Look guys, I've got an urgent lead on a crime. I just need to see him, even if only for a minute."

The three men looked at each other for what seemed an eternity. Finally, they agreed, and I stepped by them, pushing the door to the hospital room open into a completely different world. The lights inside were excessively bright. The sound of a heart monitor filled the room with a steady, death defying beep, a mechanical rhythm interrupting the chamber's eerie calm. The man lying on the bed—FBI Special Agent Reginald Williams—had tubes all over his body. His head was grossly swollen. Although I felt guilty about being in there, I hoped that Reggie would be able to talk. I needed to figure out who Lyle was for sure.

I walked over to the side of the bed and sat down on a metal stool nearby, placing my hand softly on the wrist of my fellow agent. I was surprised when Reggie's eyes cracked open and he turned his head, his glazed look reflecting an awareness of his condition, but a wish for ignorance of his pain. I had so many questions, but I first needed to introduce myself.

"Reggie," I began, speaking quietly. "I'm Billy Tucker. FBI. I was sent into Tremont Heights undercover by Robert O'Donnell to find out about the Polowski murder."

It felt strange to refer to Lucy's death like a street cop might. There was no response.

"Reggie. I said I'm Billy Tucker. Jayme's brother."

Again, no response. Just a look of bare, glassy curiosity. I continued.

"You didn't know I was with the FBI, did you?"

I paused, but continued again.

"I definitely had no idea who you were when I heard your name at the party last night, although O'Donnell told me there was another agent hanging around."

It was then that the bedridden Special Agent pressed his eyes tight. I could tell that he was struggling, and I let him come to grips with the mounting pressure facing him.

Reggie Williams shook his head ever so slightly.

"What?" I asked. "What is it Reggie?"

His eyes started to well up with tears. He blinked, and the water poured down his cheeks. His lips moved, but his voice was feeble and dry.

"So you're it." He paused, continuing to struggle. "This whole time, you're my exit strategy. I should have known. And O'Donnell should have told me."

Reggie gasped for air.

"Tell O'Donnell to fuck himself. I told him you were in town after I heard about you in the jail cell. He never told me you were FBI. All he told me was not to waste time on you. O'Donnell, his big ideas and his f..." Reggie paused, pained by his effort.

I waited. It took him several seconds to continue.

"I thought Lyle Jasper was working with me. Turns out he was working for Ronnie Luca. Nothing's like it seems kid; nothing at all. Don't ever forget that. Fucking O'Donnell."

Reggie Williams closed his eyes.

"Tell my wife I love her, kid. Don't forget that either. I'm not going to make it."

I was losing Reggie. The FBI, the world, was losing him. I thought he was descending into delirium when I heard his next words: "Love is sacred. Love is blind. When the Bureau takes that from you, you lose your mind."

Poor guy, I thought. *The Bureau took him from his wife. He's losing it.*

But Reggie hadn't lost it yet at all, and his next words hit me like a falling rock, crushing all that gave me support.

"That's a little rhyme my friend, Victoria Summers, told me when she got her last assignment."

"S-s-summers?" I stammered, my heart pounding. "Victoria Summers, a rookie from San Diego?"

Reggie Williams cracked open his eyes and nodded. My head spun in confusion. A line of sweat streaked from Reggie's forehead toward his ear. I lifted the corner of the sheet to wipe it away.

"She's no rookie."

"What?" I demanded, my desperate whisper now filling the room.

"Shit, kid," Reggie managed, but his lips barely moved. "Summers has been in the Bureau three years. She was furious when they gave her some bullshit assignment back in Quantico."

My breath stopped in my throat. I couldn't swallow.

"You're...you're..." Reggie tried to continue. I gripped his hand. "My wife. My kids. Tell them Billy. Tell them for me."

My eyes watered as I attempted hopeless words of reassurance. "Hang in there Williams. You've got to hang in there," I finished letting go of his grip.

Then, sliding back from the bed, I made my way out the door, unable to hide the tears in my eyes from the three men outside.

"How's he doing?" one of them asked as I made my way by them.

I looked back but didn't focus on anyone in particular. I was unable to speak. I only shook my head to signal the worst.

When I found my way to the exit door and back to Jayme's bike, it was 10:15 a.m. I was exhausted, but the fresh air, coupled with a sudden surge of denial brought back some adrenaline.

"It couldn't be. It can't be," I muttered. "It's the FBI, for Christ's sake. It can't be." Then, my throat vibrating with the echoes of my pain, I belted aloud: "No!!!!"

I pedaled as fast as I could until I found a pay phone.

Chapter Fifty-Seven

"Hello," she answered. "Victoria Summers."

Her voice no longer comforted me, I noticed. "You're at work," I said.

"Where are you?" she responded anxiously.

"I'm just getting back from the hospital visiting an FBI agent named Reggie Williams."

"Never heard of him."

"Never?" I asked. "He's a part of O'Donnell's team too."

The line was silent on the other end.

"Never heard of him," she confirmed. "What gives?"

"Say it isn't so Victoria," I pleaded. "Say it isn't so. Tell me your feelings for me are real. Tell me you love me again. Fly to Boston now. Say it to my face. Tell me that everything I've been feeling for you is real, that you've been feeling it too; all through training, when I saw you in New York, when I talked to you on the telephone."

"Billy, I…" she started.

"Wait," I interrupted. "Just wait a minute. I thought that it was strange when it took you so long to come out into the lobby to see me in New York, and when after I called you, O'Donnell came first. Say it isn't so, Victoria. Say it's real."

With each moment that passed, my heart began to ache, my soul to disintegrate.

"Billy, I can explain."

"Oh my God," I started. "Oh my God."

"Billy, stop that. I can explain. I never wanted this assignment but O'Donnell…."

"This *assignment*?" I questioned. "Assignment? I'm your assignment, aren't I? O'Donnell put you up to it, didn't he?"

"Billy," she began.

"Stop Victoria," I interrupted. "It's a yes or no question. Did or did he not put you up to it?"

The line was silent.

"Answer me!!"

"Where are you, Billy?"

"Answer me!!" I repeated.

"I'm calling O'Donnell," she said. "Give me your whereabouts."

"I was ready to give you my life an hour ago, Victoria! Now, you're getting nothing from me."

I hung up the telephone, and pressed my eyelids tightly, hoping that somehow, shutting off my vision of the world, it would all go quickly away.

Jayme, I thought. *She's all that I've got.*

* * *

When Victoria heard the dial tone, she immediately paged Robert O'Donnell.

"Cover's blown, sir."

"What?"

"Billy visited Reggie Williams at the hospital."

"So! Reggie doesn't know about you!"

Victoria stared at the receiver, drawing a deep breath. "Billy must have figured it out, sir. Cover's blown."

"Fuck!!" O'Donnell screamed, slamming down the receiver.

"This assignment was a stupid idea in the first place," Victoria muttered into the empty end of her line. "Nothing like being a woman in the Bureau."

And then, to no one in particular, but loud enough for others in the room to hear: "Asshole O'Donnell."

Chapter Fifty-Eight

That morning, Nathan and Jayme slept in each other's arms, a symbol of pure love and trust. But when Nathan awoke, he was startled and anxious, and he had a different feeling about himself as he dressed. His story was now out there, *but to someone I trust*, he reminded himself, although the reminder did not help ease his anxiety. He dressed quickly and headed downtown, to the usual spot. Ronnie always had meetings in the afternoon on Sundays, to wrap up the weekend and talk about the week ahead.

"Mr. Luca," Nathan started, a hesitant tone to his words as he observed the serious faces around the table. He feared Ronnie Luca might somehow have learned about Jayme. There was nowhere either of them could hide if Ronnie knew that. "What's going on?"

No one even looked his way. Except Ronnie. "You look tired, kid," he started, and then he paused to take a drag on his cigar. "How was the party?"

Nathan shrugged. It seemed like a loaded question. "It was a party. Not much to it."

"I wouldn't say that," Ronnie Luca added, offering a sarcastic laugh. "Bad scene, kid. Real bad scene. You hear the news?"

"I've been sleeping," Nathan defended, swallowing hard.

"Well, I'll be the first to tell you then. Our guy at the party, the one I told you about, had to take a swim. You know what I'm saying? Tell him Joey."

Joey Luca shrugged at his father's urging. "Ah," Joey said in disgust. "It's history. How was the party?"

Nathan didn't know what to make of the questions. He tried to deflect attention.

"Someone fucked up?" Nathan asked.

Ronnie Luca stood from the table. He walked over to the bar and reached across to the wooden shelves on the other side. "Wild turkey," he said. "It always calms the nerves."

"What going on, Mr. Luca?" Nathan now felt his anxiety turn to paranoia.

His story was out there. No longer was it in the tight, loyal hands of Jayme Tucker. There was now one more tongue to fear. Ronnie Luca tended to know everything, and Nathan figured that Ronnie knew he had blabbed to me.

"You notice any commotion at the party?" Ronnie asked. "I'm a little worried our guy went overboard."

"The same one that went swimming?" Nathan asked, knowing better than to say the real words.

"No loud words? No pushing? No fights?"

"Not that I noticed, but then again…"

"Our man Lyle Jasper took a crowbar to the undercover fibbi last night," Ronnie finally blurted. "Dumb shit. He sure made a bad mistake there."

Nathan knew not to ask or say anything more, and he was relieved, actually. It was a simple logic equation. Ronnie's man had beaten up the undercover FBI agent. The FBI would hunt him down. They would find him. He would be questioned, interrogated for hours. He would be sleep deprived, starved and fatigued and maybe, just maybe, Ronnie Luca feared, his man would turn 'rat.' Then, Ronnie himself would be in danger.

For situations like this, Nathan understood that Ronnie Luca sent only Joey. He sent his son because Joey had the biggest interest in seeing that his father was never in danger. He could handle Lyle Jasper just fine. All Joey needed was some cover.

* * *

Special Agent Reginald Williams died in a hospital bed of internal bleeding and brain swelling. Robert O'Donnell took a moment to offer the usual apologies to his family.

I wanted him out of there. It had gone on too long. I'm so sorry. This was just bad timing. Wrong place. Wrong time. I don't know what happened. I think it could have even been an accident. The guy might not have ever known he was FBI. These are mean streets. We've got to clean them up. Your husband was a brave man.

* * *

While all of this was happening, I headed over to Fuller Street, to pay a visit to a man I had never spoken to in my entire life. I knew him only through the eyes of his daughter.

The shades were down when I arrived. They were tinted orange and torn in a couple of spots along the edges. I couldn't see inside, but the word was that Denny Polowski lived alone, and rarely emerged. He was a loner even before his daughter died.

The last time I had seen him was at her funeral. He had worn black-out sunglasses that wrapped around his temples. He looked up from the ground maybe once or twice. He also looked worn, as if he hadn't slept at all and as if he was the lifeless one hidden within the wooden box.

I watched him nearly the entire time. It was as if he couldn't talk, couldn't engage. There were people next to him and around. The Priest stood beside him and said several prayers. He didn't need any of it at all. He needed his daughter back. She had been taken from him. She hadn't moved on to a better life, or relocated to experience something different. She wouldn't be coming home for the holidays, sending him birthday cards, curling up on the couch next to him, or bending over to kiss him good night in front of the television set. She wouldn't be doing anything more for him at all.

When he finally opened the door, squinting in the sunlight, a putrid waft of stale air exited his house.

"Mr. Polowski," I said. "I was a friend of Lucy's. I went to school with her. My name is Billy Tucker."

Denny Polowski looked me up and down, measuring my age and maturity.

"I'm just out of college," I said. "I never got a chance to offer you my condolences in person at her funeral, and I wanted to come by."

He waved his hand and motioned for me to come inside, as if it was too much effort to speak. To say that his home wasn't well kept would have been an understatement. *But who could blame him*? I thought.

"Fanta?" he asked, finally opening his mouth just barely wide enough to get the one word out.

I considered my thirst and the fact that he might not have too many groceries lying around, so I declined. He went ahead and helped himself in the refrigerator.

"Not much to say about Lucy," he muttered with a sigh. "Cops are still clueless. I call them every now and then when I get the chance."

I shrugged and nodded. I wondered if it was better he didn't know the truth.

"Probably that Italian prick she met at the club," he said. "I never even heard the guy's name until the cops came knocking. Damn nightclubs."

We then sat in silence for a while, the stench from his living room reminding me that I did not want to make an afternoon of it.

"So college, huh?" he said more than asked. "I always wanted Lucy to go to college. She was smart cookie, that one."

"We talked about it once," I jumped in. "She would have gone someday."

I remembered her visit with Nathan that weekend. *Lucy would have fit in just fine,* I knew.

"She was one magnetic girl," I continued. "Nathan was the envy of the school."

Denny Polowski looked away. "Nathan," he repeated sarcastically, but he didn't seem sure of what he wanted to say. "Nathan will end up like me someday if he doesn't watch out."

I studied Denny Polowski's frame in the easy chair. I searched for some hint of a prior life, toned and strong, like Nathan, but I couldn't find any. Denny had barely been out of his house for over a year now. He probably had no clue what had become of Nathan. For all he knew, Nathan was still wrapped up in gambling and spending the bulk of his time watching his bets on T.V.

"You know what I last remember about her?" Denny said more than asked. "Seeing her standing in front of the mirror in the bathroom and running a brush through her hair, her gorgeous red hair. God was she gorgeous. Just like her mother, in more ways than one. Lucy had her own agenda too. She always did. But some guy would have stayed around for the ride just to look at her, just like me with her mother. Maybe it would have been Nathan. Maybe this Italian prick. Who knows? It definitely would have been somebody. And for the rest of that somebody's life, that somebody would be holding on for dear life."

The thought of Bobby Reed swinging Lucy around the Sigma Phi Delta living room came to my mind, but then quickly exited as I watched Denny's determined expression turn sour, and then sullen. He dropped his chin to his chest and pressed his eyes closed tight. His shoulders shook.

"God I miss her."

I looked away. It had been too long for me to miss her that way. Besides, I only missed an image, a thought of what might have been.

"I miss her too," I added.

He sniffed and looked away. I felt that I had violated his solace by laying claim to a part of his emotions.

"You know what I miss the most? Reading to her in bed, her breathing so steady and pure, a dim night lamp illuminating one side of her face, her fingers touching the edges of the pages as she followed along, the way she would look up at me if I paused, the way she trusted me to continue, to bring her to the end, the intelligent little questions she would ask.

Why is the frog sad? How come they won't let the other one play? Can I touch a rainbow? she would say.

"I remember it all as if it were yesterday. Funny thing is, though, the last time I did that, she was five years old. It was long before we ever came to Tremont Heights, long before her mother left us and long before she ever found her way to that damn nightclub downtown. But that was my Lucy. That was my girl. And whenever I looked at her, I didn't care if she was sixteen or eighteen, that's who I saw. My little girl. My blood. My life."

The lump in my throat paralyzed my ability to respond. The loss I had just felt over Victoria paled in comparison to what Denny Polowski must have felt everyday without Lucy.

"She died trying," I told him. "I know she died trying. That was Lucy. She was always trying." I wanted to tell him about his little girl and how she spent her final moments, but sitting with him there, I decided he didn't need any new information.

I stood and leaned over to shake his hand. "Thank you for talking," I continued. "If there is anything I can do, anything at all, please let me know."

Chapter Fifty-Nine

When I stepped outside, I headed straight for Tremont Heights Park. I hoped that there, amidst the rubber skids along the cement and the multitude of ball marks and memories against the wall, I would find my answers. The loss of Victoria was settling in. My emotional visit with Lucy's father had worn me out.

It was raw and cold, an early autumn day, and the smell of dried-out leaves was pervasive. A light breeze blew rustling bunches of brown along the ground. I kicked at a few along the way lost in thought, searching for what might be the right decision.

What did Nathan Marks deserve? And what did I owe to him? To Jayme? Did I owe anything at all to the FBI? And where did I fit into this entire picture? Did I owe anything to myself?

I resented what Robert O'Donnell had done to me. I tried to see opportunity, but I only saw despair; personal despair; despair in what I might be doing to Nathan and Jayme; and never ending despair for Denny Polowski if I kept the lid on the truth.

"What am I going to do?" I called out.

I was startled to hear an answer behind me. It was Nathan.

"When you start talking to yourself, Billy, it's time to call the men in the white coats."

I turned to him. "Call them," I said. "Tell them to come quick."

"Nah," he said. "You just need a little athletic therapy."

"Is that a challenge?" I asked. "I thought you didn't bother with this game anymore."

He rotated his shoulder to loosen up. "Couldn't hurt to give it a try," he said, and then he removed a pink rubber ball from his pocket.

"You still know how to hold it?" he teased.

"Like riding a bike," I responded, eyeing him.

Nathan shook his head at my analogy. "We've had some tough times," he said.

I nodded, "I know."

Nathan flipped the ball in his hand a couple of times and then asked me if I was ready. I crouched and stared at the wall until, with a *hiss!* of air and a *pop!* against the backboard, our game was underway. Nathan's first shot had no angle, and I scooped it up with barely any lateral movement. I then hurled my arm sideways, maximizing the right to left spin and ensuring that Nathan would have to move far to his left to get it. He did it. I was impressed with his speed, but he was now poised to get me. Nathan aimed low and picked the perfect angle. This was always a killer shot. I never had a chance. I went to the wall to take my licks.

"You'll be lucky to come within a foot!" I taunted, but Nathan would have nothing of it.

I counted aloud, hoping that Nathan would wait too long and lose his chance. "One, one-thousand. Two, one-thousand. Three, one-thousand."

Just as my hope of hitting "Five" rose, my right ear rattled as the rubber ball missed my head by less than a foot.

"That one was to shut you up," Nathan called to me. Then, he finished: "This one's for a point!"

But Nathan's second shot missed as well, just outside my lower back.

"You got nothing," I taunted again. "I always used to carry us anyway!"

I had barely finished my last word when Nathan's last ball caught me in the upper thigh.

"That's one chump," Nathan called, claiming victory. "And it's probably all I'll need."

The training I had done in Quantico was good for my game, though. I stayed with Nathan the entire time. I had more stamina than him. Had our game been up to 25, instead of 11, I think I would have taken him.

I blew my chance when I had him 9-8. Nathan slipped and missed the pick up off the wall. He claimed his sneakers were too worn out. I saw it differently. I was wearing him down. With Nathan lined up at the wall, I missed my first toss, but connected on my second one, a strategic lob at his back. My goal with that kind of a throw was always to make sure I got the point. 10-8. I was almost there.

"You're not going to end this with one of those fag lobs?" he challenged, egging me out of my game.

And I decided Nathan was right. I reared back and fired, going for the hard kill, but my ball curled high and to the left. Nathan turned around and laughed.

"Now you're toast," he said, stepping back next to me over the line.

Holding the ball in his hand, Nathan put his whole body into his arm.

When the pink rubber blurred the air, I swear the ball was shaped like an egg. It came off the wall on an erratic line, skipping and spinning the entire time. I missed it and now, Nathan had three throws.

Fierce competitor that he had always been, this was the end of the game for me. With a one-two punch, dead center on my back, Nathan evened the score. He threatened mercy. He suggested we should leave the game as it was. A tie.

"I'll have none of that," I said, turning back to him for a moment and knowing that I hadn't offered the same sportsmanship. "If you don't take me down now, you've lost your chance."

Nathan shrugged and motioned for me to turn back around. "So be it," he called, and my body cringed as he fired his last shot, just barely nicking my upper thigh.

"Game," Nathan said. "One for the good guys."

I considered the irony. We connected fists. *Good game*, the gesture said.

We both then walked over to the bleachers at the side of the court and took a seat on the first bench.

"I just got back from a meeting with Ronnie Luca," Nathan started.

"Yeah? Well, I just got back from talking to Denny Polowski."

"You didn't tell him, did you?"

I shot Nathan a look. "Give me a little more credit than that."

We both sat in silence for several minutes. I thought back to what I had learned that morning from Nathan and Jayme.

"What did good old Ronnie Luca have to say for himself?"

As far as I knew, Nathan didn't have anymore secrets. I, of course, still had a major one I was keeping from him. I planned to tell him, but I was just waiting for the proper moment, if it was ever possible that there could be one.

Nathan proceeded to tell me about his meeting with Ronnie Luca and his gang. He also told me what he knew about Lyle Jasper.

"Did Ronnie tell you Joey shot him?" I asked when he finished.

Nathan shook his head.

"How about Joey, then?" I asked eagerly, now seeing an opportunity for us all. "Did Joey tell you what he did?"

But Nathan didn't answer. He didn't respond at all, at least not in words. Instead, Nathan looked at me, curiously, for a long time. There was no expression in his eyes. It was as if he was measuring his past against his present as he considered my question and what it meant.

I felt that I had gone too far, and I was disappointed with myself, but the fact remained that I was now desperate. I wanted to break rank, pull out my credentials and tell him why I had really come back home. I resisted, though, unsure of where that would really get me at this point.

I didn't even know what I really wanted then anyway. Sure, I wanted Nathan to give me the evidence to get to Joey and Ronnie Luca, but for the last few months, I had been set on making the case against them for Lucy. Justice for her. Victoria Summers and I together when it was over. That's what I had been able to hang on to. Now, knowing the truth behind Lucy's shooting and not having any clue who Victoria Summers really was, the landscape had changed.

* * *

The truth behind Lucy's shooting was unsettling to say the least. Apparently, I'd bragged a little too much one night about what I'd learned in legal studies class in college.

"Self-defense," I'd told Nathan, nearly three years earlier. "It clears you of any crime."

The night Joey Luca threatened Nathan at *Fire!* he headed home and went straight for the bottle of Jack Daniels. *Self-defense?* he wondered silently, fearing a visit from Joey and heeding my words. Then, he took a long gulp.

"What are you doing to yourself?" Jayme asked him as she watched.

My little sister had started spending time with Nathan when Lucy Polowski was not around. Nathan had even begun to call Jayme when he knew he'd be alone. He didn't like it when Lucy went out. Nathan confessed to me that with Jayme near him, he also felt close to me.

That night, Nathan told Jayme that he needed to go out for a while. Jayme asked why.

"It's cold and late," Jayme told him. "Why do you want to do that? What's even open?"

"It's been a long night, Jayme," Nathan replied. "A lot has happened. I need some air. I need to take a little walk and be alone."

Nathan spoke as he pulled on his sneakers. Jayme knew exactly what she was going to do. She would follow him. He would never even know it.

Just look and see which way he goes, give him twenty seconds, and then I won't be far behind, Jayme thought to herself, and that is what she did. She watched him. She waited. She pulled on her own shoes. And then, she was out the door, catlike, unsuspected and undetected.

Nathan walked straight toward the expressway. Jayme wondered why he didn't just head to the Park. That was a more pleasant walk. Her heart was pounding. For a moment, she feared he was suicidal.

The night air was cool. Autumn had most definitely arrived. The smell of the dying leaves on the trees surrounded them. It was time to prepare for winter. In the still of the night, they heard only themselves breathing. Jayme stayed far enough back. Nathan later said that he sensed she was there.

"And that comforted me," he said. "I was never worried about Jayme seeing me do something wrong."

And 'something wrong' is what Nathan had set out to do; a break-in at The Chocolate Cone; an invasion of the cash register and the safe. He had watched Addison Parker out of the corner of his eye on more than one occasion. He swore to himself that he would never do it, but this was life or death. On that understanding, and thanks to my advice about self-defense, Nathan made sure he found his way to Addison's gun. Addison had told Nathan and me about it one night when we were young, after the news broke about a shooting of a gas station attendant in Mattapan. He said we were the only two who knew, other than his wife, Betsy.

Jayme nodded at me as Nathan told me the story. She shrugged. "That was all he was doing," she said, "looking for some cash and a gun, either one could save his life."

I should have known. The way Addison challenged me about the cops not finding a murder weapon, I should have thought of it. There was something omniscient in his eyes that day. After Lucy was shot, Addison knew damn well his gun was missing and he knew damn well the only one who was capable of taking it.

Nathan continued. He got to Addison's store and hooked around the back dumpster, freeing the metal pole which held it shut. Nathan swung hard, with all of the strength in his shoulders and chest. Sparks tore out of the metal box and the night lights inside The Chocolate Cone went down. So did its alarm.

Jayme jumped back in the night as she saw the sparks fly. Nathan was not just out for a walk. He was heading for bigger trouble, and the next thing she heard was broken glass. Then, all was silent again. Jayme crept closer to the store. She could make out Nathan's figure crawling around the counter. She was afraid to get too close, though, for fear that her footsteps would alert him that he had been followed. She worried. She hoped. She prayed. She heard Nathan swear and grunt.

And then, in the distance, a car pulled off the expressway and began to descend the off-ramp into Tremont Heights. Jayme could hear its engine drone lower, losing speed as it left the highway. Most of the locals would have taken note of the darkened sign for The Chocolate Cone, she knew. Its lights welcomed home all who stayed out too late. Jayme wondered whether the darkened anomaly in front of her and Nathan's mischief within would pass without observation.

The next thing Jayme saw was Nathan exiting the store and beginning a jog toward home. Jayme lay back at first, then she started to jog too. She stopped dead in her tracks, though, when she heard a familiar shriek. *It was Lucy Polwoski.*

Nathan stopped too. Then, after no more than a moment's hesitation, he changed his course toward the expressway, opening up his strides into an all out sprint. Jayme followed, hopelessly exasperated and trailing continuously further behind.

Nathan's throat pounded with the pulse in his heart. He arrived at the scene to see the passenger door of a Black Corvette opening, and Lucy's shrill voice rising beyond comprehension. All he heard were the words, *Dumb-ass!* as she slammed the door of the car and tried to flee.

Around the other side of the car came the bounding body of Joey Luca. This time, seeing Joey, Nathan did not go pale. In the chaos of the situation, he assumed a familiar, yet quiet, self-directed confidence. His entire life, Nathan was always most sure of himself when he had to rely on his body.

"Nathan!" Lucy yelped when she saw him on the other side of the street. "It's a miracle! It's you. Help me," she roared.

"Marks?" Joey questioned as he followed Lucy toward the underpass. "Two times in one night? You'd better be getting my money."

"What's going on?" Nathan asked, standing tall, far from the stature he had taken before Joey Luca earlier in the night.

"What's it to you?" Joey belted, his chest rising as he continued to stride in Nathan's direction.

"Get him Nathan. Get him now." Lucy called. "He fuckin' slapped me."

Lucy circled behind Nathan, but he directed her away. "Go over there," he pointed.

"Don't you tell me what to do!" Lucy protested, starting to cry. "You son of a bitch, Nathan. Get him now!" she repeated between sobs, backing away.

Joey glared. "Look at that Marks. You made her cry. You made my girl cry. I don't like it when ANYONE makes MY girl cry."

"Lay off, Joey," Nathan warned. "This isn't your town." But Nathan's warning fell flat.

Joey stepped right up to Nathan and pressed his nose in his face. "If I'm correct here, buddy boy, you owe me money. So until you friggin' pay me…"

Jayme gasped as she arrived at the scene, crouching behind a mailbox. Joey had pulled a knife, and as he stood toe to toe with Nathan, he began running the blade against Nathan's shoulder, using its flat surface to scope Nathan's neck. But Nathan barely flinched the entire time, causing Joey to up the ante, digging the knife's edge into the soft tissue around Nathan's shoulder blade, smiling through gritted teeth as he did.

"Stop it, Joey!" Lucy screamed. "You sick bastard. Do something Nathan!"

And Lucy's next words ran together in a slow, agonized but deliberate tone.

"F-o-r -o-n-c-e-i-n-y-o-u-r-l-i-f-e, N-a-t-h-a-n, d-o-s-o-m-e-t-h-i-n-g!"

With a cat-like quickness, Nathan's right hand grabbed Joey's wrist, twisting the knife away from his body while his left landed an uppercut beneath Joey's chin. Joey Luca stepped back to deliver his own blow, but by then, it was too late. Nathan had pulled Addison's gun from his waistband. He told me that while he pointed it at Joey first, he actually turned and directed its barrel at Lucy.

"Do NOT talk to me like that Lucy," he yelled.

Her mouth gaped in shock. "How dare you!" she called between gritted teeth.

Joey Luca rubbed his chin between his thumb and his index finger and Jayme swore she saw him smile.

It was then that Nathan shook his head and rotated his body and his outstretched arms back toward Joey. Nathan said his eyes blurred in his concentration and in the confusion of the moment, and the next thing he knew, Lucy's hands crashed into his shoulder, and a shot fired into the night. All three them froze, checking themselves for holes.

"This isn't a game Marks!" Joey called. "Are you trying to shoot me?"

Lucy backed away.

"Are you?" Joey continued. "Huh?" he asked, but he wasn't backing away at all. Now, he was walking right at Nathan, whose quiet calm gave way to a nervous quiver after the gun fired. Jayme had never seen Nathan like this, and Joey must have sensed his weakening resolve. Joey turned for Lucy and, although she tried to side-step him, he grabbed her wrist and twisted it behind her back using her body to shield himself.

"Go ahead Marks. Take a shot now," Joey taunted. "Let's see what you got. But don't hit the red head. There are no points for that."

Lucy tried to wrestle free and she bent her body at the waist and tried to stomp on Joey's toes.

"Cut the shit, Lucy," Joey called. "I'll shoot you myself."

Finally, Nathan regained his composure and spoke. "Let her go Joey."

Lucy stopped struggling. With her back against Joey's body, she now leaned toward Nathan and mouthed two words: "shoot him."

It was then that Joey threw Lucy aside and charged at Nathan. "Give me that fuckin' gun. I'm going to shoot both of you!"

Nathan held the gun far in his right hand, trying to shield Joey away with his left. Joey reached and pulled at Nathan's body. Nathan grunted as Joey drove a fist into his ribcage. The gun slid across the ground. Joey ran for it, but Nathan dove and swiped at his ankles.

Now Lucy tried to step over them, tried to get to the gun herself. She stumbled as she ran, and Nathan reached up and pulled her down. She fell on top of Joey, giving Nathan enough time to rise and dart a few steps to his right to regain control of the weapon.

Lucy, seeing the weapon back in the hands of the boy she loved to torment, then tore at Nathan with her tongue: "You good for nothing brainless thug," she said. "You ripped my skirt, you no good, going nowhere, pathetic dumb-ass…"

But Lucy's tirade was interrupted when a second *pop!!* echoed in the air.

Jamie said Lucy's body seemed as if it was tossed back two feet when, eyes bulging, she landed on her heels and fell to the ground.

Joey, who had regained his footing, looked back.

"Jesus," Joey said as he eyed Lucy and shook himself away. "What the fuh? What the fuh? What the fuh?" he stuttered.

And as Joey Luca struggled for the words, he sidestepped toward his car, twisting as he ran in fear, anger and confusion, and wanting nothing more than to be long gone. He hopped inside his Corvette, slammed his hands on the steering wheel in frustration, ignited the car's engine and tore away.

When Joey's Corvette was out of sight, and when the only remaining sound in the air was the buzz from the highway above, Nathan stepped toward Lucy and dropped to his knees.

"Oh no," he said, but his panic was interrupted.

"Don't touch her!!" Jayme screamed, and Nathan turned, startled to see her at the scene. "Don't touch her!!" Jayme screamed again as she ran toward him.

And Nathan listened, if for no other reason than because he had no idea what else to do. Jayme held back her dinner as she saw Lucy Polowski lying there wide-eyed and empty, but most importantly, she told me, "I made sure Nathan's hands never touched her body."

"No clues," she said, and I couldn't believe what I was hearing from my little sister. She was right. It was brilliant. If Nathan didn't touch her, the only person who could finger him would be Joey Luca.

"But Joey Luca would never do that," Jayme added, beaming at me in our living room with bitter conviction. "Because the first thing Nathan and I would do is pin the murder on him. Two against one. Motherless girl from Tremont Heights and handsome boyfriend out for a late night walk. A gangster's kid didn't stand a chance before a jury."

I was speechless. *Perjury. Conspiracy to commit perjury. Aiding and abetting.* These were only a few of the crimes that first came to my mind. This was my sister, my seventeen year-old sister.

And then Jayme's voice turned low: "As far as we know, Billy, the Luca's still don't know I'm the young girl they're looking for, but at least they know enough about Nathan to understand what's at stake. A young girl from Tremont Heights witnesses a crime? Who's she going to side with? It sure as hell won't be Joey Luca. It's Nathan that's the legend in this town."

* * *

And that was the end of their story to me. They had re-lived the moment so many times together, but they had never told a soul, not until they told me. They told me because they trusted me, deeply, both of them. They told me because they needed to tell someone and needed to get it out. It was killing them, eating them alive, particularly after I came home. They needed to purge.

So many thoughts enveloped me. Oddly, the one that stood out, hearing Nathan and Jayme together, was how brilliant Robert O'Donnell's idea had been. Brilliant, that is, until he considered the emotions, most notably mine.

Chapter Sixty

As I sat on the bleachers with Nathan, despite all of the pain I knew could cause, a part of me still wanted to do my job for the FBI. After eighteen weeks in Quantico and countless oaths, that was what I was supposed to do. That was my mission and what I had been training for. That was Robert O'Donnell's plan. Revealing the truth, and flipping Nathan into an informant, was what Victoria had wanted me to do as well.

I thought about my past, my friendship with Nathan, my relationship with my sister, what it was and what it could be, my years in college, my hope for a career in the Bureau, and my oath to uphold the Constitution and seek justice and truth. At that moment, in an overwhelming conflict of my loyalties, I knew that something had to give. I wondered who, or what, in the end, would bear the burden of my betrayal. Of course, I didn't rule out that it could be me.

I turned to Nathan and pushed the issue again. "Did Joey tell you he shot Lyle?" I asked.

This time, Nathan nodded, and I breathed a sigh of relief. I now had my out, all that I needed to know. It was time, at last, to tell Nathan the secret I had been keeping from him.

My heart lurched inside my chest as I considered how I would begin.

"What?" Nathan said looking at me. "What's that funny look for? You going to sell me down the river?"

I shook my head, allowing his words to sink in. I started with something simple.

"Why are you even bothering with Ronnie Luca?" I said. "Why not keep things on the straight and narrow?"

Nathan sniffed out a laugh. "Ronnie takes care of me," he said. "All he asks for is my loyalty."

"Why?" I pushed. "You don't need that? Where's it going to lead? You know you're going to be answering to Joey some day, and based on what you told me this morning happened with Lucy, that's never going to be a comfortable situation. So where is this going?"

Nathan looked down at his toes and started shaking his head rapidly back and forth, as if he didn't want to hear what I was saying. I continued.

"I'll tell you one place this could go. "You could end up *swimming,*" I emphasized, "with Lyle Jasper."

Nathan lifted his chin, and then, offered me a response I did not expect.

"I know," he said. "I know. You think I haven't thought about it. When I met up with the guys yesterday, it was all I was thinking about. But you know what keeps me safe and sure?" he asked, but indicated he would answer his own inquiry. "Being open. Being honest. Showing loyalty. That's all Ronnie asks for. That's all I give. I work for him. I do what he says. And I won't have a problem, ever. I'm doing what's best for me."

"Are you?" I snapped.

Nathan paused and stared at me, perturbed that I would question him. "I am," he confirmed, his eyes tearing into mine.

"Are you doing what's best for Jayme?" I returned, changing the focus.

"Ahh." he said with a wave of his hand brushing off my inquiry, but I continued to push.

"No seriously, Nathan. Have you thought about where you're bringing Jayme? Have you thought about what she deserves? Your love for her aside, have you thought about giving her the world as her option, instead of Tremont Heights."

"What's wrong with you, man? You're still in love with Lucy, aren't you?"

I wasn't sure we were even having the same conversation and shook my head in confusion.

"Aren't you?" he asked again.

I shook my head to say 'no' but he continued. "You still blame me for keeping her here with me, instead of telling her to ride off to college with you, don't you? You still don't understand it, do you? Why she, or any other girl, would give up everything you got to experience for life here in Tremont Heights with me?"

I didn't know what to say. I wanted to tell Nathan that he was being ridiculous, that I had found true love in Victoria, something that took any feelings I once had for Lucy out the equation completely. But now, with what had just happened, I wasn't even sure of those feelings anymore.

"I don't know what love is," I said to Nathan. "I thought I knew once, but not anymore. As far as I'm concerned, the only thing I love in this world is Jayme, and I may have made some mistakes in the past, but I'm going to do everything I can now to protect her.

"You don't need to," he interrupted. "I'm already doing that."

"You don't get it, Nathan. A life with Ronnie and Joey Luca, and trusting that they won't turn on you when they figure out your secret isn't exactly *protecting* Jayme Tucker."

"So what do you suggest, Billy? That is my life. That's the life I'm leading now. Jayme loves me. I love her. That's all there is right now. I'd bury the man who interferes with that."

I felt my skin raise all over my body. I thought back to that moment at the party when I saw Jayme and Nathan dancing together. I thought of all of the moments I had with Victoria, and it pained me to consider how wrong I'd been. I wouldn't interfere. I couldn't interfere. Even Lucy Polowski, the same girl who had whipped a rubber ball at Nathan's head when we were 15 and who took his bullet just over five years later, wouldn't have wanted me to interfere.

I then turned to Nathan and considered at least five different ways to do it, but I finally decided on the one I had practiced the most.

"I do have a suggestion, Nathan," I said, picking up on his cue. "There's something you need to know."

He looked at me oddly and shrugged. "What?" he challenged.

"It's a new day. These are new times. We each have our own thing going. You have yours. I have mine, and I'm not just your old pal Billy, anymore."

Nathan waited.

"I'm undercover with the FBI."

I watched as Nathan's face drained, no doubt our years of laughter and friendship giving way to lies and betrayal. I pulled out my credentials and handed them to him. Nothing dramatic. I stayed seated as I did. Just showing an old friend an ID card. Nathan took it from my hand. He looked at it. He nodded. He handed it back.

"How about that," he said. "Not a bad picture of you."

I took it back, looked at it and agreed.

"Are you wearing a wire?" he asked.

"No," I said.

And then, as if Robert O'Donnell had scripted the scene himself, Nathan asked, "what are we going to do now?"

I stared at him, accepted what he was offering and considered the irony of it all. "You're going to have to trust me," I said. "Just like you've been doing now."

"I've got to get Jayme. She's going to need…" he started, but I stopped him.

"I'll take care of talking to her, Nathan. I should really be the one to tell her."

He agreed.

Chapter Sixty-One

It was Sunday night, 11:30 p.m. Robert O'Donnell stood by the receiver fuming, gulping from his ninth cup of coffee for the day. It had been over fifteen hours since our last contact; he had already lost one agent; he had called Victoria Summers over twenty times to see if she heard from me again. He was about ready to leave the field office to search for me himself. He paced and swore, paced and swore. It was moments like this that made him hate his job, hate being a supervisor and depending on others. It was moments like this when he needed the bottle and needed it bad. He wanted to scream at the top of his lungs.

"Discipline. Control," he reminded himself as he wrung his hands together and shook his head rapidly back and forth.

Just then, the static sound filled the room from the receiver, and I was on the other end of the telephone.

"Special Agent Billy Tucker reporting, sir," I said, and afraid of the ramifications if I offered a pause, I continued. "Takedown cleared."

I could hear O'Donnell gasp. At first, he didn't respond at all, but then, assuming an authoritative tone, he spoke.

"Confirm Tucker."

I drew a deep breath when O'Donnell spoke. I feared where this moment might lead, but knew I couldn't look back. I had made my decision, put my faith in my training, my ideals and finally, for the first time in my life, myself.

On behalf of the Federal Bureau of Investigation, over my mother's grave, out of love for my sister, and despite my respect for an old friend and that blazing red head with the green butterfly on her back, I reached deep within myself and crushed the memories of my childhood, the bonds of my youth and the innocence of my past. I radioed back to Robert O'Donnell.

I said all the words we had practiced in Quantico. "Billy Tucker. FBI Badge ID number 88030, code zero-zero red. Signal confirmed. Takedown cleared."

* * *

Robert O'Donnell's hands were still shaking at 2:00 a.m. when he had lined everyone up. Better to strike in the wee hours of the morning, he knew. His men were poised and ready. They had been so for two hours.

When they got the signal, thirty-two federal agents, wearing bullet proof vests and armed with laser assault rifles, instantly bolted into action. The doors to the homes of Ronnie Luca, Joey Luca, cousin Frankie, Uncle Arnie, Morton Jamison and six others who frequented The Tavern at odd hours to talk business, fell down almost simultaneously. The orders of the intruders woke them all from their once pleasant slumbers. The arrest warrants were executed, and Robert O'Donnell's plan had hit its second phase.

O'Donnell still needed me though, and he knew it. He didn't know why I had cleared the takedown, but we had gone over several times what it had to mean if I did. O'Donnell would have to wait until the next day to speak to me, though. After I got some sleep, I planned to bring him Nathan Marks.

Chapter Sixty-Two

We arrived at Center Plaza two of the more rested ones in the room. When Robert O'Donnell saw me come through the doors with Nathan, his expression was an odd mixture of anger, hope, relief and anguish. He was on his seventeenth cup of coffee in 28 hours. His breath smelled of rot.

Nathan knew exactly what he had to say. We had gone over it twice in the car. I drove. The black T-Bird was not such a bad ride, but for where we were going, what the T-Bird stood for was about to be over.

Robert O'Donnell introduced himself to my old pal. He struggled not to slur his words. "Didn't sleep much last night, or the night before," he said boldly, trying to take back the edge he had clearly lost in the all-nighter. "Let's step into a private room and go over what we've got." He nodded at me. "Billy," he said, "I'll take it from here."

Nathan looked at me, and I shook my head. "I'll join you," I said to my supervisor. "Just to make sure you get it all right."

O'Donnell eyed me suspiciously, but he was too tired to care. "Coffee?" he asked, making his way over to the glass pot on the counter, but neither Nathan nor I wanted any.

When we sat down in the room, O'Donnell didn't speak. He waited, patiently, to see which one of us would start. Nathan waited as well.

"Go ahead, Nathan. Tell him what we talked about," I finally said.

Nathan began by telling Robert O'Donnell things O'Donnell already knew; his deteriorating relationship with Lucy; his gambling; her trips into Kenmore; his streak of bad luck; heading into town after her; seeing Jocy; feeling desperate; feeling scared; feeling threatened; and going for the cash and a gun at The Chocolate Cone.

O'Donnell's ears and senses perked up when Nathan started into the territory of the unknown. And just as we had rehearsed, Nathan told Robert O'Donnell what 'had happened.'

"We struggled with the gun," Nathan began. "I know I was holding it, but

I know Joey was too. I know Lucy was screaming. I know I felt pressure on my finger from Joey's grip. All I could think about was pointing the gun away from my body to hit Joey. I was just afraid that in our struggle, the barrel of the gun was pointing at me, or something like that."

Robert O'Donnell studied Nathan as he spoke. He even looked me directly in the eyes to test his suspicion. He was clearly a seasoned agent who had heard it all before. My insides churned. Thankfully, Nathan held that same stone-faced look I had remembered from the snack line in high school. He was cool under pressure, and I didn't do so badly either.

Nathan knew he had to be good. He knew that his life, and Jayme's life depended on it. And me, well, I knew that Nathan could do it. I had never seen, nor could I even imagine, Nathan cracking under pressure. He was Nathan. He had that cold, blank stare. He was using it now. I was sure it would work.

"And then, you know the rest," Nathan finished. "Lucy took the bullet. And Joey, well, Joey ran. I stayed with her for a few minutes. I didn't know what to do. And then, like Joey, I ran."

When Nathan paused, my body tightened. He had left out a detail, and I knew Robert O'Donnell would not forget.

"Jayme Tucker," O'Donnell demanded. "She was at the scene."

"She was at the scene," Nathan confirmed. "She wanted to go to the police and tell them what happened. It was my fault. I told her she couldn't. I told her I would go to prison. I told her that if she talked, or even if we tried to blame Joey alone, that would be the end of us. Ronnie Luca would never stand for it."

"Did Ronnie tell you that himself," O'Donnell asked eagerly. "He came to see you that next day, right? Did he tell you that himself?"

"He came to see me," Nathan confirmed. "He wanted to see where I stood. He had no idea about Jayme being at the scene, though. I guess you guys had it all on him there."

O'Donnell's body tilted slightly back and upright, proud of what the FBI knew.

"I told him there was someone there, but I just didn't tell him it was Jayme."

To me, this was the beauty of the whole situation. Ronnie Luca had no knowledge of my sister at all.

"Why did you tell him that?" O'Donnell challenged, and I figured that his lack of sleep slowed his mind a bit.

"I told him to protect myself and to make sure he knew that he had two people to worry about."

O'Donnell pressed his eyes and nodded.

"So we had a mutual interest in my mind: keeping this thing quiet. It was valuable to him. He forgave my debt and told me I could work it off easily by working for him." Nathan shrugged. "And then," Nathan added, for no reason in particular, "he told me to never skip out on a meal again."

Nathan figured he was talking above O'Donnell. I knew that he was not.

I looked at O'Donnell out of the corner of my eye. *So far,* I figured, *he must be frustrated. So far, he had nothing, so I was sure he was waiting for more.* His next words confirmed my thoughts.

"Billy," he said, right in front of Nathan and clearly with an intent to intimidate. "Your buddy here better have some more. So far all I see is manslaughter for Joey *and* Nathan and a conspiracy to cover it up by *Jayme*," he emphasized. "Conspiracy charges for Ronnie, Joey and *Jayme and Nathan*," he emphasized again. "There isn't much juice in that for anyone to get off easy," he threatened, now looking back at Nathan. Not even a pretty boy and his teenage doll."

I felt a stab of anger as, by threatening Jayme, O'Donnell was now threatening me. I thought again about everything O'Donnell had done to me, and I grew confident that I was doing the right thing. The way O'Donnell had manipulated me into this project, I was now sure I was doing the right thing to get myself out.

I let Nathan tell a little lie to Robert O'Donnell, but O'Donnell would get everything he wanted from his project with me anyway. We gambled that O'Donnell would recognize that no prosecutor would want to charge Nathan for an accidental homicide when, as far as they knew, it wasn't even him who pulled the trigger. Sure, O'Donnell still threatened Nathan with prosecution, but in the end, he knew he had little to do so. In the end, we knew that O'Donnell would be more interested in what Nathan could tell him about Lyle Jasper.

"So I'll tell you what I can," Nathan then continued. "I know you're after Ronnie. I can't give him to you like you want him, though. All I can give you is Joey. I can give you Joey good and then it will be up to you to do the rest."

O'Donnell shifted in his seat. "I'm going to start the recorder," he said, and then, pressing his index finger over two buttons on the machine, he began to speak. "The date is November 17, 2000. The time is 12:34 p.m. Present is Assistant Special Agent in Charge Robert O'Donnell with Special Agent Billy Tucker. Speaking is Nathan Marks of Tremont Heights." Then, O'Donnell looked up at Nathan. "Your microphone Nathan. Speak slowly and clearly if you can. These words can be used against you."

Nathan then began to tell the tale of Lyle Jasper, a wildcard of sorts, but one that I knew I could play fairly. Unfortunately, the card came up in the deck at the expense of Reggie Williams. Were it not for this odd set of events, there would be no clean way to get Joey and to try to get to Ronnie. Without Lyle Jasper, it would be a prolonged series of wiretaps, document searches and other long nights of piecing together minor bits of evidence. With Lyle Jasper, Robert O'Donnell had a mob hit, and he could use it as he wished. If he wanted to use it outright, he could. He could pull the plug on Joey right away.

But Nathan and I figured O'Donnell wouldn't want to do that. Robert O'Donnell would want to use the information about Lyle's shooting to manipulate the group he had just arrested. O'Donnell was the expert, and he would determine how to use it best. What he did wasn't my concern, I decided. Nor was my career with the FBI.

And truthfully, keeping Nathan out of the mess wasn't my biggest concern either. My biggest concern was Jayme. If Nathan admitted he was the only one holding the gun that night, Robert O'Donnell would have never let him out. That was too much to let go. And I knew Nathan. I knew him at his core. He needed to get out. He needed to start again. But most of all, so did Jayme. Jayme needed to get out of this as cleanly as possible. I knew the love she felt for Nathan. Painfully now, I knew how deep those feelings ran.

So it would be relocation and witness protection for Nathan. Jayme would go away too, but it would be to college. She could go to school somewhere near Nathan, but not too close. I wanted her to have a fair opportunity to experience something more, without any ties to Tremont Heights.

When I made my decision, I knew it was right. It was right for everyone involved, even Denny Polowski. Denny really had no interest or need to hear anything more than a story of tragic accident, and that was what Jayme would tell him. I would take her there myself.

And as for Nathan? Well, Nathan Marks would never be able to show his face around Tremont Heights again, and I worried for him in that way more than any. Although I would always be pleased that he would remain free, I wondered whether Nathan would ever be able to live a normal life again.

And for me? The bottom line was that even after all of this growing up was said and done, I still allowed the past to dictate my future. But maybe that was the way it was supposed to be.

So at the end of the whole ordeal, as much as Nathan and I had grown apart, lived entirely distinct and separate lives and shared vastly different experiences, we actually stayed together. But that was only part of Lucy Polowski's legacy. As I saw it, a greater part of her legacy was my return to Tremont Heights and the opportunity to rescue Jayme. For a conscience wracked with guilt, I appreciated the opportunity O'Donnell had given me.

But after what the FBI allowed to happen with Victoria, I didn't care to work with anyone there again. I took a trip to New York to speak to Victoria face to face after it was all over. She'd tried to call me several times, and I decided that I needed the closure too. Victoria offered nothing of the sort. Instead, sitting on the railing of the Promenade in Brooklyn Heights, staring at the skyline of lower Manhattan, she told me that, despite it all, she'd fallen in love.

"Bullshit," I responded.

"It's true," she chimed, but her pleading eyes were no longer a sight to behold. "I protested this damned assignment all the way up to the Undercover Review Committee. I swear I did."

I raised my hand telling her not to bother.

"Don't look at me like that, Billy. You know what Robert O'Donnell is capable of. He tried to assure me—and he apparently convinced the Committee—that it was unlikely to work. 'Just an experiment,' he said. 'The FBI undercover on itself.' He actually had the gall to laugh when he talked about it."

I shook my head in frustration.

"And I felt so bad for you," she continued. "I couldn't believe what was happening to you. From the minute I met you, I thought you were so sweet. The way you tried to insist that I go in the door ahead of you. The way you admired my notes."

My thoughts trailed off when she called me 'sweet.' That was Lucy's word for me. Lucy alone owned the right to call me that.

"But it's just sixteen weeks, I thought," Victoria continued. "O'Donnell was all fired up about it. 'If you do this,' he promised me, 'you'll be golden in the Bureau. I'll make sure of it.'"

Of course, I recognized those words as the same O'Donnell had said to me. My face grew hot.

Victoria's imitation of O'Donnell did not stop. "Psychological control, he continued to me. 'It's the best control I can have in this situation. Love is probably my only chance of keeping Billy in check.'"

I shook my head in anger when she told me that. *Little did he know,* I considered, *what Billy Tucker would do when he did see true love.* I was referring to Nathan and Jayme, of course, but Victoria Summers could not know that.

Then, Victoria proceeded to tell me that after she met me, when she got to know me, she did fall in love. It was exactly the way I felt that it would happen to me someday. *I wasn't ever going to wow anyone,* I always figured.

It would take time. Victoria's betrayal now seemed to even take that away from me.

"It's not fair, Billy," she commented when she must have read my eyes. "I struggled. It was hard to love you and keep this a secret, hard to love you and not look out for your best interests as well. I tried to walk the line, Billy, hoping it would all turn out well in the end. But it didn't. You found out. I was always planning to tell you, just like I'm telling you now. You found out before you were supposed to, before you heard the words from me."

Her eyes welled-up with tears. Mine did too, but I didn't feel close to her. I felt further away than we'd ever been. I believed her, but didn't trust anything she was telling me. I wanted to, though. I wanted to badly, but too much had happened too quickly. I needed time away. I needed to regroup.

I slid off the railing and faced Victoria Summers. I didn't know what to say, so instead, I touched her hand, held it briefly, and then brought my fingers to my lips. In a simple, quiet, but unmistakable gesture, I blew her a kiss. Then, watching her shake her head in disappointment, as I backed off, I turned and walked away.

The funny thing was, as I strode off alone, my emotions laid bare and my life in a new state of disarray, I needed to talk to the one person I could not, one who once challenged me with such simple words on a park bench so many years ago.

Who do you like, Billy, Lucy Polowski asked.

I could have answered the question then. Years later, despite so much having changed, I could answer the question now. There was something pure and simple about Lucy Polowski. She didn't belong to anybody. Nobody would own her or rule her, not Nathan, not Joey, not school, not a career, and not even her father. In all of the time I knew her, Lucy Polowski lived by her own rules, something I now realized I did too. Victoria Summers lived by the rules of the FBI, and I didn't blame her for it. I just didn't think that I could ever love her again.

So when I think about Lucy Polowski's legacy to me.... or rather, Lipstick's legacy, I think of her words, and I long to be with her on that park bench again. This time I would answer her, and I would answer her bravely.

Epilogue

The story I've just told all happened in twelve months, December 1999 to December 2000: the FBI's information session, my interview with Robert O'Donnell, training in Quantico, meeting Victoria, getting my assignment from O'Donnell, and, of course, returning to Tremont Heights and changing my life and the lives of Nathan and Jayme forever.

But when I think of that year and everything it meant to me, I'm taken all the way back to a street corner on Mother's Day. I'm twelve years old. I'm hurt. I'm afraid. I'm surrounded by tragedy, guilt and shame and there, with me, is Nathan. Old memories of Nathan, of course, always bring me back to Lucy Polowski.

With Lucy, I'm frozen in time. I'm in high school. I'm in line at the snack bar. I'm at a Halloween dance. I'm at the Sigma Phi Delta beach bash. I'm a loner, an observer, one who will not make his own way unless and until he goes far away. That was the solution, I was sure at the time, and it had the added effect of removing me from the unconscionable place I'd left Jayme.

I keep coming back to that as my motive to leave town. It seems right. It seems plausible. I can't quite buy into it, though. Removing myself was not the solution. I was a fool to think it would be. The FBI so much as told me. I really never found my own way until the FBI sent me back home.

But even that doesn't work. Even there, I fail. The decision I made at the end was the best decision I could make for Jayme and Nathan. It was not the best decision I could make for me. I did the same thing that night in Sigma. I ran from the decision that was best for me.

I consider the possibility of 'self-sacrifice.' I try to use it as a precept to bring together all that has happened to me, and all of the decisions I have made.

Wisdom through silence. Strength in observation.

But where is the wisdom in keeping my needs silent? Is there strength with no experience, with only observation? What exactly would living by those ideals cause me to continue to sacrifice?

The months that passed after I realized Lipstick's legacy were lonely months, some of the loneliest I have ever had. I went for long walks through the cold, winter streets. I spent hours staring at the walls, pushing repeat on the CD player for my favorite sad songs. I needed somewhere to turn for support, and I couldn't bring myself to burden Jayme. Nathan and I had forever grown apart. My allegiance to him in the end, I realized, was nothing more than my failure to let go of the past.

Not surprisingly, I guess, I found solace in the companionship of Addison Parker. Addison's failure to come forward with material evidence about the murder weapon may have been distasteful, even a crime to someone who didn't know him, but that person was not me. In the end, my position on Nathan was not much different than Addison's. To me, Addison was like an old Redwood tree: strong, and increasingly majestic and imposing with the passage of time. Any effort to cut down the lifestyle and morals he lived by would be just flat wrong, do no one any good.

After spending far too many hours with Addison at The Chocolate Cone, though, I began to grow restless. I also started to worry. There was something more for Billy Tucker out there. Addison actually planted the seed once when we were talking.

"You have your own sense of justice, Billy. That's a gift. Not a burden."

I disagreed. It was a burden, I was sure.

"What possible good can come of it?" I asked.

Addison just shrugged and held his stare, long enough for me to realize the good that already had.

*

Printed in the United States
35362LVS00005B/55-213

9 781413 782400